# Crimson Snow

D0006560

# Crimson Snow

## Winter Mysteries

### Edited by Martin Edwards

Poisoned Pen Press

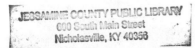

JESSAMINE COUNTY PUBLIC LIBRARY
600 South Main Street
Nicholasville, KY 40356

Introduction and notes copyright © 2016 Martin Edwards
Published by Poisoned Pen Press in association with the British Library

'The Case of the Man with the Sack' by Margery Allingham reprinted by permission of Peters Fraser & Dunlop (www.petersfraserdunlop.com) on behalf of the Estate of Margery Allingham.
'The Carol Singers' reproduced with permission of Curtis Brown Group Ltd, London, on behalf of the Estate of Josephine Bell.
'Deep and Crisp and Even' reproduced with permission of Curtis Brown Group Ltd, London, on behalf of the Estate of Michael Gilbert.
'Death in December' © Estate of Victor Gunn.
'Mr. Cork's Secret' by Macdonald Hastings reprinted by permission of Peters Fraser & Dunlop (www.petersfraserdunlop.com) on behalf of the Estate of Macdonald Hastings.
'Off the Tiles' © Estate of Ianthe Jerrold.
'Christmas Eve' © Estate of Sir Sydney Roberts.
'The Santa Claus Club' reproduced with permission of Curtis Brown Group Ltd, London, on behalf of the Estate of Julian Symons.

First Edition 2016
First US Trade Paperback Edition

10 9 8 7 6 5 4 3 2 1

Library of Congress Catalog Card Number: 2016937064
ISBN: 9781464206757          Trade Paperback

All rights reserved. No part of this publication may be reproduced, stored in, or introduced into a retrieval system, or transmitted in any form, or by any means (electronic, mechanical, photocopying, recording, or otherwise) without the prior written permission of both the copyright owner and the publisher of this book.

Poisoned Pen Press
6962 E. First Ave., Ste. 103
Scottsdale, AZ 85251
www.poisonedpenpress.com
info@poisonedpenpress.com

Printed in the United States of America

# Contents

# Introduction

*Crimson Snow* gathers vintage crime stories set in winter. The mysterious events chronicled by a distinguished array of contributors frequently take place at Christmas. There's no denying that the supposed season of goodwill is a time of year that lends itself to detective fiction. On a cold night, it's tempting to curl up by the fireside with a good mystery—and rather more pleasurable than indulging in endless online shopping. And more than that, claustrophobic Christmas house parties, when people may be cooped up with long-estranged relatives, can provide plenty of motives—and opportunities, as some of these stories demonstrate—for murder.

Winter also offers interesting possibilities for the crime writer. The 'impossible crime' story, a favourite sub-genre with readers ever since Edgar Allan Poe wrote *The Murders in the Rue Morgue*, is a striking example. An appealing variant on the concept of murder in a locked room, with no apparent means by which the killer could get in or out, is to have a crime committed somewhere surrounded by snow—with no footprints leading to or from the corpse.

The classic Christmas crime story has enjoyed a remarkable resurgence of popularity in recent years. J. Jefferson Farjeon's long-forgotten *Mystery in White* was a runaway best-seller in the final weeks of 2014, and twelve months later, two more titles published in the British Library's Crime Classics series also enjoyed remarkable success. One was Muriel Doriel Hay's *The Santa Klaus Murder*, an even more obscure title first published in the 1930s, and the other was the anthology *Silent Nights*, in which I collected a variety of short Yuletide mysteries by authors as diverse as Sir Arthur Conan Doyle and Dorothy L. Sayers. The British Library's lead has been followed by other publishers, who have revived several crime novels set at the festive season, occasionally giving them new titles to underline their suitability as presents for the crime fan in one's life. There is, it seems clear, a real enthusiasm for snow splashed with crimson…

Excellent as many Christmas mysteries are, it is inevitably the case that the seasonal background is more relevant in some novels than in others. The same is true when it comes to short crime fiction, but arguably the shorter form of mystery is better suited to making the most of such a setting. In the space of a few weeks, *Silent Nights* became one of the UK's fastest-selling crime anthologies for many years, and sales were matched by a very positive reception from reviewers. Duly encouraged, the British Library asked me to delve into its vaults once again, to see if there was scope for another book of classic tales set amid the mist and snow.

As with previous anthologies in the Crime Classics series, my approach was to look for a mix of stories, some of them rarities, some of them slightly more familiar (at least to connoisseurs of vintage mysteries). I was pleasantly surprised by the quality of material available. Assisted by the invaluable know-how of experts in the field, such as Jamie Sturgeon and Barry Pike, I managed to track down a number of previously hidden gems. Only one author, Margery Allingham, features both in *Silent Nights* and this book.

I have been struck by the sheer number of leading crime writers who have, over the years, tried their hand at a seasonal mystery. No fewer than seven of the eleven authors featured here were members of the prestigious Detection Club, the world's first social network for crime writers. Yet two of their stories are exceptionally obscure—those written by Christopher Bush and Macdonald Hastings, which feature their regular detectives, Ludovic Travers and Mr. Cork respectively.

In keeping with the playful nature of the puzzle story—which during the Golden Age of Murder between the two world wars often saw authors laying down an explicit 'challenge to the reader' to guess whodunit and why—Hastings' story was published in the form of a Christmas prize competition. It appeared in the December issue of the monthly magazine *Lilliput*, and the solution was printed several months later after all the entries had been judged. The prize winners proved themselves to be excellent detectives, and readers of this book will have the chance to emulate their success: the solution to Hastings' conundrum appears at the end of this book.

The other contributors include Julian Symons, whose reputation is as a stern critic of the light-hearted detective story who much preferred psychological suspense. Yet 'The Santa Claus Club' demonstrates that, especially in the early years of his career as a writer of fiction, Symons enjoyed indulging himself in the old-fashioned pleasures of the puzzle story. His friend of many years, Michael Gilbert, who was less bashful about his enthusiasm for the traditional mystery, is represented here by a characteristically readable tale.

Gilbert was an accomplished but unpretentious crime writer who never made any secret of the fact that his primary aim as an author was to entertain, and that is an aim I share as an anthologist. I think of the stories in *Crimson Snow* as comparable to the contents of a luxurious box of assorted chocolates. Their purpose is to give pleasure. I hope that the variety and quality of the selection as a whole will provide plentiful enjoyment for readers, and help for a few hours to take their minds off the cold reality of winter.

Martin Edwards
www.martinedwardsbooks.com

# The Ghost's Touch

## Fergus Hume

Fergus Hume was one of the most intriguing crime writers of the nineteenth century. His real name was Fergusson Wright Hume, and he was born to Scottish parents in England in 1859, before moving with them in infancy to a new life in New Zealand. He studied law, and was called to the New Zealand Bar, but promptly emigrated to Australia, where he worked as a law clerk while seeking to develop a career as a playwright. After studying the crime fiction of the French writer Emile Gaboriau, he wrote a murder mystery set in Melbourne. Failing to interest a traditional publisher, he resorted to self-publishing, and *The Mystery of a Hansom Cab* (which appeared in 1886, a year before Sherlock Holmes made his debut in *A Study in Scarlet*) became a best-seller. Unwisely, Hume sold his copyright; the company which bought it later became insolvent, and the rights passed to the British publisher Jarrolds, who persuaded Hume to revise the book, cutting out some of the 'local colour'.

Hume returned to Britain in 1888, which became his home for the rest of his life. A highly prolific writer, he lived until 1932, but his many later novels or stories have been almost wholly overshadowed by *The Mystery of a Hansom Cab*, which 'caught the moment' in a manner achieved by few crime novels. 'The Ghost's Touch' is set in an English country house, but as elsewhere in Hume's fiction, the events have their roots in Australia. This highly traditional mystery is a period piece, yes, but also offers a reminder that Hume was a capable storyteller; he deserves more than to be remembered solely on the strength of a single book.

I shall never forget the terrible Christmas I spent at Ringshaw Grange in the year '93. As an army doctor I have met with strange adventures in far lands, and have seen some gruesome sights in the little wars which are constantly being waged on the frontiers of our empire; but it was reserved for an old country house in Hants to be the scene of the most note-worthy episode in my life. The experience was a painful one, and I hope it may never be repeated; but indeed so ghastly an event is not likely to occur again. If my story reads more like fiction than truth, I can only quote the well-worn saying, of the latter being stranger than the former. Many a time in my wandering life have I proved the truth of this proverb.

The whole affair rose out of the invitation which Frank Ringan sent me to spend Christmas with himself and his cousin Percy at the family seat near Christchurch. At that time I was home on leave from India; and shortly after my arrival I chanced to meet with Percy Ringan in Piccadilly. He was an Australian with whom I had been intimate some years before in Melbourne: a dapper little man with sleek fair hair and a transparent complexion, looking as fragile as a Dresden china image, yet with plenty of pluck and spirits. He suffered from heart disease, and was liable to faint on occasions; yet he fought against his mortal weakness with silent courage, and with certain precautions against over-excitement, he managed to enjoy life fairly well.

Notwithstanding his pronounced effeminacy, and somewhat truckling subserviency to rank and high birth, I liked the little man very well for his many good qualities. On the present occasion I was glad to see him, and expressed my pleasure.

'Although I did not expect to see you in England,' said I, after the first greetings had passed.

'I have been in London these nine months, my dear Lascelles,' he said, in his usual mincing way, 'partly by way of a change and partly to see my cousin Frank—who indeed invited me to come over from Australia.'

'Is that the rich cousin you were always speaking about in Melbourne?'

'Yes. But Frank is not rich. I am the wealthy Ringan, but he is the head of the family. You see, Doctor,' continued Percy, taking my arm and pursuing the subject in a conversational manner, 'my father, being a younger son, emigrated to Melbourne in the gold-digging days, and made his fortune out there. His brother remained at home on the estates, with very little money to keep up the dignity of the family; so my father helped the head of his house from time to time. Five years ago both my uncle and father died, leaving Frank and me as heirs, the one to the family estate, the other to the Australian wealth. So—'

'So you assist your cousin to keep up the dignity of the family as your father did before you.'

'Well, yes, I do,' admitted Percy, frankly. 'You see, we Ringans think a great deal of our birth and position. So much so, that we have made our wills in one another's favour.'

'How do you mean?'

'Well, if I die Frank inherits my money; and if he dies, I become heir to the Ringan estates. It seems strange that I should tell you all this, Lascelles; but you were so intimate with me in the old days that you can understand my apparent rashness.'

I could not forbear a chuckle at the reason assigned by Percy for his confidence, especially as it was such a weak one. The little man had a tongue like a town-crier, and could no more keep his private affairs to himself than a woman could guard a secret. Besides, I saw very well that with his inherent snobbishness he desired to impress me with the position and antiquity of his family, and with the fact—undoubtedly true— that it ranked amongst the landed gentry of the kingdom.

However, the weakness, though in bad taste, was harmless enough, and I had no scorn for the confession of it. Still, I felt a trifle bored, as I took little interest in the chronicling of such small beer, and shortly parted from Percy after promising to dine with him the following week.

At this dinner, which took place at the Athenian Club, I met with the head of the Ringan family; or, to put it plainer, with Percy's cousin Frank. Like the Australian he was small and neat, but enjoyed much better health and lacked the effeminacy of the other. Yet on the whole I liked Percy the best, as there was a sly cast about Frank's countenance which I did not relish; and he patronized his colonial cousin in rather an offensive manner.

The latter looked up to his English kinsman with all deference, and would, I am sure, have willingly given his gold to regild the somewhat tarnished escutcheon of the Ringans. Outwardly, the two cousins were so alike as to remind one of Tweedledum and Tweedledee; but after due consideration I decided that Percy was the better-natured and more honourable of the two.

For some reason Frank Ringan seemed desirous of cultivating my acquaintance; and in one way and another I saw a good deal of him during my stay in London. Finally, when I was departing on a visit to some relatives in Norfolk he invited me to spend Christmas at Ringshaw Grange—not, as it afterwards appeared, without an ulterior motive.

'I can take no refusal,' said he, with a heartiness which sat ill on him. 'Percy, as an old friend of yours, has set his heart on my having you down; and—if I may say so—I have set my heart on the same thing.'

'Oh, you really must come, Lascelles,' cried Percy, eagerly. 'We are going to keep Christmas in the real old English fashion. Washington Irving's style, you know: holly, wassail-bowl, games, and mistletoe.'

'And perhaps a ghost or so,' finished Frank, laughing, yet with a side glance at his eager little cousin.

'Ah,' said I. 'So your Grange is haunted.'

'I should think so,' said Percy, before his cousin could speak, 'and with a good old Queen Anne ghost. Come down, Doctor, and Frank shall put you in the haunted chamber.'

'No!' cried Frank, with a sharpness which rather surprised me, 'I'll put no one in the Blue Room; the consequences might be fatal. You smile, Lascelles, but I assure you our ghost has been proved to exist!'

'That's a paradox; a ghost can't exist. But the story of your ghost—'

'Is too long to tell now,' said Frank, laughing. 'Come down to the Grange and you'll hear it.'

'Very good,' I replied, rather attracted by the idea of a haunted house, 'you can count upon me for Christmas. But I warn you, Ringan, that I don't believe in spirits. Ghosts went out with gas.'

'Then they must have come in again with electric light,' retorted Frank Ringan, 'for Lady Joan undoubtedly haunts the Grange. I don't mind as it adds distinction to the house.'

'All old families have a ghost,' said Percy, importantly. 'It is very natural when one has ancestors.'

There was no more said on the subject for the time being, but the upshot of this conversation was that I presented myself at Ringshaw Grange two or three days before Christmas. To speak the truth, I came more on Percy's account than my own, as I knew the little man suffered from heart disease, and a sudden shock might prove fatal. If, in the unhealthy atmosphere of an old house, the inmates got talking of ghosts and goblins, it might be that the consequences would be dangerous to so highly strung and delicate a man as Percy Ringan.

For this reason, joined to a sneaking desire to see the ghost, I found myself a guest at Ringshaw Grange. In one way I regret the visit; yet in another I regard it as providential that I was on the spot. Had I been absent the catastrophe might have been greater, although it could scarcely have been more terrible.

Ringshaw Grange was a quaint Elizabethan house, all gables and diamond casements, and oriel windows, and quaint terraces, looking like an illustration out of an old Christmas number. It was embowered in a large park, the trees of which came up almost to the doors, and when I saw it first in the moonlight—for it was by a late train that I came from London—it struck me as the very place for a ghost.

Here was a haunted house of the right quality if ever there was one, and I only hoped when I crossed the threshold that the local spectre would be worthy of its environment. In such an interesting house I did not think to pass a dull Christmas; but—God help me—I did not anticipate so tragic a Yuletide as I spent.

As our host was a bachelor and had no female relative to do the honours of his house the guests were all of the masculine gender. It is true that there was a housekeeper—a distant cousin, I understood—who was rather elderly but very juvenile as to dress and manner. She went by the name of Miss Laura, but no one saw much of her as, otherwise than attending to her duties, she remained mostly in her own rooms.

So our party was composed of young men—none save myself being over the age of thirty, and few being gifted with much intelligence. The talk was mostly of sport, of horse-racing, big game shooting, and yacht-sailing: so that I grew tired at times of these subjects and retired to the library to read and write. The day after I arrived Frank showed me over the house.

It was a wonderful old barrack of a place, with broad passages, twisting interminably like the labyrinth of Daedalus; small bedrooms furnished in an old-fashioned manner; and vast reception apartments with polished floors and painted ceilings. Also there were the customary number of family portraits frowning from the walls; suits of tarnished armour; and ancient tapestries embroidered with grim and ghastly legends of the past.

The old house was crammed with treasures, rare enough to drive an antiquarian crazy; and filled with the flotsam and jetsam of many centuries, mellowed by time into one soft hue, which put them all in keeping with one another. I must say that I was charmed with Ringshaw Grange, and no longer wondered at the pride taken by Percy Ringan in his family and their past glories.

'That's all very well,' said Frank, to whom I remarked as much; 'Percy is rich, and had he this place could keep it up in proper style; but I am as poor as a rat, and unless I can make a rich marriage, or inherit a comfortable legacy, house and furniture, park and timber may all come to the hammer.'

He looked gloomy as he spoke; and, feeling that I had touched on a somewhat delicate matter, I hastened to change the subject, by asking to be shown the famous Blue Chamber, which was said to be haunted. This was the true Mecca of my pilgrimage into Hants.

'It is along this passage,' said Frank, leading the way, 'and not very far from your own quarters. There is nothing in its looks likely to hint at the ghost—at all events by day—but it is haunted for all that.'

Thus speaking he led me into a large room with a low ceiling, and a broad casement looking out onto the untrimmed park, where the woodland was most sylvan. The walls were hung with blue cloth embroidered with grotesque figures in black braid or thread, I know not which. There was a large old-fashioned bed with tester and figured curtains and a quantity of cumbersome furniture of the early Georgian epoch. Not having been inhabited for many years the room had a desolate and silent look—if one may use such an expression—and to my mind looked gruesome enough to conjure up a battalion of ghosts, let alone one.

'I don't agree with you!' said I, in reply to my host's remark. 'To my mind this is the very model of a haunted chamber. What is the legend?'

'I'll tell it to you on Christmas Eve,' replied Ringan, as we left the room. 'It is rather a blood-curdling tale.'

'Do you believe it?' said I, struck by the solemn air of the speaker.

'I have had evidence to make me credulous,' he replied dryly, and closed the subject for the time being.

It was renewed on Christmas Eve when all our company were gathered round a huge wood fire in the library. Outside, the snow lay thick on the ground, and the gaunt trees stood up black and leafless out of the white expanse. The sky was of a frosty blue with sharply twinkling stars, and a hard-looking moon. On the snow the shadows of interlacing boughs were traced blackly as in Indian ink, and the cold was of Arctic severity.

But seated in the holly-decked apartment before a noble fire which roared bravely up the wide chimney we cared nothing for the frozen world out of doors. We laughed and talked, sang songs and recalled adventures, until somewhere about ten o'clock we fell into a ghostly vein quite in keeping with the goblin-haunted season. It was then that Frank Ringan was called upon to chill our blood with his local legend. This he did without much pressing.

'In the reign of the good Queen Anne,' said he, with a gravity befitting the subject, 'my ancestor Hugh Ringan was the owner of this house. He was a silent misanthropic man, having been soured early in life by the treachery of a woman. Mistrusting the sex he refused to marry for many years; and it was not until he was fifty years of age that he was beguiled by the arts of a pretty girl into the toils of matrimony. The lady was Joan Challoner, the daughter of the Earl of Branscourt; and she was esteemed one of the beauties of Queen Anne's court.

'It was in London that Hugh met her, and thinking from her innocent and child-like appearance that she would make him a truehearted wife, he married her after a six months' courtship and brought her with all honour to Ringshaw Grange. After his marriage he became more cheerful and less distrustful of his fellow-creatures. Lady Joan was all to him that a wife could be, and seemed devoted to her husband and child—for she early became a mother—when one Christmas Eve all this happiness came to an end.'

'Oh!' said I, rather cynically. 'So Lady Joan proved to be no better than the rest of her sex.'

'So Hugh Ringan thought, Doctor; but he was as mistaken as you are. Lady Joan occupied the Blue Room, which I showed you the other day; and on Christmas Eve, when riding home late, Hugh saw a man descend from the window. Thunderstruck by the sight, he galloped after the man and caught him before he could mount a horse which was waiting for him. The cavalier was a handsome young fellow of twenty-five, who refused to answer Hugh's questions. Thinking, naturally enough, that he had to do with a lover of his wife's, Hugh fought a duel with the stranger and killed him after a hard fight.

'Leaving him dead on the snow he rode back to the Grange, and burst in on his wife to accuse her of perfidy. It was in vain that Lady Joan tried to defend herself by stating that the visitor was her brother, who was engaged in plots for the restoration of James II, and on that account wished to keep secret the fact of his presence in England. Hugh did not believe her, and told her plainly that he had killed her lover; whereupon Lady Joan burst out into a volley of reproaches and cursed her husband. Furious at what he deemed was her boldness Hugh at first attempted to kill her, but not thinking the punishment sufficient, he cut off her right hand.'

'Why?' asked everyone, quite unprepared for this information.

'Because in the first place Lady Joan was very proud of her beautiful white hands, and in the second Hugh had seen the stranger kiss her hand—her right hand—before he descended from the window. For these reasons he mutilated her thus terribly.'

'And she died.'

'Yes, a week after her hand was cut off. And she swore that she would come back to touch all those in the Blue Room—that is who slept in it—who were foredoomed to death. She kept her promise, for many people who have slept in that fatal room have been touched by the dead hand of Lady Joan, and have subsequently died.'

'Did Hugh find out that his wife was innocent?'

'He did,' replied Ringan, 'and within a month after her death. The stranger was really her brother, plotting for James II, as she had stated. Hugh was not punished by man for his crime, but within a year he slept in the Blue Chamber and was found dead next morning with the mark of three fingers on his right wrist. It was thought that in his remorse he had courted death by sleeping in the room cursed by his wife.'

'And there was a mark on him?'

'On his right wrist red marks like a burn; the impression of three fingers. Since that time the room has been haunted.'

'Does everyone who sleeps in it die?' I asked.

'No. Many people have risen well and hearty in the morning. Only those who are doomed to an early death are thus touched!'

'When did the last case occur?'

'Three years ago' was Frank's unexpected reply. 'A friend of mine called Herbert Spencer would sleep in that room. He saw the ghost and was touched. He showed me the marks next morning—three red finger marks.'

'Did the omen hold good?'

'Yes. Spencer died three months afterwards. He was thrown from his horse.'

I was about to put further questions in a sceptical vein, when we heard shouts outside, and we all sprang to our feet as the door was thrown open to admit Miss Laura in a state of excitement.

'Fire! Fire!' she cried, almost distracted. 'Oh! Mr. Ringan,' addressing herself to Percy, 'your room is on fire! I—'

We waited to hear no more, but in a body rushed up to Percy's room. Volumes of smoke were rolling out of the door, and flames were flashing within. Frank Ringan, however, was prompt and cool-headed. He had the alarm bell rung, summoned the servants, grooms, and stable hands, and in twenty minutes the fire was extinguished.

On asking how the fire had started, Miss Laura, with much hysterical sobbing, stated that she had gone into Percy's room to see that all was ready and comfortable for the night. Unfortunately the wind wafted one of the bed-curtains towards the candle she was carrying, and in a moment the room was in a blaze. After pacifying Miss Laura, who could not help the accident, Frank turned to his cousin. By this time we were back again in the library.

'My dear fellow,' he said, 'your room is swimming in water, and is charred with fire. I'm afraid you can't stay there tonight; but I don't know where to put you unless you take the Blue Room.'

'The Blue Room!' we all cried. 'What! The haunted chamber?'

'Yes; all the other rooms are full. Still, if Percy is afraid—'

'Afraid!' cried Percy indignantly. 'I'm not afraid at all. I'll sleep in the Blue Room with the greatest of pleasure.'

'But the ghost—'

'I don't care for the ghost,' interrupted the Australian, with a nervous laugh. 'We have no ghosts in our part of the world, and as I have not seen one, I do not believe there is such a thing.'

We all tried to dissuade him from sleeping in the haunted room, and several of us offered to give up our apartments for the night—Frank among the number. But Percy's dignity was touched, and he was resolute to keep his word. He had plenty of pluck, as I said before, and the fancy that we might think him a coward spurred him on to resist our entreaties.

The end of it was that shortly before midnight he went off to the Blue Room, and declared his intention of sleeping in it. There was nothing more to be said in the face of such obstinacy, so one by one we retired, quite unaware of the events to happen before the morning. So on that Christmas Eve the Blue Room had an unexpected tenant.

On going to my bedroom I could not sleep. The tale told by Frank Ringan haunted my fancy, and the idea of Percy sleeping in that ill-omened room made me nervous. I did not believe in ghosts myself, nor, so far as I knew, did Percy, but the little man suffered from heart disease—he was strung up to a high nervous pitch by our ghost stories—and if anything out of the common—even from natural causes—happened in that room, the shock might be fatal to its occupant.

I knew well enough that Percy, out of pride, would refuse to give up the room, yet I was determined that he should not sleep in it; so, failing persuasion, I employed stratagem. I had my medicine chest with me, and taking it from my portmanteau I prepared a powerful narcotic. I left this on the table and went along to the Blue Room, which, as I have said before, was not very far from mine.

A knock brought Percy to the door, clothed in pyjamas, and at a glance I could see that the ghostly atmosphere of the place was already telling on his nerves. He looked pale and disturbed, but his mouth was firmly set with an obstinate expression likely to resist my proposals. However, out of diplomacy, I made none, but blandly stated my errand, with more roughness, indeed, than was necessary.

'Come to my room, Percy,' I said, when he appeared, 'and let me give you something to calm your nerves.'

'I'm not afraid!' he said, defiantly.

'Who said you were?' I rejoined, tartly. 'You believe in ghosts no more than I do, so why should you be afraid? But after the alarm of fire your nerves are upset, and I want to give you something to put them right. Otherwise, you'll get no sleep.'

'I shouldn't mind a composing draught, certainly,' said the little man. 'Have you it here?'

'No, it's in my room, a few yards off. Come along.'

Quite deluded by my speech and manner, Percy followed me into my bedroom, and obediently enough swallowed the medicine. Then I made him sit down in a comfortable armchair, on the plea that he must not walk immediately after the draught. The result of my experiment was justified, for in less than ten minutes the poor little man was fast asleep under the influence of the narcotic. When thus helpless, I placed him on my bed, quite satisfied that he would not awaken until late the next day. My task accomplished, I extinguished the light, and went off myself to the Blue Room, intending to remain there for the night.

It may be asked why I did so, as I could easily have taken my rest on the sofa in my own room; but the fact is, I was anxious to sleep in a haunted chamber. I did not believe in ghosts, as I had never seen one, but as there was a chance of meeting here with an authentic phantom I did not wish to lose the opportunity.

Therefore when I saw that Percy was safe for the night, I took up my quarters in the ghostly territory, with much curiosity, but—as I can safely aver—no fear. All the same, in case of practical jokes on the part of the feather-headed young men in the house, I took my revolver with me. Thus prepared, I locked the door of the Blue Room and slipped into bed, leaving the light burning. The revolver I kept under my pillow ready to my hand in case of necessity.

'Now,' said I grimly, as I made myself comfortable, 'I'm ready for ghosts, or goblins, or practical jokers.'

I lay awake for a long time, staring at the queer figures on the blue draperies of the apartment. In the pale flame of the candle they looked ghostly enough to disturb the nerves of anyone: and when the draught fluttered the tapestries the figures seemed to move as though alive. For this sight alone I was glad that Percy had not slept in that room. I could fancy the poor man lying in that vast bed with blanched face and beating heart, listening to every creak, and watching the fantastic embroideries waving on the walls. Brave as he was, I am sure the sounds and sights of that room would have shaken his nerves. I did not feel very comfortable myself, sceptic as I was.

When the candle had burned down pretty low I fell asleep. How long I slumbered I know not: but I woke up with the impression that something or someone was in the room. The candle had wasted nearly to the socket and the flame was flickering and leaping fitfully, so as to display the room one moment and leave it almost in darkness the next. I heard a soft step crossing the room, and as it drew near a sudden spurt of flame from the candle showed me a little woman standing by the side of the bed. She was dressed in a gown of flowered brocade, and wore the towering head dress of the Queen Anne epoch. Her face I could scarcely see, as the flash of flame was only momentary: but I felt what the Scotch call a deadly grue as I realized that this was the veritable phantom of Lady Joan.

For the moment the natural dread of the supernatural quite overpowered me, and with my hands and arms lying outside the counterpane I rested inert and chilled with fear. This sensation of helplessness in the presence of evil was like what one experiences in a nightmare of the worst kind.

When again the flame of the expiring candle shot up, I beheld the ghost close at hand, and—as I felt rather than saw—knew that it was bending over me. A faint odour of musk was in the air, and I heard the soft rustle of the brocaded skirts echo through the semi-darkness. The next moment I felt my right wrist gripped in a burning grasp, and the sudden pain roused my nerves from their paralysis.

With a yell I rolled over, away from the ghost, wrenching my wrist from that horrible clasp, and, almost mad with pain I groped with my left hand for the revolver. As I seized it the candle flared up for the last time, and I saw the ghost gliding back towards the tapestries. In a second I raised the revolver and fired. The next moment there was a wild cry of terror and agony, the fall of a heavy body on the floor, and almost before I knew where I was I found myself outside the door of the haunted room. To attract attention I fired another shot from my revolver, while the Thing on the floor moaned in the darkness most horribly.

In a few moments guests and servants, all in various stages of undress, came rushing along the passage bearing lights. A babel of voices arose, and I managed to babble some incoherent explanation, and led the way into the room. There on the floor lay the ghost, and we lowered the candles to look at its face. I sprang up with a cry on recognizing who it was.

'Frank Ringan!'

It was indeed Frank Ringan disguised as a woman in wig and brocades. He looked at me with a ghostly face, his mouth working nervously. With an effort he raised himself on his hands and tried to speak—whether in confession or exculpation, I know not. But the attempt was too much for him, a choking cry escaped his lips, a jet of blood burst from his mouth, and he fell back dead.

Over the rest of the events of that terrible night I draw a veil. There are some things it is as well not to speak of. Only I may state that all through the horror and confusion Percy Ringan, thanks to my strong sleeping draught, slumbered as peacefully as a child, thereby saving his life.

With the morning's light came discoveries and explanations. We found one of the panels behind the tapestry of the Blue Room open, and it gave admittance into a passage which on examination proved to lead into Frank Ringan's bedroom. On the floor we discovered a delicate hand formed of steel, and which bore marks of having been in the fire. On my right wrist were three distinct burns, which I have no hesitation in declaring were caused by the mechanical hand which we picked up near the dead man. And the explanation of these things came from Miss Laura, who was wild with terror at the death of her master, and said in her first outburst of grief and fear, what I am sure she regretted in her calmer moments.

'It's all Frank's fault,' she wept. 'He was poor and wished to be rich. He got Percy to make his will in his favour, and wanted to kill him by a shock. He knew that Percy had heart disease and that a shock might prove fatal; so he contrived that his cousin should sleep in the Blue Room on Christmas Eve; and he himself played the ghost of Lady Joan with the burning hand. It was a steel hand, which he heated in his own room so as to mark with a scar those it touched.'

'Whose idea was this?' I asked, horrified by the devilish ingenuity of the scheme.

'Frank's!' said Miss Laura, candidly. 'He promised to marry me if I helped him to get the money by Percy's death. We found that there was a secret passage leading to the Blue Room; so some years ago we invented the story that it was haunted.'

'Why, in God's name?'

'Because Frank was always poor. He knew that his cousin in Australia had heart disease, and invited him home to kill him with fright. To make things safe he was always talking about the haunted room and telling the story so that everything should be ready for Percy on his arrival. Our plans were all carried out. Percy arrived and Frank got him to make the will in his favour. Then he was told the story of Lady Joan and her hand, and by setting fire to Percy's room last night I got him to sleep in the Blue Chamber without any suspicion being aroused.'

'You wicked woman!' I cried. 'Did you fire Percy's room on purpose?'

'Yes. Frank promised to marry me if I helped him. We had to get Percy to sleep in the Blue Chamber, and I managed it by setting fire to his bedroom. He would have died with fright when Frank, as Lady Joan, touched him with the steel hand, and no one would have been the wiser. Your sleeping in that haunted room saved Percy's life, Dr. Lascelles, yet Frank invited you down as part of his scheme, that you might examine the body and declare the death to be a natural one.'

'Was it Frank who burnt the wrist of Herbert Spencer some years ago?' I asked.

'Yes!' replied Miss Laura, wiping her red eyes. 'We thought if the ghost appeared to a few other people, that Percy's death might seem more natural. It was a mere coincidence that Mr. Spencer died three months after the ghost touched him.'

'Do you know you are a very wicked woman, Miss Laura?'

'I am a very unhappy one,' she retorted. 'I have lost the only man I ever loved; and his miserable cousin survives to step into his shoes as the master of Ringshaw Grange.'

That was the sole conversation I had with the wretched woman, for shortly afterwards she disappeared, and I fancy must have gone abroad, as she was never more heard of. At the inquest held on the body of Frank the whole strange story came out, and was reported at full length by the London press to the dismay of ghost-seers: for the fame of Ringshaw Grange as a haunted mansion had been great in the land.

I was afraid lest the jury should bring in a verdict of manslaughter against me, but the peculiar features of the case being taken into consideration I was acquitted of blame, and shortly afterwards returned to India with an unblemished character. Percy Ringan was terribly distressed on hearing of his cousin's death, and shocked by the discovery of his treachery. However, he was consoled by becoming the head of the family, and as he lives a quiet life at Ringshaw Grange there is not much chance of his early death from heart disease—at all events from a ghostly point of view.

The Blue Chamber is shut up, for it is haunted now by a worse spectre than that of Lady Joan, whose legend (purely fictitious) was so ingeniously set forth by Frank. It is haunted by the ghost of the cold-blooded scoundrel who fell into his own trap; and who met with his death in the very moment he was contriving that of another man. As to myself, I have given up ghost-hunting and sleeping in haunted rooms. Nothing will ever tempt me to experiment in that way again. One adventure of that sort is enough to last me a lifetime.

# The Chopham Affair

## Edgar Wallace

Edgar Wallace (1875–1932) was a legendary figure whose life was stranger than any fiction. A journalist who became a hugely successful novelist and playwright, he stood for Parliament, and made and spent a fortune. His was a household name—so much so that, even thirty years after his death, *Edgar Wallace Mysteries* became a popular and long-running television series with a theme tune that was a Top Ten hit for the Shadows. G.K. Chesterton said not long after his death that Wallace was 'a mass-producer…a huge furnace and factory of fiction'. Subtlety was not his strongest point; as Chesterton said, 'We have all enjoyed his ingenious plots, but there was inevitably something in his type of plotting that recalls our shyness in the presence of the Omnipresent Chinaman or the League of the Scarlet Scorpion.'

Wallace's contemporaries, in other words, recognized that he often relied on lurid and melodramatic scenarios to achieve his effects, but nobody could deny that he was the most popular thriller writer of his day. Vivid, engaging, and energetic, his short stories have arguably stood the test of time better than the majority of his novels. He had a knack of conjuring up a character or a setting in a couple of sentences, and in 'The Chopham Affair', he tackles a Christmas mystery with his customary verve.

Lawyers who write books are not, as a rule, popular with their confrères, but Archibald Lenton, the most brilliant of prosecuting attorneys, was an exception. He kept a case-book and published extracts from time to time. He has not published his theories on the Chopham affair, though I believe he formulated one. I present him with the facts of the case and the truth about Alphonse or Alphonso Riebiera.

This was a man who had a way with women, especially women who had not graduated in the more worldly school of experience. He described himself as a Spaniard, though his passport was issued by a South American republic. Sometimes he presented visiting cards which were inscribed 'Le Marquis de Riebiera', but that was only on very special occasions.

He was young, with an olive complexion, faultless features, and showed his two rows of dazzling white teeth when he smiled. He found it convenient to change his appearance. For example: when he was a hired dancer attached to the personnel of an Egyptian hotel he wore little side whiskers which, oddly enough, exaggerated his youthfulness; in the casino at Enghien, where by some means he secured the position of croupier, he was decorated with a little black moustache. Staid, sober and unimaginative spectators of his many adventures were irritably amazed that women said anything to him, but then it is notoriously difficult for any man, even an unimaginative man, to discover attractive qualities in successful lovers.

And yet the most unlikely women came under his spell and had to regret it. There arrived a time when he became a patron of the gambling establishments where he had been the most humble and the least trusted of servants, when he lived royally in hotels where he once was hired at so many piastre per dance. Diamonds came to his spotless shirt-front, pretty manicurists tended his nails and received fees larger than his one-time dancing partners had slipped shyly into his hand.

There were certain gross men who played interminable dominoes in the cheaper cafés that abound on the unfashionable side of the Seine, who are amazing news centres. They know how the oddest people live, and they were very plain-spoken when they discussed Alphonse. They could tell you, though heaven knows how the information came to them, of fat registered letters that came to him in his flat in the Boulevard Haussmann. Registered letters stuffed with money, and despairing letters that said in effect (and in various languages): 'I can send you no more—this is the last'. But they did send more.

Alphonse had developed a well-organized business. He would leave for London, or Rome, or Amsterdam, or Vienna, or even Athens, arriving at his destination by sleeping-car, drive to the best hotel, hire a luxurious suite—and telephone. Usually the unhappy lady met him by appointment, tearful, hysterically furious, bitter, insulting, but always remunerative.

For when Alphonse read extracts from the letters they had sent to him in the day of the Great Glamour and told them what their husbands' income was almost to a pound, lira, franc or guilder, they reconsidered their decision to tell their husbands everything, and Alphonse went back to Paris with his allowance.

This was his method with the bigger game; sometimes he announced his coming visit with a letter discreetly worded, which made personal application unnecessary. He was not very much afraid of husbands or brothers; the philosophy

which had germinated from his experience made him contemptuous of human nature. He believed that most people
were cowards and lived in fear of their lives, and greater fear
of their regulations. He carried two silver-plated revolvers,
one in each hip-pocket. They had prettily damascened bar-
rels and ivory handles carved in the likeness of nymphs. He
bought them in Cairo from a man who smuggled cocaine
from Vienna.

Alphonse had some twenty 'clients' on his books, and
added to them as opportunity arose. Of the twenty, five were
gold mines (he thought of them as such), the remainder
were silver mines.

There was a silver mine living in England, a very lovely,
rather sad-looking girl, who was happily married, except when
she thought of Alphonse. She loved her husband and hated
herself and hated Alphonse intensely and impotently. Having
a fortune of her own she could pay—therefore she paid.

Then in a fit of desperate revolt she wrote saying: 'This is
the last, etc.' Alphonse was amused. He waited until Septem-
ber when the next allowance was due, and it did not come.
Nor in October, nor November. In December he wrote to
her; he did not wish to go to England in December, for
England is very gloomy and foggy, and it was so much nicer
in Egypt; but business was business.

His letter reached its address when the woman to whom it
was addressed was on a visit to her aunt in Long Island. She
had been born an American. Alphonse had not written in
answer to her letter; she had sailed for New York feeling safe.

Her husband, whose initial was the same as his wife's,
opened the letter by accident and read it through very carefully. He was no fool. He did not regard the wife he wooed
as an outcast; what happened before his marriage was her
business—what happened now was his.

And he understood these wild dreams of her, and her wild, uncontrollable weeping for no reason at all, and he knew what the future held for her.

He went to Paris and made enquiries: he sought the company of the gross men who play dominoes, and heard much that was interesting.

Alphonse arrived in London and telephoned from a call-box. Madam was not at home. A typewritten letter came to him, making an appointment for the Wednesday. It was the usual rendezvous, the hour specified, an injunction to secrecy. The affair ran normally.

He passed his time pleasantly in the days of waiting. Bought a new Spanza car of the latest model, arranged for its transportation to Paris and, in the meantime, amused himself by driving it.

At the appointed hour he arrived, knocked at the door of the house and was admitted...

Riebiera, green of face, shaking at the knees, surrendered his two ornamented pistols without a fight...

At eight o'clock on Christmas morning Superintendent Oakington was called from his warm bed by telephone and was told the news.

◇◇◇

A milkman driving across Chopham Common had seen a car standing a little off the road. It was apparently a new car, and must have been standing in its position all night. There were three inches of snow on its roof, beneath the body of the car the bracken was green.

An arresting sight even for a milkman who, at seven o'clock on a wintry morning, had no other thought than to supply the needs of his customers as quickly as possible and return at the earliest moment to his own home and the festivities and feastings proper to the day.

He got out of the Ford he was driving and stamped through the snow. He saw a man lying face downwards, and in his grey hand a silver-barrelled revolver. He was dead. And then the startled milkman saw the second man. His face was invisible: it lay under a thick mask of snow that made his pinched features grotesque and hideous.

The milkman ran back to his car and drove toward a police-station.

Mr. Oakington was on the spot within an hour of being called. There were a dozen policemen grouped around the car and the shapes in the snow; the reporters, thank God, had not arrived.

Late in the afternoon the superintendent put a call through to one man who might help in a moment of profound bewilderment.

Archibald Lenton was the most promising of Treasury Juniors that the Bar had known for years. The Common Law Bar lifts its delicate nose at lawyers who are interested in criminal cases to the exclusion of other practice. But Archie Lenton survived the unspoken disapproval of his brethren and, concentrating on this unsavoury aspect of jurisprudence, was both a successful advocate and an authority on certain types of crime, for he had written a textbook which was accepted as authoritative.

An hour later he was in the superintendent's room at Scotland Yard, listening to the story.

'We've identified both men. One is a foreigner, a man from the Argentine, so far as I can discover from his passport, named Alphonse or Alphonso Riebiera. He lives in Paris, and has been in this country for about a week.'

'Well off?'

'Very, I should say. We found about two hundred pounds in his pocket. He was staying at the Nederland Hotel, and bought a car for twelve hundred pounds only last Friday, paying cash. That is the car we found near the body. I've been on the 'phone to Paris, and he is suspected there of being a blackmailer. The police have searched and sealed his flat, but found no documents of any kind. He is evidently the sort of man who keeps his business under his hat.'

'He was shot, you say? How many times?'

'Once, through the head. The other man was killed in exactly the same way. There was a trace of blood in the car, but nothing else.'

Mr. Lenton jotted down a note on a pad of paper.

'Who was the other man?' he asked.

'That's the queerest thing of all—an old acquaintance of yours.'

'Mine? Who on earth—?'

'Do you remember a fellow you defended on a murder charge—Joe Stackett?'

'At Exeter, good lord, yes! Was that the man?'

'We've identified him from his fingerprints. As a matter of fact, we were after Joe—he's an expert car thief who only came out of prison last week; he got away with a car yesterday morning, but abandoned it after a chase and slipped through the fingers of the Flying Squad. Last night he pinched an old car from a second-hand dealer and was spotted and chased. We found the car abandoned in Tooting. He was never seen again until he was picked up on the Chopham Common.'

Archie Lenton leant back in his chair and stared thoughtfully at the ceiling.

'He stole the Spanza—the owner jumped on the running-board and there was a fight'—he began, but the superintendent shook his head.

'Where did he get his gun? English criminals do not carry guns. And they weren't ordinary revolvers. Silver-plated, ivory butts carved with girls' figures—both identical. There were fifty pounds in Joe's pocket; they are consecutive numbers to those found in Riebiera's pocket-book. If he'd stolen them he'd have taken the lot. Joe wouldn't stop at murder, you know that, Mr. Lenton. He killed that old woman in Exeter, although he was acquitted. Riebiera must have given him the fifty—'

A telephone bell rang; the superintendent drew the instrument toward him and listened. After ten minutes of a conversation which was confined, so far as Oakington was concerned, to a dozen brief questions, he put down the receiver.

'One of my officers has traced the movements of the car; it was seen standing outside "Greenlawns", a house in Tooting. It was there at nine forty-five and was seen by a postman. If you feel like spending Christmas night doing a little bit of detective work, we'll go down and see the place.'

They arrived half an hour later at a house in a very respectable neighbourhood. The two detectives who waited their coming had obtained the keys, but had not gone inside. The house was for sale and was standing empty. It was the property of two old maiden ladies who had placed the premises in an agent's hands when they had moved into the country.

The appearance of the car before an empty house had aroused the interest of the postman. He had seen no lights in the windows, and decided that the machine was owned by one of the guests at the next door house.

Oakington opened the door and switched on the light. Strangely enough, the old ladies had not had the current disconnected, though they were notoriously mean. The passage was bare, except for a pair of bead curtains which hung from an arched support to the ceiling.

The front room drew blank. It was in one of the back rooms on the ground floor that they found evidence of the crime. There was blood on the bare planks of the floor and in the grate a litter of ashes.

'Somebody has burnt paper—I smelt it when I came into the room,' said Lenton.

He knelt before the grate and lifted a handful of fine ashes carefully.

'And these have been stirred up until there isn't an ash big enough to hold a word,' he said.

He examined the blood-prints and made a careful scrutiny of the walls. The window was covered with a shutter.

'That kept the light from getting in,' he said, 'and the sound of the shot getting out. There is nothing else here.'

The detective-sergeant who was inspecting the other rooms returned with the news that a kitchen window had been forced. There was one muddy print on the kitchen table which was under the window, and a rough attempt had been made to obliterate this. Behind the house was a large garden and behind that an allotment. It would be easy to reach and enter the house without exciting attention.

'But if Stackett was being chased by the police why should he come here?' he asked.

'His car was found abandoned not more than two hundred yards from here,' explained Oakington. 'He may have entered the house in the hope of finding something valuable, and have been surprised by Riebiera.'

Archie Lenton laughed softly.

'I can give you a better theory than that,' he said, and for the greater part of the night he wrote carefully and convincingly, reconstructing the crime, giving the most minute details.

That account is still preserved at Scotland Yard, and there are many highly placed officials who swear by it.

And yet something altogether different happened on the night of that 24th of December...

The streets were greasy, the car-lines abominably so. Stackett's mean little car slithered and skidded alarmingly. He had been in a bad temper when he started out on his hungry quest; he grew sour and savage with the evening passing on with nothing to show for his discomfort.

The suburban high street was crowded too; street cars moved at a crawl, their bells clanging pathetically; street vendors had their stalls jammed end to end on either side of the thoroughfare; stalls green and red with holly wreaths and untidy bunches of mistletoe; there were butcher stalls, raucous auctioneers holding masses of raw beef and roaring their offers; vegetable stalls; stalls piled high with plates and cups and saucers and gaudy dishes and glassware, shining in the rays of the powerful acetylene lamps…

The car skidded. There was a crash and a scream. Breaking crockery has an alarming sound… A yell from the stall owner; Stackett straightened his machine and darted between a tramcar and a trolley…

'Hi, you!'

He twisted his wheel, almost knocked down the policeman who came to intercept him, and swung into a dark side street, his foot clamped on the accelerator. He turned to the right and the left, to the right again. Here was a long suburban road; houses monotonously alike on either side, terribly dreary brick blocks where men and women and children lived, were born, paid rent, and died. A mile further on he passed the gateway of the cemetery where they found the rest which was their supreme reward for living at all.

The police whistle had followed him for less than a quarter of a mile. He had passed a policeman running toward the sound—anyway, flatties never worried Stackett. Some of his ill humour passed in the amusement which the sight of the running copper brought.

Bringing the noisy little car to a standstill by the side of the road, he got down, and, relighting the cigarette he had so carefully extinguished, he gazed glumly at the stained and battered mudguard which was shivering and shaking under the pulsations of the engine...

Through that same greasy street came a motorcyclist, muffled to the chin, his goggles dangling about his neck. He pulled up his shining wheel near the policeman on point duty and, supporting his balance with one foot in the muddy road, asked questions.

'Yes, sergeant,' said the policeman. 'I saw him. He went down there. As a matter of fact, I was going to pinch him for driving to the common danger, but he hopped it.'

'That's Joe Stackett,' nodded Sergeant Kenton of the C.I.D. 'A thin-faced man with a pointed nose?'

The point-duty policeman had not seen the face behind the wind-screen, but he had seen the car, and that he described accurately.

'Stolen from Elmer's garage. At least, Elmer will say so, but he probably provided it. Dumped stuff. Which way did you say?'

The policeman indicated, and the sergeant kicked his engine to life and went chug-chugging down the dark street.

He missed Mr. Stackett by a piece of bad luck—bad luck for everybody, including Mr. Stackett, who was at the beginning of his amazing adventure.

Switching off the engine, he had continued on foot. About fifty yards away was the wide opening of a road superior in class to any he had traversed. Even the dreariest suburb has its West End, and here were villas standing on their own acres—very sedate villas, with porches and porch lamps in wrought-iron and oddly coloured glass, and shaven lawns, and rose gardens swathed in matting, and no two villas were alike. At the far end he saw a red light, and his heart leapt with joy. Christmas—it was to be Christmas after all, with good food and lashings of drink and other manifestations of happiness and comfort peculiarly attractive to Joe Stackett.

It looked like a car worth knocking off, even in the darkness. He saw somebody near the machine and stopped. It was difficult to tell in the gloom whether the person near the car had got in or had come out. He listened. There came to him neither the slam of the driver's door nor the whine of the self-starter. He came a little closer, walked boldly on, his restless eyes moving left and right for danger. All the houses were occupied. Bright lights illuminated the casement cloth which covered the windows. He heard the sound of revelry and two gramophones playing dance tunes. But his eyes always came back to the polished limousine at the door of the end house. There was no light there. It was completely dark, from the gabled attic to the ground floor.

He quickened his pace. It was a Spanza. His heart leapt at the recognition. For a Spanza is a car for which there is a ready sale. You can get as much as a hundred pounds for a new one. They are popular amongst Eurasians and wealthy Hindus. Binky Jones, who was the best car fence in London, would pay him cash, not less than sixty. In a week's time that car would be crated and on its way to India, there to be resold at a handsome profit.

The driver's door was wide open. He heard the soft purr of the engine. He slid into the driver's seat, closed the door noiselessly, and almost without as much as a whine the Spanza moved on.

It was a new one, brand new... A hundred at least.

Gathering speed, he passed to the end of the road, came to a wide common and skirted it. Presently he was in another shopping street, but he knew too much to turn back toward London. He would take the open country for it, work round through Esher and come into London by the Portsmouth Road. The art of car-stealing is to move as quickly as possible from the police division where the machine is stolen and may be instantly reported, to a 'foreign' division which will not know of the theft until hours after.

There might be all sorts of extra pickings. There was a big luggage trunk behind and possibly a few knick-knacks in the body of the car itself. At a suitable moment he would make a leisurely search. At the moment he headed for Epsom, turning back to hit the Kingston by-pass. Sleet fell—snow and rain together. He set the screen-wiper working and began to hum a little tune. The Kingston by-pass was deserted. It was too unpleasant a night for much traffic.

Mr. Stackett was debating what would be the best place to make his search when he felt an unpleasant draught behind him. He had noticed there was a sliding window separating the interior of the car from the driver's seat, which had possibly worked loose. He put up his hand to push it close.

'Drive on, don't turn round or I'll blow your head off!'

Involuntarily he half turned to see the gaping muzzle of an automatic, and in his agitation put his foot on the brake. The car skidded from one side of the road to the other, half turned and recovered.

'Drive on, I am telling you,' said a metallic voice. 'When you reach the Portsmouth Road turn and bear toward Weybridge. If you attempt to stop I will shoot you. Is that clear?'

Joe Stackett's teeth were chattering. He could not articulate the 'yes'. All that he could do was to nod. He went on nodding for half a mile before he realized what he was doing.

No further word came from the interior of the car until they passed the race-course; then unexpectedly the voice gave a new direction:

'Turn left toward Leatherhead.'

The driver obeyed.

They came to a stretch of common. Stackett, who knew the country well, realized the complete isolation of the spot.

'Slow down, pull in to the left... There is no dip there. You can switch on your lights.'

The car slid and bumped over the uneven ground, the wheels crunched through beds of bracken...

'Stop.'

The door behind him opened. The man got out. He jerked open the driver's door.

'Step down,' he said. 'Turn out your lights first. Have you got a gun?'

'Gun? Why the hell should I have a gun?' stammered the car thief.

He was focused all the time in a ring of light from a very bright electric torch which the passenger had turned upon him.

'You are an act of Providence.'

Stackett could not see the face of the speaker. He saw only the gun in the hand, for the stranger kept this well in the light.

'Look inside the car.'

Stackett looked and almost collapsed. There was a figure huddled in one corner of the seat—the figure of a man. He saw something else—a bicycle jammed into the car, one wheel touching the roof, the other on the floor. He saw the man's white face... Dead! A slim, rather short man, with dark hair and a dark moustache, a foreigner. There was a little red hole in his temple.

'Pull him out,' commanded the voice sharply.

Stackett shrank back, but a powerful hand pushed him toward the car.

'Pull him out!'

With his face moist with cold perspiration, the car thief obeyed; put his hands under the armpits of the inanimate figure, dragged him out and laid him on the bracken.

'He's dead,' he whimpered.

'Completely,' said the other.

Suddenly he switched off his electric torch. Far away came a gleam of light on the road, coming swiftly toward them. It was a car moving towards Esher. It passed.

'I saw you coming just after I had got the body into the car. There wasn't time to get back to the house. I'd hoped you were just an ordinary pedestrian. When I saw you get into the car I guessed pretty well your vocation. What is your name?'

'Joseph Stackett.'

'Stackett?'

The light flashed on his face again. 'How wonderful! Do you remember the Exeter Assizes? The old woman you killed with a hammer? I defended you!'

Joe's eyes were wide open. He stared past the light at the dim grey thing that was a face.

'Mr. Lenton?' he said hoarsely. 'Good God, sir!'

'You murdered her in cold blood for a few paltry shillings, and you would have been dead now, Stackett, if I hadn't found a flaw in the evidence. You expected to die, didn't you? You remember how we used to talk in Exeter Gaol about the trap that would not work when they tried to hang a murderer, and the ghoulish satisfaction you had that you would stand on the same trap?'

Joe Stackett grinned uncomfortably.

'And I meant it, sir,' he said, 'but you can't try a man twice—'

Then his eyes dropped to the figure at his feet, the dapper little man with a black moustache, with a red hole in his temple.

Lenton leant over the dead man, took out a pocket case from the inside of the jacket and at his leisure detached ten notes.

'Put these in your pocket.'

He obeyed, wondering what service would be required of him, wondered more why the pocket-book with its precious notes was returned to the dead man's pocket.

Lenton looked back along the road. Snow was falling now, real snow. It came down in small particles, falling so thickly that it seemed that a fog lay on the land.

'You fit into this perfectly… a man unfit to live. There is fate in this meeting.'

'I don't know what you mean by fate.'

Joe Stackett grew bold: he had to deal with a lawyer and a gentleman who, in a criminal sense, was his inferior. The money obviously had been given to him to keep his mouth shut.

'What have you been doing, Mr. Lenton? That's bad, ain't it? This fellow's dead and—'

He must have seen the pencil of flame that came from the other's hand. He could have felt nothing, for he was dead before he sprawled over the body on the ground.

Mr. Archibald Lenton examined the revolver by the light of his lamp, opened the breech and closed it again. Stooping, he laid it near the hand of the little man with the black moustache and, lifting the body of Joe Stackett, he dragged it toward the car and let it drop. Bending down, he clasped the still warm hands about the butt of another pistol. Then, at his leisure, he took the bicycle from the interior of the car and carried it back to the road. It was already white and fine snow was falling in sheets.

Mr. Lenton went on and reached his home two hours later, when the bells of the local Anglo-Catholic church were ringing musically.

There was a cable waiting for him from his wife:

*A Happy Christmas to you, darling.*

He was ridiculously pleased that she had remembered to send the wire—he was very fond of his wife.

# The Man with the Sack

*Margery Allingham*

Along with Agatha Christie, Dorothy L. Sayers, and Ngaio Marsh, Margery Louise Allingham (1904–66) was one of those 'Queens of Crime' who helped to transform the detective fiction genre in the 1930s. Albert Campion, her series character, is a rather more enigmatic figure than most 'great detectives' of the Golden Age, but no less interesting for that. He made his first appearance in *The Crime at Black Dudley* (1929), although he played a subordinate role to Dr. George Abbershaw. Before long, he took centre stage, and after Allingham's death, her husband Philip Young-man Carter completed the last Campion novel, and wrote a couple more himself. In recent years, continuation novels featuring Campion have been penned by Mike Ripley, while the flourishing state of the Margery Allingham Society more than half a century after her death is testament to the endur-ing appeal of a highly engaging author.

Allingham was a prolific writer of short stories, and the disciplines of the short form seemed to bring out the best in her. This Yuletide tale was first published as 'The Case of the Man with the Sack' in the *Strand Magazine* in 1936, and was included in *Mr Campion: Criminologist* the following year; an abbreviated version, 'The Man with the Sack', appeared many years later. The text reprinted here is the original.

'Albert dear,

'We are going to have a quiet family party at home here for the holiday, just ourselves and the dear village. It would be *such fun* to have you with us. There is a train at 10.45 from Liverpool Street which will get you to Chelmsworth in time for us to pick you up for lunch on Christmas Eve. You really must *not* refuse me. Sheila is being rather difficult and I have the Welkins coming. Ada Welkin is a dear woman. Her jewellery is such a responsibility in a house. She *will* bring it. Sheila has invited such an undesirable boy, the son in the Peters crash, absolutely penniless, my dear, and probably quite desperate. As her mother I am naturally anxious. Remember I rely on you.

'Affectionately yours,
'Mae Turrett.

'P.S. Don't bring a car unless you must. The Welkins seem to be bringing two.'

Mr. Albert Campion, whom most people described as the celebrated amateur criminologist, and who used to refer to himself somewhat sadly as a universal uncle, read the letter a second time before he expressed himself vulgarly but explicitly and pitched it into the waste-paper basket. Then, sitting down at the bureau in the corner of the breakfast-room, he pulled a sheet of notepaper towards him.

'My Dear Mae,' he wrote briefly, 'I can't manage it.
You must forgive me. My love to Sheila and George.
'Yours ever,
'Albert.

'P.S. My sympathy in your predicament. I think I can
put you on to just the man you need: P. Richards,
13 Acacia Border, Chiswick. He is late of the Metropolitan Police and, like myself, is clean, honest and
presentable. Your guests' valuables will be perfectly
safe while he is in the house and you will find his fee
very reasonable.'

He folded the note, sealed it, and addressed it to Lady Turrett, Pharaoh's Court, Pharaoh's Field, Suffolk.

'In other words, my dear Mae,' he said aloud, as he set it
on the mantelpiece, 'if you want a private dick in the house,
employ one. We are not high-hat, but we have our pride.'

He wandered back to the breakfast-table and the rest of
his correspondence. There was another personal letter under
the pile of greeting cards sent off a week too soon by earnest
citizens who had taken the Postmaster-General's annual
warning a shade too seriously, a large blue envelope addressed
in a near-printing hand which proclaimed that the writer
had gone to her first school in the early nineteen-twenties.

Mr. Campion tore it open and a cry from Sheila Turrett's
heart fell out.

'My Darling Albert,
'Please come for Christmas. It's going to be poisonous. Mother has some queer ideas in her head and
the Welkins are frightful. Mike is a dear. At least I
like him and you will too. He is Mike Peters, the son
of the Ripley Peters who had to go to jail when the

firm crashed. But it's not Mike's fault, is it? After all, a good many fathers ought to go to jail only they don't get caught. I don't mean George, of course, bless him (you ought to come if only for his sake. He's like a depression leaving the Azores. It's the thought of the Welkins, poor pet). I don't like to ask you to waste your time on our troubles, but Ada Welkin is *lousy* with diamonds and Mother seems to think that Mike might pinch them, his father having been to jail. Darling, if you are faintly decent do come and back us up. After all, it *is* Christmas.

> 'Yours always (if you come),
> 'Sheila.

'P.S. I'm in love with Mike.'

For a moment or so Mr. Campion sat regarding the letter and its pathetic postscript. Then, rather regretfully, but comforted by a deep sense of virtue, he crossed the room and, tearing up the note he had written to Lady Turrett, settled himself to compose another.

On Christmas Eve the weather decided to be seasonable; a freezing overhead fog turned the city into night and the illuminated shop fronts had the traditional festive appearance even in the morning. It was more than just cold. The damp, soot-laden atmosphere soaked into the bones relentlessly and Mr. Campion's recollection of Pharaoh's Court, rising gaunt and bleak amid three hundred acres of ploughed clay and barren salting, all as flat as the estuary beyond, was not enhanced by the chill.

The thought of Sheila and her father cheered him a little, almost but not quite offsetting the prospect of Lady Mae in anxious mood. Buttoning himself into his thickest overcoat, he hoped for the best.

The railway station was a happy pandemonium. Everybody who could not visit the East Coast for the holiday was, it seemed, sending presents there, and Mr. Campion, reminded of the custom, glanced anxiously at his suitcase, wondering if the box of cigars for George was too large or the casket of perfume for Mae too modest, if Sheila was still young enough to eat chocolates, and if there would be hordes of unexpected children who would hang round his room wistfully, their mute glances resting upon his barren luggage.

He caught the train with ease, no great feat since it was three-quarters of an hour late, and was sitting in his corner idly watching the excited throng on the platform when he caught sight of Charlie Spring. He recognized the face instantly, but the name came to him slowly from the siftings of his memory.

Jail had done Mr. Spring a certain amount of good, Mr. Campion reflected as his glance took in the other man's square shoulders and developed chest. He had been a weedy wreck six months ago standing in the big dock at the Old Bailey, the light from the roof shining down upon his small features and his low forehead, beneath which there peered out the stupidest eyes in the world.

At the moment he seemed very pleased with himself, a bad omen for the rest of the community, but Mr. Campion was not interested. It was Christmas and he had troubles of his own.

However, from force of habit he made a careful mental note of the man and observed that he had been 'out' for some little time, since he had lost all trace of jail shyness, that temporary fit of nerves which even the most experienced exhibit for a week or so after their release. He saw also that

Mr. Spring looked about him with the same peculiar brain-less cunning which he had exhibited in the dock.

He boarded the train a little lower down and Mr. Campion frowned. There was something about Charlie Spring which he had known and which now eluded him. He tried to remember the last and only time he had seen him. He himself had been in court as an expert witness and had heard Mr. Spring sentenced for breaking and entering just before his own case had been called. He remembered that it was breaking and entering and he remembered the flat official voice of the police detective who gave evidence.

But there was something else, something definite and personal which kept bobbing about in the back of his mind, escaping him completely whenever he tried to pin it down. It worried him vaguely, as such things do, all the way to Chelmsworth.

Charlie left the train at Ipswich in the company of one hundred and fifty joyous fellow travellers. Mr. Campion spotted him as he passed the window, walking swiftly, his head bent and a large new fibre suitcase in his hand.

It occurred to Campion that the man was not dressed in character. He seemed to remember him as a dilapidated but somewhat gaudy figure in a dirty check suit and a pink shirt, whereas at the moment his newish navy greatcoat was a model of sobriety and unobtrusiveness. Still, it was no sartorial peculiarity that haunted his memory. It was something odd about the man, some idiosyncrasy, something slightly funny.

Still faintly irritated, Mr. Campion travelled a further ten miles to Chelmsworth. Few country railway stations present a rustic picturesqueness, even in summer, but at any time in the year Chelmsworth was remarkable for its windswept desolation. Mr. Campion alighted on to a narrow slab of concrete, artificially raised above the level of the small town in the valley, and drew a draught of heady rain and brine-soaked air into his lungs. He was experiencing the first shock of finding it not unattractive when there was a clatter of brogues on the concrete and a small russet-clad figure appeared before him. He was aware of honey-brown eyes, red cheeks, white teeth, and a stray curl of red hair escaping from a rakish little tweed cap in which a sprig of holly had been pinned.

'Bless you,' said Sheila Turrett fervently. 'Come on. We're hours late for lunch, they'll all be champing like boarding-house pests.'

She linked her arm through his and dragged him along.

'You're more than a hero to come. I am so grateful and so is George. Perhaps it'll start being Christmas now you're here, which it hasn't been so far in spite of the weather. Isn't it glorious?'

Mr. Campion was forced to admit that there was a certain exhilaration in the air, a certain indefinable charm in the grey-brown shadows chasing in endless succession over the flat landscape.

'There'll be snow to-night.' The girl glanced up at the featherbed sky. 'Isn't it grand? Christmas always makes me feel so excited. I've got you a present. Remember to bring one for me?'

'I'm your guest,' said Mr. Campion with dignity. 'I have a small packet of plain chocolate for you on Christmas morning, but I wished it to be a surprise.'

Sheila climbed into the car. 'Anything will be welcome except diamonds,' she said cheerfully. 'Ada Welkin's getting diamonds, twelve thousand pounds' worth, all to hang round a neck that would disgrace a crocodile. I'm sorry to sound so catty, but we've had these diamonds all through every meal since she came down.'

Mr. Campion clambered into the car beside her.

'Dear me,' he said. 'I had hoped for a merry Christmas, peace and goodwill and all that. Village children bursting their little lungs and everybody else's eardrums in their attempts at religious song, while I listened replete with vast quantities of indigestible food.'

Miss Turrett laughed. 'You're going to get your dear little village kids all right,' she said. 'Two hundred and fifty of 'em. Not even Ada Welkin could dissuade Mother from the Pharaoh's Court annual Christmas Eve party. You'll have just time to sleep off your lunch, swallow a cup of tea, and then it's all hands in the music room. There's the mothers to entertain, too, of course.'

Mr. Campion stirred and sighed gently as he adjusted his spectacles.

'I remember now,' he murmured. 'George said something about it once. It's a traditional function, isn't it?'

'More or less.' Sheila spoke absently. 'Mother revived it with modern improvements some years ago. They have a tea and a Christmas tree and a Santa Claus to hand round the presents.'

The prospect seemed to depress her and she relapsed into gloomy silence as the little car shot over the dry, windswept roads.

Mr. Campion regarded her covertly. She had grown into a very pretty girl indeed, he decided, but he hoped the 'son in the Peters crash' was worth the worry he saw in her forehead.

'What about the young gentleman with the erring father?' he ventured diffidently. 'Is he at Pharaoh's Court now?'

'Mike?' She brightened visibly. 'Oh yes, rather. He's been there for the best part of a week. George honestly likes him and I thought for one heavenly moment that he was going to cut the ice with Mother, but that was before the Welkins came. Since then, of course, it hasn't been so easy. They came a day early, too, which is typical of them. They've been here two days already. The son is the nastiest, the old man runs him close and Ada is ghastly.'

'Horrid for them,' said Mr. Campion mildly.

Sheila did not smile.

'You'll spot it at once when you see Ada,' she said, 'so I may as well tell you. They're fantastically rich and Mother has been goat-touting. It's got to be faced.'

'Goat-touting?'

Sheila nodded earnestly.

'Yes. Lots of society women do it. You must have seen the little ads in the personal columns: "Lady of title will chaperone young girl or arrange parties for an older woman." Or "Lady X. would entertain suitable guest for the London season." In other words, Lady X. will tout around any socially ambitious goat in exchange for a nice large, ladylike fee. It's horrid, but I'm afraid that is how Mother got hold of Ada in the first place. She had some pretty heavy bridge losses at one time. George doesn't know a thing about it, of course, poor darling—and mustn't. He'd be so shocked. I don't know how he accounts for the Welkins.'

Mr. Campion said nothing. It was like Mae Turrett, he reflected, to visit her sins upon her family. Sheila was hurrying on.

'We've never seen the others before,' she said breathlessly. 'Mother gave two parties for Ada in the season and they had a box at the Opera to show some of the diamonds. I couldn't understand why they wanted to drag the menfolk into it until they got here. Then it was rather disgustingly plain.'

Mr. Campion pricked up his ears.

'So nice for the dear children to get to know each other?' he suggested.

Miss Turrett blushed fiercely. 'Something like that,' she said briefly and added after a pause, 'Have you ever met the sort of young man who's been thrust into a responsible position in a business because, and only because, he's Poppa's son? A lordly, blasé, sulky young man who's been kow-towed to by subordinates who are fifty times as intelligent as he is himself? The sort of young man you want to kick on sight?'

Mr. Campion sighed deeply. 'I have.'

Sheila negotiated a right-angle turn. Her forehead was wrinkled and her eyes thoughtful.

'This'll show you the sort of man Kenneth Welkin is,' she said. 'It's so petty and stupid that I'm almost ashamed to mention it, but it does show you. We've had a rather difficult time amusing the Welkins. They don't ride or shoot or read, so this morning, when Mike and I were putting the final touches to the decorations, we asked Kenneth to help us. There was a stupid business over some mistletoe. Kenneth had been laying down the law about where it was to hang and we were a bit tired of him already when he started a lot of silly horseplay. I don't mind being kissed under the mistletoe, of course, but—well, it's the way you do these things, isn't it?'

She stamped on the accelerator to emphasize her point, and Mr. Campion, not a nervous man, clutched the side of the car.

'Sorry,' said Sheila and went on with her story. 'I tried to wriggle away after a bit, and when he wouldn't let me go Mike suddenly lost his temper and told him to behave himself or he'd damned well knock his head off. It was awfully melodramatic and stupid, but it might have passed off and been forgotten if Kenneth hadn't made a scene. First he said he wouldn't be talked to like that, and then he made a reference to Mike's father, which was unforgivable. I thought they were going to have a fight. Then, right in the middle of it, Mother fluttered in with a Santa Claus costume.

She looked at Mike and said, "You'd better try it on, dear. I want you to be most realistic this afternoon." Before he could reply, Kenneth butted in. He looked like a spoilt kid, all pink and furious. "I didn't know you were going to be Father Christmas," he said.'

Miss Turrett paused for breath, her eyes wide.

'Well, can you imagine anything so idiotic?' she said. 'Mike had offered to do the job when he first came down because he wanted to make himself useful. Like everyone else, he regarded it as a fatigue. It never dawned on him that anyone would *want* to do it. Mother was surprised, too, I think. However, she just laughed and said, "You must fight it out between you" and fluttered away again, leaving us all three standing there. Kenneth picked up the costume. "It's from Harridge's," he said. "My mother was with Lady Mae when she ordered it. I thought it was fixed up then that I was to wear it.""

Mr. Campion laughed. He felt very old.

'I suppose Master Michael stepped aside like a little gent and Master Kenneth appears as St. Nicholas?' he murmured.

'Well no, not exactly.' Sheila sounded a little embarrassed. 'Mike was still angry, you see, because Kenneth really had been infernally casual. He suddenly decided to be obstinate. Mother had asked him to do the job, he said, and he was going to do it. I thought they were going to have an open row about it, which would have been quite too absurd, but at that moment the most idiotic thing of all happened. Old Mr. Welkin, who had been prowling about listening as usual, came in and told Kenneth he was to "give way" to Mike— literally, in so many words! It all sounds perfectly mad now I've told it to you, yet Mike is really rather a darling.'

Mr. Campion detected a certain wistfulness in her final phrase and frowned.

◇◇◇

Pharaoh's Court looked unexpectedly mellow and inviting as they came up the drive some minutes later. The old house had captured the spirit of the season and Mr. Campion stepped out of a cold grey world into an enormous entrance hall where the blaze from the nine-foot hearth flickered on the glossy leaves of the ivy and holly festooned along the carved beams of the ceiling.

George Turrett, grey haired and cherubic, was waiting for them. He grasped the visitor's hand with fervour. 'So glad you've come,' he murmured. 'Devilish glad to see you, Campion.'

His extreme earnestness was apparent and Sheila put an arm round his neck.

'It's a human face in the wilderness, isn't it, darling?' she murmured.

Sir George's guilty protest was cut short by the first luncheon bell, a reminder that the train had arrived late, and Mr. Campion was rushed upstairs to his room by a harassed manservant.

He saw the clock as he came down again a moment or so later. It burst upon him as he turned a corner in the corridor and came upon it standing on a console table. Even in his haste it arrested him. Mae Turrett had something of a reputation for interior decoration, but large country houses have a way of collecting furnishing oddities, however rigorous their owner's taste may be.

Although he was not as a rule over-sensitive to artistic monstrosities, Mr. Campion paused in respectful astonishment before this example of the mid-Victorian baroque. A bewildered-looking bronze lady, clad in a pink marble nightgown, was seated upon a gilt ormolu log, one end of which had been replaced by a blue and white enamel clock face. Even as he stared the contraption chimed loudly and aggressively, while downstairs a second luncheon bell rang.

He passed on and forgot all about the clock as soon as he entered the dining-room. Mae Turrett sprang at him with little affected cries which he took to indicate a hostess's delight.

'Albert *dear!*' she said breathlessly. 'How marvellous to see you! Aren't we wonderfully festive? The gardener assures me it's going to snow to-night, in fact he's virtually promised it. I do love a real old family party at Christmas, don't you? Just our very own selves… too lovely! Let me introduce you to a very dear friend of mine: Mrs. Welkin—Mr. Campion…'

Campion was aware of a large middle-aged woman with drooping cheeks and stupid eyes who sniggered at him and looked away again.

Lunch was not a jolly meal by any means. Even Lady Turrett's cultivated chatter died down every now and again. However, Mr. Campion had ample opportunity to observe the strangers of whom he had heard so much.

Mike Peters was a surprise to him. He had expected a nervy, highly-strung young man, afflicted, probably, with a generous dose of self-pity, as the innocent victim of his father's misdeeds or misfortunes, but found instead a sturdy silent youngster with a brief smile and a determined chin. It was obvious that he knew what he wanted and was going for it steadily. Mr. Campion found himself wishing him luck.

Since much criticism before a meeting may easily defeat its own ends, Mr. Campion had been prepared to find the Welkin family pleasant but misunderstood people, round pegs in a very square hole. But here again he was mistaken. Kenneth Welkin, a fresh-faced, angry-eyed young man in clothes which managed to look expensive while intending to appear nonchalant, sat next to Sheila and sulked throughout the meal. The only remark he addressed to Mr. Campion was to ask him what make of car he drove and to disapprove loudly of the answer to his question.

A closer inspection of Mrs. Welkin did not dispel Mr. Campion's first impression, but her husband interested him. Edward Welkin was a large man with a face that would have been distinguished had it not been for the eyes, which were too shrewd, and the mouth, which was too coarse. His attitude towards his hostess was conspicuously different from his wife's, which was ingratiating, and his son's, which was uneasy and unnecessarily defensive. The most obvious thing about him was that he was complacently alien. George he regarded quite clearly as a nincompoop and Lady Turrett as a woman who so far had given his wife value for money. Of everyone else he was sublimely unconscious.

His plus-fours, of the best Savile Row old-gentleman variety, had their effect ruined by the astonishing quantity of jewellery he chose to display at the same time. He wore two signet rings, one with an agate and one with a sapphire, and an immense jewelled tiepin, while out of his waistcoat pocket peeped a gold and onyx pen with a pencil to match, strapped together in a bright green leather case. They were both of them as thick round as his forefinger and looked at first glance like the insignia of some obscure order.

Just before they rose from the table Mrs. Welkin cleared her throat.

'As you're going to have a crowd of *tenants* this evening, Mae, dear, I don't think I'll wear it, do you?' she said with a giggle and a glance at Mr. Campion.

'Wear what, dear?' Lady Turrett spoke absently and Mrs. Welkin looked hurt.

'The necklace,' she said reverently.

'Your diamonds? Good heavens, no! Most unsuitable.' The words escaped her ladyship involuntarily, but in a moment she was mistress of herself and the situation. 'Wear something very simple,' she said with a mechanical smile. 'I'm afraid it's going to be very hard work for us all. Mike, you do know exactly what to do, don't you? At the end of the evening, just before they go home, you put on the costume and come into the little anteroom which leads off the platform. You go straight up to the tree and cut the presents off, while all the rest of us stand round to receive them and pass them on to the children.'

Mrs. Welkin bridled. 'I should have liked to have worn them,' she said irritatingly. 'Still, if you say it's not safe…'

'Mother didn't say it wasn't safe, Mrs. Welkin,' said Sheila, who was fond of the village and resented bitterly any aspersions on its honesty. 'She said it wasn't suitable.'

Mrs. Welkin blushed angrily and forgot herself.

'You're not very polite, young lady,' she said, 'and if it's a question of suitability, where's the suitability in Mr. Peters playing Santa Claus when it was promised to Kenny?'

The mixture of muddled logic and resentment startled everyone. Mike and Sheila grew scarlet, Sir George looked helplessly at his wife, Kenneth Welkin turned savagely on his mother, and Edward Welkin settled rather than saved the situation.

'That'll do,' he said in a voice of thunder. 'That's all been fixed, Ada. I don't want to hear any more from either of you on the subject.'

It was altogether a very awkward moment and the table broke up with relief. Sir George tugged Campion's arm.

'Cigar—library,' he murmured, and faded quietly away. Campion followed him.

◇◇◇

There were Christmas decorations in the big book-filled study and, as he settled himself in a wing chair before a fire of logs and attended to the tip of a Romeo y Julieta, Mr. Campion felt once more the return of the Christmas spirit.

Sir George was anxious about his daughter's happiness.

'I like young Peters,' he said earnestly. 'Fellow can't help his father's troubles. Mae objects he hasn't any money, but, between you and me, Campion, I'd rather see her in rags tied to a decent fellow than sittin' up in a Rolls-Royce beside that little Welkin bounder in the next room.'

Mr. Campion agreed with him and he went on.

'The boy Mike's an engineer,' he said, 'and makin' good at his job slowly, and Sheila seems fond of him, but Mae talks about hereditary dishonesty. Taint may be there. What do you think?'

Mr. Campion had no time to reply to this somewhat unlikely theory. There was a flutter and a rustle outside the door and a moment later Mr. Welkin senior came in with a flustered lady. George got up and held out his hand.

'Ah, Miss Hare,' he said. 'Glad to see you. Come on your annual visit of mercy?'

Miss Hare, who was large and inclined to be hearty, laughed.

'I've come cadging again, if that's what you mean, Sir George,' she said cheerfully, and went on, nodding to Mr. Campion as if they had just been introduced. 'Every Christmas Eve I come round collecting for my old women. There are four of 'em in the almshouse by the church. I only ask for a shilling or two to buy them some little extra for the Christmas dinner. I don't want much. Just a shilling or two.'

She glanced at a little notebook in her hand.

'You gave me ten shillings last year, Sir George.'

The Squire produced the required sum and Mr. Campion felt in his pocket.

'Half a crown would be ample,' said Miss Hare encouragingly. 'Oh, that's very nice of you. I assure you it won't be wasted.'

She took the coin and was turning to Welkin when he stepped forward.

'I'd like to do the thing properly,' he said. 'Anybody got a pen?'

He took out a cheque-book and sat down at George's desk uninvited.

Miss Hare protested. 'Oh no, really,' she said, 'you don't understand. This is just for an extra treat. I collect it nearly all in sixpences.'

'Anybody got a pen?' repeated Mr. Welkin.

Campion glanced at the elaborate display in the man's own waistcoat pocket, but before he could mention it George had meekly handed over his own fountain-pen.

Mr. Welkin wrote a cheque and handed it to Miss Hare without troubling to blot it.

'Ten pounds?' said the startled lady. 'Oh, but really…!'

'Nonsense. Run along.' Mr. Welkin clapped her familiarly on the shoulder. 'It's Christmas time,' he said, glancing at George and Campion. 'I believe in doing a bit of good at Christmas time—if you can afford it.'

Miss Hare glanced round her helplessly.

'It's very—very kind of you,' she murmured, 'but half a crown would have been ample.'

She fled. Welkin threw George's pen on the desk.

'That's the way I like to do it,' he said.

George coughed and there was a faraway expression in his eyes.

'Yes, I—er—I see you do,' he said and sat down. Welkin went out.

Neither Mr. Campion nor his host mentioned the incident. Campion frowned. Now he had two minor problems on his conscience. One was the old matter of the little piece of information concerning Charlie Spring which he had forgotten, the other was a peculiarity of Mr. Welkin's which puzzled him mightily.

The Pharaoh's Court children's party had been in full swing for what seemed to Mr. Campion at least to be the best part of a fortnight. It was half-past seven in the evening and the relics of an enormous tea had been cleared away, leaving the music-room full of replete but still energetic children and their mothers, dancing and playing games with enthusiasm, but their eyes never straying for long from the next sensation of the evening, the fourteen-foot tree ablaze with coloured lights and tinsel.

Mr. Campion, who had danced, buttled, and even performed a few conjuring tricks, bethought him of a box of his favourite cigarettes in his suitcase upstairs and, feeling only a little guilty at leaving George still working like a hero, he stole away and hurried up the deserted staircase to his room.

The main body of the house was deserted. Even the Welkins were at work in the music-room, while the entire staff were concentrated in the kitchen washing up.

Mr. Campion found his cigarettes, lit one, and pottered for a moment or two, reflecting that the Christmases of his youth were much the same as those of to-day, but not so long from hour to hour. He felt virtuous and happy and positively oozing with goodwill. The promised snow was falling great soft flakes plopping softly against his window.

At last, when his conscience decreed that he could absent himself no longer, he switched off the light and stepped into the corridor, to come unexpectedly face to face with Father Christmas. The saint looked as weary as he himself had been and was stooping under the great sack on his shoulders. Mr. Campion admired Harridge's costume. The boots were glossy, the tunic with its wool border satisfyingly red, while the benevolent mask with its cotton-wool beard was almost lifelike.

He stepped aside to let the venerable figure pass and, because it seemed the moment for jocularity, said lightly:

'What have you got in the bag, Guv'nor?'

Had he uttered a spell of high enchantment, the simple words could not have had a more astonishing effect. The figure uttered an inarticulate cry, dropped the sack, which fell with a crash at Mr. Campion's feet, and fled like a shadow.

For a moment Mr. Campion stood paralysed with astonishment. By the time he had pulled himself together the crimson figure had disappeared down the staircase. He bent over the sack and thrust in his hand. Something hard and heavy met his fingers and he brought it out. It was the pink marble, bronze and ormolu clock.

He stood looking at his find and a sigh of satisfaction escaped him. One of the problems that had been worrying him all day had been solved at last.

◇◇◇

It was twenty minutes later before he reappeared in the music-room.

No one saw him come in, for the attention of the entire room was focused upon the platform. There, surrounded by enthusiastic assistants, was Father Christmas again, peace-fully snipping presents off the tree.

Campion took careful stock of him. The costume, he decided, was identical, the same high boots, the same tunic, the same mask. He tried to remember the fleeting figure in the corridor upstairs, but the costume was a deceptive one and he found it difficult.

After a time he found a secluded chair and sat down to await developments. They came.

As the last of the visitors departed, tired and smiling, their coats buttoned against the snow, and Lady Turrett threw herself into an arm-chair with a sigh of happy exhaustion, Pouter, the Pharaoh's Court butler, came quietly into the room and murmured a few words in his master's ear. From where he sat Mr. Campion heard George's astonished 'God bless my soul!' and rose immediately to join him. But although he moved swiftly Mr. Welkin was before him and, as Campion reached the group, his voice resounded round the room.

'A burglary? While we've been playing the fool in here? What's gone, man? What's gone?'

Pouter, who for some obscure reason of his own objected to the form of address, regarded his master's guest coldly.

'A clock from the first floor west corridor, a silver-plated salver, a copper loving-cup from the hall, and a brass Buddha and a gilt pomander box from the first-floor landing, as far as we can ascertain, sir,' he said.

'Bless my soul!' said George again. 'How extraordinary!'

'Extraordinary be damned!' ejaculated Welkin. 'We've got *valuables* here. Ada!'

'The necklace!' shrieked Mrs. Welkin, consternation suddenly welling up in her stupid eyes. 'My necklace!'

She scuttled out of the room and Sheila came forward with Santa Claus, who had taken off his mask and pushed back his hood to reveal the stolid but not unhandsome features of Mike Peters.

Lady Turrett did not stir from her chair, and Kenneth Welkin, white-faced and bewildered, stared down at her.

'There's been a burglary,' he said. 'Here, in this house.'

Mae Turrett smiled at him vaguely. 'George and Pouter will see to it,' she said. 'I'm so tired.'

'Tired!' shouted Edward Welkin. 'If my wife's diamonds—'

He got no further. Ada Welkin tottered into the room, an empty steel dispatch case in her trembling hands.

'They've gone,' she said, her voice rising in hysteria. 'They've gone. My diamonds…My room's been turned upside down. They've been taken. The necklace has gone.'

It was Mike who had sufficient presence of mind to support her to a chair before she collapsed. Her husband shot a shrewd, preoccupied glance at her, shouted to his son to 'Look after your mother, boy!' and took command of the situation.

'Now this is serious. You, Pigeon, whatever your name is, get all the servants, every one who's in this house, to come here in double-quick time, see? I've been robbed.'

Pouter looked at his master in mute appeal and George coughed.

'In a moment, Mr. Welkin,' he said. 'In a moment. Let us find out what we can first. Pouter, go and find out if any stranger has been seen about the house or grounds this evening, will you, please?'

The manservant went out instantly and Welkin raged.

'You may think you know what you're doing,' he said, 'but my way was the best. You're giving the thief time to get away, and time's precious, let me tell you. I've got to get the police up here.'

'The police?' Sheila was aghast.

He gaped at her. 'Of course, young woman. Do you think I'm going to lose twelve thousand pounds? The stones were insured, of course, but what company would pay up if I hadn't called in the police? I'll go and 'phone up now.'

'Wait a moment, please,' said George, his quiet voice only a little ruffled. 'Here's Pouter again. Well?'

The butler looked profoundly uncomfortable.

'Two maids, sir,' he said, 'the under housemaid and Miss Sheila's maid, Lucy, were waiting in the hall to tell me that they saw a man running down the drive just before the Christmas tree was begun.' He hesitated. 'They—they say, sir, he was dressed as Father Christmas. They both say it, sir.'

Everyone looked at Mike and Sheila's cheeks flamed.

'Well?' she demanded.

Mr. Welkin suddenly laughed. 'So that's how it was done,' he said. 'The young blackguard was clever, but he was seen. You weren't so bright as you thought you were, my lad.'

Mike moved forward. His face was pale and his eyes were dangerous. George laid a hand upon his arm.

'Wait,' he commanded. 'Pouter, you may go. Now,' he continued as the door closed behind the man, 'you, Mr. Welkin, you'll have to explain, you know.'

Mr. Welkin kept his temper. He seemed almost amused.

'Well, it's perfectly simple, isn't it?' he said. 'This fellow has been wandering about in this disguise all the evening. He couldn't come in here because her ladyship wanted him to be a surprise to the children, but he had the rest of the house to himself. He went round lifting anything he fancied, including my diamonds. Suppose he had been met? No one would think anything of it. Father Christmas always carries a sack. Then he went off down the drive, where he met a confederate in a car, handed over the stuff and came back to the party.'

Mike began to speak, but Sheila interrupted him.

'What makes you think Mike would do such a thing, Mr. Welkin?' she demanded, her voice shaking with fury.

Edward Welkin's heavy mouth widened in a grin.

'Dishonesty's in the family, isn't it?' he said.

Mike sprang, but George clung to him. 'Hold on, my boy, hold on,' he said breathlessly. 'Don't strike a man old enough to be your—'

He boggled at the unfortunate simile and substituted the word 'mother' with ludicrous effect.

Mr. Campion decided it was time to interfere.

'I say, George,' he said, 'if you and Mr. Welkin would come along to the library I've got a suggestion I'd like to make.'

Welkin wavered. 'Keep an eye on him then, Ken,' he said over his shoulder to his son. 'I'll listen to you, Campion, but I want my diamonds back and I want the police. I'll give you five minutes, no longer.'

◇◇◇

The library was in darkness when the three men entered, and Campion waited until they were well in the room before he switched on the main light. There was a moment of bewildered silence. One corner of the room looked like a stall in the Caledonian Market. There the entire contents of the sack, which had come so unexpectedly into Mr. Campion's possession, was neatly spread out. George's cherubic face darkened.

'What's this?' he demanded. 'A damned silly joke?'

Mr. Campion shook his head. 'I'm afraid not. I've just collected this from a gentleman in fancy dress whom I met in the corridor upstairs,' he said. 'What would you say, Mr. Welkin?'

The man stared at him doggedly. 'Where are my diamonds? That's my only interest. I don't care about this junk.'

Campion smiled faintly. 'He's right, you know, George,' he said. 'Junk's the word. It came back to me as soon as I saw it. Poor Charlie Spring—I recognized him, Mr.

Welkin—never had a successful coup in his life because he can't help stealing gaudy junk.'

Edward Welkin stood stiffly by the desk.

'I don't understand you,' he said. 'My diamonds have been stolen and I want to call the police.'

Mr. Campion took off his spectacles. 'I shouldn't if I were you,' he said. 'No you don't—!'

On the last words Mr. Campion leapt forward and there was a brief struggle. When it was over Mr. Welkin was lying on the floor beside the marble and ormolu clock and Mr. Campion was grasping the gold pen and pencil in the leather holder which until a moment before had rested in the man's waistcoat pocket.

Welkin scrambled to his feet. His face was purple and his eyes a little frightened. He attempted to bluster.

'You'll find yourself in court for assault,' he said. 'Give me my property.'

'Certainly. All of it,' agreed Mr. Campion obligingly. 'Your dummy pen, your dummy pencil, and in the little receptacle which they conceal, your wife's diamonds.'

On the last word he drew the case apart and a glittering string fell out in his hand.

There was a long, long pause.

Welkin stood sullenly in the middle of the room.

'Well?' he said at last. 'What are you two going to do about it?'

Mr. Campion glanced at George, who was sitting by the desk, an expression of incredulity amounting almost to stupefaction upon his mild face.

'If I might suggest,' he murmured, 'I think he might take his family and spend a jolly Christmas somewhere else, don't you? It would save a lot of trouble.'

Welkin held out his hand.

'Very well. I'll take my diamonds.'

Mr. Campion shook his head. 'As you go out of the house,' he said with a faint smile. 'I shouldn't like them to be—lost again.'

Welkin shrugged his shoulders. 'You win,' he said briefly. 'I'll go and tell Ada to pack.'

He went out of the room, and as the door closed behind him George bounced to his feet.

'Hanged if I understand it...' he began. 'D'you mean to say the feller put up this amazing cock-and-bull story simply so that he could get Mike accused of theft?'

Mr. Campion remained serious. 'Oh no,' he said. 'That was an artistic afterthought, I imagine. The cock-and-bull story, as you call it, was a very neat little swindle devised by our unpleasant friend before he came down here at all. It was very simple to stage a burglary here on Christmas Eve, especially when he had heard from his wife that Mae had ordered a Santa Claus costume from Harridge's. All he had to do was to go and get one there too. Then, armed with the perfect disguise, he enlisted the services of a genuine burglar, to whom he gave the costume. The man simply had to walk into the house, pick up a few things at random, and go off with them. I think you'll find if you go into it that he hired a car at Ipswich and drove out here, changing somewhere along the road.'

◇◇◇

George was still puzzled. 'But his own son Kenneth was going to play Santa Claus,' he said. 'Or at least he seemed to expect to.'

Campion nodded. 'I know,' he said. 'Welkin had foreseen that difficulty and prepared for it. If Kenneth had been playing Father Christmas and the same thing had happened I think you would have found that the young man had a pretty convincing alibi established for him. You must remember the burglar was not meant to be seen. He was only furnished with the costume in case he was. As it happened, of course, when Welkin *père* saw that Mike was not too unlike his burglar friend in build, he encouraged the change-over and killed two birds with one stone—or tried to.'

His host took the diamonds and turned them over. He was slow of comprehension.

'Why steal his own property?' he demanded.

Mr. Campion sighed. 'You have such a blameless mind, George, that the wickedness of some of your fellow-men must be a constant source of astonishment to you,' he murmured. 'Did you hear our friend Welkin say that he had insured this necklace?'

George's eyebrows rose.

'God bless my soul!' he said. 'The bounder! In our house, too,' he added as an afterthought. 'Miracle you spotted it, Campion. God bless my soul! Draw the insurance and keep the diamonds... Damnable trick.'

He was still wrathful when the door burst open and Mae Turrett came in, followed by Mike and Sheila.

'The Welkins are going. They've ordered their cars. What on earth's happened, George?'

Her ladyship was startled but obviously relieved.

Mr. Campion explained. 'It had been worrying me all day,' he said after the main part of the story had been told. 'I knew Charlie Spring had a peculiarity, but I couldn't think what it was until I pulled that clock out of the bag. Then I remembered his penchant for the baroque and his sad habit of mistaking it for the valuable. That ruled out the diamonds instantly. They wouldn't be big enough for Charlie. When that came back to me I recollected his other failing. He never works alone. When Mr. Spring appears on a job it always means he has a confederate in the house, usually an employee, and with these facts in my hand the rest was fairly obvious.'

Mike moved forward. 'You've done me a pretty good turn, anyway,' he said.

George looked up. 'Not really, my boy,' he said. 'We're not utter fools, you know, are we Mae?'

Lady Turrett blushed. 'Of course not, Mike my dear,' she said, and her smile could be very charming. 'Take Sheila away and cheer her up. I really don't think you need wait about to say good-bye to the Welkins. Dear me, I seem to have been very silly!'

Before she went out Sheila put her hand into Mr. Campion's.

'I told you I was glad to see you,' she said.

As the two cars containing the Welkins, their diamonds and all that was theirs disappeared down the white drive, George linked his arm through Mr. Campion's and led him back to the library.

'I've been thinking,' he said. 'You spotted that pen was a dummy when Miss Hare came in this afternoon.'

Mr. Campion grinned. 'Well, it was odd the man didn't use his own pen, wasn't it?' he said, settling himself before the fire. 'When he ignored it I guessed. That kind of cache is fairly common, especially in the States. They're made for carrying valuables and are usually shabby bakelite things which no one would steal in the ordinary way. However, there was nothing shabby about Mr. Welkin—except his behaviour.'

George leant back in his chair and puffed contentedly.

'Difficult feller,' he observed. 'Didn't like him from the first. No conversation. I started him on shootin', but he wasn't interested, mentioned huntin' and he gaped at me, went on to fishin' and he yawned. Couldn't think of anything to talk to him about. Feller hadn't any conversation at all.'

He smiled and there was a faintly shamefaced expression in his eyes.

'Campion,' he said softly.

'Yes?'

'Made a wonderful discovery last week.' George had lowered his voice to a conspiratorial rumble. 'Went down to the cellar and found a single bottle of Cockburn's 'sixty-eight. 'Sixty-eight, my boy! My father must have missed it. I was saving it for to-morrow, don't you know, but whenever I looked at that feller Welkin, I couldn't feel hospitable. Such a devilish waste. However, now he's gone—' His voice trailed away.

'A very merry Christmas indeed,' supplemented Mr. Campion.

# Christmas Eve

## *S.C. Roberts*

Sir Sydney Castle Roberts (1887–1966) was a renowned publisher who played a leading part in Cambridge academic and literary life. Born in Birkenhead, he studied at Pembroke College, Cambridge, and joined Cambridge University Press in 1922. He became Master of Pembroke College in 1948, and Vice-Chancellor of the University from 1949–51, thereafter serving as Chairman of the British Film Institute. His diverse publications included *Lord Macaulay: the pre-eminent Victorian* (1927) and *Samuel Johnson* (1954).

Roberts was also a distinguished Sherlockian, whose enjoyable parodies and pastiches of the great consulting detective included a splendid story, 'The Case of the Megatherium Thefts'. In a book of memoirs, he recalled playing golf with Conan Doyle in 1911, when the author came to stay with a family friend, and explained how, years later, Ronald Knox's writings about Holmes inspired his own work in the field, such as *Doctor Watson: Prolegomena to the Study of a Biographical Problem* (1931). 'For myself,' he wrote in the year of his death, 'I never cease to marvel at the vitality of the Holmesian cult.' Half a century later, that vitality remains as marvellous as ever. This little play reflects the lighter side of Sherlock.

◇◇◇

(Sherlock Holmes, *disguised as a loafer,*
*is discovered probing in a sideboard cupboard*
*for something to eat and drink.*)

HOLMES: Where in the world is that decanter? I'm sure I—

(*Enter* Dr. Watson, *who sees only the*
*back of* Holmes's *stooping figure*)

WATSON: (*Turning quickly and whispering hoarsely offstage*) Mrs. Hudson! Mrs. Hudson! My revolver, quick. There's a burglar in Mr. Holmes's room. (Watson *exits*)

HOLMES: Ah, there's the decanter at last. But first of all I may as well discard some of my properties. (*Takes off cap, coat, beard, etc., and puts on dressing gown*) My word, I'm hungry. (*Begins to eat sandwich*) But, bless me, I've forgotten the siphon! (*Stoops at cupboard in same attitude as before*)

(*Enter* Watson, *followed by* Mrs. Hudson)

WATSON: (*Sternly*) Now, my man, put those hands up.

HOLMES: (*Turning round*) My dear Watson, why this sudden passion for melodrama?

WATSON: Holmes!

HOLMES: Really, Watson, to be the victim of a murderous attack at your hands, of all people's—and on Christmas Eve, too.

WATSON: But a minute ago, Holmes, there was a villainous-looking scoundrel trying to wrench open that cupboard—a really criminal type. I caught a glimpse of his face.

HOLMES: Well, well, my dear Watson, I suppose I ought to be grateful for the compliment to my make-up. The fact is that I have spent the day loafing at the corner of a narrow street leading out of the Waterloo Road. They were all quite friendly to me there... Yes, I obtained the last little piece of evidence that I wanted to clear up that case of the Kentish Town safe robbery—you remember? Quite an interesting case, but all over now.

Mrs. Hudson: Lor', Mr. 'Olmes, how you do go on. Still, I'm learnin' never to be surprised at anything now.

HOLMES: Capital, Mrs. Hudson. That's what every criminal investigator has to learn, isn't it, Watson? (*Mrs. Hudson leaves*)

WATSON: Well, I suppose so, Holmes. But you must feel very pleased to think you've got that Kentish Town case off your mind before Christmas.

HOLMES: On the contrary, my dear Watson, I'm miserable. I like having things on my mind—it's the only thing that makes life tolerable. A mind empty of problems is worse even than a stomach empty of food. (*Eats sandwich*) But Christmas is commonly a slack season. I suppose even criminals' hearts are softened. The result is that I have nothing to do but to look out of the window and watch other people being busy. That little pawnbroker at the corner, for instance, you know the one, Watson?

WATSON: Yes, of course.

HOLMES: One of the many shops you have often seen, but never observed, my dear Watson. If you had watched that pawnbroker's front door as carefully as I have during the last ten days, you would have noted a striking increase in his trade; you might have observed also some remarkably well-to-do people going into the shop. There's one well-set-up young woman whom I have seen at least four times. Curious to think what her business may have been... But it's a shame to depress your Christmas spirit, Watson. I see that you are particularly cheerful this evening.

WATSON: Well, yes, I don't mind admitting that I am feeling quite pleased with things today.

HOLMES: So 'Rio Tintos' have paid a good dividend, have they?

WATSON: My dear Holmes, how on earth do you know that?

HOLMES: Elementary, my dear Watson. You told me years ago that 'Rio Tintos' was the one dividend which was paid in through your bank and not direct to yourself. You come into my room with an envelope of a peculiar shade of green sticking out of your coat pocket. That particular shade is used by your bank—Cox's—and by no other, so far as I am aware. Clearly, then, you have just obtained your pass-book from the bank and your cheerfulness must proceed from the good news which it contains. *Ex hypothesi*, that news must relate to 'Rio Tintos.'

WATSON: Perfectly correct, Holmes; and on the strength of the good dividend, I have deposited ten good, crisp, five-pound notes in the drawer of my dressing table just in case we should feel like a little jaunt after Christmas.

HOLMES: That was charming of you, Watson. But in my present state of inertia I should be a poor holiday companion. Now if only—(*Knock at door*) Come in.

Mrs. Hudson: Please sir, there's a young lady to see you.

HOLMES: What sort of young lady, Mrs. Hudson? Another of these young women wanting half a crown towards some Christmas charity? If so, Dr. Watson's your man, Mrs. Hudson. He's bursting with banknotes today.

Mrs. Hudson: I'm sure I'm very pleased to 'ear it, sir; but this lady ain't that kind at all, sir. She's sort of agitated, like… very anxious to see you and quite scared of meeting you at the same time, if you take my meaning, sir.

HOLMES: Perfectly, Mrs. Hudson. Well, Watson, what are we to do? Are we to interview this somewhat unbalanced young lady?

WATSON: If the poor girl is in trouble, Holmes, I think you might at least hear what she has to say.

HOLMES: Chivalrous as ever, my dear Watson—bring the lady up, Mrs. Hudson.

Mrs. Hudson: Very good, sir. (*To the lady outside*) This way, Miss.

(*Enter* Miss Violet de Vinne, *an elegant but distracted girl of about twenty-two*)

HOLMES: (*Bowing slightly*) You wish to consult me?

Miss de Vinne: (*Nervously*) Are you Mr. Sherlock Holmes?

HOLMES: I am—and this is my friend and colleague, Dr. Watson.

WATSON: (*Coming forward and holding out hand*) Charmed, I am sure, Miss—

HOLMES: (*To* Miss de Vinne) You have come here, I presume, because you have a story to tell me. May I ask you to be as concise as possible?

Miss de Vinne: I will try, Mr. Holmes. My name is de Vinne. My mother and I live together in Bayswater. We are not very well off but my father was… well… a gentleman. The Countess of Barton is one of our oldest friends—

HOLMES: (*Interrupting*) And the owner of a very wonderful pearl necklace.

Miss de Vinne: (*Startled*) How do you know that, Mr. Holmes?

HOLMES: I am afraid it is my business to know quite a lot

about other people's affairs. But I'm sorry. I interrupted. Go on.

Miss de Vinne: Two or three times a week I spend the day with Lady Barton and act as her secretary in a casual, friendly way. I write letters for her and arrange her dinner-tables when she has a party and do other little odd jobs.

HOLMES: Lady Barton is fortunate, eh, Watson?

WATSON: Yes, indeed, Holmes.

Miss de Vinne: This afternoon a terrible thing happened. I was arranging some flowers when Lady Barton came in looking deathly white. 'Violet,' she said, 'the pearls are gone.' 'Heavens,' I cried, 'what do you mean?' 'Well,' she said, 'having quite unexpectedly had an invitation to a reception on January 5th, I thought I would make sure that the clasp was all right. When I opened the case (you know the special place where I keep it) it was empty— that's all.' She looked as if she was going to faint, and I felt much the same.

HOLMES: (*Quickly*) And did you faint?

Miss de Vinne: No, Mr. Holmes, we pulled ourselves together somehow and I asked her whether she was going to send for the police, but she wouldn't hear of it. She said Jim (that's her husband) hated publicity and would be furious if the pearls became 'copy' for journalists. But of course she agreed that something had to be done and so she sent me to you.

HOLMES: Oh, Lady Barton sent you?

Miss de Vinne: Well, not exactly. You see, when she refused to send for the police, I remembered your name and implored her to write you… and… well… here I am and here's the letter. That's all, Mr. Holmes.

HOLMES: I see. (*Begins to read letter*) Well, my dear lady, neither you nor Lady Barton has given me much material on which to work at present.

Miss de Vinne: I am willing to answer any questions, Mr. Holmes.

HOLMES: You live in Bayswater, Miss Winnie?

WATSON: (*Whispering*) 'De Vinne,' Holmes.

HOLMES: (*Ignoring* Watson) You said Bayswater, I think, Miss Winnie?

Miss de Vinne: Quite right, Mr. Holmes, but—forgive me, my name is de Vinne.

HOLMES: I'm sorry, Miss Dwinney—

Miss de Vinne: De Vinne, Mr. Holmes, D...E...V...

HOLMES: How stupid of me. I think the chill I caught last week must have left a little deafness behind it. But to save further stupidity on my part, just write your name and address for me, will you? (*Hands her pen and paper, on which* Miss de Vinne *writes*) That's better. Now, tell me, Miss de Vinne, how do you find Bayswater for shopping?

Miss de Vinne: (*Surprised*) Oh, I don't know. Mr. Holmes, I hardly—

HOLMES: You don't care for Whiteley's, for instance?

Miss de Vinne: Well, not very much. But I can't see...

HOLMES: I entirely agree with you, Miss de Vinne. Yet Watson, you know, is devoted to that place—spends hours there...

WATSON: Holmes, what nonsense are you—

HOLMES: But I think you are quite right, Miss de Vinne. Harrod's is a great deal better in my opinion.

Miss de Vinne: But I never go to Harrod's, Mr. Holmes, in fact I hardly ever go to any big store, except for one or two things. But what has this got to do—

HOLMES: Well, in principle, I don't care for them much either, but they're convenient sometimes.

Miss de Vinne: Yes, I find the Army and Navy stores useful now and then, but why on earth are we talking about shops and stores when the thing that matters is Lady Barton's necklace?

HOLMES: Ah, yes, I was coming to that. (*Pauses*) I'm sorry, Miss de Vinne, but I'm afraid I can't take up this case.

Miss de Vinne: You refuse, Mr. Holmes?

HOLMES: I am afraid I am obliged to do so. It is a case that would inevitably take some time. I am in sore need of a holiday and only today my devoted friend Watson has made all arrangements to take me on a Mediterranean cruise immediately after Christmas.

WATSON: Holmes, this is absurd. You know that I merely—

Miss de Vinne: Dr. Watson, if Mr Holmes can't help me, won't you? You don't know how terrible all this is for me as well as for Lady Barton.

WATSON: My dear lady, I have some knowledge of my friend's methods and they often seem incomprehensible. Holmes, you can't mean this?

HOLMES: Certainly I do, my dear Watson. But I am unwilling that any lady should leave this house in a state of distress. (*Goes to door*) Mrs. Hudson!

Mrs. Hudson: Coming, sir. (Mrs. Hudson *enters*)

HOLMES: Mrs. Hudson, be good enough to conduct this lady to Dr. Watson's dressing room. She is tired and a little upset. Let her rest on the sofa there while Dr. Watson and I have a few minutes' quiet talk.

Mrs. Hudson: Very good, sir.

(*Exeunt* Mrs. Hudson *and* Miss de Vinne,
*the latter looking appealingly at* Dr. Watson)

HOLMES: (*Lighting cherry-wood pipe*) Well, Watson?

WATSON: Well, Holmes, in all my experience I don't think I have ever seen you so unaccountably ungracious to a charming girl.

HOLMES: Oh, yes, she has charm, Watson—they always have. What do you make of her story?

WATSON: Not very much, I confess. It seemed fairly clear as far as it went, but you wouldn't let her tell us any detail. Instead, you began a perfectly ridiculous conversation about the comparative merits of various department stores. I've seldom heard you so inept.

HOLMES: Then you accept her story?

WATSON: Why not?

HOLMES: Why not, my dear Watson? Because the whole thing is a parcel of lies.

WATSON: But, Holmes, this is unreasoning prejudice.

HOLMES: Unreasoning, you say? Listen, Watson. This letter purports to have come from the Countess of Barton. I don't know her Ladyship's handwriting, but I was struck at once by its laboured character, as exhibited in this note. It occurred to me, further, that it might be useful to obtain a specimen of Miss de Vinne's to put alongside it—hence my tiresome inability to catch her name. Now, my dear Watson, I call your particular attention to the capital B's which happen to occur in both specimens.

WATSON: They're quite different, Holmes, but—yes, they've both got a peculiar curl where the letter finishes.

HOLMES: Point No. 1, my dear Watson, but an isolated one. Now, although I could not recognize the handwriting, I knew this notepaper as soon as I saw and felt it. Look at the watermark, Watson, and tell me what you find.

WATSON: (*Holding the paper to the light*) A. and N. (*After a pause*) Army and Navy... Why, Holmes, d'you mean that—

HOLMES: I mean that this letter was written by your charming friend in the name of the Countess of Barton.

WATSON: And what follows?

HOLMES: Ah, that is what we are left to conjecture. What will follow immediately is another interview with the young woman who calls herself Violet de Vinne. By the way, Watson, after you had finished threatening me with that nasty-looking revolver a little while ago, what did you do with the instrument?

WATSON: It's here, Holmes, in my pocket.

HOLMES: Then, having left my own in my bedroom, I think I'll borrow it, if you don't mind.

WATSON: But surely, Holmes, you don't suggest that—

HOLMES: My dear Watson, I suggest nothing—except that we may possibly find ourselves in rather deeper waters than Miss de Vinne's charm and innocence have hitherto led you to expect. (*Goes to door*) Mrs. Hudson, ask the lady to be good enough to rejoin us.

Mrs. Hudson: (*Off*) Very good, sir.

(*Enter* Miss de Vinne)

HOLMES: (*Amiably*) Well, Miss de Vinne, are you rested?

Miss de Vinne: Well, a little perhaps, but as you can do nothing for me, hadn't I better go?

HOLMES: You look a little flushed, Miss de Vinne; do you feel the room rather too warm?

Miss de Vinne: No, Mr. Holmes, thank you, I —

HOLMES: Anyhow, won't you slip your coat off and—

Miss de Vinne: Oh no, really. (*Gathers coat round her*)

HOLMES: (*Threateningly*) Then, if you won't take your coat off, d'you mind showing me what is in the right-hand pocket of it? (*A look of terror comes on* Miss de Vinne's *face*) The game's up, Violet de Vinne. (*Points revolver, at which* Miss de Vinne *screams and throws up her hands*) Watson, oblige me by removing whatever you may discover in the right-hand pocket of Miss de Vinne's coat.

WATSON: (*Taking out note-case*) My own note-case, Holmes, with the ten five-pound notes in it!

HOLMES: Ah!

Miss de Vinne: (*Distractedly*) Let me speak, let me speak. I'll explain everything.

HOLMES: Silence! Watson, was there anything else in the drawer of your dressing table besides your note-case?

WATSON: I'm not sure, Holmes.

HOLMES: Then I think we had better have some verification.

Miss de Vinne: No, no. Let me—

HOLMES: Mrs. Hudson!

Mrs. Hudson: (*Off*) Coming, sir.

HOLMES: (*To* Mrs. Hudson *off*) Kindly open the right-hand drawer of Dr. Watson's dressing table and bring us anything that you may find in it.

Miss de Vinne: Mr. Holmes, you are torturing me. Let me tell you everything.

HOLMES: Your opportunity will come in due course, but in all probability before a different tribunal. I am a private detective, not a Criminal Court judge. (Miss de Vinne *weeps*)

(*Enter* Mrs. Hudson *with jewel case*)

Mrs. Hudson: I found this, sir. But it must be something new that the doctor's been buying. I've never seen it before. (Mrs. Hudson *leaves*)

HOLMES: Ah, Watson, more surprises! (*Opens case and holds up a string of pearls*) The famous pearls belonging to the Countess of Barton, if I'm not mistaken.

Miss de Vinne: For pity's sake, Mr. Holmes, let me speak. Even the lowest criminal has that right left him. And this time I will tell you the truth.

HOLMES: (*Sceptically*) The truth? Well?

Miss de Vinne: Mr. Holmes, I have an only brother. He's
a dear—I love him better than anyone in the world—
but, God forgive him, he's a scamp… always in trouble,
always in debt. Three days ago he wrote to me that he
was in an even deeper hole than usual. If he couldn't raise
fifty pounds in the course of a week, he would be done
for and, worse than that, dishonoured and disgraced
forever. I couldn't bear it. I'd no money. I daren't tell my
mother. I swore to myself that I'd get that fifty pounds
if I had to steal it. That same day at Lady Barton's, I was
looking, as I'd often looked, at the famous pearls. An
idea suddenly came to me. They were worn only once or
twice a year on special occasions. Why shouldn't I pawn
them for a month or so? I could surely get fifty pounds
for them and then somehow I would scrape together
the money to redeem them. It was almost certain that
Lady Barton wouldn't want them for six months. Oh, I
know I was mad, but I did it. I found a fairly obscure
little pawnbroker quite near here, but to my horror he
wouldn't take the pearls—looked at me very suspiciously
and wouldn't budge, though I went to him two or three
times. Then, this afternoon, the crash came. When Lady
Barton discovered that the pearls were missing I rushed
out of the house, saying that I would tell the police. But
actually I went home and tried to think. I remembered
your name. A wild scheme came into my head. If I could
pretend to consult you and somehow leave the pearls
in your house, then you could pretend that you had
recovered them and return them to Lady Barton. Oh, I
know you'll laugh, but you don't know how distraught I
was. Then, when you sent me into that dressing room, I
prowled about like a caged animal. I saw those banknotes
and they seemed like a gift from Heaven. Why shouldn't
I leave the necklace in their place? You would get much

more than fifty pounds for recovering them from Lady
Barton and I should save my brother. There, that's all…
and now, I suppose, I exchange Dr. Watson's dressing
room for a cell at the police station!

HOLMES: Well, Watson?

WATSON: What an extraordinary story, Holmes!

HOLMES: Yes, indeed. (*Turning to* Miss de Vinne) Miss
de Vinne, you told us in the first instance a plausible
story of which I did not believe a single word; now you
have given us a version which in many particulars seems
absurd and incredible. Yet I believe it to be the truth.
Watson, haven't I always told you that fact is immeasur-
ably stranger than fiction?

WATSON: Certainly, Holmes. But what are you going to do?

HOLMES: Going to do? Why—er—I'm going to send for
Mrs. Hudson. (*Calling offstage*) Mrs. Hudson!

Mrs. Hudson: (*Off*) Coming, sir. (*Enters*) Yes, sir.

HOLMES: Oh, Mrs. Hudson, what are your views about
Christmas?

WATSON: Really, Holmes.

HOLMES: My dear Watson, please don't interrupt. As I was
saying, Mrs. Hudson, I should be very much interested
to know how you feel about Christmas.

Mrs. Hudson: Lor', Mr. 'Olmes, what questions you do ask.
I don't hardly know exactly how to answer but… well…
I suppose Christmas is the season of good will towards
men—and women too, sir, if I may say so.

HOLMES: (*Slowly*) 'And women too.' You observe that,
Watson.

WATSON: Yes, Holmes, and I agree.

HOLMES: (*To* Miss de Vinne) My dear young lady, you
will observe that the jury are agreed upon their verdict.

Miss de Vinne: Oh, Mr. Holmes, how can I ever thank you?

HOLMES: Not a word. You must thank the members of the jury... Mrs. Hudson!

Mrs. Hudson: Yes, sir.

HOLMES: Take Miss de Vinne, not into Dr. Watson's room this time, but into your own comfortable kitchen and give her a cup of your famous tea.

Mrs. Hudson: How do the young lady take it, sir? Rather stronglike, with a bit of a tang to it?

HOLMES: You must ask her that yourself. Anyhow Mrs. Hudson, give her a cup that cheers.

(*Exeunt* Mrs. Hudson *and* Miss de Vinne)

WATSON: (*In the highest spirits*) Half a minute, Mrs. Hudson. I'm coming to see that Miss de Vinne has her tea as she likes it. And I tell you what, Holmes (*Looking towards* Miss de Vinne *and holding up note-case*), you are not going to get your Mediterranean cruise.

(*As* Watson *goes out, carol-singers are heard in the distance singing 'Good King Wenceslas.'*)

HOLMES: (*Relighting his pipe and smiling meditatively*) Christmas Eve!

Curtain

# Death in December

## *Victor Gunn*

Victor Gunn was one of several pseudonyms used by Edwy Searles Brooks (1889–1965). Although not a best-seller to compare with Edgar Wallace, or as accomplished a stylist as Margery Allingham, he enjoyed a long career as a 'mass producer' of lively popular fiction. It was his proud—and remarkable—boast that he never earned a penny of his living other than from writing, and he produced well over one hundred novels as well as two thousand other stories. These figures appear on an impressively detailed website, www.edwysearlesbrooks.com, which explains that his unusual first name came from a Welsh king called Edwy the Fair. He was born in Hackney, the son of a Congregational minister who was also a seasoned political journalist.

*Footsteps of Death*, the first Victor Gunn novel featuring Chief Inspector Bill 'Ironsides' Cromwell, appeared in 1939. The dust jacket blurb summed him up as 'essentially human, vividly alive—and refreshingly different. Bill Cromwell seldom does anything without a grumble, and the unconventional methods he sometimes employs would certainly get him dismissed from the Force if his Scotland Yard superiors knew anything about them. Not that Ironsides ever takes the slightest trouble to camouflage his actions. He is supremely contemptuous of official regulations and red tape. He ambles through an investigation in his own sweet way—and gets there every time.' 'Death in December' comes from *Ironsides Sees Red*, originally published in 1943, in which the great man encounters mysterious crimes during the course of three separate holidays.

## I. The Thing Which Left No Footprints

'For years,' said Johnny Lister, as he peered through the snow-flecked windscreen, 'my old dad has been longing to meet you, Ironsides; and at last his wish is going to be fulfilled. You'd better let me go in first, so that I can brace him up with a couple of quick snifters.'

'If he's anything like his son, I'm the one who'll need the snifters,' retorted Bill Cromwell. 'How the hell I ever let you talk me into accepting this Christmas invitation is more than I can understand. I hate parties. I hate noise. I hate crazy young people who drag you into drivelling games. I'm not sure that I don't hate you. In other words, I'm nothing but a fool!'

Johnny chuckled. His respected—not very respected— chief had been grumbling all the way from London, and now that the speeding Alvis was well into the wild and hilly country of Derbyshire, he was more caustic than ever. For snow was falling and the broad road was a gleaming ribbon of white under the glare of the headlamps. And Ironsides, it appeared, hated snow too.

'Cheer up, Old Iron,' said Johnny lightly. 'You're going to like the old man; he has his faults and his funny ways, but he's a good sport. You're going to like Cloon Castle, too.'

'The name's enough to give you a fit of depression,' growled the Chief Inspector. 'It's a wonder they didn't call it Gloom Castle, and have done with it. By what I can see, it's situated on the top of a damned mountain! How much longer have we got to climb this scenic railway?'

'You should worry!' said Johnny. 'As long as we've got a good engine, and good brakes, what does it matter about hills? Or didn't you know that the Peak District is largely composed of hills? Cloon Castle has belonged to the Cloon branch of our family since old Noah accidentally hit one of the peaks with his Ark. But the Cloons died out a couple of hundred years ago—'

'Well, that's something,' said Cromwell, brightening.

'And since then the Lister branch has done all the lording,' continued the streamlined sergeant. 'The last survivor of that particular clan was an aunt of mine, Lady Julia Lister. She handed in the bucket years ago, and Cloon Castle was scooped in by the old man. Until now he has done nothing with the place, and I haven't even seen it. I spent all my boyhood and flowering youth at the family's Essex hovel, a little cottage of about five hundred rooms—and one of them a bathroom, too. The old man thought it would be a good idea to open up Cloon Castle, and this house-party is a kind of Christmas house-warming.'

'All I can say,' grunted Bill Cromwell, 'is that it's disgusting that one family should possess so many whacking great mansions. It isn't decent. It's the kind of thing that creates class warfare.'

'Class warfare, my big toe!' said Johnny, grinning. 'Why, the opening up of Cloon Castle alone has given good jobs to twenty or thirty people. As for this Christmas party, I understand it's going to be a humdinger. Dancing...'

'I hate dancing.'

'Winter sports...'

'I loathe winter sports.'

'Amateur theatricals...'

'I'd crawl a mile not to see amateur theatricals.'

'There's even a cold, gloomy, family crypt, where you can lie down and die,' said Johnny. 'Now tell me you hate lying down and dying, and I won't believe you. For all I know, there's a ghost haunting the place. It wouldn't be a real ancestral castle without a ghost, would it? All I hope is that the old boy haunts you every night.' He paused reflectively. 'But, of course, it might be a beautiful girl ghost. In that case, I hope she haunts me every night.'

'I'll bet you'll be haunted by girls, and they won't be ghosts,' said Ironsides caustically.

'Here, steady! Not at night, in my bedroom!'

'I wouldn't put it past 'em,' said Cromwell, with a sniff. 'I know these country house-parties.'

'I think,' said Johnny carefully, 'that we'll change the subject. This one has every indication of developing into a recital of your shady past.'

The subject changed itself, as a matter of fact, for a finger-post, standing drunkenly at the side of the road, said, 'Cloon C.—½ m.,' and pointed uncertainly into the opening of a narrow side road. For a mile or two the Alvis had been purring sweetly along a perfectly level road, and Johnny and his passenger seemed to have reached a kind of plateau. Just within the range of the headlights there were low stone walls bordering the road, and here and there stunted hedges and wind-swept trees. A somewhat desolate wilderness, in fact.

The snow was not falling heavily, but in fine feathery flakes, and there was only about half an inch of it on the roads; not sufficient to affect Johnny's driving. But the sky was black and solid and heavy, and any native of the district could have told Johnny that a lot of snow was on its way.

'Christmas Eve, now, and sundry log fires awaiting us,' said Johnny gaily, as he turned the Alvis's long nose into the lane. 'Ironsides, old sourpuss, we're going to have the time of our lives. No routine—no murders—no crooks. Nothing but jollity and laughter.'

Ironsides grunted, and by the expression on his face it seemed that he preferred crooks and murders. He was not, in fact, much of a mixer, and parties always frightened him. For one thing, he had to wear respectable clothes, and brush his hair, and smoke cigars instead of his evil-smelling pipe. All in all, he wasn't too happy about this binge.

An ancient stone wall, rather like a miniature Wall of China, soon loomed up on the left hand, and presently a great gateway came into view, with the gates standing wide open, and a dazzling electric light overhead, turning the night into day. There were faint tracks of other cars, but they had been almost obliterated by the freshly fallen snow—so that the drive, when the Alvis went gliding along it, was a broad white expanse in the gleam of the headlamps.

'What price your Gloom Castle now?' asked Johnny slyly, as they turned a bend in the drive. 'We're in good time to dress for dinner, and do full justice to the cocktails.'

The castle was in full view—a cheery picture of gleaming lights from almost every window. It stood somewhat to the left, so the drive evidently took another turn a bit farther on.

'Here, am I seeing things, Old Iron?' ejaculated Johnny suddenly. 'Who's that rummy looking old cove?'

There was every reason for his surprised utterance. A couple of hundred yards in front of them, and just within full range of the headlights, an extraordinary figure was making its way directly across the drive, after emerging from the bushes to the right. Cromwell caught a glimpse of a queer, old-fashioned cape, and a high-crowned, wide-brimmed hat. There was something unnatural and grotesque in the stumbling gait of the cloaked figure, and never once did the man turn his face towards the approaching car, as one would have expected. 'I say, he must be ill!' muttered Johnny.

He slowed down, but by the time they reached the spot, and looked into the trees beside the drive, there was no sign of any living presence. Johnny drove on almost reluctantly, and he turned and gave Ironsides a strange look.

'Stop the car!' said the Chief Inspector, in a queer voice.

'Damn it, Ironsides, you don't think...'

'I don't know what I think,' interrupted Bill Cromwell. 'Either I'm mad, or blind—but I'll swear that there were no footprints in the snow. Didn't you notice?'

Johnny's shapely jaw sagged a couple of cogs.

'No footprints——!' he began incredulously.

Then he stopped, swung the car straight across the drive and turned it about. He crawled back along his own tracks, his heart thudding. The drive was flooded with light, and suddenly Ironsides called a halt.

'Just about here,' he said, hopping out.

Down the centre of the drive were the clear-cut tracks of the Alvis, and the almost-obliterated tracks of previous cars underneath. To the right and left, and in the centre, a half-inch carpet of freshly-fallen virgin snow!

'But, damn my eyes, it's impossible!' protested Johnny, staring up and down the drive. 'We saw the fellow, Old Iron. We must have made a mistake; the spot was farther down...'

'This,' interrupted Ironsides, 'is the spot.'

'But...'

'You know damned well that we only travelled ten or fifteen yards past the place, and we have come that distance back,' went on Cromwell. 'Besides, there's this old stump sticking out of the snow, on the grass verge. The figure we saw crossed the drive within a couple of yards of the stump.'

A tingling quiver ran up and down Johnny Lister's spine, rather like an electric shock. When he looked at his own and Cromwell's footprints, they were clear-cut and distinct. Cromwell had now left the hard concrete of the drive, and was peering into the trees at the side—where the mysterious figure had last been seen. The snow, here, was patchy, on account of the evergreens, and the ground was hard from the recent frost.

'I say,' Johnny was hesitant. 'I don't want to be imaginative, or anything like that, old thing, but this business is uncommonly eerie. I mean to say, we *both* saw that johnnie in the light of our headlamps, and anything human would have left tracks in this soft snow. Look at our own tracks.'

Cromwell grunted.

'A fine place to bring me to for Christmas,' he said sourly. 'Ghosts all over the place before we even get indoors!'

'Come off it!' protested Johnny. 'You don't believe in ghosts, you old fraud! Neither do I.'

'I believe the evidence of my own eyes,' said Ironsides, who was bending down over the snow, and inspecting it carefully. 'And I know it's physically impossible for any flesh-and-blood human to walk over a snow-covered drive without making footprints. It occurred to me that somebody might be playing a practical joke with a suspended dummy, but we can rule out that possibility.'

He indicated the ancient trees on one side of the drive, and the low bushes on the other.

'There's no way in which such a dummy could have been suspended,' he added. 'Besides, I'm not blind. The figure we saw was no dummy—and it *walked* straight across the drive.'

'Then what's the answer? Somebody walking on stilts? I once read a story…'

'Stilts would have left marks,' interrupted Ironsides, frowning.

'Then what *is* the answer?'

'Am I supposed to tackle riddles?' asked Cromwell, with a shrug. 'I didn't want to come to this God-forsaken mountain fastness in the first place. You see what happens? Before we've got our noses through the front door, we see apparitions!'

He climbed back into the car, and Johnny, with a last mystified look at the white carpet of snow, joined him. The usually cheery young sergeant was looking so thoughtful and grave when he greeted his father, a few minutes later, that the latter gave him a very sharp look.

'What's the matter with you, Johnny?' demanded General Lister, in his direct way. 'Are you ill—or in love?'

'Eh?' Johnny started. 'Ill? In love? No, dad, I'm perfectly fit. By the way, did I introduce Ironsides?'

'I've been waiting for you to do so,' replied his father gruffly. 'And I'm not going to wait any longer. There's no need for formalities, eh, Mr. Cromwell? Delighted to meet you, sir. This is a pleasure I have long awaited.'

He seized the Chief Inspector's hand in a huge country-squire grip and wrung it like a pump handle. General John Everett Lister, D.S.O., was a big, genial man of middle age, and he exactly fitted the huge oak-raftered hall, with its blazing log fire, in which he stood.

He put Cromwell at his ease at once; not that Cromwell really needed any putting. The great hall, with its glow of concealed electric lighting, its holly and its gay Christmas decorations, had already had a warming effect on Ironsides. Immense doors were standing open, giving a glimpse into other well-lighted rooms, and there were all sorts of cheery looking people moving about, and the air was filled with a constant sound of chatter and laughter.

'I owe you a big debt, Mr. Cromwell,' continued General Lister, regarding Ironsides with brotherly warmth. 'When my son shocked me, some years ago, by entering the Metropolitan Police, I practically cut him out of my will. But I've changed my opinion now. His association with you, my dear sir, has made a man of him.'

'I can't say that I've noticed it,' replied Ironsides bluntly. 'Ever since he's been my assistant, he's done nothing but make my life a misery.'

But the general refused to be drawn into an argument on the merits or demerits of his hopeful son. Johnny, in fact, had warned him just what to expect from Ironsides.

'Before we mingle with the happy throng, dad, there's one thing I'd like to ask in your private ear,' murmured Johnny mysteriously. 'Is it usual for the ghost of Cloon Castle to do his walking out-of-doors, comparatively early in the evening?'

General Lister started, and looked at Johnny very hard.

'Ghost!' he repeated sharply. 'You don't mean…'

'So there *is* a ghost of Cloon Castle?' asked Johnny, as his father hesitated.

'Nothing of the sort!' said the general hastily. 'How the devil did you get such a ridiculous idea?' He looked at Johnny harder than ever. 'Don't you think it would have been better if you had left your drinking until after you got here?'

'Be yourself, guv'nor,' protested Johnny. 'I haven't touched a drop since lunch-time. Can't you see how my tongue is hanging out? Ask Old Iron. He saw the bally ghost, or whatever it was, just as clearly as I did.'

General Lister looked puzzled and concerned when he was told about the 'appearance' on the drive. He might have doubted Johnny's veracity, but when Cromwell corroborated the story in every detail, he became quite serious.

'I don't pretend to understand what it was you saw, but I hope to heaven you'll keep it to yourselves,' said Johnny's father earnestly. 'The very last thing I want is a lot of ghost talk. I've had trouble enough, God knows, to make this infernal place look cheerful. Ancestral castles are all very well, but give me my Mayfair flat every time. I've had about forty thousand electricians working on the place for a month, and the dark corners they haven't succeeded in lighting up are legion.'

'Well, they'll come in handy for hide-and-seek,' said Johnny philosophically. 'You've got to admit that's something.'

Any further discussion was interrupted by the arrival of another guest. The very sight of this newcomer caused Ironsides to wince and hurriedly retreat. Even Johnny looked pained, and he saw a spasm flit across his father's face.

'Young Ronnie Charton!' whispered General Lister, in a tone of apology. 'Had to invite the young bounder because of his brother Gerry. You needn't meet him now.'

Johnny had no wish to meet him, and he escaped with Ironsides while his father was cordially shaking Ronnie Charton's hand. This Ronnie Charton was a young fellow with a pale face, long hair, and a queer tie. He had the air of a dreamy intellectual, and his manner suggested that he was doing the general a tremendous favour by coming to the party at all.

'I've heard he's an insufferable blister,' said Johnny, as he and Cromwell went upstairs to find their rooms. 'The Chartons are neighbours, sort of. Live in a big place two miles away. Gerry, I understand, is a right guy, well liked by all. I believe he used to pop over the castle wall as a boy, and pinch Lady Julia's apples, and this endeared him to her. But the blighter Ronnie would sooner listen to a Bach fugue than pinch anybody's apples. A dashed Eric-or-Little-by-Little, in fact, and therefore nobody's meat and drink.'

Later, Ironsides had an opportunity of verifying Johnny's graphic description. Dressed in 'white tie and tails,' and thoroughly uncomfortable, Mr. Cromwell did a certain amount of mingling. He was well on scene at the cocktail bar, and here he met both the Chartons—Gerry, cheery, frank and likeable; and Ronnie, supercilious and full of psycho-this and psycho-that. Even Gerry, who was the life and soul of the party, was clearly uncomfortable in his younger brother's presence.

Most of the other guests were thoroughly happy people, full of the Christmas spirit—or, at least, filling up. Most of them were General Lister's old friends, and their friends, including many nice couples and a really surprising number of pretty girls.

Ironsides, as observant as ever—although strictly off duty—found only one other guest, in addition to Ronnie Charton, who could be classed as eccentric. It never occurred to Cromwell to include himself in this class. The man he singled out for the honour was the famous Dr. Spencer Ware, of Wimpole Street. Dr. Ware was a brain specialist, although nobody was supposed to know this. He described himself as a healer of nervous disorders; and he was eccentric in Ironsides' view, only because he looked the very antithesis of his calling. He was a huge, boisterous-voiced, bronzed man with a laugh like a blare of trumpets, and a thoroughly surprising store of witty anecdotes. He looked exactly like a big game hunter—which was not very surprising, because big-game hunting was his hobby, when he could drag himself away from his patients.

The party went with a fine swing. Soon, everybody knew everybody else, and Johnny found at least three pretty girls who were vastly interested in him, not merely because of his good looks, but because of his association with Scotland Yard. Even Ironsides became genial under the influence of several cocktails and a really excellent dinner.

There was no dancing to-night, but any amount of good cheer, with a spot of excitement now and again as tardy guests put in an arrival. The excitement was caused by the rapid worsening of the weather conditions. The gentle snow of the earlier evening had become a veritable blizzard. On two occasions there had been S.O.S. calls for young men to dash out to the rescue of late arrivals who had failed to negotiate the drive, which was fast becoming a thick snowdrift.

The wind had risen to a gale, and it was howling and screaming round the ancient walls like a million demons.

A fitting setting for a Christmas party—and grim mystery!

## II. The Death Room

Bill Cromwell and Johnny Lister quite naturally found themselves in a little gathering of men round the library fire after the ladies and most of the other guests had retired for the night. There was some excellent hot toddy going, and, incidentally, going fast. Everybody round the fire was very talkative and affable; men who had not met one another until that same evening were pouring confidences into one another's ears, and forgetting all about them the next minute

There were many favourite topics of conversation, such as cursing the Government, deciding who was the prettiest girl in the party, and so on. General Lister's chief concern, at the moment, was a check-up on his guests, and when he was satisfied that everybody had safely arrived, he allowed himself to relax.

'It's a good thing they have all arrived,' he remarked to Johnny. 'By the look of things, we shall be thoroughly snowed up before the morning. Mr. and Mrs. Carstairs, who were the last to get in, had the very devil of a time. They were stuck in three different places, and it took them the best part of three hours to cover a couple of miles. I hear that the lane between here and the main road is already seven feet deep in snow. What it'll be like by the morning, God knows!'

'Who cares?' replied Johnny lightly. 'I take it that you've got plenty of grub and provisions generally? And drink? It'll be rather fun, being snowed up on Christmas Day.'

What with the howling of the wind, and the beating of the snow on the library windows, and the occasional down-draught in the great fireplace, the conversation quite naturally and automatically drifted along to the subject of ghosts. Any gathering of men, taking a last drink in a big old country house at Christmas time will inevitably talk of ghosts sooner or later.

'You're not going to tell me that there isn't a ghost of Cloon Castle,' said one man emphatically. 'There must be a ghost of Cloon Castle! Dammit, it wouldn't be an authentic old English castle without some Veiled Lady, or Headless Knight, or Hooded Monk.' He turned, glass in hand, and looked at General Lister reprovingly. 'What about it, Lister? You're not going to hold out on us, are you?'

'I think,' retorted the general gruffly, 'that it's time we all went to bed.'

'Not before you tell me whether the ghost walks in my corridor or somebody else's corridor!'

'Don't be a fool, Drydon…'

'For all I know, my very bedchamber may be haunted,' continued Drydon, as he refilled his glass. 'Is it haunted, Lister? Have you bunged me in…'

'The Death Room?' suggested somebody else.

Drydon looked round, as if to find out who had spoken. Ironsides was watching General Lister, and there was such a change in the genial host that other men, too, fell silent.

'Why Death Room?' asked Johnny curiously.

'I wasn't aware that anybody here knew about the Death Room,' said the general, half angrily. 'Which one of you brought up the subject?'

The men looked at one another, but nobody seemed to know.

'Not that it matters,' continued the host. 'I'm certainly not going to have the matter discussed at this time of night…'

He was interrupted by a chorus of protest. Even Johnny joined in. Having said so much, General Lister would have to say more.

'You've got to play the game, sir,' urged Gerry Charton, with a grin. 'Any one of us may be sleeping in the Death Room, and it's only fair that we should know something…'

'Nobody is sleeping in the Death Room,' interrupted the general, almost curtly. 'The Death Room is downstairs, and it is always kept heavily locked, so there's no sense in discussing it at all. It has been locked for over a hundred years.'

Naturally, this statement made the group round the fireside more curious than ever. Ordinarily, perhaps, being gentlemen, they would have respected their host's obvious hint that the subject was not one that he cared to discuss. But the toddy had been going round pretty freely, and this fact, added to the general Christmas feeling, disposed of all reticence. Men who were usually discreetness itself, clamoured for General Lister to tell them more about the Death Room.

'I only know that the room is situated at the end of the south corridor, on the ground floor, and that it is reputed to be haunted,' said the host reluctantly. 'I shall be obliged, gentlemen, if you will now change the subject…'

'But what's the story?' demanded somebody. 'If there's a haunted room, there must be a story connected with it. Don't be so damned mysterious, Lister. You're making us more curious than ever. Let's have the story.'

'I tell you, there is no story,' retorted the general angrily.

But his very vehemence hinted that he was holding something back. Johnny, knowing that his father desired no 'ghost talk,' did his best to rally round. He shrewdly pointed out that somebody must have been murdered in the apartment, otherwise it would not be called the Death Room; and who wanted to have a look at a musty old chamber like that, anyway?

'By God, young Lister, that's an idea!' chuckled Drydon. 'Let's all go along, and have a look at the Death Room! Who's game?'

Everybody, apparently, was game—with the exception of the host, who, judging by the glance he bestowed on his hopeful son, did not seem to think that Johnny had helped much.

'The trouble with you fellows,' said Ronnie Charton, taking part in the conversation for the first time, 'is that you're all drunk.'

For the first time that evening, General Lister looked at Ronnie almost affectionately. The statement was not true, for nobody was beyond the merry stage, but it caused an awkward hiatus in the babble of talk. It was the sneering, supercilious tone in Ronnie's voice, quite as much as his words, which brought about the pause.

'What does it matter whether you look at the room, or whether you don't look at the room?' continued Ronnie, with a curl of his lip. 'Any room that has been locked up for a hundred years will look mysterious and ghostly. It's merely a question of mind over matter. You might just as well go up and look at one of the attics. It'll be just as dusty and just as gloomy.'

'Curse it, Ronnie, you're not going to talk us out of seeing the Death Room,' protested Gerry. 'I'm not mad enough to suggest that anybody should spend the night in the Death Room, but there's no harm in having a look.'

So many of the others seconded this proposal that General Lister could see that he would either have to unlock the Death Room for a few minutes, or quarrel with his guests. He was very irritated, but tried not to show it. In the end, he walked out of the library, and the others followed like a lot of schoolboys. Johnny, as keen as the rest, noticed that Ironsides was making for the big staircase.

'Aren't you coming, Old Iron?'

'Why should I come?' demanded Cromwell. 'I don't believe in ghosts, and I'm not going to get any pleasure out of looking into a dusty old room. I'd rather go to bed.'

But he accompanied Johnny readily enough, after Johnny had argued for a minute, and when Johnny thought things over later, he came to the conclusion that Ironsides had meant to see the Death Room from the first—but he liked to be persuaded. This was just one of his little ways.

'One of the old man's dark corners,' murmured Johnny, when they got to the end of the south corridor.

Certainly, the electricians had made no attempt to illuminate this particular stone-flagged passage. It was very gloomy at the far end, and a wave of dank cold air swept over the little crowd of men when General Lister unlocked a heavy door and pushed it open on its creaking hinges.

'There are no lights,' said the general briefly.

They crowded in, and most of them possessed either matches or automatic lighters. These were struck into flame, and the aggregation made a fair light.

There was no longer a babble of talk. The very atmosphere of the room struck a chill into the explorers—and it was not only the cold. The solid, heavy furniture, with its layer of age-old dust, the great empty fireplace, and the blackened oak beams—all this made a picture, in the feeble, flickering light that struck an exceedingly eerie note. The shrieking of the wind outside did not help.

'I'm beginning to think, you fellows, that we shouldn't have come,' said Gerry Charton softly. 'Hell! I've got the creeps already. I shall dream about this beastly room.'

His brother laughed in a superior way.

'I never had any suspicion, Gerry, that you were neurotic,' he chaffed. 'I can assure you that the room won't have the slightest effect upon my sleep. Haunted houses or rooms are only haunted by—atmosphere. The mind does the rest. Healthy minds remain unaffected. Neurotic minds react in a great variety of ways. What they see in a haunted room is nothing but the figment of their own imagination.'

'That's rather an interesting argument,' admitted Gerry. 'As it happens, none of us know what this room *is* haunted by, because the general won't tell us—admitting that it is haunted at all. So if one of us stayed the night in the room and—well, saw things—those things would be nothing but the phantoms of his own mind.'

'Naturally,' agreed Ronnie, with a shrug. 'In just the same way, people hear stories of a certain haunting, they keep watch, and they see the supposed ghost. Actually, they only see what they have been led to expect, and it is purely imaginary.' He walked farther into the room and looked about him contemptuously. 'Eeriness is merely a condition of mind,' he said. 'This room doesn't affect me in the least. Why should it? Its history is no concern of mine, and therefore it is nothing but a drab, cold, dusty-looking room. With a fire glowing in the grate, and lights everywhere, it would be just the same as any other room.'

'But we do not all possess such strong nerves,' murmured Dr. Ware dryly. 'In my experience, it is only the extremely bold and the extremely foolish who take pleasure in sleeping in haunted chambers. The first-named are proof against any shocks, and the second are far too brainless to possess any imagination. In just the same way, regrettable as it is to admit it, it is the clod who sometimes earns the V.C. in battle—although he doesn't always get it. He has no imagination to picture the dangers into which he is hurling himself.'

'Well, let's clear out of the place before our lighters burn out,' said Gerry Charton, with a laugh. 'Nobody's going to sleep the night in here—not even the bold, fearless Ronnie. He obviously comes into Dr. Ware's first category, because everybody knows he's not a fool.'

Ronnie flushed with annoyance.

'There's always something damned unpleasant in your humour, Gerry,' he said. 'If you're suggesting that I wouldn't spend the night in this room… Blast you, I *will* spend the night in the room!'

'Come, come, Charton!' said General Lister sharply. 'There's no need for you to be piqued. Your brother didn't mean any reflection on your courage…'

'None whatever,' put in Gerry. 'He just makes me sick, that's all. He's got no more sense of humour than a carrot. Even when we were boys at school together…' He suddenly laughed. 'I'm beginning to think Ronnie was right. He's the only sober one amongst us.'

There was a stubborn, sulky look on Ronnie's face, which had now returned to its normal pallor.

'I meant what I said!' he muttered haughtily.

'Don't be a fool, Ronnie,' said Gerry, with quick concern. 'Hang it, man, I was only kidding. Can't you ever take a joke? Only a fool or a braggart would keep up that nonsense about spending a night…'

'All right—I'm a fool,' flared Ronnie. 'I'm a braggart! If I don't spend the night in the room now, everybody will think I'm yellow.'

'Nonsense!' laughed Dr. Ware. 'You're taking the whole thing far too seriously, my boy. What do you think, Mr. Cromwell?' he added, turning to Ironsides, who happened to be standing beside him.

'I think I'm going to bed,' replied Ironsides, yawning.

He apparently thought that the whole discussion would fizzle out, once the men had returned to the library—and the hot toddy. But Ronnie Charton was one of those pig-headed, insufferable young men who possess an extraordinarily inflated opinion of their own importance. Anybody else might have responded to the chaff with a laugh, and the whole thing would have been over. But not the magnificent Ronnie.

The inevitable outcome was that some of the other men decided to take him at his word, and there was talk of getting candles and lamps, and lighting a fire in the Death Room.

'It'll do the young swine a heap of good,' murmured Drydon into Johnny's ear. 'Who the hell does he think he is, anyway? What he needs is a lesson. I don't mind having a side bet that he comes squealing out of the room within half an hour.'

Johnny grinned.

'Isn't it more usual for the house-party to find the occupant of the haunted room stretched out cold and stark on the floor?' he chuckled.

General Lister, at first angry, then concerned, was helpless. If he forbade Ronnie to spend the night in the Death Room, he would undoubtedly make an enemy of the young ass—and Johnny's father was a friendly soul, and the host to boot. The other men took the whole thing into their own hands, and in a very short time a great fire was blazing in the Death Room, and half a dozen candles were burning on the mantelpiece, to say nothing of an old-fashioned standard oil lamp, with a hideous rose shade, in one of the darkest corners.

'Listen, Ronnie!' said Gerry Charton earnestly. 'Nobody wants you to do this potty thing. If I annoyed you, I'm most frightfully sorry. Why not call it all off?'

'What's the matter—getting scared?' retorted Ronnie, with a sneer. 'I'm going to spend the night in the Death Room—not you. What's more, I'm going to sleep. You surely don't think I'm nervous, do you?'

Gerry looked at him helplessly.

'Go ahead,' he said, with a shrug. 'I give up.'

The others were not so considerate. With their tongues in their cheeks, they solemnly advised Ronnie to keep a sharp look-out for the ghost; they suggested that he should leave the door slightly ajar, so that he could make a quick getaway at the first rattle of bones. A final drink, and a large one, was pressed on Ronnie, and it was noticed by one and all that he drank it at a gulp.

Then, after he had shut himself in the Death Room, a big shout of laughter went up when the heavy key was heard turning in the lock. If one of the humorists had not suggested that Ronnie should leave the door ajar, he would probably have left it unlocked, at the very least.

'Silly young chump!' growled Johnny, as he and Ironsides at last went up to bed. 'Between you and me, old bean, the pater is worried more than somewhat. I can't say I think a lot of the binge myself.'

'Um!' grunted Mr. Cromwell vaguely.

'Who the devil started the talk about the Death Room, anyhow?'

'I don't know who started it, but you helped the talk along very nicely,' said Ironsides, with a sniff. 'This is my room, isn't it? Where's yours? Next door? Well, I suppose the walls are pretty thick in an old house like this, so I ought to be able to get some sleep.'

Johnny was not listening.

'Just between ourselves, Old Iron, it's a priceless opportunity for some evilly disposed person to bump that young blighter, and no questions asked,' he said. 'The castle is congested with people who would like to see Ronnie Charton lying stark and stiff, with his face frozen into an expression of livid fear.'

'Go to bed!' said Cromwell, yawning.

And down in the Death Room, Ronnie Charton was sitting in a big chair in front of the blazing fire, smoking with an air of calm nonchalance. For Ronnie belonged to that large class of people who continually fool themselves, but fool nobody else. In his heart, he was not a bit keen on this vigil, but he would not have admitted it to himself for a sum of ten thousand pounds, cash on the spot.

The brightly blazing fire, and the lights, did no more than half dispel the eerie gloom of the long, draughty chamber, with its deeply-recessed windows and its shadowy corners. The flickering shadows on the raftered ceiling took all sorts of queer shapes, and Ronnie found himself getting jumpy.

He was strong enough, he told himself, to make his mind a blank. The best thing in a situation like this was to think of nothing whatever. It annoyed him to find that he kept conjecturing on the possible appearance of the supposed ghost. It was perfectly senile of General Lister to withhold the story of the Death Room—for it was quite palpable to Ronnie that his lordship did know something. The unfortunate young man was left entirely to his own imagination.

For some little time he heard the vague talking of his late companions out in the great hall, and an occasional burst of laughter. Whereupon he gritted his teeth and chewed up a couple of perfectly good cigarettes. Presently, the voices died away, and the only sounds which came to his ears were caused by the crackling of the fire, the howling of the wind outside, and an occasional mysterious creak from odd corners of the room. These creaks rather got on his nerves—although his common sense should have told him that a room, left for years without a fire, would do quite a lot of creaking with an unaccustomed heat spreading throughout its length and breadth.

After a while he got to his feet and walked to one of the windows. Clearing the steamy glass with his hand, he peered outside. But he could see little, for the snow was piled high on the ledge, and flakes were whirling in millions. It was a wild and fearful night, even for the Peak District of Derbyshire.

Ronnie gave the room a cool, careless glance as he walked back to the fireplace. As he had known from the first, there was nothing in spending a night in a haunted room. He was even feeling sleepy—a sure proof that his nerves were rock steady. He piled more logs on the fire, which was burning rapidly, and sat down in the big easy chair again.

He lit a cigarette and yawned. He puffed lazily for a few minutes, and felt strangely drowsy and at peace.

'Haunted rooms!' he murmured. 'The bunk!'

The cigarette drooped in his lips, and he took it out and tossed it into the fire. He closed his eyes, and his head fell back…

Ronnie Charton started up in his chair with a horrible screaming cry ringing in his ears. His head was throbbing painfully, and his vision was blurred. For a moment or two he did not even know where he was; and then, as he saw the fire, and the big chair, memory came flooding back.

But that cry…?

He must have been dreaming, although he had no recollection of it. His brain seemed solid and dull. It was some little time before he realized, with a start, that the long candles had nearly burned themselves out, and the fire was low. It seemed to him that he had put those fresh logs on only a few minutes ago; but a couple of hours, at least, must have elapsed.

He rose unsteadily to his feet, and looked into the depths of the room. The sky had apparently cleared, for a shaft of moonlight was slanting from the end window on to the parquet floor, *and there was something lying in the moonbeam!* Ronnie stood stock still, and his heart faltered. He braced himself and tried to control the sudden shivering of his limbs. There was nothing over there on the floor… There couldn't be anything… Just a shadow…

An awful driving force seemed to compel him forward—something entirely outside his own will. His brain was still thick and heavy, and he groped in a dense mental fog. He found himself looking down at the floor where the moonbeam slantingly fell—and the thing he saw brought a shuddering sob of horror into his semi-paralysed throat.

A man was lying there, face upwards, his sightless eyes flatly and fearfully reflecting the moonlight; a man quaintly dressed in an old-time cape, with a cravat showing behind the rumpled collar. Knee breeches and buckled shoes… But Ronnie Charton saw nothing beyond the figure's middle. Driven clean through the heart was a broken and jagged-ended iron stake, two feet of which was sticking straight upwards. And a glistening pool on the parquet floor had spread out from the body. Not merely one pool… The polished flooring was drenched with blood all round, and the air was full of an awful nauseating *smell*…

'My God!' screamed Ronnie Charton wildly.

Panic seized him—an awful, crazy, nightmare panic. He flung himself round towards the door, his shoes slipping and slithering on the floor, so that he lost his balance and crashed into the end of the heavy table. Rebounding from this, he tottered to the door, and managed to turn the key in the lock. He was breathing in great sobbing gulps, his face turned over his shoulder, staring... staring...

How he got the door open he never knew, but he flung himself out, and went running insanely down the stone-flagged passage, scream after scream issuing from his throat in hideous crescendo. As he ran he crashed into obstacle after obstacle, gashing his head, his hands, and his knees. But he felt no pain; he only knew that his brain was on the point of bursting with an unnamed terror.

He reached the great hall, where a single electric light was burning. He tried to reach the staircase, but failed, and collapsed into a shuddering, quivering heap on the floor.

## III. Ghost, Or...?

It was significant that of all the people in Cloon Castle, Chief Inspector Cromwell was the first man to appear. In spite of his professed indifference, as expressed to Johnny Lister, he must have been very much on the alert—or, at least, sleeping with one eye open and one ear slightly flapping.

Quick as he was, however, to hurry out of his bedroom, Johnny and his father were right on his heels as he went loping down the big staircase not unlike a great shaggy bear—a particularly lean and loose-limbed bear—with his hair pointing to all points of the compass, and his dressing-gown waving.

'In God's name, Johnny, what has happened?' panted General Lister, as he caught up with his son, and pulled at his arm.

'No good asking me, dad,' replied Johnny. 'Something woke me up—shrieks and things—and as soon as I got out of my room I found Ironsides streaking along in front of me. I suppose you heard the shrieks, too?'

'Everybody in the castle must have heard them,' said his distracted father. 'It's that young fool, Charton! I knew what would happen if he went into the Death Room! But I blame myself more than... Well, Cromwell? What are you standing there for? What's that on the floor?'

The general and Johnny had just got to the bottom of the stairs, and, turning the angle, they saw that Ironsides was bending over something a few feet away.

'A little more light would help,' said Cromwell briefly.

Johnny dashed to the switches, and pressed them. The hall became flooded with light. A babble of voices from upstairs and flitting figures on the great balcony indicated that many other members of the house-party were aroused and coming down to find out what was wrong. A considerable fluttering, rather like a disturbed hen-roost, accompanied by frightened squeaks, proved that the feminine element was on the job, too.

'It's young Charton,' said Cromwell unemotionally, as his host reached his side. 'No, he's not dead. Not by a mile. But he's the most frightened man I've ever had the misfortune to see. Poor devil! He's knocked himself about a bit, too, by the look of it—bumping into walls, no doubt, as he ran from the Death Room.'

Johnny, without waiting, made a dash for the library, and returned with the brandy decanter.

'Good man,' muttered Ironsides. 'That is what he needs.'

A booming voice from upstairs, urging the ladies to be calm, announced the arrival of Dr. Spencer Ware. He did yeoman work, and General Lister was grateful. He succeeded in bunching the ladies on the balcony, and keeping them there. A lithe young figure in a dressing-gown came tearing downstairs. Gerry Charton, although well over thirty, was as athletic as a youth in his 'teens.

'What's happened?' he asked huskily, as his startled eyes beheld the limp form of his brother in Cromwell's arms. 'Is Ronnie hurt? I warned him…'

'Steady, young man,' interrupted Ironsides. 'His physical hurts are trivial. All I know is that he let out some of the most fearful screams I had ever heard, and he has had a pile-driving shock. Overwrought nerves, perhaps…'

'It's in there,' babbled Ronnie Charton, partially recovering after a big swig of brandy. 'In the Death Room! I saw it, lying on the floor, in the moonlight! I saw it, I tell you…'

He broke off, shuddering, and, covering his face with both hands, he sobbed convulsively, his whole body racked. Bill Cromwell allowed him to keep this up for nearly a minute, waving the others back with an authoritative hand. Then, as gentle as a woman, the loose-limbed Yard man gave Ronnie another pull of brandy, and eased him into a more comfortable position. 'If you're feeling strong enough…'

'I'm all right—I'm a lot better,' panted Ronnie, his eyes still wild with fear. 'I must have fallen asleep… When I woke up I saw that *Thing* on the floor… Oh-h-h-h!'

He broke off, and clutched at Ironsides as a child might have clutched at its mother.

'Take it easy, Ronnie, old lad,' said Gerry gently. 'You couldn't have seen anything, really…'

'A man—all funnily dressed—a man lying face upwards, dead,' breathed Ronnie. 'There was blood all round—pools of it, gleaming in the moonlight. And right through his heart, a great iron stake!'

'My God!' whispered General Lister.

His tone was so strange that Ironsides shot him a quick, searching glance. There was a startling change in the general; his usually healthy, ruddy face was as white as a sheet of paper, his eyes were full of a great horror. Then, without a word, and running unsteadily, he dashed towards the south corridor.

'Look after your brother, Mr. Charton,' muttered Cromwell.

Gerry nodded, and Ironsides and Johnny were right on the general's heels when he entered the Death Room. There were one or two other men in the party, too. Johnny's father was walking round the table, staring at the floor, searching all about. Cromwell helped matters by flashing on a powerful electric torch, and the white beam of light slashed the darkness like a miniature searchlight.

'Nothing!' said General Lister, more to himself than to the others. 'Nothing at all. I knew it. There *couldn't* be anything.'

'I say, dad, you're worrying me,' protested Johnny, taking his father's arm. 'You're looking nearly as bowled over as that young fellow in the hall. Why?'

His father did not seem to hear. He was still looking at the floor, particularly where the moonlight streamed into the room. There was nothing but the parquet wood—no body—no pools of blood—nothing! The floor was bone dry and bare. Before Ronnie had commenced his vigil, the whole floor had been thoroughly swept, and the furniture dusted.

'God help him!' muttered the general.

'But what on earth...'

'Ronnie Charton saw an apparition in this room,' said General Lister steadily. 'Call it a ghost, if you like. I've never really believed in ghosts—until now.'

'Here, steady, guv'nor! The poor chap simply worked himself into a state of terror, and saw things,' objected Johnny. 'The imagination can play frightfully queer tricks...'

'Perhaps so—but it was not imagination in this case,' interrupted his father. 'Two hundred years ago Sir Travers Cloon, the then lord of the manor, was foully murdered in this very room. He was found lying on the floor in a great pool of blood, with a broken iron stake through his heart.'

'Whew! That's just what Ronnie said.'

'Yes,' agreed the general. 'That's just what Ronnie said.'

There was a silence. All the men in that gloomy room looked at one another strangely. For a few moments the only sound was the whistling of the wind outside.

'Very rum,' said Ironsides softly. 'Very rum, indeed!'

'The boy knew nothing of this story,' continued the general, his manner almost fierce. 'Nobody in the house knew it—except me. When you asked me to tell you the story of the Death Room, I refused. Ronnie knew nothing at all, I tell you. What he saw was an apparition. He couldn't have *imagined* something of which he had absolutely no knowledge.'

He walked towards the door, and all the others, except Ironsides, promptly followed him. Even Johnny, whose nerves were composed of a mixture of catgut and tungsten, felt an inclination to be elsewhere. When they got back into the hall they found that Ronnie Charton was on his feet. As he saw them coming he took an impulsive step towards them.

'Well?' he asked hoarsely.

'It's all right, my boy,' said General Lister kindly. 'Your brother had better take you up to your room. You've had a very nasty dream…'

'Dream!' shouted Ronnie, in amazement. 'What do you mean—dream? Why do you try to treat me like a child? You've seen the body, haven't you?'

'There is no body, Charton,' said the general. 'Nobody has been killed. There's nothing in the Death Room…'

'You're mad!' panted Ronnie hoarsely.

He pushed past them, and ran unsteadily into the south corridor. When he dashed into the Death Room, he found Cromwell pottering about with his electric torch.

'It was here—lying on the floor, right on this spot!' said Ronnie, pointing. 'Why are you trying to trick me?' He spun round angrily on his host and his brother, who had followed him in. 'You've taken the body away…'

'Come, come, my boy,' said General Lister quietly. 'Nobody's trying to trick you. Look for yourself. You say the body was here? But the floor is bone dry, and even if some ill-disposed practical joker played a cruel trick on you, it would have been quite impossible to remove the body *and wipe up the blood* in so short a space of time. Scarcely five minutes elapsed between your cries and our entry into this room. But the very idea of such a practical joke is too outrageous to be given a moment's consideration.'

Ronnie Charton had a relapse. All he could do as he stood looking at the dry floor was to babble incoherently. He was led away by his brother and another man, and as they took him upstairs he sobbed and shook. It was fortunate that Dr. Ware was a member of the house-party, and he promised General Lister that he would do everything possible.

When Johnny went back into the Death Room, he found Cromwell still prowling about. Cromwell, for some reason, was taking a keen interest in the apartment.

'There's something funny about this affair, my Johnny,' said Ironsides confidentially. 'I've read stories about haunted rooms. If young Charton had been found stiff and cold, the whole thing would have been just the same as the situation in nine ghost stories out of ten.'

'Exactly,' agreed Johnny. 'This damned business is all wrong. Not according to Hoyle at all. It's the bloke who spends the night in the haunted chamber who always cops it in the neck. Ronnie copped it to a certain extent, but he's still in the land of the living. What's the answer, Old Iron? Who was the bloke on the floor?'

Ironsides did not appear to be listening. He was continuing his perambulations round the room, and Johnny went on talking. He had an idea that he was talking to himself, but it amused him.

'Personally, I don't believe there was any bloke on the floor,' he said. 'How could there have been? Ronnie locked himself in this room, sat in front of the fire, and proceeded to get a large attack of the heebie-jeebies. Being an absolute chump, he wouldn't admit that the room was getting him down, and in the end he saw things... How do we know that Ronnie had never heard the story of the Death Room? The old man didn't trot it out in the library, but Ronnie might have heard it years ago. You know what I mean, a sort of subconscious knowledge. Then his imagination starts working overtime...'

'What the hell are you drivelling about?' asked Cromwell tartly. 'I was the first to get to the young blighter, wasn't I? He didn't see any spooks. He was scared in quite a different way.'

Johnny walked across. Ironsides was on his hands and knees, and his electric torch was lying on the floor, sending its shaft of light across the parquet. And with the point of a pencil, Ironsides was gently turning over some tiny scraps of something.

'What have you got there?' asked Johnny curiously.

'Can't you see? Earth, my good Johnny—little particles of *damp* earth!'

And Bill Cromwell's manner caused Johnny Lister to look at him in wonder; for Cromwell had suddenly become very happy—a sure sign that he was exceedingly puzzled.

# IV. The Crypt

Christmas Day found the Cloon Castle house-party gay and happy. The blizzard of the night was over, the sun was shining, and there was snow everywhere. It was the kind of Christmas Day one sometimes reads about in old-time novels, but rarely experiences.

With the bright winter's sunshine streaming through the windows, Ronnie Charton's adventure of the night seemed perfectly ridiculous. Most members of the house-party—and the servants, too—had been reassured when it had been established that there was no gruesome body lying in the Death Room, as Ronnie had stated. There was not even the slightest evidence of a ghost.

'Nerves—that's all it was, just nerves,' was the general verdict. 'The young ass shut himself up in that gloomy old room and his imagination did the rest. Serves him right!'

Which was all the sympathy Ronnie Charton got. His fellow guests were laughing at his misfortune. Ronnie himself kept to his room this morning, and it was felt by one and all that this was the best place for him. The party was a great deal more pleasant without him.

Nearly all the talk at the breakfast table was concerned with the prospects of tobogganing, winter sports generally, and the great blizzard of the night. General Lister's prophecy proved correct. Cloon Castle was completely snowed up. Every available manservant had been working for hours to cut a way through a ten-foot drift in one of the rear court-yards, for it appeared that three unfortunate grooms were marooned in an out-building. The difficulties of this task indicated how thoroughly the castle was shut off from the outside world. For the drifts in the drive, and elsewhere, were even deeper. Some enthusiasts conceived the idea of climbing to the castle's highest turret, and taking a look at the countryside through binoculars. So, directly after breakfast, a crowd of laughing young men and girls went off on this quest, and Johnny was roped in as head man.

After a dizzy climb up endless circular steps, the turret of the highest tower was reached—and then it was seen that the house-party was cut off from the world in very truth. The air was as clear as crystal, and one could see for miles in every direction. The Half Mile Lane, which was the only connecting link with the main road, had completely disappeared; even the tops of the hedges had vanished. The main road itself could not be identified. In every direction snow, and nothing but snow.

'Well, if this isn't ye olde Christmasse weather,' remarked Johnny, 'go find me some. I'm told that the telephone is as dead as mutton, so the wires must have been blown down during the night. How do you like being marooned, Phyllis, my child?'

Phyllis, the girl who had attached herself to Johnny this morning, laughed happily.

'As long as there's enough grub in the place to carry us over the vacation, who cares?' she replied, with practical common sense. 'That was one of the first questions I asked when I came down this morning, and they tell me that the castle is so stacked with fodder we can have double rations at every meal for a month, and the pile wouldn't look any smaller.'

'We should worry about snow, then,' said Johnny, grinning.

The Christmas spirit so possessed him that he joyously agreed to join a party of daring young people who were planning to go out and make a toboggan run. But when he went up to his room, to obtain a woollen scarf and heavy gloves, he encountered Ironsides in the wide corridor; and Ironsides was looking so serenely and disgustingly happy that Johnny stopped dead.

'Dammit, Old Iron, you don't mean to say that you're still thinking about that blighting business of Ronnie Charton and the Death Room?' asked Johnny. 'A whole gang of us is going out into the cold, cold snow. Aren't you coming?'

'What do you take me for—a lunatic?' retorted Cromwell, with a snort. 'I can see all the snow I want from the windows—and a hell of a sight more than I want! But go ahead with your childish pleasures, if you want to. You're on vacation, so I can't expect you to work.'

'Work!' ejaculated Johnny, staring.

'You disappoint me, Johnny,' said Ironsides, with regret. 'It's a relief to know that most of the featherbrains in this house believe that young Charton was merely the victim of his own jitters. But you're different—or you ought to be. There's a grim mystery waiting to be solved in the Death Room, but don't let that interfere with your pleasures.'

And Bill Cromwell brushed past, and walked into Ronnie Charton's bedroom. Johnny followed, his interest in the proposed outdoor jaunt practically dead.

Ronnie looked practically dead, too. He was lying in bed as still as a corpse, his face pallid and drawn, even in sleep. General Lister and Gerry Charton and Dr. Spencer Ware were in the room, too, standing by the bed and looking down at its motionless occupant.

'Am I intruding?' asked Ironsides mildly. 'I was going to ask Ronnie a few questions about last night.'

The general shook his head.

'I don't think you'll be able to question him for some days, Mr. Cromwell,' he replied. 'His nerves are in such a dreadful state that Dr. Ware was obliged to give him a sleeping draught.'

Gerry, who was looking haggard, suddenly cursed.

'If we hadn't been sozzled last night, we wouldn't have allowed the young idiot to do such a crazy thing,' he said fiercely. 'I haven't had a wink of sleep since—it happened. I was with Ronnie until six o'clock, and he was so wild and violent that I was jolly glad when Dr. Ware came in. Damn all haunted castles and haunted rooms!'

General Lister, who was a kindly man, made allowances for Gerry's overwrought condition, and he was not even offended.

'The present trouble, I'm afraid, is going to be the least of our worries,' said the brain specialist, his manner very grave. 'I've had a great deal of experience of nervous disorders, gentlemen, and this unfortunate young man will need very careful treatment and nursing if he is to be restored to perfect health.'

The general and Ironsides looked at him hard, and Dr. Ware, who was standing in such a position that Gerry could not see him, tapped his head significantly.

'A great deal depends upon Ronnie himself,' continued the doctor. 'I'm afraid he's not the strong man he pretends to be. You must forgive me for being frank, Gerry.'

'You're not telling me anything, Dr. Ware,' growled Gerry Charton. 'I've always known that Ronnie was nothing but a windbag and a braggart. It was his poses that always made me see red.'

'I have too often found that such mentalities are the quickest to crumble under the influence of a great shock,' said Dr. Ware. 'Men like Ronnie go through life fooling themselves constantly. They think they are very fine fellows; they express contempt for almost every known convention. It is only when they experience a sudden shock that their innate weakness is exposed. To use a colloquialism, they just can't take it.'

Cromwell and Johnny left the bedroom a moment or two before their host. Johnny was looking uncomfortable.

'Does the old boy mean that Ronnie will eventually be shoved into the loony bin?' he murmured.

'It seems to be the general idea,' replied Ironsides. 'And why not? He wouldn't be the first young fool to go crazy after spending a night in a haunted room.'

'But I thought you said…'

'That the room was not really haunted?' supplied Cromwell. 'What difference does it make? Ronnie *thought* it was haunted, and he saw a dreadful apparition—and it comes to exactly the same thing.'

They were joined by Johnny's father.

'This is a damnable business, my boy,' said the general worriedly. 'Thank God we've got a doctor on the premises. Snowed up as we are, and quite unable to obtain medical aid from outside, we should have been in a fine pickle with Ronnie… By the way, Johnny,' he added suddenly. 'You, too, Mr. Cromwell. I hope to God you won't discuss the boy's condition with any of my other guests. It would be grievous to spoil their enjoyment of Christmas Day. Far better to let them believe that Ronnie is peacefully sleeping.'

'Can I have the key of the Death Room?' asked Ironsides, in his abrupt way.

'Do you really think we should go in there again?' said the general, frowning.

'Come with me, sir, and I'll show you whether we should go in again!' retorted Cromwell calmly. 'I tried to get into the room before breakfast, but I found that you had locked it after I left the apartment during the night.'

Johnny's father was not enthusiastic, but there was something very compelling in Cromwell's manner. They succeeded in reaching the Death Room without attracting the attention of anybody else—for, by this time, the outdoor party had made a noisy exit, and could be heard yelling and laughing in the snow outside.

'The reason I asked you to come, sir, is this,' said Ironsides, getting straight to the point. 'Where does this lead to?'

Having closed the door, he had taken long, loose strides across the room to a narrow stone arch in a corner of the Death Room. Almost hidden in the shadows at the back of this arch was an enormously strong door. It was made of solid age-old oak, and heavily studded with metal. There was a keyhole of great size, but no key.

'Why do you want to know what lies beyond this door, Mr. Cromwell?' asked General Lister, in a strange voice. 'The door has not been unlocked. I keep the key in my safe—and the key, incidentally, weighs about half a hundredweight.'

'All the same, sir, I'd like to know what's on the other side,' insisted Ironsides gently.

'There are some stone steps leading downwards, a comparatively short arched tunnel, and then—the family crypt of the Cloons,' said the general quietly. 'If you are going to suggest that I should open the door, Mr. Cromwell, I must emphatically refuse.'

Johnny started.

'I say! This is hot,' he exclaimed, in a shocked voice. 'The family crypt, what? So the spectre of old Sir Travers doesn't have to make much of a journey when he gives his midnight performance?'

'You talk like a child, Johnny,' said his father, annoyed. 'How the authorities at Scotland Yard can employ you as a detective constantly baffles me. It is a scathing indictment of the slipshod methods of the police authorities.'

'Anybody might think you were Ironsides, dad,' protested Johnny. 'He's always saying things like that about me. I don't see where I went off the rails. The ghost did appear in this room, and if it's only a few steps from here to the crypt, where the bones of Sir Travers Cloon are resting...'

'There is no need, Johnny, to make it worse,' snapped his father. 'This facetiousness is most distasteful. You know perfectly well that Ronnie Charton saw no ghost.'

Ironsides had been waiting patiently for the argument to finish.

'I want,' he said, 'the key of this door.'

'Really, Mr. Cromwell, I've already told you…'

'Breaking the door down,' mused Cromwell, 'would make a considerable amount of noise, and probably attract attention.'

General Lister jumped.

'Good God, man, you're not proposing…'

'Not at all,' murmured Ironsides. 'How much easier to use a key—even if it is a bit cumbersome.'

There was something hypnotic in the lean Yard man's persistence. His complete and utter calmness, too, made his host feel extremely helpless. In the end, of course, Ironsides had his way. Johnny's father hurried off to get the key.

'Aren't you a bit high-handed, old thing?' hinted Johnny. 'Quite apart from the fact that you're a guest in this house, and in no position to give orders, don't you think it's a bit thick to disturb the mouldering bones of dead and bygone Cloons? I deprecate this morbid streak in your nature, Old Iron. Admitting that you look somewhat like Frankenstein…'

'You know,' said Ironsides reflectively, 'your father was quite right, Johnny. How the hell the Yard authorities continue to be bluffed into believing that you possess brains is simply incredible.'

Johnny Lister sagged a bit.

'You mean, you've spotted something that I've completely missed?' he said. 'Well, damn it, man, be a sport! I haven't been concentrating. I mean, Christmas and all that…'

At this point his father returned with an object which looked rather like the ceremonial key which is presented to a man about to receive the Freedom of the City. Cromwell took it, and examined it closely.

'I don't know what you're looking for,' said the general impatiently. 'The key has not been used, and the door has not been unlocked for ten years. The last body to be interred in the crypt was that of Lady Julia Lister, my sister, and she died ten years ago.'

Ironsides did not answer. Having satisfied himself that the key had not been recently used—for he was obviously unwilling to accept even his host's word—he thrust it into the great keyhole and turned it. As he did so he crouched down and listened intently, his ear close to the door. He looked up, and there was a smile in his eyes beneath their shaggy brows.

'Very strange!' he murmured.

'What is very strange?' asked the general wonderingly. 'I didn't hear anything, Mr. Cromwell.'

'No,' agreed Mr. Cromwell. 'That's what's very strange.'

Leaving his host completely puzzled, he pushed on the heavy door and thrust it open. As he did so, he shot a glance at Johnny, and Johnny—who was now concentrating—began to tremble with a queer inward excitement. It was not merely the prospect of entering a dank crypt which caused this reaction.

General Lister had apparently noticed nothing peculiar in the opening of the door. But Johnny had noticed it. Ironsides had pushed the heavy door quite gently, and it had presumably not been opened for ten years. Yet the door swung back without the slightest whisper of sound.

'If you don't mind,' murmured Ironsides, 'I'll go first.'

But he did not go immediately. He stood on the threshold, throwing the light of his powerful electric torch on to the ancient stone steps which led steeply downwards into the black and mysterious depths. The steps were quite dry and showed no traces of dust. But after Cromwell had descended a few treads, he bent down and scraped something from the edge of the hard stone.

'What have you got there, Mr. Cromwell?' asked the general, from behind.

'Nothing much,' grunted Ironsides.

But Johnny had seen the little scrap of damp earth between the Chief Inspector's fingers.

They continued descending cautiously, Cromwell slow and unflurried, Johnny excited, and his father thoroughly impatient. When they reached the bottom of the steps, there was an earthy tunnel stretching before them. The walls and the arched roof were of ancient brick, but the floor was just hard earth, damp in places. Johnny was breathing very quickly as they pushed on and entered the family vault of the Cloons.

It was not a pleasant spot. The air was filled with the vague, indefinable dankness of age—and the grave. Overhead, the roof arched to a point, and along the walls there were supporting pillars, on which the roof rested. All round, on stone slabs, in deep recesses, were the caskets of the dead. Many had almost crumbled away with age; others were in bad condition; a few still had the appearance of freshness.

General Lister shivered.

'I must insist, Mr. Cromwell, upon an explanation,' he said angrily. 'If I thought for one moment that nothing but idle curiosity brought you here, I should be very annoyed.'

Ironsides, who was prowling softly round the vault, took not the slightest notice. And the general did not protest again. He, like Johnny, was rather fascinated by Cromwell's intent manner; he reminded them of a lean and shaggy hound on the track of a buried bone. And the simile, after all, was apt enough!

He had made a three-quarter circuit of the crypt when he paused, and he reminded his companions even more of a hound, for he held his head back, his nostrils twitched, and he sniffed the air slowly and deliberately.

'What on earth...' began the general.

Cromwell turned to a magnificent coffin which stood on a slab near him. It looked almost new, and he held his electric torch close over the lid, examining it with great care. He looked round suddenly.

'Who sleeps in here?' he asked softly.

'That is the casket of Lady Julia Lister,' replied his host. 'I beg of you, Mr. Cromwell, to... Good God, man, what are you doing?'

It was perfectly obvious what Ironsides was doing. He was giving the heavy coffin-lid a great heave, and to General Lister's consternation and stupefaction, the lid appeared to be minus its heavy screws. For it fell back into the space between the coffin and the wall.

'Just as I thought,' grunted Bill Cromwell grimly.

Johnny and his father, with their hearts nearly in their mouths, ran to the coffin. The torchlight was streaming into it—full upon the body of a man, dressed in strange clothing, who had been dead for no more than a few hours!

## V. Mystery

The grisly discovery was not much of a shock for Johnny Lister. Knowing Cromwell's methods, he had half anticipated some dramatic development. But to his father, the finding of the dead man in Lady Julia's coffin was a sheer nightmare. For some moments he was speechless with stupefied horror.

'Now,' murmured Ironsides, 'we're getting somewhere.'

'I'm damned glad to know it, old boy!' said Johnny, wiping the cold sweat from his forehead. 'You old fraud! You knew, all the time…'

'I knew nothing until I had taken a look into this casket,' interrupted Cromwell. 'I suspected that a body was tucked away somewhere, but I knew nothing for certain. I should advise you to take a grip on yourself, sir,' he added, turning to his host. 'This is a mighty ugly situation.'

'In God's name, Cromwell, what is the meaning of it all?' asked the general, finding his voice at last. 'I'm bewildered. I'm stunned. I can't understand anything. What an appallingly ghastly business!'

As his brain started work again, he became excited.

'Who are the vandals who have dared to desecrate this sacred tomb?' he went on. 'And Lady Julia——! Good God! What have they done with the remains of Lady Julia?'

'Nothing, I fancy,' replied Ironsides. 'I've no doubt that she is still wrapped in her shroud beneath this dead man— what there is left of her after ten years.'

General Lister shuddered. Much as he liked Chief Inspector Cromwell, and respected him, he could not help likening Ironsides to a ghoul. For Ironsides, far from looking horrified, was apparently exceedingly pleased with himself, and he was bending over the coffin, making a further examination.

'It's lucky that we three came down here just by ourselves, sir,' he went on. 'Do you know who this man is? He hasn't been dead for many hours, and he was killed by some jagged instrument which entered his heart with great force. He must have died without a struggle… Hallo! What's this?'

An acute note had entered his voice, and Johnny saw that he was directing his torchlight into the dead man's eyes.

'What is what?' asked Johnny curiously.

'Can't you see? No, you wouldn't,' said Ironsides. 'Never mind. Forget it. But I think I can understand why the poor devil made no struggle.'

'I don't know this man.' General Lister, fighting back his repugnance, had taken a long, searching look at the face of the corpse. 'I've never seen him before in my life. What does it mean, Cromwell? If you know something, for God's sake speak!'

'All I *know* is that Ronnie Charton was tricked into believing that he saw an apparition in the Death Room,' replied Cromwell, in a hard voice. 'He awoke from a sleep beside the fire—probably aroused by some sharp sound. When he looked about him he saw a perfectly genuine murdered man on the floor; and seeing a thing like that, in such a room, was quite sufficient to send him screaming out into the hall. He *knew* it was real. We know now that it was real. But when young Charton was told that there was no body, no blood—nothing at all, in fact, to support his story—then he was forced to the conclusion that he had seen an apparition. That meant shock number two, with such dire consequences that the young chap is a mental wreck.'

'But why?' asked the general, spreading his hands in helpless terror. 'Who in the name of all that's devilish could have played such a ghastly trick?'

'Somebody in your house-party, sir.'

'What! No, damn it, Cromwell! You don't mean...'

'Listen, sir,' interrupted Ironsides grimly. 'When young Charton saw the supposed ghost in the Death Room, the time was approximately two-thirty. *At that hour Cloon was snowbound,* and it was physically impossible for any person to get away. So it stands to reason that the murderer is still in this house.'

'But not one of my guests!'

'One of the servants, then?' countered Cromwell, with ill-concealed contempt. 'You seriously believe that one of your servants had such intimate knowledge of the family history of the Cloons that he could accurately duplicate the death scene of Sir Travers Cloon? And which of your servants, may I ask, is so interested in Ronnie Charton...'

'I'm sorry, Cromwell; you needn't go on,' interrupted General Lister. 'It is, of course, preposterous to suppose that any one of the servants could have perpetrated this appalling act. But the alternative is even more preposterous,' he added helplessly. 'Ronnie Charton is not popular, I know, and I can well believe that some of the young spirits would play an ill-natured practical joke. But there's a murdered man to explain.'

'Exactly,' agreed Ironsides. 'But the elements are on our side.'

He did not explain the meaning of this cryptic remark for some minutes. He walked to the shadowy end of the crypt, and flashed his light on a great slab of solid stone, which not only possessed hinges, but heavy bolts.

'I see there's another exit. This door, I presume, leads into the chapel?'

'At one time it led into the chapel,' agreed Johnny's father. 'But now it leads more or less into the open air, for the chapel is nothing but a ruin. The roof fell in a century ago, and it was never restored. The walls are crumbling away beneath festoons of ivy and other creepers.'

Ironsides nodded.

'Then I was right about the elements,' he said placidly. 'Last night's snowstorm put a big kink in the killer's plans. Everything was arranged, I believe, to the last detail—but all the killer's calculations were frustrated by the weather.'

'I'm afraid I don't understand.'

'The original idea, quite obviously, was to allow Ronnie Charton to see the dead body, and then to convey it through the crypt and out into the open air. Is there a river close at hand? Or a lake?'

'There's a lake at the bottom of the gardens. It is very deep in places, too.'

'We're getting along,' nodded Cromwell. 'Another proof that the killer has intimate knowledge of Cloon Castle and the Cloon history. I'll bet my pension that he meant to carry the dead body to the lake, and dump it into the deepest part. What chance should we have had, then, of proving anything? What chance should we have had of knowing that young Charton's "apparition" was not, in fact, an apparition?'

'I wonder,' murmured Johnny musingly, 'if the killer knew that you had been invited, Old Iron?'

'There are not many of my guests who know of Mr. Cromwell's calling, even now,' put in his father.

'But the snow, coming so unexpectedly and so abundantly, made the killer change his plans,' continued Ironsides. 'He found it impossible to take the body out through this second door into the open. I'll guarantee there's a snowdrift fifteen feet deep within the crumbling walls of the chapel. The programme had been arranged, and could not be postponed—why, I'm hoping to learn in due course. So the body had to be hurriedly concealed. And where better than in one of these coffins?'

'Pretty good, Ironsides,' said Johnny admiringly. 'A dashed shrewd deduction. Dad would never have dreamed of looking into the coffins. For that matter, neither would I. Only an old ghoul like you… Well, you know what I mean. And I'll bet the killer is still ignorant of the fact that you are one of the Yard's cleverest sleuths. Any professional crook, of course, would have known you a mile off. But there's no professional touch about this business.'

'Which gives us a certain advantage, Johnny,' murmured Cromwell. 'The fact that we three are the only ones to know of this discovery gives us a further advantage. We can investigate without alarming Mr. Killer.'

Johnny scratched his head.

'You know, Old Iron, I still don't get it,' he said. 'Young Charton swears that there were pools of blood on the floor, but the floor was clean and dry.'

'Come and look here,' said Cromwell briefly.

He flashed his torchlight into the coffin, and Johnny and his father saw what he meant. Underneath the body, but partially visible, was a rubber waterproof sheet, sticky with patches of blood—*and painted on one side, so that it exactly resembled an old parquet floor!*

'Well, blow me down!' said Johnny.

'Indisputable evidence that the crime was deliberately premeditated,' nodded Bill Cromwell placidly. 'Also, if it comes to that, it proves that the killer knew just how to duplicate the floor of the Death Room. With this sheet laid on the floor, it was impossible—in a weak light—to notice the tricky deception.'

'I find the whole affair fantastic and incredible,' said General Lister, grievously troubled. 'You are asking us to believe, Cromwell, that the murderer made all his gruesome preparations in the Death Room while young Charton was dozing in the chair before the fire?'

'Not dozing, sir—sleeping very soundly.'

'Drugged, you mean?' put in Johnny quickly.

'Of course he was drugged,' said Ironsides. 'One of the first things I did was to examine his eyes and feel his pulse. I'm no doctor, but there are some things I *do* know. The drug might have been administered in any one of a number of ways—a drink, a cigarette, even the fumes from the fire.'

'It is all very horrible,' muttered Johnny's father.

'Murder generally is, sir—particularly a premeditated murder,' agreed Cromwell. 'You say this dead man is quite unknown to you. He's not a guest, neither is he a servant. Yet he was here fairly early last night, for the snowstorm was at its height before eleven o'clock, and he could not have arrived after that. It is certain that the man was invited to the castle by one of your guests, secretly admitted, and then done to death.'

'But why?' broke out General Lister. 'In God's name, man, why? And, above all else, why was the body carried into the Death Room to frighten poor Charton? It all seems so senseless...'

'That's only because we don't know the inner facts,' interrupted Cromwell. 'Now, sir, about these guests of yours. How about making a list of likely suspects? Take the men who were in the library last night, for instance—the men who practically egged Ronnie Charton to sleep in the Death Room. They can't all be in the murder plot. All of them except one, perhaps, acted quite innocently—and more or less under the influence of drink. Let's take these men one by one.'

'It's a perfectly ghastly task, but I presume it has got to be done,' said Johnny's father worriedly. 'There are several men—including yourself, Cromwell, and my son—who can be eliminated at once. I trust you can eliminate me, too. Damn it, man, we can eliminate everybody who was in the library last night! I refuse to believe...'

'If you'd been in my line of business as long as I have, sir, you wouldn't refuse to believe anything,' interrupted Ironsides gruffly. 'Neither would you be squeamish. Supposing we start with the man who brought up the subject of ghosts? Drydon, I think his name is. A pleasant, genial sort of fellow, as far as I can judge...'

'Howard Drydon is a wealthy stockbroker, and a personal friend of mine,' interrupted the general stiffly. 'At least...' He paused uncertainly. 'What I mean is, I've frequently met him at my club. Perhaps it is not exactly truthful to say that he is wealthy, for it is being whispered in the City that his financial position is not very sound.'

'I see,' said Ironside gently. 'And Ronnie Charton? Has Ronnie ever had any business connections with Drydon?'

'I believe he has—I'm not sure,' answered the troubled host. 'Ronnie has many interests; he is quite wealthy, and naturally employs a stockbroker. But if you're suggesting that Drydon...'

'We'll mark Mr. Drydon off for the time being, and take Dr. Spencer Ware,' pursued Cromwell imperturbably.

'Nonsense, sir,' said the general, annoyed. 'Dr. Ware can be eliminated just as quickly as yourself. He was wholeheartedly opposed to Ronnie spending the night in the Death Room. Until yesterday he had never met Ronnie in his life, and can have no personal interest in him. Moreover, he's wealthy, with one of the most lucrative practices in Wimpole Street.'

'Yes, that seems to dispose of Dr. Ware satisfactorily enough,' said Cromwell dryly. 'In the same way, we can rule out Brother Gerry, who did all he could to stop the affair. There was another young man—Bayne, or Bates...'

'You mean young Philip Bayle,' said General Lister—and then he started. 'Oh, but really...'

'You were saying?' murmured Cromwell, as the general paused.

'Bayle is a member of young Charton's own set, and I've just remembered that he was once engaged to a girl named Audrey Woods,' said the general. 'Quite a nice girl, I believe, and a member of the Gaiety chorus. Anyhow, the engagement was broken, and after that Audrey was seen about a great deal with Ronnie Charton.'

'*Cherchez la femme,*' murmured Johnny. 'Spurned lover finds rival in same house-party and rubs out same. Simple!'

'Too simple, I'm afraid, Johnny,' said his father, with a faint smile. 'You have no doubt noticed that Bayle is a most innocuous young man. For weeks, in fact, he has been telling his friends that he has had a very lucky escape.'

'But we've got to admit him as a possible,' said Ironsides. 'You can't always trust these innocuous looking fellows. Take your own son, for example. Anybody, to look at Johnny, would say that he had no wits at all—and they would be just about half right. It's quite possible that Philip Bayle has nursed a bitter resentment against young Charton for stealing his girl. As for the other men in the library...' He rubbed his chin reflectively. Let me see, there was Lord Springton, elderly and affable; Colonel Scrumthorpe, and the Hon. Gerald Morley. All of them, I believe, are strangers to Ronnie. H'm! We don't seem to get far, do we?'

He took another look at the coffin, as though he liked it.

'We still don't know who this poor blighter is, or how he got into the castle,' he continued. 'His clothes don't give us a clue, because his own clothes were removed before he was killed—probably while he was unconscious. And don't forget this, sir—*it was never intended by the killer that the body or the clothes should ever be examined.* Even now the killer has no suspicion that his devilish plan has half failed—and that should help us a lot. Well, we'd better get out of here as quietly as possible. I'll make a thorough examination of the body later.'

He carefully replaced the coffin lid, and they all went back to the Death Room, and the heavy door was closed and locked. Cromwell kept the key.

'Christmas Day and my house full of guests—and this dreadful thing has to happen,' said General Lister distractedly. 'I beg of you, Cromwell, to keep this shocking business as quiet as possible.'

'You don't expect me to go and shout it from the house-top, do you?' retorted Ironsides gruffly. 'My plain duty, of course, is to inform the coroner and the local police.' He paused, and his eyes twinkled. 'But I can't do either, because we're snowed up. It'll be a refreshing change to conduct an inquiry without a lot of incompetent busybodies cluttering up the place and getting in my way. I'd like you to go along to the billiard room, sir, and generally mix with your guests. Don't let 'em see that anything is wrong. The younger ones are all out of doors, fooling about in the snow—so it's a good opportunity for me to do a bit of prowling.'

The general promised to do his best, and he went off at once. Cromwell and Johnny followed, and they had only gone a few steps down the south corridor when Ironsides paused and peered into a dark, gloomy opening.

'Thought so. A back staircase—leading straight up to the rear of the main landing. Easy enough for the killer to have slipped upstairs after hiding the body, and to have mingled with the other guests—as though he had just been aroused out of his sleep. We'll go this way. I'm going to pop into some of the bedrooms and have a quick look round.'

The staircase proved to be short and direct, and it communicated with the main landing just as Cromwell had guessed. Johnny was instructed to stroll up and down the big main corridor, and if any of the guests should happen along, he was to start whistling. Ironsides, meanwhile, was to enter the bedrooms and give them a keen once-over.

Before putting this plan into effect, however, they both went along to see how Ronnie Charton was. His brother was sitting by his bedside, and Gerry looked tired and haggard.

'He's no different,' he said worriedly. 'I'm glad you've come,' he added, suddenly getting to his feet, and staring strangely at the newcomers. 'Dr. Ware thinks he's fooling me, but he's not. He keeps telling me that Ronnie will be all right—but I know damned well that he privately believes that Ronnie's mind will always be—you know. Has he said anything to either of you to that effect?'

'No, nothing—not a word,' replied Johnny quickly.

But he could not help remembering how the specialist had tapped his head behind Gerry's back, and he wondered if Gerry had seen anything of that significant motion.

'I don't believe in these high-toned experts,' went on the young man, almost fiercely. 'Do you think Ware cares a hoot whether Ronnie recovers or not? He's just a new subject—an experiment—an interesting case. I'm almost ready to believe that Ware *wants* Ronnie to wake up half loony, if only to prove that his theories are right.'

Cromwell did not get into an argument. He tried to say a few comforting words, but he was not particularly good at that sort of thing, and was glad enough to escape.

As he and Johnny passed the balcony that overlooked the great hall, they heard the booming voice of Dr. Ware from below; and Ironsides, seizing his advantage, had a look into Dr. Ware's bedroom as a beginning. He was soon out, and then he went into other bedrooms—Johnny, meanwhile, strolling aimlessly about, ready to whistle at a moment's notice.

Five or six times Ironsides dodged out of one room and into another, and he was just repeating the manoeuvre when Johnny caught a glimpse of a shadowy figure at the dark end of a branch corridor. The figure stood motionless, staring at the disappearing form of Cromwell as the latter slipped into the bedroom—which was exactly opposite the passage. Johnny, strolling leisurely past, saw the figure for a moment only, for it turned abruptly and vanished. Like a hare the immaculate sergeant sped down the passage, and at the end of it he found a staircase leading down steeply.

'The bally place is full of dashed staircases,' he murmured, realizing that it would be a waste of time to descend.

Whistling, he retraced his steps, and met Ironsides in the main corridor. He quickly related what he had seen.

'Might have been one of the servants,' said Cromwell, frowning. 'Too late to do anything now, of course. It's a pity you didn't keep a sharper watch...'

'Well, I like that!' protested Johnny. 'Do you think I've got X-ray eyes? I only saw the bloke for a jiffy, and as soon as he twigged that I was looking at him he took a powder.' He eyed Cromwell narrowly. 'And what's the result of your perambulations? You don't look particularly triumphant.'

Ironsides made noises indicative of disgust.

'I found—smells!' he grunted. 'Perfume in Gerry Charton's room; perfume which reminded me of that saucy-eyed girl with the fluffy hair (the young ass ought to be more careful when he invites girls into his room); the whiff of stinking stale Turkish cigarettes in Drydon's; and a particularly ghastly brilliantine niff in young Bayle's. On the whole, not a bad fifteen minutes' work.'

'You think smells are going to help us?'

'You'd be surprised!' said Cromwell.

'What the devil...'

But Ironsides refused to amplify his remark, and they both went downstairs. They were silent as they descended, and as they turned an angle they came within sight of the great fireplace. They saw Philip Bayle talking earnestly to Howard Drydon, the stockbroker.

The two men looked strangely startled as they glanced up and recognized the pair on the staircase; then, without another word, they walked quickly out of the hall.

## VI. *The Killer Strikes*

It seemed to Johnny that Bill Cromwell lost interest in the mystery; for, during the rest of the morning, he pottered about in an aimless sort of way, wandering in and out of the Death Room, and up and down stairs.

This, at least, appeared to be the sum total of Ironsides' activities. Even Johnny, accustomed as he was to the Chief Inspector's wiles, did not see through the scheme. Cromwell was actually making a careful examination of the dead body in the crypt; but he performed this task piecemeal, so that he should show himself sauntering idly about, as though bored. Furthermore, he was keeping an eye on Ronnie Charton, and those in Ronnie's room never quite knew when Ironsides would butt in.

It was very cleverly done—so cleverly that Johnny had no suspicion of what was going on. At lunch-time the house-party was as jolly and merry as ever. Even Gerry, relieved from duty in the sick-room, bucked up a lot. Cromwell sat moodily silent during most of the meal, and those on either side of him came to the conclusion that he was nothing but a boor. Not that Ironsides cared a toss what they thought.

After lunch he was more gloomy than ever, and Johnny became suspicious.

'Come across, you old humbug,' he said accusingly. 'You're looking so dashed fed up that you must have got somewhere. Give, old boy—and give freely.'

'I shall have got somewhere in about three minutes,' admitted Cromwell. 'Come along, and I'll show you.'

He walked to the library, selected the biggest chair, and sank luxuriously into its depths.

'Well?' demanded Johnny.

'What's the matter? Are you blind?' said Cromwell, with a yawn. 'Can't you see I've got somewhere? In this chair, my lad, and I'm going to stay in it for the rest of the afternoon. What's the good of being on vacation if you can't sleep most of the time?'

Johnny gave it up. His father happened to come in just then, and he could not help noticing the surprised look on the general's face. A few minutes later they left the library together, and General Lister wanted to know why Cromwell was taking things so easily.

'You're asking me!' said Johnny, with a shrug. 'I've been with him for two or three years, but I'm damned if I know what to make of him. If this inactivity means anything at all, it means that Ironsides has hit the trail, and is marking time. He knows that the killer can't get away, and it's good policy to let the blighter think that he's sitting soft.'

'Well, it all seems very strange,' frowned the general. 'At the same time, I'm relieved. If we can keep the tragedy a secret until after Christmas, so much the better. But when I think of that body lying in Lady Julia's coffin I go cold all over!'

'That's an easy one, dad,' said Johnny. 'Don't think of it.'

Since there was nothing for him to do—for Ironsides had given him no instructions—he went out snow-larking with a laughing, cheery crowd of the younger people. There was a good deal of activity round and about the castle, every available able-bodied man of the staff working hard at clearing the snow.

There were fine slopes in the park, where tobogganing was indulged in freely, and Johnny had a thoroughly good time. He went back to the castle towards dusk, but most of the others remained out, tea having no attractions for them.

'So you haven't broken your neck?' was Cromwell's greeting, as he met Johnny in the hall. 'No, don't take your overcoat off. We're going out. It's practically dark, and everything's quiet. The elderly ladies are in the drawing-room swilling tea, the elderly gents are in the billiard room playing billiards, and the youngsters are somewhere in the park.'

When they got outside, Cromwell explained why he had waited until now. First, what he had to do had better be done in the dark; and, secondly, squads of men had been busy all the afternoon clearing the drive.

'Why, you cunning old fraud,' said Johnny. 'I'll bet it was you who asked the old man to have the drive cleared of snow. I thought it was a potty idea when I saw the men at work—because I knew it was impossible for them to progress far.'

'Yes, we're still snowed up and cut off from the world,' said Ironsides complacently, as they crunched over the frozen snow. 'But, at least, we can get to the spot in the drive where we saw the "apparition." I wonder if you noticed, when we were on the spot last night, a particularly hefty tree close by?'

'Can't say that I did.'

'I've half an idea that that tree will help us,' said Cromwell. 'Anyway, we shall soon see.'

The snow had been cleared for about twenty yards beyond this spot, and it was piled in great heaps on one side of the drive. The other side—where there were many trees—was comparatively free of snow. Cromwell pointed to one particular tree, and he proceeded to climb it with remarkable agility for one who was always complaining about his bodily ills.

'Huh! Thought so!' came a satisfied grunt from Cromwell. 'The tree's as hollow as your head, Johnny. Come up and have a look. While we were looking for our "ghost" last night, he was hiding in this tree.'

'Here, steady, Old Iron; that's only a guess.'

Johnny was wrong; it was no guess. After he had climbed up, he looked down into a surprisingly large hollow space.

Ironsides was holding his electric torch well down, so that the interior of the tree was lighted. At the same time, none of the rays escaped. As Cromwell remarked, he did not want people to come along and ask footling questions.

But even the astute Ironsides did not allow for people—one person, at least—with powerful night glasses at an upper window of the castle. A dim, shadowy figure stood there, watching Bill Cromwell's activities with intense interest. The watcher was even more interested when he saw Johnny climb the tree, and stare into the hollow interior.

'Funny!' said Johnny, in surprise.

The space into which he looked was littered at the bottom with ancient and rotted leaves, twigs, and little patches of powdery snow, which had drifted in during the night. Also, Johnny saw a pair of very old boots, and there was something peculiarly different about these boots.

'What the dickens are those spikes, Ironsides?'

'We'll soon find out,' said Cromwell.

He had brought a crooked stick with him, and, leaning far over, he fished up one of the boots. Projecting from the sole were three two-inch spikes, and one from the heel.

'Crude, but effective,' commented Cromwell. 'The boots were evidently prepared in a hurry—our unknown friend having decided to take advantage of the light snow that was falling. You see what he did? He drove two and a half-inch nails clean through the boots, uppers and all. Once driven home, it was easy enough to tear the uppers free, and the holes didn't matter. The nails were in position, spikes downwards. All the gentleman had to do was to walk carefully, picking his feet up clean, and he left no footprint in the snow.'

'Damned ingenious,' said Johnny, half admiringly. 'The wheeze could not have been worked so easily in frozen snow, for the nails would have made *some* marks. But with the snow all powdery, the nails hardly disturbed it. No wonder we were puzzled. This killer bloke is a bit of an opportunist, old boy. He no sooner sees that it's snowing than he thinks up this brain wave.'

Cromwell fished up the other boot, switched off the light, and they both dropped to the ground.

'But why?' demanded Johnny, appealing to the night air.

'Why what?'

'Why should anyone try to scare *us*?'

Ironsides gave a snort like a peeved hippo, and refused to make any comment. He trudged along towards the castle in silence for some time. When he did speak, it was to ask a question.

'During lunch,' he said, 'I heard you talking to Gerry Charton about cars, and that murdering projectile of yours in particular. Did Charton happen to mention what make of car his brother Ronnie drives?'

'Yes. Alvis—like mine.'

'Well, then, there's your answer.'

'Answer? What answer? Oh! You mean... Ironsides, you deep blighter, I get it. The killer aimed to scare Ronnie Charton. He heard the sweet purr of my Alvis...'

'You mean, the machine-gun-like roar—but go on.'

'He heard this glorious sound,' said Johnny firmly, 'and naturally assumed that it was young Charton breezing in. So on with the ghost act. By the time he had extricated himself from the hollow tree—before he could do it, in fact—he heard another Alvis, and then it was too late. You remember that Ronnie Charton arrived immediately after us?'

'Of course I remember it—I've remembered it all the time,' retorted Cromwell. 'Your brains, apparently, are only just beginning to thaw out. It's perfectly clear that the killer decided, on seeing the snow falling, to give Ronnie a preliminary dose of the jitters before administering the full dose. He would have done so if your Alvis hadn't fooled him.'

'Well, that's one point cleared up; although I can't see that it gets us any forrarder,' said Johnny. 'We still don't know who used to belong to the dead body; we still don't know who the killer is; we still don't know...' He suddenly stopped and looked at Ironsides searchingly. 'Or do we?' he added, with a start.

'*We*—don't,' replied Ironsides tartly.

And he refused to say another word as they continued their way towards the castle.

Within the ancient pile all was peace and quiet. It was the slack period before the dressing-gong was due to boom. Scarcely a soul was upstairs, and the mysterious figure who slipped like a shadow into Cromwell's bedroom did so without being observed by any eye. Once in the room, he closed the door and locked it, but did not switch on the light. A fire was burning cheerfully in the grate, and by its ruddy glow the intruder could see all that he wanted to see.

He worked quickly and efficiently, moving with a sure step and a devil's purpose. As he crossed the room to an antique chest of drawers, his shadow, cast by the fire, was like a great monster on the wall and ceiling. And how true that shadow was! For no matter how much this figure resembled a normal man, his soul was that of a demon from hell.

He shifted the chest from the wall, and half-dragged, half-carried it to the side of the fine antique four-poster bed, with its solidly made oak canopy, so exquisitely carved. Leaping on to the chest, he was able to reach right over the top of the canopy, at the head of the bed. A swift, careful scrutiny, and he saw that the heavy framework was securely held in position by a slot device.

It needed an iron nerve and great strength for the next move. With a slow, gradual heave, his shoulder beneath the underside of the great fixture, he raised it clear of the slots—and then allowed it to come to rest again. But now it was so placed that the smallest jar of the bed would bring it crashing down. So delicately was the balance adjusted that the intruder himself, in getting down, did so with extreme caution—lest his very movements should cause premature collapse.

He was even more cautious in shifting the chest back to its original position. Having done this, he moved away from the fire, where he stood, a shadowy figure in the gloom. He was breathing hard from his exertions, but he gave himself only a moment's rest. He padded across to the big bay window. Here, overhead, just in front of the dressing table, hung the main electric light of the room. Reaching up, the intruder sharply tapped the electric bulb—once, twice, three times. The jarring was sufficient to break the delicate filament and render the lamp useless. So much more subtle than removing the lamp from its socket, or tampering with the switch. So much safer—for it left no evidence.

He crept to the door and silently pressed the switch down. No result. The lamp was dead. He turned his head and gazed at the bed, so solid looking and massive. At the head of the bed, in the very centre, hung a length of flex, with a switch at the end.

'It can't miss!' muttered the intruder.

It was, indeed, a subtle and ingenious trick. Cromwell, coming into the bedroom to dress for dinner, and finding the main light out of action, would naturally turn to the bedside lights, both of which were operated by the central hanging switch. It was a very wide bed—in fact, enormous, as judged by the standard of modern beds. In order to reach that switch, Ironsides would be compelled to reach over... and lean against the side of the bed... and kneel on the bed...

## VII. The Invisible Clue

When Bill Cromwell and Johnny reached the great terrace in front of the castle they found a gang of young men and girls, fresh from their winter sports, collected in a semi-circle on the wide steps, lustily bawling a Christmas carol. It was not a particularly pleasant sight, and Ironsides viewed the scene distastefully.

'Don't you like carols?' grinned Johnny.

'As a matter of fact, I'm rather partial to a well-sung Christmas carol,' replied Ironsides. 'But if you think I'm going to admire this yowling, caterwauling mob of half-wits, you'd better think again! Why don't you join 'em, Johnny? Just about your stamp.'

'Thanks,' said Johnny, 'for nothing.'

He was forced to admit that the carol singing, as carol singing, was both poor and unmelodious, and especially unmelodious.

'I wonder,' bawled Cromwell, 'if I can be permitted to pass?'

There was a shout of laughter, and the roisterers parted with mock bows, and opened up a lane.

'Only our fun, Mr. Cromwell,' grinned Phil Bayle, who was much in evidence. 'But this is only just the beginning. Wait until we get properly worked up after dinner.'

'Whoopee!' cried some of the girls.

'Whoopee with knobs on,' sang out another young man. 'Dancing—games—charades—and tons of fun. We'll make this old castle burst its sides before we've finished.'

'And Mr. Cromwell's going to join in, too,' said one of the young ladies, linking her arm in Ironsides' and looking saucily into his eyes. 'Are you any good at games, Mr. Cromwell? I like the creepy ones. Last Christmas we played a marvellous game called "Dead Man" or "Murder" or something…'

'No, confound it, not that!' interrupted young Bayle, losing all his boisterous good humour.

He looked so pale and shaken that much of the laughter died down, and Johnny saw that Ironsides was looking at Philip Bayle with more than passing interest.

'Don't you like the parlour game of "Murder," Mr. Bayle?' he murmured gently.

'No, I'm damned if I do,' replied Bayle. 'I played it once, years ago...' He paused awkwardly. 'I wasn't scared, but two of the girls in the party—mere youngsters—had fits of hysterics that lasted for hours. I think those sort of games are rotten.'

'Mr. Bayle,' said Ironsides, 'I'm with you.'

And he passed indoors without another word. He and Johnny walked upstairs together, and when they reached Cromwell's door, Johnny paused before going to his own bedroom.

'Rather funny, that "murder game" incident,' he remarked. 'You saw how the Bayle bloke went ashen about the gills? I'm beginning to wonder...'

'Don't,' interrupted Cromwell sourly. 'You're bound to be wrong.'

And, leaving Johnny flat, he went into his bedroom and shut the door. The firelight flickered cheerfully. He clicked the light switch, and nothing happened. He clicked it again, and glanced over at the hanging light, with its modern shade, by the dressing-table. The fault was obviously local, since the corridor was a perfect blaze of happy, cheerful light.

'Why,' asked Cromwell bitterly, 'should my light, of all lights, be the one to give up the ghost?'

He remembered the bedside lights, and moved in that direction. It was an instinctive act. Every step he took was a step nearer to—death. But his subconscious mind was already putting in some fast work. Why, indeed, should it be *his* light to fail? Beneath Ironsides' matter-of-fact, sleepy exterior, his senses were acute with a razor-edged fineness. They had been so all the afternoon, and nobody—not even Johnny Lister—had guessed that Cromwell had been putting on a brilliant act. For the shaggy, long-legged Yard man was well aware of the hideous dangers that lurked in this old castle.

Ordinarily, perhaps, he would have thought nothing of the light failure—until it was too late. But this evening he was ready for any kind of trouble. He was half expecting trouble. In the privacy of his own room it was no longer necessary to maintain his pose, and he shed it like a cloak, standing revealed as eleven-stone-nine-pounds of human electricity.

'By God!' murmured Bill Cromwell.

Half-way to the bed he stood as though powerful magnets had fastened him to the floor. Never in his career had he so much resembled a shaggy, ungainly bloodhound; for his sensitive nostrils were twitching visibly as he sniffed at the air. He detected a faint, illusory odour—so vague, so transient that at times it nearly eluded him. But it was there, in the room, and he recognized it. And, recognizing it, his muscles stiffened and his eyes grew as hard as frozen flint.

Ironsides had got hold of his first real clue—and it was an invisible clue. A clue that drifted in the warm atmosphere of this age-old bedroom.

'The light,' whispered Cromwell shrewdly. 'I find the light out of commission, and I walk across to the bed and reach over for the hanging switch. In reaching over, I lean against the bed and shake it... Pretty! Devilish pretty!'

He gazed musingly up at the massive canopy, with its sombre hangings, and a cold grip encircled his heart.

'H'm! Treacherous things, these infernal canopies,' he observed. 'I've always hated them—always had a horror that they might fall on top of me—*like this*!'

He reached out a long leg, gave the bed a sharp push, and leaped back. As he did so, he saw the heavy oaken framework part company with its moorings at the head of the bed, and fall.

Cra-a-a-a-ash—thud!

The noise was not excessive. Just a splintering of wood as the fixture split at the foot of the bed, and the head part fell like a ton of bricks on to the pillows. The thing fell with appalling force, and Ironsides knew that if he had been reaching for the switch at that crucial second, the heavy wooden bar would have crushed his head in like an eggshell.

And then, the tension over, he thought of—Johnny. His face twitched slightly, and his jaw came together until his lips set in a thin, hard line. In three long strides he was at the door. He went out, shut the door, locked it, and in a couple of seconds he was with Johnny—who was half undressed.

'Here, I say, dash it… Oh, it's you, Old Iron,' said Johnny. 'Why the devil can't you knock when you come into a chap's room? I was thinking of what you said about the girls…'

'Forget the girls,' interrupted Ironsides, in so strained a voice that Johnny stood stock still. 'H'm! Everything seems to be all right here. The killer has come to the conclusion that you're not worth bothering about.'

'If you'll cease talking hokus bolonus, and tell me what the hell you mean, I shall be somewhat obliged,' said Johnny, drawing on a pair of evening dress trousers with creases that could have been used to carve a joint. 'Damn it, Ironsides, you look shaken. I didn't know you *could* be shaken. What's happened?'

'Nothing, you blithering idiot!' replied Ironsides. 'Can't you see I'm still alive? But I shouldn't have been alive if I had walked into the ingenious trap our mutual pal laid for me. The general scheme was to drop several tons of weight on my head and expose my brains to view.'

'A thing which simply couldn't be done,' said Johnny promptly.

But he ceased to be facetious after Ironsides had briefly explained.

'Hell's bells! This is getting a bit thick,' he commented, and then started. 'What was that crack you made when you first came in? So I'm not worth bothering about? Rats! The blighter's obviously saving me up for the next reel.'

'Don't bother to finish dressing,' said Cromwell. 'I want you to come back with me to my room—and help me to put that canopy to rights. *Somebody* in this house-party thinks I'm dead by this time, and I shall be interested in certain faces when I walk downstairs in one piece.'

They hurried out, but before they reached the next bedroom, Cromwell paused. His super-sensitive wits were at work again. He had heard a faint crackle of ice on the path, below, and he stepped quickly to the window. It was freezing sharply outside, and he knew that this particular window overlooked the path which led to the ruined chapel—and it was a path that had been cleared of snow during the afternoon. The fragments of snow left on the crazy paving of the path were as brittle as glass.

Shading his face with both hands he peered out into the darkness. And down there, on the chapel path, he saw a shadowy, stealthily moving shape.

'By God! I didn't expect... Quick, Johnny! Come with me.'

'Hang it, I haven't got a collar on...'

'Blast your collar! Come!'

Ironsides grabbed Johnny's arm in a vice-like grip, and whirled him downstairs. It was useless for Johnny to protest. Luckily, there was nobody in the hall, for all the guests were dressing for dinner and there were no servants about at the moment. Johnny was glad when he reached the shadows of the south corridor.

They went through the Death Room like a gale, and Ironsides took out the great key of the metal-studded door and turned it. They ran down the steps and a moment later they were in the crypt.

'Hold this!' snapped Cromwell.

Johnny held it—the electric torch. Cromwell heaved at the heavy lid of Lady Julia's casket—and cursed. The body of the unknown man had gone.

'But where?' ejaculated Johnny, in startled astonishment. 'How the dickens was the body taken through the house without anybody seeing?'

'Through the house, nothing!' snapped Ironsides, swinging round to the stone door that gave on to the ruined chapel. 'I thought I felt a draught! The door's not even fastened. Quick, Johnny. He's only been gone a minute—perhaps less.'

Johnny was bewildered as Cromwell pulled the heavy door open, and they went out into the keen air of the frosty evening.

'Hey, where's all that blinking snow?'

'Why do you suppose I was sleeping most of the afternoon?' retorted Cromwell tartly. 'Because I had done the brainwork, and others were doing the manual labour. If you hadn't been late for lunch you would have heard your father stating to the company in general—at my suggestion—that he was going to have the path leading from the castle to the lake cleared of snow. He had hinted that there might be good skating to-morrow. And everybody more or less cheered.'

'You wily old…'

'Cut the compliments, and keep your voice down,' warned Ironsides. 'The men, in clearing the path, took a short cut through the chapel ruins, and it seemed quite natural that they should heave the snow away from the crypt door. A little trap of mine, if only you had the sense to see it.'

'Ironsides, old thing, you're priceless,' murmured Johnny admiringly. 'I get it now. A temptation to the killer to get the body out and duly deposit it on the lake, as per the original script.'

'Exactly,' said Cromwell, as they cautiously advanced along the cleared path between piled masses of snow. 'But I didn't expect the blighter to act until the middle of the night. He's in a panic, my lad; he wouldn't have monkeyed with my bed if he hadn't been in a panic. He's found out that I know something, and his idea was to ensure that I met with an unfortunate "accident" so that he could do his body removing without fear of interruption. But the fool has overreached himself, as most murderers do, and we've got him.'

As he spoke, he pointed. They had turned a bend of the path, and here it sloped slightly, the surface treacherous under their feet; and right ahead they could see the wide expanse of the snow-covered lake, shadowed, on the farther side, by a belt of tall trees. And on the lake, vaguely visible against the background of white, a strange, shapeless figure was moving.

Johnny felt his heart pumping painfully. There was something so grotesque, so monstrous about that figure that his usually steady nerve was shaken. Then he drew in his breath with a little gulp of relief, and felt sheepish. The dark figure looked monstrous because he was carrying a heavy, bulky burden across his shoulders. And even as Ironsides and Johnny slithered down to the edge of the lake, the unknown dropped his grisly parcel on to the ice.

'Better leave this to me!' whispered Cromwell grimly. 'He'll probably be dangerous. See that hole in the ice? He must have made it in advance. He knows that it'll be frozen over again by the morning... Hey, you!'

Cromwell uttered the last two words in a voice of loud command, and at the same moment he switched on his electric torch and flashed it out upon the figure on the frozen lake. The man turned, startled and dumbfounded by that unexpected shout, and the backward step he took was quite involuntary. Also it was fatal.

The body was lying on the edge of the broken hole in the ice, and the living man's weight, suddenly added to that of the dead man, proved too much for the ice. There was a splintering crash, a wild shriek of indescribable horror, and the living and the dead plunged into the black water.

And for a moment, a moment that would be photographed in Johnny Lister's mind for years, the light of Ironsides' torch lit up the face that slid beneath the troubled surface; and it was the face of Dr. Spencer Ware!

## VIII. Ironsides Pounces

'Hell and damnation!' swore Cromwell angrily.

He ran with long strides over the ice, but put the brake on with caution as he approached the jagged hole. The torchlight showed a turbulent disturbance of the black water—and some bubbles. But Dr. Spencer Ware had vanished for ever from this life.

'Can't we do something, Old Iron?' asked Johnny, horrified. 'Damn it, he only plunged in a moment ago. He's bound to come up…'

'He'll never come up—until we fish him up with grappling irons!'

'But that's crazy…'

'Would you come up, if you sank into a deep lake with your pockets filled with heavy weights?' interrupted Cromwell grimly. 'Can't you see how it happened? Ware laid the body at the edge of the hole, ready for him to attach the weights. Probably a few big stones; quite sufficient to keep any dead body down. Quite sufficient, by the same token, to keep a live body down in icy-cold water. When the ice broke, Ware plunged straight down, and he stayed down. There's nothing we can do.'

It was horrible, but true. In spite of the shudder that rippled through Johnny's frame, he could not help seeing that there was poetic justice in this accident. The murderer had been carried into Eternity with his victim.

'You know,' muttered Johnny slowly, 'I had half an idea that Ware was guilty. It seemed a bit fishy to me, the way he doped Ronnie Charton with drugs. He was a bit hasty, too, in hinting that Ronnie had gone loony. What's behind it, Ironsides? Why did Dr. Ware kill one man, and try to drive another out of his senses?'

'We'd better get away from here,' said Cromwell, ignoring the questions. 'The sooner we can tell your father about this infernal business, the better. No time like the present. Everybody is still upstairs.'

They hurried back to the castle, and Johnny was glad enough to get away from the lake. The water in that jagged hole had ceased to ripple, and it told its own story.

Passing through the Death Room, they crossed the great hall, with its bright lights and gay decorations, and mounted the stairs. On the landing they encountered Gerry Charton, resplendent in evening dress. He started like a frightened horse as he caught sight of the pair.

'Great Scott! What are you walking about like that for, Lister?' he ejaculated. 'Do you know that you're collarless and that your hair is all ruffled? Has something happened?'

'Plenty has happened, Mr. Charton,' said Cromwell, before Johnny could speak. 'I'm glad we met you. I've got something to say to the general, and I'd like you to be present.'

'You're damned mysterious,' said Gerry Charton, staring. 'Has somebody been trying to bump you off?' he added, with a laugh. 'I think the general is in Ronnie's bedroom. I asked him to take over for a bit while I dressed. Dr. Ware has been on the job most of the day, and I believe he's gone out for a breath of fresh air.'

'I think he's had it,' said Ironsides carefully.

They went into Ronnie's room and found Johnny's father sitting by the bedside.

'I say, damn it, Johnny, must you go about the place half dressed?' asked the general. 'I'm glad you've come, Charton. Your brother has been restless. I think one of you should fetch the doctor.'

Cromwell bent over the patient and took a searching look into Ronnie Charton's staring, lack-lustre eyes. The young man was only half conscious, but his eyes were very wide open and the expression in them was unnatural and frightening.

'There's nothing you can do, Mr. Cromwell,' said Gerry, with a worried shake of his head. 'Dr. Ware tells me that there's little hope of Ronnie ever getting back to normal. You can see how his eyes reflect the disordered condition of his mind.'

Ironsides looked up.

'I can see how his eyes reflect the filthy drugs that Ware has been feeding him on,' he retorted in a hard voice. 'Twenty-four hours of normal sleep and a week of cheerful society and your brother will be as healthy as ever—both in mind and body.'

'Good God, Cromwell, what are you saying?' demanded General Lister, while Gerry stood transfixed. 'You're hinting that Dr. Ware is responsible...'

'This is no time for hints, sir,' interrupted Cromwell bluntly. 'It's time to speak plainly. Last night a man not included in your list of guests was admitted into the castle. He was drugged with chloroform, left in that condition until after midnight, and then stabbed to death while he was still unconscious. Before being stabbed, however, his own clothing was removed and old-time costume substituted. I believe he was actually stabbed on the floor of the Death Room while Ronnie Charton slept in a chair. But he didn't cry out. The cry that aroused Ronnie from his drugged sleep was uttered by the murderer. The body, as you know, was then hidden in the vault…'

'Are you drunk, Cromwell? What fantastic story is this?' broke in Gerry Charton in amazement. 'Do you actually mean that Dr. Ware killed somebody?'

Ironsides turned to him squarely.

'No,' he replied. '*You* killed that somebody!'

For a breathless moment there was such a silence in the room that it could be felt like some heavy cloud of oppressive solidity. The first man to move was Johnny.

'I think not!' said Johnny softly.

He was standing right beside Gerry Charton, and his hand went like a piston to Gerry's hip-pocket—a fraction of a second before the young man's hand reached the same objective. The sergeant's slim fingers closed over a small automatic, which gleamed in the electric lights.

'Have you all gone mad?' shouted General Lister, starting agitatedly to his feet.

Gerry Charton's face was ashen.

'I've done nothing,' he said, the veins throbbing on his temples. 'It was Ware who killed Nayton. He deserved to die, the blackmailing skunk! He…' Gerry pulled himself up with a sobbing intake of breath, realizing that in his panic he was saying too much. 'You blundering fool, Cromwell, you've made a crazy mistake!'

'I've made mistakes in my life, I'll admit, but this time I've scored a bull's-eye,' retorted Ironsides. 'Sit down, Mr. Charton. No sense in getting all melodramatic. The game's up, and you know it. Your confederate, Dr. Spencer Ware, is dead; he plunged to the bottom of the lake with your victim and Lister and I were unable to save him. I can't compel you to say anything, and I'm not sure that I want you to say anything. After we have recovered the body of Nayton, it won't take the Yard long to establish his identity.'

The general was looking stunned; and, indeed, he was so appalled that the flood of questions he wanted to ask became tangled up with his vocal cords, and he remained dumb.

'You'll pay for this, Cromwell,' said Gerry Charton contemptuously. 'Do you think I'd try to drive my own brother insane?'

'The history of crime tells us that such a thing has been done before,' replied Cromwell, nodding. 'Furthermore, the number of brothers who have murdered their own flesh and blood is legion. While I was out of doors a short while ago, you fixed up a very nice death-trap in my bedroom, didn't you?'

'I don't know what the hell you're talking about!'

'No? Then perhaps you'll suggest that Ware did it?' snapped Cromwell. 'You're no professional crook, Charton. You make too many blunders. You made a bad slip on the landing, when you asked if somebody had been trying to bump me off. *You* knew about the death-trap, but nobody else did—because I locked the door of my bedroom, and nobody could have got in. I also happen to know that Dr. Ware was in this room with Ronnie for a full hour prior to the death-trap incident. You were the one, therefore, who set that interesting scene.'

'If you think you can prove…'

'But there's something else,' continued Ironsides imperturbably. 'When you drugged Nayton last night you used chloroform—probably after you had made him doze with a doped cigarette. But the smell of chloroform hangs about. When I entered your bedroom this morning it fairly reeked of perfume, and a man of your stamp hasn't much ordinary use for perfume. You pinched some from that fluffy-haired girl, didn't you?—perhaps without her knowledge. Chloroform is hard to conceal, Charton. I was seeking for traces of it, and that helped me. You see, I know the effects of chloroform, and I saw them in the dead man.

'When I went into my bedroom and found the light wouldn't come I detected a very faint perfume in the air. Normally, I don't think I should have noticed it; but I was half-expecting trouble. You came straight out of your own bedroom, Charton, and into mine. You carried with you some of that perfume—and you left that invisible clue to condemn you. I knew, then, that it was *you* who had monkeyed with the canopy of my bed… It couldn't have been the girl… To turn away from that subject, it was rather a neat dodge of yours to put spikes in a pair of old boots and walk across the drive, thinking to give your brother a scare…'

'Lies—all lies!' said Charton contemptuously. 'How do you know it wasn't Ware who played that trick?'

'Because Ware's feet were large feet—and he could not have got them into those boots,' retorted Ironsides crushingly. 'Ware was a stranger to Cloon Castle, whereas you know every inch of it. You spent your childhood in the neighbourhood, and I'll warrant you played in these very grounds—yes, and concealed yourself in that hollow tree.'

Point after point Cromwell was driving home with devastating force, and under those hammer blows Gerry Charton's confidence was crumbling.

'You know, at one time I was half inclined to suspect young Bayle and that Drydon chap,' murmured Johnny. 'Especially after they gave us such queer looks, Ironsides, as we went downstairs.'

'A perfectly natural incident,' said Ironsides impatiently. 'Bayle happened to see me going into somebody else's bedroom, and he thought it a bit queer. He saw you looking at him and he dodged down some back stairs. He was telling Drydon about my mysterious movements when we happened upon them. You mustn't take too much notice of trifles, Johnny.'

'Okay, Chief,' said Johnny humbly.

It was not surprising that Gerry Charton suddenly broke down and babbled out his black part in the sordid crime. As Ironsides had said, he was not a professional criminal, and the strain on his nerves during the past twenty-four hours had been acute. This sudden denouement, coupled with the certain conviction that the net was tightly about him, proved too much for his self-control.

To the world at large Gerry Charton had always been a cheery fellow and a great sport, worth pots of money. But for years he had been drained by a slimy crook named Cecil Nayton, who knew something ugly in Gerry's past. It was not generally known that Ronnie was only half-brother to Gerry, and Ronnie's fortune was considerably larger, on account of an inheritance from his dead mother.

Gerry had played for big stakes—but the murder plot had only been evolved after he had accidentally discovered that Dr. Spencer Ware, the eminent Wimpole Street specialist, was also a victim of Nayton, the blackmailer. Gerry and Ware had got together, and it was through Gerry that the brain specialist had been invited to Cloon Castle for Christmas. Gerry knew the castle inside out; as a boy he had heard the story of the Death Room and he knew all the details. It was easy enough to duplicate that age-old crime.

So he had arranged for Nayton to come secretly to Cloon Castle, presumably to receive a large sum of 'black' money. He had taken Nayton upstairs by a back way; and once Nayton was in Gerry's bedroom, he had been easily drugged—and left lying unconscious in a great old-fashioned cupboard during dinner and afterwards. Then his clothing had been changed, and the rest of the grim business had been carried out.

Before this, however, Gerry Charton had cunningly brought the talk in the library round to ghosts, and this had led up to the discussion about the Death Room. It was Gerry who had really egged Ronnie on to spending the night in the Death Room—although most of the men present at that discussion would have sworn that Gerry had done his best to persuade his brother to abandon the whole thing.

Cromwell pointed out that in spite of his apparent sleepiness, he had been very much on the alert—remembering, as he did, the curious incident on the drive. He took particular note of the fact that although it was Drydon who handed Ronnie a large drink just before he entered the Death Room, that drink had been put into Drydon's hand by Gerry Charton. A cunning and subtle move.

But the snow had defeated the plans. The plotters had been obliged to hide the body in the crypt, instead of taking it through, and out to the lake. Ware was to have done the carrying, whilst Gerry mingled with the alarmed guests. But as they merely dumped the body into the crypt, they were able to slip up the back staircase, and mingle with the guests—both of them—within a very few minutes. It was during the later hours of the night that Gerry had used his duplicate keys to get into the crypt and unfasten Lady Julia's casket.

The schemers had guessed that Ronnie, awakening from a drugged sleep and finding the body, would rush straight out of the Death Room—and this would give them the time they needed.

The set-up was perfect. At one blow, Gerry Charton and Dr. Spencer Ware got rid of the man who had been blackmailing them for years—and Ronnie would be sent insane. Easy enough for a man of Dr. Ware's reputation to fool another doctor into signing a lunacy certificate—particularly with Ronnie cleverly doped into stupidity. With Ronnie safely confined in Dr. Ware's 'nursing home'—in other words, a private lunatic asylum—Gerry would have had control of his younger brother's money.

And if the plan had gone as originally mapped out, no dead body would have come to light in the crypt, and thus the blackmailer—whose presence at Cloon Castle was unsuspected—would have disappeared without a trace, and it was certain that none would have mourned him or made inquiries as to his disappearance.

Cromwell was very diplomatic. He learned, by casual questions, that there were some very fine old dungeons in Cloon Castle. And he and Johnny Lister, unknown to a soul, escorted their prisoner by devious ways to the strongest of these dungeons. Here the wretched man was locked in—and later food and a bed were smuggled to him, to say nothing of a large supply of blankets. As it was impossible for Ironsides to hand over his prisoner to the Derbyshire police, he was keeping him well locked up until the roads were clear.

And General Lister's Christmas guests went on their merry way, serenely unconscious of the grim tragedy that had been enacted under their very noses. A murdered man, and a co-murderer at the bottom of the lake, and another murderer in the castle dungeons... And the party made whoopee without a suspicion… Truly, one of the strangest situations imaginable.

Everybody believed that Dr. Ware and Gerry Charton were kept away from the merrymaking because of Ronnie's illness, and it was not until days later, when Gerry was formally charged at the local police court, that the truth came out. And by that time Christmas was over—and Ronnie Charton, incidentally, was not only well on the way to recovery, but he was in many respects a better man.

# Murder at Christmas

## Christopher Bush

Christopher Bush, whose real name was Charlie Christmas Bush, was born on Christmas Day in Great Hockham, in Norfolk's Brecklands. He was educated locally and read languages at King's College, London, before becoming a school teacher. His first crime novel, *The Plumley Inheritance*, appeared in 1926, but three years passed before the publication of his second, *The Perfect Murder Case*. This early example of the 'serial killer whodunit', written long before the term 'serial killer' had been coined, received widespread critical acclaim, and from then on, Bush did not look back. Prolific as a mystery writer, he also produced novels of Breckland life under the name Michael Home.

Bush (1885–1973) continued to write about his detective, Ludovic Travers, until the late 1960s, and over the course of time, Travers evolved as a character, even if he did not age much. In his early days, he was a financial wizard working for an agency called the Durangos Conglomerate, and was presented as 'a dilettante with economics as a passionate hobby'. Later, he became a more conventional private eye.

In this entertaining story, he gives a first-hand account of a Yuletide puzzle.

I drove to Worbury on the afternoon before Christmas Eve. My wife had been called away to help nurse an aged and ailing aunt, and so I rang Bob Valence and asked if his invitation was still on for, say, the Christmas week-end. He wanted me to make it a week.

Worbury—which isn't its real name—is a town of some 2,000 people, and Robert Valence is its Chief Constable. He and I have run up against each other a lot professionally, since I'm at odd moments what the Yard chooses to call an unofficial expert, and he seems to think he's in my debt. In any case. I like him. He knows his job but makes no boasts, and he's genuine all through.

I was looking forward to that holiday. There's more futility than festivity alone in a London flat for Christmas, and, as I said, I liked Valence. He's a bachelor, by the way, and has a very nice service flat within a few hundred yards of his headquarters.

I'd been told to bring my golf clubs. We should have played on the morning of Christmas Eve, but there'd been a burglary in Marshwell, a village nearby, and Valence was called there well before we were thinking of starting for golf. But to get to Marshwell one goes through Rendham, which is two miles from Worbury, and the golf-course is there. So our golf bags went in the car and the new plans were for an early lunch at the clubhouse and a quick getaway after it, and with the certainty of a comfortable finish before dusk and a possible fog. December was commonly open that year, and when you get sun in the day you're almost bound to get fog at night.

That robbery at Marshwell Hall took up more of Valence's time than we'd thought and it was getting on for one o'clock when we left. It's three miles from there to Rendham, and as we came to the first house of the straggling village Valence suddenly slowed the car.

'See this chap coming towards us. Know who he is?'

I had five seconds, perhaps, in which to look, and what I saw was a man of sixty or more, short and with thin, stooping shoulders. I placed him as a retired professional man.

'Don't know,' I said.

'He's Brewse. John Block Brewse!'

My eyes popped a bit. 'Good Lord! What's he doing down here?'

'He has to live somewhere,' Valence told me dryly. 'Suppose he thought Rendham'd be as good as anywhere else. He has that first house back there. The one with the walled garden.'

'Any of his victims here?'

'One at least here,' he said, 'and one or two in Worbury. I doubt if there's a town in the country where there isn't.'

I supposed he was right. Brewse was the last of the line of financial swindlers, and it says a good deal for his plausibility that even among his victims there were still those who could judge him more unlucky than guilty. But he'd been put away for eight years and, considering the misery he had brought to thousands, I thought him lucky to have had so short a sentence.

'How long's he been here?'

'About a year,' he said. 'Almost as soon as he came out. The house, I gather, was bought beforehand in his housekeeper's name, so Rendham didn't guess what it was in for.'

'There was a bit of a stir?'

He laughed. '"Stir" isn't the word. A man named All-good—has a big furniture store in Worbury—was behind it. There was writing on Brewse's wall and his house. No jailbirds wanted, and that sort of things, and then when someone set fire to his shed, I had to step in.'

'And all's quiet now on the Rendham front?'

'I think so. Rice, the local man, hasn't reported anything lately, and Brewse lives very quietly. Just goes out for his daily walk and that's all.'

Then suddenly he was braking the car and looking to the right. We were through the actual village and almost at the entrance to the course, and he was looking along what was little more than a metalled track that made a sort of ride in a long stretch of wood. Drawn among the trees just off that track was a van. Valence took a long squint at it. Then he smiled.

'That'll be So-and-So,' he said. 'Thought it might be one of our Gipsy friends. Rice has been chasing them quite a lot. They come round the woods after holly and greenery and hawk it round the town.'

Through the thinned, leafless tops of the oaks I could see a quick-rising upland of green, which was the golf-course, and almost at once we were turning in at the gates. Quite a few cars were in the park.

'We'll just have a cold snack and some beer,' Valence said, 'then we can get away at once. Suit you all right?'

So we had sandwiches and beer in the bar. When we went to the locker-room, a couple of men were just going out. One was a tall, powerful looking chap in the late thirties and the other a plump, but far from flabby, parson in the forties.

'Hallo, Padre,' Valence said. 'Having another crack at the Demon?'

'Well, yes,' the parson said blandly. 'Trying to exercise is perhaps the better term.'

Valence laughed. 'And how're you, Prowse?' he said to the other chap. 'This is a friend of mine, Ludovic Travers. This is Mayne and this is Prowse.'

Mayne, he added, was the local vicar and Prowse the golf demon. A good-looking fellow, Prowse, with the very devil of a grip. Then when they'd gone, Valence told me some more. Mayne was a four man not long, but exasperatingly straight, and positively deadly round the greens. Prowse was plus one.

'Wait a minute,' I said. 'Did not he put up quite a good show in last year's Amateur? Or have I got the name wrong?'

'You're quite right,' he said. 'He was actually in the last eight. Got knocked out by a winner.'

We had quite a good game: I'm six feet, three inches and lean as a lamppost, and when I hit them just right they go the devil of a way. Valence is a lusty hitter, too, especially with his irons. At the dog-legged thirteenth he actually took an iron from the tee and played well out to the left. The hole itself lay behind an out-jutting spur of the wood which ran along that track—Frog's Lane, it was called—where Valence thought he had spotted a Gipsy. The cracks, like Prowse, could carry that spur of wood and get an easy four.

I almost had a go at it myself, but I was two down and didn't like to risk it, so I too took an iron and kept away to the left. And, of course, I overdid it, and that was to put me three down. But it did give me the chance to see Prowse driving at the sixteenth—a terrific crack that went straighter and farther than my incredible best.

When we got back to the clubhouse Prowse and the Vicar had gone, but the steward told us that Prowse had won by two up. Valence and I had tea and then cut in for bridge. We were in the second rubber when he was called to the telephone. He came back all apologies. Something had cropped up and he had to go.

When we stepped outside there was a fog that might have been much worse. It was more like a heavy mist, with a visibility of about fifty yards, which made it more of a nuisance than a menace.

'Sorry to have to rush you about like this,' Valence said. 'It may be for nothing, after all, but some man or other just rang the station and said there was a man's body in Catley Wood. That's about half-way home.'

And that was all he knew. Clare—his Chief-Inspector— had rung him about that anonymous call, and was on the way himself to Catley Wood. Hoax or not, he had at least to make sure.

A mile on the homeward road and there on the left was the stretch of wood. A car was drawn up on the verge and we stopped just short. Clare was in the wood and we saw the flash of his torch. Valence hailed him and his own torch flashed ahead through the sparse trees. But there was practically no undergrowth, and thirty yards on we picked up Clare and Sprat, the police-surgeon.

'No hoax, sir,' Clare said, and held his torch to what was on the ground. A small man lay there. An elderly man in a dark overcoat face sideways and arms flung wide. Valence's own torch caught the face and stayed.

'Good God!' he said. 'See who it is, Brewse!'

Brewse it was. But he got down on one knee and turned the face round. He looked at the eyes and pried open the mouth.

'What killed him, Sprat?'

'Manual strangulation,' Sprat said. 'There's a contusion on the point of the chin, so it looks as if he was knocked out first.'

'When?'

'Don't know,' Sprat said. 'Three hours ago—more or less. Tell you when I've got him away. Might do something with that stomach content.'

Valence got to his feet. It was dark in that wood—black as black hogs, as they say in Suffolk—and I could barely see the lighter blackness that was his face.

'Sorry about this, Travers. I'll have you run back and then you could get a meal at the Lion. Or would you rather stay?'

It was after eight when we got back to town, though Brewse's body had gone well before that. In Valence's office we had a look at his clothes, which had come in from the surgeon's room, and the contents of his pockets. There was a fairish sum of money in what seemed an intact wallet. As for the clothes, the overcoat had lichen stains on the back.

'Almost looks as if he was leaning against a tree in that wood, waiting for someone,' Valence said.

'A queer spot, surely, to fix for an appointment?' I said. 'No undergrowth, and only twenty yards from the road. Anyone could have seen both him and whomever it was he was meeting.'

'Depends when it was.'

'I don't know,' I said. 'If the appointment was for after dark, why should Brewse go all that way? Anywhere would have done. His house, for example. If the appointment was for daylight, then that wood was useless as a screen.'

'I've got a vague idea that'd explain some of that,' he said. 'The appointment might have been with someone coming from here, and if so, that wood was about halfway.'

'Anyone special in mind?'

He frowned. 'Well, there's always that chap Allgood I told you about. He lost a packet over Brewse. It was an employee of his whom Rice caught tarring a threatening message on the side of Brewse's house.'

'Anyone in Rendham who lost money over Brewse?'

'There is,' he said. 'Mayne did. Only indirectly. An aunt of his lost quite a lot.'

'And what about the man who rang the station about the body?'

'Just an anonymous voice. Might have been the man of a courting couple, going in there and finding the body. A local call, so it can't be traced. About time, by the way, that we had something from Sprat.'

He rang through to the mortuary. From his grunts and monosyllables I could guess what he was being told. But the news did turn out to be definite. Brewse's last meal had been at one o'clock. The stomach content showed death as taking place as so near to three o'clock it made no difference.

Valence said he'd like to see that housekeeper, so off we went through the mist to Rendham and Brewse's house. The elderly housekeeper was called Callaby. She was a loyal sort of soul who'd been with Brewse and his people most of her life. She confirmed that he had had his lunch that day at one o'clock sharp.

'Any letters this morning?'

She said there were none.

'Any telephone calls?'

He'd explained to me that the telephone had had to be disconnected soon after Brewse's arrival in Rendham. Scurrilous and threatening messages were always being received. But now the phone was in use again.

'There was a call early this morning,' she said. 'Just about nine o'clock.'

'You don't know from whom?'

She didn't know a thing, except that Brewse himself took the call. But she had been thinking. It now struck her that he had been just a bit perturbed after that call. And he had gone out for a walk, which was a queer thing for him. His walks were invariably in the afternoons. He had left for that afternoon walk about a quarter to three. She had seen him from her bedroom.

That was about all. Valence asked if he might use the telephone, and after he'd finished, we thanked her and left. Valence told me the morning call had been a local one. He added that we might as well drop in on Prowse. I asked no questions, though I didn't see why.

Prowse looked surprised to see us. His daily woman had gone and he was in slippers, with a drink at a side-table by his chair. He wanted us to have a drink too. Valence said he was technically on duty, and told him about Brewse.

'This has to be strictly confidential,' he said, 'but it's obvious that if Brewse was murdered, the likely suspects are those whose money he took. My superiors will expect me to question them. But I'd rather not question Mayne.'

Prowse smiled. 'You're surely not suggesting—'

'I'm not suggesting anything,' Valence told him bluntly. 'I'm telling you in strict confidence what I have to do as part of my job. All I'm asking is that you'd be prepared to swear, if necessary, that Mayne was never out of your sight this afternoon.'

'But of course he wasn't!'

'You never broke off the game?'

'Not for a second. We played straight on.'

'Good enough,' Valence said. 'Keep what I've asked you under your hat. Call it red-tape or what you will. And now I think we'll have that drink you offered us.'

Prowse poured the drinks and he noticed me looking round.

'Something struck me as unusual,' I said, 'and I've just found out what. This is Christmas Eve, but there's no holly.'

'No holly for me,' he said. 'I'm a widower, with no chick or child. Christmas is just something you've got to forget.'

One of my minor hobbies is to spot accents, and by that I mean to identify a person's native country. Prowse, when I asked him, said he was a Londoner. He'd been in Rendham only a few years. The property had actually been bought just before his wife died, and he'd then intended to sell it again. Then he'd changed his mind, fallen in love with the countryside and had become virtually a Rendhamian.

We'd been talking just for sociability over the drinks, and in about ten minutes we left. Allgood was waiting in the annex to Valence's room and Valence had him in at once. He was a beefy-looking man of about sixty. Valence told him about Brewse, and before he'd recovered from what seemed a shock, talked about red-tape and so on.

'You didn't like Brewse.'

'I hated the swine,' Allgood told him. 'I don't give a damn if he's dead or alive. I still hate him.'

'Then, just for the records, where were you at three o'clock this afternoon?'

'Well—' His eyes suddenly goggled. 'That's funny. At three o'clock I was within a stone's-throw of Brewse's place. Tell you how it was. I had a man to see at Cambridge and I was on my way when I got a puncture just where I said, and when I got the wheel off and the spare on, I found I hadn't got my pump with me, so I had to wait till a car came by, and that wasn't till just on three. I happened to stop a lorry and the driver gave me a hand.'

'Name and name of his firm? Still just for the records.'

'Darned if I know,' Allgood said. 'He drew up his lorry ahead of me, so I didn't see any name. And I didn't think to ask him his. I did tip him half-a-dollar.'

'That's all right,' Valence said. 'Suppose you didn't happen to see Brewse by any chance?'

'Matter of fact, I did. I happened to look round and there he was, walking towards the village. I hadn't seen him come out of his house, because I'd been busy over that spare.'

'What'd be the time when you saw him?'

'Be about a quarter to three,' he said. 'He was just short of the turn.'

'Well, that's that,' Valence said when Allgood had gone. 'Confirms what that Miss Callaby said about Brewse going out. And I'd say he was going to see the one who rang him this morning.'

'Then he couldn't have been killed before a quarter past three,' I said. 'He wasn't a fast walker and it'd have taken him half an hour to get to Catley Wood. It's a good mile and a half.'

'Stomach content isn't accurate to a second,' Valence said. 'A quarter of an hour either way is good enough. I don't know about you, but I'm damnably hungry.'

We managed to get sandwiches and coffee brought in. Valence asked me if I had any ideas, and I said I'd never a one.

'Just one thing that's rather footling,' I said. 'I'm pretty sure that Prowse told me a lie.'

His eyebrows raised at that.

'Nothing to do with Brewse,' I hastened to say. And I told him about that hobby of mine and how I was dead sure—as a Suffolk man myself—that Prowse was a Suffolk or South Norfolk man. Certain subtleties of accent and intonation had made that unmistakable.

Valence seemed rather amused. If he was interested, it was only out of politeness. I said it wasn't important, but I just happened to have a tidy mind: one that resented being cluttered up with irreconcilables.

He left me to finish the sandwiches while he went to Clare's room. While I was lighting my pipe I happened to drop my pouch on the floor, and when I picked it up, my fingers had a red stain. I looked at the pouch and that was where the red came from. For a moment I thought of blood, but I hadn't scratched my hand. Then I looked on the floor and there was a crushed holly berry, and I had to smile. I even thought of those lines from the old carol—

*The holly bears a berry*
*As red as any blood.*

and I didn't think any more, because Valence had to come back just then and he was saying that everything was well in hand and we might as well get along to the flat and have a real, belated meal.

Two days went by and Valence was making no headway. A search of the wood where the body was found had revealed never a thing. Someone had simply come up to Brewse, given him that quick upper-cut to the jaw, strangled him, and gone. But Valence did have some other, faint ideas. Allgood might have gone after Brewse and had words with him and lost his temper and strangled him, and then carted the body to where it was found.

After all, a puncture was an easy thing to fake. Even if the supposed lorry driver was found, Allgood still had no real alibi. But *might* was what they call the operative word, and what Valence was anxiously dreading was having to call in the Yard. The Allgood theory was largely hope.

And I couldn't tag along all day at Valence's heels. I had plenty of time to myself not that that worried me. I was more concerned about Valence's really pathetic apologies, which persisted even when I assured him that I was happy doing nothing in particular.

But one can't have leisure without thought, and I did quite a lot of thinking, and I have what's known as a harum-scarum mind. Unsolved mysteries nag at me, however insignificant they may seem, and I was pestered by a wonder why Prowse had told me that lie, for lie I was sure it was. Then I happened to run into Rice, the constable, who'd been at Rendham for some years. I had to be tactful in mentioning Prowse, and only as a golfer.

'How long's he been at Rendham, Rice?'

'Mr. Prowse?' he frowned. 'Be just seven years come January.'

'Of course!' I said it as if I'd just remembered. 'A London firm brought his things, didn't they?'

'That's right,' he said. 'Two vans. Harridges it was. I know, because I had a few words about a smashed gate-post with one of the drivers.'

So Prowse had come from London, and somehow I was wrong. But I still didn't know. To come from London doesn't make one a Londoner. So I did some more thinking, and when thinking got unbearable I rang the Broad Street Detective Agency. This was in the days when Bill Ellice owned it.

I told him about Prowse and gave a full description. He was to find out what he could from Harridges. That was early in the morning.

At seven that evening he rang me as arranged. The furniture had indeed been collected by Harridges, but not from a London address. It had come from a little village called Felling, which is near Bury St. Edmunds, in Suffolk.

'Right, Bill,' I said. 'Get busy on this at once. Get a good man down to this Felling place and have him find out everything he can about Prowse. Give me a ring this time tomorrow night.'

Then when I'd hung up I wondered why the devil I'd given him that assignment. It wasn't the expense that bothered me, but merely an apprehension of futility. Why worry one's head about Prowse when he, like his partner, Mayne, could not conceivably have had anything to do with the killing of Brewse? The only answer was that I was both hunch-ridden and curiosity-ridden, and it would probably cost me a couple of ten-pound notes.

Meanwhile Valence was worried. He'd found that lorry driver, but the Allgood theory was unaffected, and to carry that theory forward into proof was proving beyond him.

While he had found someone who had seen Allgood's car on its way through Rendham to Cambridge, nobody had seen it going back towards Worbury, as it must have done if he had been carrying Brewse's body.

Valence, in fact, was on the point of calling in Scotland Yard. Any man takes pride in his job, and it more than irked him that this, a murder case that had naturally excited a pretty general interest, should need the Yard for its solving. I was sorry for him, but there was nothing I could do to help.

I ran into Mayne as I was leaving the cinema that early evening. He told me he was playing Prowse again in a day or so.

'Plucky of you challenging him on level terms,' I said.

'The last time it was he who challenged me,' he said. 'But it doesn't work out too dear at ten bob a time. Sooner or later I'll be at the collecting end.'

I wished him luck and went on to the post office for Ellice's call. And I got one of the surprises of my life. Prowse's wife had been Brewse's niece, and Felling village reckoned that it was the disgrace of her uncle's imprisonment that had killed her. But there was more to come. Prowse's name wasn't Prowse at all. His name was Palfrey. He had changed to Prowse after leaving Felling.

Valence was in the flat when I got back. In the morning, he said, he'd be meeting his Watch Committee and recommending calling in the Yard. Just to take his mind off things, I told him what I'd unearthed about Prowse.

'Where's it get us?' he said, and shrugged his shoulders. 'We know he couldn't have killed Brewse. Besides, he had to change his name and dig himself in anonymously down here on account of the Brewse business. He wouldn't want his wife's name, or his own, connected in any way.'

Of course he was right, and yet again I couldn't help thinking. He had to go out after dinner and that left me to the thoughts, and when they'd circled so as almost to drive me mad, I suddenly remembered something. So I got through to the Yard.

Brewse's clothes had gone there for a laboratory check, and all I wanted was an answer to a certain question. I was promised it by the morning—and early. Then I rang Mayne and asked him a question, and after that I began to feel as if I might get a good night's rest.

It was during breakfast that the call came for me from the Yard, and it gave me just what I wanted.

'I wonder if you'd like to try a gamble before you see your Watch Committee,' I said to Valence. 'Let's run out to Rendham at once and see Prowse.'

'But why?'

'Just to try out a hunch,' I said. 'It won't cost a thing. And let me do the talking.'

'You really think—?'

'Yes,' I said. 'I think we might get something out of Prowse. Better take a couple of men with us. One for Prowse's back door and the other for his garage.'

He didn't ask any more questions, though he was hard put to it while we were making for Rendham.

Prowse looked mightily surprised at the sight of us at that early hour.

'Just a thing or two you might help us about,' Valence said, Prowse was ushering us in.

'Sorry I can't offer you coffee. Unless you'd wait a minute or two while I make it.'

'We've just had breakfast,' I replied. 'All we want is some information.'

'Not about poor old Mayne again?'

'Not this time,' I said. 'What Valence is really here for is to arrest you for the murder of Brewse.'

He stared incredulously. 'You mad? Or am I? You know as well as I do that I couldn't have been within a mile of Brewse.'

I said that we were running the risk of arresting him all the same, and I duly intoned the caution.

'If you insist,' he said. 'But I warn you that you'll look a couple of fools when Mayne gets on the stand.'

'Let me change your mind for you,' I said. 'Listen to me for a minute or two while I tell you just what happened. But, starting from the beginning, your name's Palfrey. Your late wife was Brewse's niece.'

That shook him, if only for a moment. Then he was telling me to carry on, but his lips had clamped together just a bit too tight.

'It was one of those tremendous coincidences, Brewse's coming here,' I said. 'Just the last straw. I think you regarded him as the murderer of your wife and, what's more, you and he couldn't live in the same village. You might have found another name, but sooner or later he'd meet you, and you wondered what he'd do. So you planned things out. You yourself fixed that game of golf with Mayne, and because Mayne didn't like Brewse either. In the event of any unforeseen slip-up over that alibi of yours, he'd keep his mouth shut or swing things your way.

'But you'd rung Brewse and told him who you were, though I doubt if you let him know you were living in Rendham under another name. You fixed an interview for Frog's Lane at three o'clock and your golf was timed accordingly. At just before three o'clock you were at the thirteenth. He didn't realize that you, as a golfer of the first rank, could put your ball virtually where you liked and that you really did deliberately drive into the wood.

'You told him you know just where the ball dropped, and he needn't bother to help you find it. So you went into the wood, with its holly undergrowth, and you found Brewse waiting. You knocked him out and strangled him and hid his body in a holly clump. Then you doubled back to the fairway showing a ball as if you'd found your own, *and Mayne was prepared to swear he hadn't really had you out of his sight all that afternoon.*

'Then at dusk you took the body to where it was found and you faked your voice and rang the police. You wanted the body found quickly so that there should be no doubt about when he died. Your alibi depended on that. But we know Brewse wasn't killed in Catley Wood. There's no holly there. But there was a holly-berry in the turn-up of Brewse's trousers, and it fell out on the floor of Valence's room. And Scotland Yard have found minute holly tears in his clothes and even a couple of thorns.'

'Clever,' he said. 'As a fairytale, it's clever.'

'It'll be clever enough to hang you,' Valence told him grimly.

'Two other little things,' I said. 'Brewse never went out of a morning, but he did go out that morning, and because, after that telephone conversation, he had to make sure where Frog's Lane actually was and the spot where you'd told him to meet you. The other thing is this.'

I held my clenched hand towards him. 'No holly in this house, so you didn't carry any from anywhere in your car. And yet in your car were these.'

I opened the hand and showed him a couple of holly leaves and a few berries. He stared, and then suddenly he was on his feet and through the side door.

Valence gave a yell and was after him. But he needn't have worried. Clare had him, and that was when we heard the shot. But Prowse made none too good a job of shooting himself, and it was not till two days later that he died in a hospital.

'I didn't know you had a crack at his car and found those holly berries,' Valence told me as we were leaving the hospital.

I sort of grinned and left it at that. I couldn't very well admit that I'd never seen the car.

# Off the Tiles

## *Ianthe Jerrold*

Ianthe Jerrold (1898–1977) published a book of verse in her teens, while 'The Orchestra of Death', an entertainingly macabre story, appeared in the *Strand Magazine* when she was just twenty years old. Jerrold was a versatile writer whose career as a novelist stretched from the early 1920s to the mid-1960s. Two detective novels, with well-evoked settings in London and the England-Wales border country respectively, were successful enough to earn her membership of the Detection Club, yet she promptly abandoned her pleasant if rather unmemorable amateur sleuth John Christmas.

Under the pen-name Geraldine Bridgman, Jerrold produced *Let Him Lie* (1940) and *There May Be Danger* (1948); the former is a stand-alone whodunit with a female amateur detective, while the latter veers into thriller territory. Her plotting of a mystery was never less than competent, but she seems to have found more satisfaction in writing mainstream fiction. In the 1950s, however, she did publish a handful of short mystery stories in *The London Mystery Magazine*, of which this is one.

◇◇◇

November gloom had descended on London when, at 1752 hours (5.52 p.m. on unofficial clocks), a telephone call was received at the Pine Road, Chelsea, police station. The speaker, a Mrs. Flitcroft, of 33 Chain Street, said that her next-door neighbour, a Miss Lillah Keer, had been killed by falling from the roof of her house on to the pavement. Inspector James Quy ordered an ambulance, and went at once by car to Chain Street, accompanied by P.C. Baker.

Quy knew Chain Street well, for he had recently investigated a burglary there. The houses were terrace-built, old-fashioned, stucco-faced, single-fronted, consisting each of three storeys above the ground-floor, and a basement below, with a narrow area railed off from the pavement, and several steps up to the front door. The roofs, he remembered, were of the mansard type, with small windows opening upon a leaded gutter and a low parapet. It would not be possible to fall accidentally out of such a window, and Quy therefore anticipated a case of suicide, for ladies do not usually walk about on roofs unless their nerves are disturbed and their intentions self-destructive. However, when he arrived in Chain Street, he found that the matter was by no means so simple.

Light streamed from the open front doors of Numbers 33 and 31, and there was a little knot of people gathered on the pavement at a spot almost exactly between the two houses. Looking up, Quy saw that, as he had supposed, a continuous parapet ran outside the mansard windows all along the terrace. He had time to note also that the mansard window in Number 31 was of the casement type, that in Number 33 of the sash, before three people started speaking to him all at once as he got out of his car. One was a pale young man with dark hair and a nervous blink behind horn-rimmed glasses, who said: 'Oh, Officer! If only I hadn't had my wireless on! If only I'd heard!' The second was a pale, grey-haired woman who looked pinched and wretched in a thin silk blouse, and had obviously been weeping, who said tremulously: 'I'm Mrs. Flitcroft—I rang you up!' And the third was a tall, square-faced woman in a red coat and a necklace of huge amber beads, who cried passionately: 'I'm her sister—I've only just got back! It *couldn't* have been an accident! I've done it myself often!'

Quy paused to ask:

'Done what?'

'Why, walked along the roof-gutter!' she replied. 'It's nothing, it's perfectly safe, whatever that old fool says! And so have other people done it—you couldn't fall off if you tried!'

She then glared with hatred at the other woman, and broke into tears, and Inspector Quy heard the word 'murder' as she turned aside.

'All right,' said Quy. 'Just stand by, will you? I'll want you later.' And the onlookers falling back before his uniform, he found himself facing a very old gentleman over the prone body of a middle-aged woman with a fur coat spread over her. A stethoscope dangled from the old gentleman's neck.

'The poor lady's dead,' said the old gentleman crossly.

'Did she say anything, Doctor?'

'Not to me! Broken skull, spinal injuries, and goodness knows what else! Crawling about on roofs at her age!'

'There's a lady here says it's quite safe and she's often done it herself.'

'Imagine it! Women of fifty and sixty crawling about roofs to pay calls by the attic windows, like cats! Never think of their blood-pressure, I suppose—never heard of vertigo! Heart-failure, stiff joints, poor eyesight—couldn't happen to *them*, oh no! That's what's the matter with the world to-day, if you ask me! Nobody knows his place! Insane, there's no other word for it... Well, there's nothing more I can do, so

I'll be getting home, Inspector, I'm freezing! You know where to find me if you want me.' And the very old gentleman went off, stiffly but energetically, swinging his stethoscope.

Inspector Quy turned back the fur coat that covered the body of Miss Lillah Keer, who was a slightly smaller, slightly younger, version of her sister Miss Rachel, now weeping noisily against the area railings. It was not, however, at the poor lady's face that Quy first looked, but at her hands. They were grimy, as might be expected. In a broken finger-nail on the left hand, a small piece of very dirty cotton-waste was caught. Inspector Quy took it out and carefully examined it. It had a faint scent reminiscent of turpentine. There were traces of the same kind of cotton fluff under the other nails on the left hand. Inspector Quy saw the other Miss Keer standing beside him, and asked:

'Was your sister left-handed?'

'No!' she replied fiercely. 'And she wasn't a clumsy ass, either! And I tell you, it *wasn't* an accident! It was murder, and I know who did it!'

'You can tell me about that later—in fact, you'll have to!' said Quy. 'But meanwhile, your sister was right-handed?'

'She could use both her hands pretty well, like most artists,' said Miss Keer, more quietly.

'Oh, your sister was an artist?'

'She painted with her right hand, of course, but she often used her left to mix her colours, or to clean her palette.'

'With turpentine, I suppose?'

'Yes, or some patent stuff artists' colourmen sell.'

'And cotton waste?'

'Or household rags.'

'I see,' said Inspector Quy. Further investigations were interrupted by the arrival of the ambulance and the police surgeon. When they had departed again, and the small crowd of onlookers had lingeringly dispersed, Quy took down the evidence and particulars of the inmates of the two houses. Mrs. Flitcroft of Number 33, a widow living with her son and daughter; Peter Crangley, aged twenty-four, nephew to Mrs. Flitcroft, a Civil Servant, who occupied the top floor of his aunt's house; and Miss Rachel Keer, elder sister of the deceased, a schoolteacher, who had shared Number 31 for many years with the dead lady.

'Whose fur coat is this?' asked Quy. They were standing in the ground-floor room of Miss Keer's house.

'Mine,' said Mrs. Flitcroft. 'I took it off and put it over her…'

As Quy passed it to her, there was a distinct jingle in one of its pockets. Mrs. Flitcroft heard it, and a sudden look of fright came to her careworn face.

'What is it?' asked Quy.

She said with difficulty and distress:

'The keys! Oh, they were in my coat pocket all the time!'

From one of the pockets of the fur coat she brought out with a shaking hand a small bunch of keys. 'But I'm *sure* I *felt* in my pockets!' she exclaimed, with tears.

'You *knew* they were there!' cried Miss Rachel Keer, her face distorted with hatred. 'There, Inspector! I told you! This woman murdered my sister! It was just an excuse to get Lillah out on the roof and push her over the parapet! I tell you, Inspector, this woman hated my sister; she's hated her ever since—'

'I didn't!' protested Mrs. Flitcroft tearfully. 'I don't hate people! I'm not like you!'

'No, you're the sly kind that never says what she thinks, but waits for an opportunity to hurt—stab in the back— push off the roof! You know you've hated Lillah ever since she started taking an interest in Peter—'

'Me?' exclaimed young Mr. Crangley with dramatic surprise.

'One thing at a time, please!' said Quy, as P.C. Baker, sitting at the dining-table with his helmet on a chair beside him, began to look worried over his short-hand notes. 'Tell me about the keys. What happened?'

It appeared that Mrs. Flitcroft, on returning to her house at about half-past five, had discovered that her keys were not in her hand-bag— 'though I can't *think* why not! I *never* keep them anywhere else! I thought they weren't in my pockets, either! I'm sure I felt in my pockets!'—and had rung her bell and banged on her knocker to attract the attention of her nephew, whose light she could see in the top window. She had also called to him, but he had not heard her.

'It was the damned wireless!' groaned the young man.

Mrs. Flitcroft's son and daughter were going straight from their businesses to a theatre, and would not be back until late; and since her nephew lived his own domestic life in his top flat and would not miss her, she was faced with the alternatives of staying out of her house until ten o'clock, or swallowing her pride and going next door for help. She admitted that she had had a serious quarrel with Miss Lillah Keer a month or two ago, over—over Peter, she said, glancing at that young man. She had thought it very wrong of Miss Keer to encourage her nephew in his desire to be a painter.

'Oh, you're a painter, too?' said Quy. 'I thought you said you were a Civil Servant?'

'I work in the Post Office because I have to earn my living, unfortunately.'

'That's a misfortune that occurs to a good many people,' said Quy, smiling. 'You're not at work today?'

'No, I—'

'Exactly!' said Mrs. Flitcroft with tremulous indignation. 'He doesn't stick to his work! And there she was, poor Miss Keer, telling him he had talent for art, giving him free lessons and quite turning his head! He *has* to earn his living, and his mother asked me to look after him; and even if he *could* paint, there's no living in art!'

There was no love, either, in the look exchanged between aunt and nephew.

'What happened next?' asked Quy.

Mrs. Flitcroft had asked Miss Lillah Keer if she would kindly allow her to return home via the mansard windows and the roof-gutter. It was a perfectly—well, *almost* perfectly, safe proceeding, and she and others had done it before. One had only to get out of the top window and walk along the gutter between the roof and the parapet. There was a narrow party wall of the same height as the parapet at the junction of the two houses, but there was plenty of room for a normally agile person to scramble over this without any danger of falling.

At this point, Inspector Quy asked to be conducted to the top floor so that he might judge for himself. He leant out of the small casement window of the bedroom, noted that the parapet was about two and a half feet high, and observed that the only obstacles to a walk along the gutter from end to end of the terrace were the low party walls between house and house. He also noted that a person travelling from Number 31 to Number 33 would have the roofs and the windows on his left hand.

'It certainly doesn't look very dangerous,' he commented.

'And it isn't!' said Miss Keer scornfully. 'Whatever that old fool Doctor Pellett may say! Poor Lillah *couldn't* have fallen! Somebody pushed her over!'

'How dare you?' said Mrs. Flitcroft, in angry tears.

'Why didn't you go yourself, then? It was *you* who wanted to get home!'

Inspector Quy awaited with interest the answer to this question.

'Well, of course I meant to go myself!' replied Mrs. Flitcroft tearfully. 'But I'd been out to tea and had my best things on, and Miss Keer was in her working clothes! It was very kind of her—she *insisted*!'

'So she came up here while you waited below for your nephew to open your door?'

'Well, no! I came up with her…'

'Why?'

'Well, I still thought *I* ought to go: I didn't like imposing on her good nature!'

'So you actually *saw* her fall?'

'Well, no! I saw her get out of the window, but I didn't look to see what happened—I didn't think it *could* be dangerous, you see! I was looking at that picture—it's one of Peter's—and I heard her scream, and then I heard the thud… And I rushed to the window, but of course I couldn't see over the parapet! I saw my nephew looking out of his window, and I told him what had happened, and we both rushed downstairs.'

'Who got there first?'

'I did,' said Mrs. Flitcroft. 'And I put my coat over her, and when Peter came I went to telephone you. And then Miss Rachel Keer came home—'

'Yes, and oh! If only I'd been five minutes earlier! I wouldn't have let Lillah go! I'd have told this woman to go and sit on her doorstep! I tell you, Inspector, Lillah *didn't* fall accidentally! She was pushed off!'

'A push *might* be accidental,' said Inspector Quy. He paused, glancing from one to another, but no one spoke. Inviting Peter Crangley to accompany him, he climbed out of the window and walked along the gutter towards Number 33. It was obvious, from the scratches and rubbings on the sooty coping of the parapet, that Miss Lillah Keer had fallen while negotiating the party wall, the one point at which an accident would be possible. The sash-window of Peter Crangley's room was open at the bottom. Quy climbed into the comfortable bed-sitting-room, followed by its tenant.

'Was your window open when Miss Keer fell?'

'What, in this weather? No, I opened it when I heard her scream.'

Inspector Quy sniffed.

'Turpentine—but of course! You're an artist, too. You heard her scream, then? Although you had the wireless on?'

'Good God, yes!' Peter Crangley shuddered. 'I heard her scream. I switched off the wireless, and dashed to the window.'

'What programme was on? Just a routine question.'

'The Children's Hour.'

'And what was on the Children's Hour this evening? Just routine, you know.'

The young man laughed.

'I haven't the slightest idea! I wasn't really listening, just having the thing as a sort of background noise...' He stopped rather suddenly.

'To what?' asked Quy quickly.

Peter Crangley hesitated.

'Not to house-work, by any chance?' continued Quy.

'House-work!' The young man laughed awkwardly.

'Well, it has to be done,' said Quy seriously. 'Nothing for us men to be ashamed of, nowadays. I do lashings of it when I'm off-duty. Your place looks very nice and clean—nice polished floor. Who cleans it?'

'Well, as a matter of fact you're quite right, I do it myself,' confessed Peter Crangley. 'I can't afford a housemaid on the pay of a P.O. clerk, you know! And I haven't sold any pictures yet!'

'Where do you keep your brushes?' asked Quy.

'My brushes? In that jar there!' said the young man, staring.

Quy laughed.

'Not your paint-brushes—your house-work brushes! But I suppose,' he added thoughtfully, 'you use a mop for a polished floor. My wife does.'

'It's in that cupboard,' said the young man, with a sudden odd hesitation.

Inspector Quy opened the cupboard door and took out a long-handled and very dirty floor-mop. He sniffed at its pleasant scent of turpentine, and twirled it gently round, loosing a little air-flotilla of fluff and motes into the room.

'Don't do that!' protested the young man agitatedly. He had gone very pale, and was blinking furiously.

'Not indoors, eh?' said Quy. 'No, one shouldn't. One should do it out of the window. I know, I've seen my wife do it.'

He took the mop to the window, thrust it through into the dark and twirled it over the parapet.

'That's what I meant when I said a push *might* be accidental,' he explained, desisting and returning the mop to its cupboard. 'It *might*, or it might not... Just as the window *might* have been open when the lady was coming along the gutter?'

'You don't think I'd try to hurt Lillah Keer, do you?' cried Peter Crangley in a strained, breathless voice. 'She was my best friend!'

Inspector Quy suggested gently:

'But it *might*, mightn't it, have been the *wrong lady* who was knocked over the parapet by the push that might have been accidental from the mop that might have been shaken out of the window that might have been open? I think, Mr. Crangley, you'd better come with me to the police-station. There are a few questions I'll have to ask you—not just routine, this time!'

◇◇◇

The questions, which concerned the abstraction of a bunch of keys, before her departure, from Mrs. Flitcroft's handbag, and the restoration of them to the pocket of a fur coat lying over a dead body, as well as certain other matters which soon came to light connected with Mr. Crangley's ambition for an artist's career, and his share in a trust left by his grandfather, in which his aunt had a life-interest, led eventually to the conviction of Peter Crangley for the murder of Lillah Keer, and, it is to be hoped, to apologies from Miss Rachel Keer to Mrs. Flitcroft. It also led to reflections from Inspector James Quy on the inflexibility of the criminal mind.

'If young Crangley had accepted the fact that he had unfortunately killed the wrong lady, and had carried on with the perfectly sound scheme he'd thought out for the murder of his aunt, and simply left her keys in her bedroom or somewhere, and admitted at once that he'd shaken his floor-mop out of the window just at the fateful moment, there'd almost certainly have been a verdict of accidental death. After all, a person doing house-work on the top storey can't be expected to look out in the roof gutter to make sure the coast is clear before shaking a mop over it! But no, having killed the wrong lady, he had to pursue his obsession to get rid of his aunt by trying to fasten the murder of Miss Keer on her! Too rigid-minded. Must have their way at all hazards, these criminals. Can't cut their losses. And a good job for the rest of us, eh, Baker?'

P.C. Baker, who, although he has not made much of an appearance in this story, was a bright young officer, brightly agreed.

# Mr. Cork's Secret

## *Macdonald Hastings*

Macdonald Hastings' brief career as a crime writer formed only one element of a life packed with incident. Douglas Edward Macdonald Hastings (1909–82) was the son of a journalist whose early death left his family short of money; Hastings left school, and worked briefly as a clerk at Scotland Yard before joining the publicity department of Lyons, the caterers. During his time there, he earned extra money through freelance journalism, and in 1939 he was hired by *Picture Post*. Having made his name as a reporter during the Second World War, he became editor of the legendary *Strand Magazine* until its last issue appeared in 1950.

Undaunted by the *Strand's* closure, he became 'Special Investigator' for the *Eagle*, a popular boys' comic, and established a separate reputation as a broadcaster. His first detective novel, *Cork on the Water*, appeared in 1951, and introduced the eponymous insurance investigator. Cork had a real life model, according to T.J. Binyon's study of the genre, *Murder Will Out*, a managing director of Cornhill Insurance called Claude Wilson. Cork appeared in just five novels, but they were successful enough to earn Hastings election to the Detection Club. This short story first appeared in *Lilliput* magazine, to which Hastings contributed frequently. It was presented as a Christmas competition, readers were invited to guess the nature of Mr. Cork's secret, and the lucky winners each received a prize of £150.

*'He answered all the questions which the Press reporters put to him in the de Raun case except one…'*

Monsieur Aloysia, a plump but well-made man in black jacket and striped trousers, came out of the gilded lift on the first floor of the Paradise Hotel, followed by two electricians in blue overalls. As he stepped into the passage, he gravely pointed out that one of the illuminated coloured lights on the Christmas trees flanking the lift-gates wasn't functioning. But he didn't stop. He walked on, turning right and left from one anonymous corridor to another, until he reached a room numbered 143. He pulled out a master key and turned the lock. The door wouldn't open. Keeping his hand on the key, he placed his shoulder to it and gave it a gentle shove. The door moved, but slightly.

'Shall we break it down, sir?' said one of the electricians.

M. Aloysia looked at the young man in mild rebuke.

'When you 'ave been in the 'otel business as long as I 'ave, Perkins, you will learn that an 'otelier's first regard is the comfort of 'is guests.'

He spoke in a well-fed whisper. But although he looked solemn, there was a mischievous gurgle in his voice. The way he spoke made the two electricians grin.

'Then what are we going to do, sir?' said Perkins. 'It's obvious he's blocked the door.'

'We'll try next door. You're an agile young fellow. You can slip through the window and climb along the ledge.'

Outside the adjoining bedroom, M. Aloysia knocked. Only when he was sure that the occupant was out did he use his key. The electrician, anxious to make a good showing in front of the manager, opened the window. He looked down at the semi-tropical gardens for which the Paradise, 'a West End hotel in the West Country,' is so justly famous. Then he threw his leg over the sill. He found a footing on an ornamental stone ledge running along the outside of the building. Clutching at the smelly foliage of the ivy which clothed the wall, he felt his way gingerly across the gap.

M. Aloysia occupied himself tightening a dripping tap in the wash-basin and looking under the bed to see that the maids were doing their job properly. The other electrician stood gangling at the door.

Perkins wasn't gone long. When he swung himself back into the room, the colour had drained out of his cheeks, and he licked his dry mouth with his tongue.

'What's the matter?'

There was no change in the casual tone of the manager's voice.

'He's still living, sir,' gasped the electrician, 'but he's bashed about something awful.'

'Thank you, Perkins.'

For answer, the electrician fell flat on his face in a faint.

'He'll come round in a minute,' said the manager to the other man. 'You come with me.'

Returning to Room 143, he held back the latch and put the full weight of his square frame into the door. The electrician helped. The panelling creaked under the pressure. Then, with a tearing of woodwork, the obstruction fell clear. The surviving electrician pressed forward to climb through the mess. But when he saw the inside of the room, he faltered. The manager patted him sympathetically on the shoulder.

'You wait 'ere,' he said.

He manoeuvred his way over the wreckage of the wardrobe into the bedroom. Then M. Aloysia himself gave an exclamation of horror.

'Get the door free quick,' he said over his shoulder. 'If the news of this leaks out, it'll ruin the Christmas business.'

Pushing his way through the disordered furniture, he grabbed a towel from the rail of the wash-basin and wrapped it hastily round the battered head of the man on the floor. Whatever the electrician thought, he was a corpse, and a very messy one. M. Aloysia looked ruefully at the spreading stain of blood on the new carpet.

'You and Perkins,' he ordered, 'will go straight 'ome. You will talk to nobody in the 'otel about this. Understand? Nobody. Maybe, in due course, the coroner will need you to give evidence. All right. You will tell 'im what you have seen. Now get cracking. Use the staff lift.'

The bemused electrician collected his mate and the two of them left. M. Aloysia shut himself inside the bedroom. Then he picked up the telephone.

''Allo, Miss. This is Mr. Aloysia. 'Ow are you, my dear? Splendid. Now be a good girl and put me through to Mr. Gaston in the reception. Gaston, is that you? *Comment ça va?* 'Ave you got rid of the Press people yet? So. You've told them we know nothing. Good. No, we've 'ad no news from Mr. de Raun at all. Listen, Gaston. We've got a bit of trouble 'ere in Room 143. Ring through to the police, ask them to use the staff entrance as usual, and get out the gentleman's dossier. Bill outstanding, I suppose? Pity. No, Gaston, 'e'll never pay it now.'

As soon as Gaston cut off, M. Aloysia tapped the receiver again.

'Put me through to the 'Ousekeeper... Ah, Mrs. Macpherson, 'ow are you and 'ow is your maid? You've sent 'er 'ome? Excellent. Yes, Mrs. Macpherson, it wasn't 'er imagination. It's a great nuisance and we shall 'ave to do all we can to keep the news from our other customers. The police will be 'ere soon. When they've gone, I shall 'ave to trouble you for a clean carpet from the stores.'

He glanced accusingly at the corpse.

'I'm sure I can leave it to you, Mrs. Macpherson,' he went on evenly. 'Of course, of course. Goodbye.'

He put down the receiver thoughtfully. Almost at once, the bell rang again.

'Yes, Aloysia 'ere,' he said wearily. 'Who wants 'im?'

As he heard the name, his voice changed.

'Mr. Montague Cork? Put 'im through at once, Miss. 'Ow are you, Mr. Cork? This is indeed a pleasure. And 'ow is Madame? But of course... The Paradise is at your complete disposal.'

Yet, as he listened to the august voice of the most celebrated insurance man in the world, his pink face wrinkled with anxiety. It was the pride of the Paradise that, on many occasions, Mr. and Mrs. Montague Cork had been its guests. Mr. Cork was at once one of the most respected and wealthy men in the City of London and, as the General Manager and Managing Director of the Anchor Insurance Co., he was a national figure. It was said of him that he had exposed more cases of insurance fraud than Scotland Yard. His big nose and watery eyes, dewlapped like an old bloodhound, was as familiar in the popular papers as the faces of the film

stars. And, unlike the film stars, Mr. Cork always paid his
bill in full.

M. Aloysia was in a quandary.

'If only you 'ad called me a week ago,' he said hopelessly,
'I could 'ave given you and Mrs. Cork the loveliest suite in
the 'otel, with private sitting-room and a terrace overlooking
the sea. Marvellous! But now we 'ave nothing, not even for
you, Mr. Cork. It's Christmas. We are booked full up like
an egg. Yes, we would do anything for you and Madame.
But it is Christmas Eve...'

In his desperation, he looked to the corpse for inspiration.

'But wait... I 'ave an idea, Mr. Cork. What time would you
and Madame be arriving from London? But that is perfect.
I 'ave a guest who is leaving us unexpected. The room is not
what I could wish for you, but... thank you, Mr. Cork. We
shall be delighted to welcome you again at the Paradise.'

He replaced the receiver. In spite of the studied calm of
his manner, M. Aloysia was a worried man. Only twenty-four
hours ago he was congratulating himself on the prospect of
the best Christmas business for years. The hotel was booked
right up and, to crown it all, Anton de Raun and his new
bride, Fanny Fairfield the film star, had booked the bridal
suite at the Paradise for their honeymoon. They should have
arrived after the wedding yesterday; but, so far they hadn't
turned up. They'd disappeared without a word and left him
to wrangle with the droves of reporters and Press photographers who crowded the cocktail bar and carried on as if the
hotel had lost the happy couple in the wash.

◇◇◇

And, after that, there was this. This was much worse. If it were only one of the familiar suicide cases, he could have dealt with it quite simply; but this was obviously murder. If as much as a whisper got round the hotel, he knew from experience that he'd lose half his bookings. It would call for all his skill to get the police out of the way, and the room cleaned up, before Mr. and Mrs. Cork arrived from London. But, from every point of view, the effort was worth it. And for him, Aloysia, the best hotel manager in Europe, nothing was impossible. It was Christmas Eve. Even the police were human. A bottle of whisky would work wonders. The story was bound to come out in the end but, by the grace of Heaven, there were no newspapers for another two days.

He was much too disgusted with the corpse for dislocating the business of the hotel to be more than mildly interested in what had happened. That was the affair of the police. Judging by the disorder in the room, the motive was robbery. Presumably, the murderer had climbed up the ivy from the gardens and entered, and made his exit through the open window whose curtains still flapped furiously in the sea breeze. The victim had been battered to death and the weapon, which had been thrown down on the floor, looked like a heavy iron bar; it was wrapped in a rolled newspaper. The only other object which attracted his attention was a large and elaborate leather jewel case, made in the shape of a heart. It lay on the floor, open and empty, showing the milky white silk of the lining spotted with the blood of the dead man.

There was a knock at the door. M. Aloysia opened it just enough to see who was there.

'Good morning, sir. I understand you've got a spot of trouble. I'm Detective-Sergeant O'Flaherty. The coroner's clerk will be here shortly.'

◇◇◇

For M. Aloysia, it had been a day of triumphant deception. The police had co-operated magnificently. He'd smuggled them in—the Inspector, the photographer, the doctor, the fingerprint expert, and the rest—without a breath of suspicion that anything was amiss. And he'd got the corpse out of the hotel by concealing it in an ottoman carried by undertakers' men wearing green baize aprons.

He had reported the discovery of the murder at 9.30. By cocktail time the same evening, the police had carried away the carpet and the other contents of the bedroom they needed, and Mrs. Macpherson, bless her, was organizing the refurnishing of the room. He hadn't got rid of the Inspector, who was busy interviewing various members of the hotel staff in the little office behind the reception desk. But Gaston was keeping an eye on things there.

The manager stood serenely under the crystal chandelier near the desk, with hands clasped on his breast, bowing fatly to his patrons as they drifted through on their way to dress for dinner or stopped to admire the seasonal decorations which dripped from every gilded alcove and twinkled in an avenue of Christmas trees arranged along the entire length of the Grand Foyer. People came to the Paradise Hotel to see life. It was M. Aloysia's business to make sure that they saw only what they wanted to.

His triumph was indeed complete when at the very moment he saw the grim figure of Mr. Cork arriving through the revolving doors of the main entrance, a tiny page-boy, in powder-blue uniform, brought him a message on a silver salver. It was from the hall porter. Mrs. Macpherson reported that Room 143 was ready for occupation again.

Several people looked up at Mr. Cork as he strolled across the hall to the desk. His face, with its heavy features and deep lines, was unmistakable. But, characteristically, Mr. Cork himself was quite unaware that he was a celebrity. He was only vaguely conscious of the fact that his criminal cases had made him a public figure.

As he waited for his wife, he lit a Passing Cloud and examined his chin critically in one of the rose-tinted mirrors in the hall. He'd have to shave again when he dressed for dinner. If he didn't, Phoebe was certain to complain about it. It was odd that, as he entered his sixties and the hair on his head was getting thinner, his wretched beard was sprouting more strongly than ever.

'Welcome to the Paradise, Mr. Cork.'

'Hello, Aloysia. *Noël joyeuses* to you; that's the French for it, isn't it?'

They shook hands.

'Where's Madame?'

'She'll be here in a minute. She's giving Christmas presents of warm woollen socks to some of your linkmen outside. Amazing woman, my wife. Collects friends everywhere. By the way, I'm sorry I couldn't give you longer warning. We only decided to come down here at the last moment.'

'Such a pity. A week, even a few days, could have made so much difference. The room we 'ave for you, it is not what we could wish for you and Madame.'

M. Aloysia gave a disappointed shrug.

'Never you mind, Aloysia. It was good of you to fit us in at all. I'm not surprised you're so full. I hear you've got celebrities. My wife's eating her head off to see Fanny Fairfield.'

'I'm afraid I have a disappointment for 'er.'

'Oh?'

'The bridal suite is booked but, so far, Mr. and Mrs. de Raun 'ave not arrived. We are still expecting them. Mr. de Raun's secretary phoned us only yesterday morning to confirm that they were coming. But, so far, we 'ave had no further word. Ah, Mrs. Cork!'

Mrs. Cork appeared in a mink coat, with a pink face and an armful of packages. She was as plump and smiling as a feminine Santa Claus. And, as M. Aloysia relieved her of her parcels, she bubbled gaily.

'Has this dreadful husband of mine told you what he's done? At the very last minute, Mr. Aloysia, when I'd got everything organized for a family Christmas at the farm, he suddenly decided he was coming to the Paradise instead. So here we are. Have the film stars arrived? I do so want to see them.'

'Aloysia has just told me that they haven't turned up.'

'No Fanny Fairfield. Oh, I am disappointed.'

'We are expecting them hourly, Mrs. Cork. The bridal suite is reserved.'

'The bridal suite! That sounds terribly romantic. What do you think's happened to them?'

'No use asking me,' grumbled Mr. Cork.

'I know,' said Phoebe. 'I expect the poor dears are trying to hide away from all the publicity.'

'If they had wanted to avoid publicity, Phoebe, they wouldn't have booked a suite in the Paradise and advertised the fact in every newspaper in the country.'

'The trouble with you, Monty, is that you're getting a crusty old man. You've forgotten what it means to be a young person in love.'

'You seem to be in a sentimental haze about this wedding, you and every other woman. May I remind you, Phoebe, that these "two young people" have both been married several times before; this is Anton de Raun's fourth honeymoon and Fanny Fairfield's third.'

'No, dear, it's only her second.'

'Well, whatever the score is, she's hardly a blushing young bride. And it's a lot of nonsense to suggest that these two, who've spent most of their lives making baboons of themselves in the public prints, are now sheltering shyly in a love-nest under the stars. Come on, we're keeping Aloysia waiting.'

M. Aloysia had listened to the conversation with an urbane and self-effacing smile. Privately, he was heartily in agreement with Mr. Cork. Anton de Raun was a playboy who was said to have made three fortunes, married three and lost all six. Now he was starting on Fanny Fairfield's bank balance. Still, it was good for business.

He personally escorted his distinguished guests to Room 143, protesting his apologies all the way for the inadequacy of the accommodation. He could only hope that Mrs. Macpherson had had time to fix the flowers.

He needn't have worried. When he bowed in Mr. and Mrs. Cork, every stick of furniture had been changed. There was a new carpet, a luscious bowl of flowers on the dressing-table and a basket of fresh fruit on the table between the twin beds. Gaston had sent up the champagne, all ready on the ice, for Mr. Cork, and there was a present of perfume for Mrs. Cork waiting for her on the bed.

'But this is charming,' said Phoebe. 'And you've given us one of the nice rooms with a view of the sea. It's lovely, isn't it, Monty?'

Mr. Cork gave one of his grim smiles.

'I see you remembered the champagne, too, Aloysia.'

The manager bowed in delighted satisfaction. When he closed the door behind his new guests, he looked at the number and smiled with the contentment of a milk-fed cat.

Mr. Cork was bathed and shaved. As Phoebe knotted the bow-tie of his dinner jacket for him, she said:

'Why did you want to come here? It's not business, is it, Monty? Not at Christmas?'

'Don't ask leading questions.'

'Then it is business. Another of your hunches?'

'Only a hunch, Phoebe. If I'm wrong, we can still have a good time.'

'Then I hope you're wrong.'

'There's somebody at the door. You answer it, dear. I'm going to open the champagne.'

Phoebe went to the door and collected a floppy parcel wrapped in crackling brown paper from one of the little pages.

'What is it?'

'I don't know, dear.'

'Then open it and see.'

'Great heavens. It's a pair of pyjamas. I'm sure they're not yours, Monty. You've never left your pyjamas behind when you've been here, have you?'

'After thirty years, Phoebe, you ought to know that I don't wear pyjamas like that.'

'How do I know what you get up to when you're off by yourself? They are rather sweet, aren't they? I love the frogging across the front.'

'They must have been sent up here in error. Give the valet a ring.'

Phoebe pressed the bell. But she went on admiring the pyjamas.

'It's French silk, I think. Oh yes, here's the man's name on the collar. That makes it very easy. What a funny name it is: André Guydamour. That's obviously French, isn't it?'

Mr. Cork was raising the champagne cork out of the bottle with the pressure of his thumb. He looked across at Phoebe with sudden interest as the cork popped out and hit the ceiling.

'What name was that?' he said sharply.

The champagne foamed out of the neck of the bottle over his hand.

'Look what you're doing, Monty.'

'Never mind that. What was the name?'

'Guydamour.'

'Give me those pyjamas.'

He returned the champagne bottle to its bucket of ice and, settling his half-glasses on his big nose, he examined the name carefully. When the valet answered the call, he went to the door himself.

'Did you send in these pyjamas?'

'Yes, sir.'

'Where did they come from?'

The man looked puzzled. His eyes flickered to the number on the door.

'I beg your pardon, sir, I thought the other gentleman was still here.'

'What other gentleman?'

'The guest who was in your room last night, sir. He asked me to get these pyjamas washed and return them when I came on duty this evening. He must have moved his room. I'm sorry to have troubled you, sir. I'll take them away immediately.'

'You haven't troubled me and you needn't take the pyjamas away. I'll hand them in myself at the desk downstairs.'

'Very well, sir.'

The man hesitated as if he wanted the pyjamas back, but the authority in Mr. Cork's voice made him think better of it. After all, it hardly mattered who turned them in downstairs.

'You are a funny old boy,' said Phoebe. 'What's biting you?'

Mr. Cork poured out a glass of champagne for both of them.

'When you were reading all about Fanny Fairfield, did you notice any reference to the fact that her new husband was giving her as a wedding present a valuable parure of rubies and diamonds?'

'But of course. Alouette's Worm.'

'Exactly, a collection of jewels which were supposed to have belonged, at one time, to the French singer, Alouette.'

'Have we insured them, Monty?' she said with unusual seriousness.

'We've granted temporary cover and we've laid off the risk with half a dozen other companies. It's a big sum, Phoebe. Seventy-five thousand pounds.'

'What's that got to do with the pyjamas?'

'André Guydamour is the Paris jeweller who has made the sale to de Raun. He's somewhere in the hotel. Anton de Raun is expected here with his new wife. It's evident that Guydamour has come over from France to deliver the collection.'

'That sounds quite natural. Why are you worried, dear?'

'Too much publicity, Phoebe. Every popular newspaper has been gossiping, day after day, about these jewels. De Raun has told everybody that he's giving them to his wife as a wedding present. Furthermore, he's announced to all and sundry that he's spending his honeymoon here.'

'But he hasn't turned up.'

'No, but the jeweller has. They're inviting a robbery, Phoebe.'

'So *that's* why we're spending Christmas at the Paradise.'

As he and Phoebe walked past the reception desk, Mr. Cork pushed the pyjamas, in their brown paper, across the counter to the clerk.

'My compliments to Mr. Aloysia,' he said. 'Tell him that I should like to meet the gentleman to whom these pyjamas belong.'

'But certainly, sir,' said the clerk.

After years of experience of the eccentricities of hotel guests, he knew better than to register surprise.

'Have you noticed that strange man who's following us?' whispered Phoebe.

Mr. Cork nodded.

'I wonder who he is?'

'I haven't an idea. Let's think about dinner.'

Hermann, the head waiter, raced half the length of the crowded dining-room to be there to welcome Mr. and Mrs. Cork.

'Everything is arranged,' he insisted. 'Monsieur Aloysia's personal orders. We have a special table for you and a dinner which is a poem.'

To emphasize his conviction, he pressed thumb and index-finger together and waved them in the air.

'Smoked salmon and a little caviare. *Sole en broche* with bay leaves and just a hint of onion. Roast partridge with a bottle of Mouton Rothschild…'

But before they had reached their table, the reception clerk, pale-faced, touched Mr. Cork on the shoulder.

'I'm sorry to trouble you, sir, but Inspector Trelawny would like to see you immediately in the manager's office.'

'Tell the Inspector I'll join him shortly.'

He saw Phoebe to the table. They exchanged a message with their eyebrows. Otherwise neither of them made any comment.

'Start your dinner, dear, and I'll be with you as soon as I can.'

The *maître d'hôtel* looked on with baffled resignation. It was such an exquisite dinner that he had arranged for them.

Inspector Trelawny rose from the manager's desk to greet him. The telltale pyjamas lay crumpled on the blotting-pad. M. Aloysia, all serenity gone, fluttered with agitation at the inspector's side.

'Well, Aloysia, what's all this about?' said Mr. Cork severely.

'Perhaps I can explain,' said the inspector.

M. Aloysia shrugged his shoulders miserably.

'Will you have a seat? My name's Trelawny, of the County Constabulary.'

'My name's Cork.'

'The introduction on your side is quite unnecessary, sir. It's a very great privilege meeting you.'

The Inspector waited respectfully until Mr. Cork sat down.

'I hope you'll forgive my bothering you just as you're starting dinner, but I'm engaged in making investigations into a rather serious business.'

'Robbery?' asked Mr. Cork.

The Inspector looked at him sharply.

'You knew?'

'Call it an inspired guess.'

'Your guess is the correct one. But that's not all. It's murder, too. A particularly brutal murder.'

Mr. Cork took a cigarette from his heavy gold case. The Inspector got up from the desk to light it for him.

'These pyjamas, Mr. Cork?'

'They were delivered to my room in error by the valet.'

'Not in error. The night valet, who washed them, was under the impression that the room was still occupied by the same guest who was there yesterday.'

'So I gathered.'

'I have to tell you that he was the man who was murdered and robbed in the hotel last night.'

'In my room?'

'It was the only room I 'ad available, Mr. Cork. It was the only way I could fit you in.'

'Never mind that now, Aloysia. All I have to say to you is that Mrs. Cork must never know about it.'

'But of course, of course. I would do anything not to alarm Madame.'

'May I go on?' said the Inspector coldly.

'Certainly.'

'When you handed in these pyjamas to the reception desk, you said that you wanted to talk to their owner. Naturally, I'm interested. He registered at the hotel, when he arrived yesterday morning, under the name of Franklyn. We now know, from his passport and various other papers, his real name.'

'André Guydamour,'

'Precisely. The name on the tag in the collar of these pyjamas. What can you tell us about him? We need help badly, Mr. Cork.'

'He was a Paris jeweller and clockmaker.'

'We've checked that with the *Sûreté.*'

'My own interest in him is simply that my company have had dealings with his firm in connection with an important insurance cover. Guydamour supplied us with the valuation and description of a collection of jewels we are underwriting. Because I was dissatisfied with certain aspects of the risk, I telephoned his firm in Paris early this morning. I learnt that Guydamour had travelled to England. I had reason to believe that I might find him here.'

'And the reason?'

'His purpose in coming to this country was to deliver the jewels in which we are interested to my company's client, Anton de Raun.'

'De Raun? You mean Fanny Fairfield's new husband?'

'Since you read the popular papers, you can also guess the nature of the jewels.'

'You mean Alouette's Worms?'

'You obviously do read the papers.'

'Oh God,' said the Inspector, burying his head in his hands.

'I should have thought the *Sûreté* could have told you all you want to know about the jewels.'

'That's the trouble, the whole trouble,' said the Inspector wildly. 'We can't get any information out of anybody. It's Christmas, Mr. Cork. The whole of our investigation is foxed and bewildered because everybody is thinking of Christmas.'

'You've got the ports watched, I hope?'

'We're supposed to have warned every port of exit,' said the Inspector bitterly, 'but even our own people are human. After all, all Aloysia here can think about is his Christmas business. The murderer has nearly twenty-four hours' start on us. If he's got Alouette's Worms—and he probably has because we've found a large, empty jewel case—he could be half-way across Europe by this time.'

'So you've found the case. What's it like?'

'It's a large two-decker affair in the shape of a heart.'

'Large enough to hold a complete collection: necklace, earrings, bracelet, tiara, and so on?'

'Yes, it's big enough for that. By the way, have you got a picture?'

'We've got a full description. I understand that there's also a painting in existence of Alouette wearing the jewels in their original mounting, in the Théâtre Élysées in Paris.'

'I'll get it copied.'

'It might help. May I use the 'phone?' He went on talking with his hand over the mouthpiece.

'Do you know where de Raun is?'

'So far, we haven't made any enquiries.'

'What can you do to find him? Can the newspapers help?'

'There are no newspapers for another two days.'

Mr. Cork got his number.

'Hello. This is Montague Cork. Is that Mr. Smithson's home? Yes, Smithson. May I speak to him? It's Smithson speaking? Why, man, I didn't recognize your voice. What's the matter with you? Can you hear me? Speak louder. That's better. Now listen carefully. It's about the de Raun policy. I want you to pass the complete description of the jewels we got from Guydamour to Scotland Yard immediately. What are you giggling for? There's nothing funny about it. Smithson, you're drunk. I know it's Christmas, but this is serious. It's serious. Smithson...'

Mr. Cork irritably flashed the exchange.

'What happened?'

'He's cut off.'

'You see what we're up against,' said the Inspector blandly. 'I told you that it's Christmas Eve.'

For another ten minutes the two men talked earnestly together. Infected by the force of Mr. Cork's personality, the tired policeman tackled his case with new vigour. A police message asking Anton de Raun, or anybody who had news of him, to make immediate contact was put out by the B.B.C. Scotland Yard were asked to contact Smithson, the Anchor's Claims Manager at his home, and take him to the office, however tight he was, to collect the full description of the jewels. The *Sûreté* were wired for fullest particulars about Guydamour and his background.

So far, there were no significant clues as to the murderer. It was evident that he had got into Guydamour's room by climbing up the ivy. He had battered his victim to death with a tyre lever which he had kept hidden in a roll of newspaper. Subsequently, it seemed that he had barricaded the door with the wardrobe while he searched the room for the jewels. He then left the empty case on the floor and got out the same way he had come in.

The murder, according to the police surgeon, was committed some time between 11 p.m. and 1 a.m. Suspicion was not aroused until the chambermaid brought morning coffee just before nine o'clock. It was reported to the police by the Paradise shortly after.

Trelawny's theory was that Guydamour had been followed from Paris. He said the job had the autograph of one of the gangs, or an individual out of one of the gangs, who had been terrorizing the South of France. He had already warned the police in Marseilles.

Mr. Cork was much more interested in two telephone calls, one incoming and one outgoing, which had been taken and made by Guydamour. The first was easily remembered by the operator at the hotel. Almost as soon as he arrived, she'd accepted a call from Paris.

Subsequently, Guydamour himself had made a personal call to London. The London call, an eleven-and-ninepenny one, was recorded on his unpaid bill. It had been traced to a West End hotel. The hotel was the one where Anton de Raun was staying up to the time of his marriage at the Registrar's office to Fanny Fairfield.

As they talked, Aloysia stood about the office wringing his hands and mopping away the perspiration with his handkerchief. He had given up all hope of saving the Christmas business. The way events were shaping, he'd be lucky if he had any customers left at all for the colossal celebrations he had planned for New Year's Eve.

'I think that's all we can do tonight, Inspector.'

'I can't tell you, sir, how grateful I am for your help.'

'You forget, I have a very personal interest.'

'I don't think I should feel overanxious about the jewels if I were you, sir. I can't believe that the thief can hold on to a hot packet like that for very long. The strings of rubies are said to be among the finest in the world, aren't they?'

'Guydamour described them as the most exquisite collection of Siamese gems ever assembled.'

'Then the moment the thief tries to shift them, we've got him.'

'I hope so.'

'By the way, what's the value?'

'It's been very difficult to make a figure. Alouette was said to have insured them for a million francs when francs were twenty to the golden sovereign. We were asked to give cover of £100,000. We agreed to £75,000.'

'Where did Alouette get them?'

'I thought you read the papers. The story goes that they were given to her, in the days when she was the toast of Maxims, by Izzy Loup, the South African millionaire. When she died in the South of France during the war, Goering tried to lay hands on them for his own collection. But nothing more was heard of Alouette's Worms until the papers published the story that they were safe and that the complete parure was to be offered for auction in the London Sale Rooms. Subsequently, Anton de Raun, announcing his engagement to Fanny Fairfield, said that he'd purchased them by private treaty as a wedding present.'

'I'd like to know where he got the money.'

'So would I,' said Mr. Cork enigmatically.

He looked at Aloysia.

'You appreciate, I suppose, that I must have another bedroom for my wife. She mustn't sleep in that room.'

'But we are full, Mr. Cork. We are stuffed right up. I 'ave nothing, not even an attic.'

'You've said that before. You'll have to think again.'

M. Aloysia looked at Mr. Cork with the beady eyes of a stoated rabbit. The Inspector smiled.

'The de Rauns haven't turned up. Why not put Mr. and Mrs. Cork in the bridal suite?'

'But suppose they arrive unexpected. What do I do? They 'ave reserved.'

'So much the better,' said Mr. Cork. 'If Mr. de Raun arrives unexpectedly, I shall have an early opportunity for a private conversation with him.'

M. Aloysia, the best hotel manager in Europe, threw up his hands in total surrender.

The dance floor was crowded with sad-looking people in tinsel hats. Clouds of balloons floated down from the ceiling, and the diners who were left behind at their tables solemnly amused themselves blowing out paper tubes with feathers on the end and making shrill blasts with wooden whistles. The English, in their way, were having a Gala Night.

Mr. Cork threaded through the tables to the corner where Phoebe was waiting quietly behind a Cona of black coffee. He smiled at her as he sat down.

'I suppose the news is bad,' she said.

'Not entirely. We're moving into the bridal suite.'

'Oh, why?'

'De Raun hasn't turned up, so Aloysia thought we'd like it. Aren't you pleased?'

'I've got something to tell you, Monty. You know that man who followed us when we came down from our room? He has been sitting by himself over there watching me all through dinner. He's gone now. He went off as soon as you came back.'

'Never mind him. I want something to eat.'

Phoebe was curious, but she was much too experienced a wife to pester him with questions. As they talked in a desultory way while he had his supper, she noticed that half the time he wasn't listening.

'Here comes Mr. Aloysia,' she said, after a long silence.

'I expect he's going to show us to our suite.'

'It is all prepared,' said Aloysia with something of his old panache. 'Your luggage has been moved and your suite is ready, Madame.'

'Thank you, Mr. Aloysia.'

'No. Mr. Cork, please. No bill. To-night you are the guest of the Paradise.'

Preening himself, bobbing his head to his favoured customers, the manager led them through the restaurant, along the avenue of Christmas trees, to the gilded lift. The suite was only half a floor up, but the entrée had to be arranged in style. Remembering him only a little while ago in the manager's office, Mr. Cork couldn't help admiring the manner in which the born *hôtelier* was making the best of a bad job.

'Your suite, Madame.'

M. Aloysia threw open the door which led into the lobby and the second door which opened up into the sitting-room. Out of the corner of her eye, Phoebe saw the tessellated bathroom, with its sunken rose-hued tub and ivory-capped taps. The sitting-room, with french windows opening on to a balcony overlooking the bay, was dressed with huge bowls of white and pink carnations and baskets of long-stemmed rose-buds in a froth of bows of white ribbon. Even Phoebe, accustomed to luxury, was impressed.

'So this is how film stars live,' she said.

M. Aloysia made a gallant bow.

'It is a setting more befitting to a *grande dame* like yourself, Madame.'

With open palms, he backed his way out of the suite.

'Well!' said Phoebe contentedly.

But almost at once she gave a cry of surprise. Mr. Cork, who was peeping through the curtains towards the sea, looked over his shoulder with raised eyebrows. A little man in a crumpled suit, dusted with cigarette ash, had detached himself from the deep comfort of an armchair. He was the same man who had shadowed them into the restaurant and kept a watch on Mrs. Cork throughout her dinner.

'Who the hell are you?' growled Mr. Cork. 'How did you get in?'

'I bribed the luggage porter,' said the man unconcernedly. 'My name's Chris Sparrow. I expect you've heard of me.'

'Of course I haven't heard of you.'

'But I have,' said Phoebe. 'You write in one of the papers, don't you?'

'That's me,' said Chris Sparrow. 'Do you mind if I pour myself a drink?'

He didn't wait for an invitation. Mr. Cork made a rumble in his throat like an awakening volcano.

'Damn your impudence,' he exploded.

'Granted,' said Chris Sparrow.

'My wife and I have noticed that you've been following us throughout this evening. You admit you've bribed your way in here. Before I have you thrown out, I want an explanation.'

'That's exactly what I'm here to give you. To be quite honest, Mr. Cork, I smell a good story.'

'You've discovered my name?'

'It's in the hotel register. I also know you by reputation. To be quite frank...'

'That's courteous of you.'

'I came here on the de Raun-Fanny Fairfield story. It's a flop because they haven't shown up. The other Press boys have cleared off. Suits me. It means I've got a beat on the stiff found in the hotel this morning.'

Mr. Cork glanced anxiously at his wife, but it was evident that she was uncomprehending.

'Phoebe, dear,' he said. 'I'd like to continue this conversation with Mr. Sparrow in private. Would you mind going to the bedroom?'

Mrs. Cork smiled her acquiescence.

'Don't stay up too late,' she said.

Her husband waited until she had closed the bedroom door behind her. Then he glared at Chris Sparrow.

'You needn't interpret that,' he said, 'as an invitation to extend this conversation. I am simply anxious to spare my wife the knowledge of the grisly information which you seem to have ferreted out of the hotel. Bribery again?'

Chris Sparrow grinned.

'Maybe a little palm-greasing here and there.'

'You still haven't explained what you want with me.'

'That's easy. This morning, a murder. This evening, the biggest noise in the insurance world, that's you, arrives from London. You immediately go to the room where the stiff was found. Later, you're in conference with Trelawny. To-night, you take over de Raun's suite.'

'Well?'

'It must be a big story to bring you here on Christmas Eve.'

'So that's your excuse for breaking-in to my private apartment. I suppose you expect me to give you a sensational interview.'

'That's the ticket.'

'You must be mad.'

'I'm not, you know.'

He poured himself another drink.

'I hear you're looking for Anton de Raun.'

'How do you know that?'

'Contact of mine.'

'You seem to have some unpleasant contacts.'

'This one has the unpleasant habit of keeping the radio on all day. He heard the police message you put out for de Raun about a quarter of an hour ago on the B.B.C.'

'Do you think you know where de Raun is?'

'I have a theory.'

'You lost him after the wedding.'

'Granted. He pulled a fast one. I don't know why. He meant to come here. Something must have changed his mind for him.'

'Have you waited twenty-four hours to decide that? If you're as smart a newspaperman as you act to be, I should have thought you'd have tested your theory long before this.'

'I've told you why I haven't. I've smelt a bigger story here. Besides, I rather like the Paradise.'

'What's this theory of yours?'

'Not so fast, Mr. Cork. If I can put you on to de Raun's track, what will you do to help me?'

They both lit cigarettes for themselves.

'I must warn you of the dangers of withholding important information from the police, Mr. Sparrow. This is a serious business.'

'So the story is as good as that?'

He blew the ash off the end of his cigarette as it dangled in his mouth. He studied Mr. Cork's face with concentration. Then he chuckled: 'How much are they insured for?'

Mr. Cork couldn't sleep. He slewed round and round in his bed, listening to the muffled music of the sea, rising and falling, as the rollers curled over the beach outside his bedroom window. His brain was pumping as restlessly as the waves.

The office had given cover on these wretched jewels before they'd consulted him. Not that the office was to blame; on the face of it, they'd done a good stroke of business. As the Anchor's own experts couldn't examine the gems until they were actually in de Raun's possession, they'd very properly knocked 25 per cent. off Guydamour's estimated value, raised the premium to 1½ per cent., reinsured heavily and granted temporary cover only. But, temporarily, de Raun was covered. When Smithson had brought him the file and he realized that the company was committed to carrying the risk on these over-publicized jewels, he knew in his bones that even a few days was too long. He'd tried to contact Guydamour in Paris, but he'd already left for England. The brokers had attempted to get hold of de Raun, but de Raun was getting married. He'd followed them both to the Paradise, but it was already too late: Guydamour was murdered. Anton de Raun had gone Heaven-knows-where. The company was liable on the evidence of a dead man for the theft of valuables they'd never even seen.

It was an unholy alliance that he'd entered into with this newspaper fellow. But Sparrow had proved that he had a nose for information and, if he could get a line, any sort of a line, on de Raun's whereabouts, he could have his story, and welcome. De Raun… de Raun… the very sea seemed to be hissing his name.

He must have dozed. When he stirred again, the luminous dial of his watch showed 3 a.m. He lay on his back, smoked a cigarette and longed for daylight. Unwilling to waken Phoebe, unable to contain himself any longer in bed, he fumbled for his dressing-gown and slippers. Tiptoeing through the darkness, he felt his way towards the door of the sitting-room. He turned the handle as quietly as he could. He did it so quietly that the man with a torch who was feeling the tumblers for the combination of a safe, hidden behind a picture in the wall, never noticed him.

Mr. Cork stood mouse-still until with deft gloved fingers the man swung open the door of the little safe and groped inside.

'How did you know there was a safe there?' said Mr. Cork. 'I didn't.'

Half-turning, the man plunged his hand into his pocket. Mr. Cork flicked on the lights. Dazzled by the sudden glare, the man crouched down with the cornered concentration of a rat in a drain.

'From the gesture you made just now, I imagine that you're armed,' said Mr. Cork, 'but it's quite unnecessary to invite the attentions of the hangman by shooting at me. The window, by which you entered, is still open. There's nothing to stop you leaving by the same route that you came in.'

'This is a frame-up,' muttered the man hoarsely. He used the American phrase with an affected American accent.

'I rather think it is,' said Mr. Cork, 'but I'm not the framer. Would you like a drink? You've been working very hard.'

'What's the game, guv?'

In his surprise, he relapsed into Cockney.

'I want you to tell me, if you will, what you were looking for in that safe, and who put you up to it?'

'I ain't touched nothing, guv. Honest, I haven't.'

'I know. The safe's empty. Have a drink? Come on, you've got nothing to lose and you can do yourself a bit of good by talking to me.'

'Are you going to turn me over?'

'You haven't stolen anything—that's not your fault, but you haven't—and I'll forgive you personally for breaking into my apartment in the middle of the night. If the police pick you up, and they probably will, they'll have very little to charge you with; that is, if you take the precaution to throw away that pistol.'

'O.K., guv, you can 'ave it.'

He handed the pistol over like a guilty child. Mr. Cork placed it gingerly in his dressing-gown pocket. In return he gave the burglar a whisky and soda.

'There was a murder in the hotel last night,' he said casually.

'Murder, did you say?'

'Yes, murder.'

'No wonder you copped me. I must get out.'

'Don't hurry. You may be able to help us.'

'I know nothing about it. Across m'heart, I don't.'

'Yes, you do. You and the murderer were both after the same loot. I want to know how you yourself got on to the fact that you might find Alouette's Worms in a private safe in this sitting-room to-night? Who gave you the tip?'

'Chap I met.'

'Where?'

'South of France.'

'You're operating there, are you?'

'Mostly. I got left there after the war.'

'Deserter?'

'You said you'd give me a break, guv.'

'I said nothing of the sort. I said if you helped me it might do you a bit of good. Who was this chap?'

'Dunno his name. He was a sailor off one of the English yachts at Cannes. Yacht called *Vera*, I think it was. The name was on his jersey.'

'What precisely did he tell you?'

'He told me that if I wanted to do a plumb easy job, this was it.'

'When was this?'

'Six weeks ago.'

'You mean me to believe that an unknown sailor off an English yacht at Cannes told you that if you came to this specific apartment on the night of Christmas Eve, you'd find a safe behind that picture...'

'That's right. With the stuff inside.'

'And you believed the story?'

'It was in all the papers.'

'Naturally you believe everything that you read in the papers.'

'I swear I'm telling you the truth, guv. I don't 'old with murder.'

'I think you are telling the truth. I'm only astonished at your incredible stupidity. You opened that safe with a certain skill, but you fell for a conspiracy which wouldn't trick a child.'

''Arf a mo, guv. Nobody can make a sucker o' me.'

'But they have. Now get out the way you came. If you're making for France, I warn you that all the ports are watched. If the police pick you up, I'll put in a word for you.'

The burglar looked from Mr. Cork to the window and back again.

'No, guv, I won't do it. It's a fair cop and I'll take my chance with the police.'

'You've got more sense than I gave you credit for.'

'My name's Harry. Don't tell 'em about the pistol, will you?'

Mr. Cork smiled.

'Give yourself another drink,' he said.

Chris Sparrow, yawning and unshaven, arrived in Mr. Cork's apartment looking more unkempt than ever.

'This is a fine time to turn out on Christmas Day,' he said. 'Who's this?'

'He's a friend of mine named Harry. Harry, this is Mr. Sparrow.'

The two shook hands.

'You keep early hours, don't you?' growled Sparrow.

'Harry works on a night shift,' said Mr. Cork. 'He's helping me on this case. Do you want a cup of tea to wake you up?'

'I could do with it.'

'Don't make too much noise. My wife is still in bed.'

'Where we all ought to be. What have you dug me out for at this hour? I haven't got any news yet.'

'But I have, Sparrow. I think you can help us. Do you know the South of France?'

'Ought to. I've written enough about it.'

'Have you ever heard of a big luxury yacht there, name of *Vera*?'

'Might have. Who does it belong to?'

'That's what we must find out.'

'Soon check that.'

'At this time, on Christmas morning?'

Chris Sparrow tapped his nose with his finger.

'There's one place that never shuts,' he said, picking up the 'phone. 'Get Central, London, 7440.'

'What do you know about this fellow de Raun, Sparrow?'

Chris Sparrow looked over the top of the mouthpiece.

'Handsome playboy living on his wits. Good athlete, drives racing cars, rides the Cresta Run, always marries rich film stars, does a bit of yachting...'

'Yachting?'

'I see what you're getting at. Hello, Press Association? Happy Christmas to you. This is Chris Sparrow. Can I talk to the news room? O.K... Howdye, pal... Be a good chap and look up Lloyd's Register of Yachts for me. I want to know who owns a big girl called *Vera*. Yes, I'll wait.'

◇◇◇

'You said you had a theory of your own about de Raun's whereabouts?' Mr. Cork went on.

'Yep. I know where he's garaged his car.'

'Where?'

'Not far from here.'

'Are you sure it's his car?'

'You haven't seen the car?'

'That means he came as far as Exquay, although he didn't come to the hotel.'

'That's the way of it... Hello, P.A... That sounds like it... Motor yacht of 100 tons... Southampton... Who's the owner? Who?... That's the ticket... Thanks, chum... I hope I can do the same for you some time... Happy Christmas.'

'Well?' said Mr. Cork.

'*Vera* belongs to Vic Dimitri, the film producer. He was the best man at de Raun's wedding.'

'Can we get Dimitri on the 'phone?'

'He won't like it, but we can try.'

They traced him to a number in Elstree. A sleepy voice answered the call. Yes, it was Vic Dimitri: who the hell was that?

'Tell him the police want to contact de Raun. Can he help us?'

Chris Sparrow echoed the question.

'Sure, he's honeymooning on my yacht.'

'Where is she?'

'How the hell should I know?'

He cut off.

'Ring the district officer of the Coastguards.'

'He might have headed across the Channel.'

'He might; but it's been blowing hard, and with luck he's had to hug the coast.'

'How do you ring the Coastguards?'

'I imagine you just ask for them like the police.'

It worked. Another sleepy voice promised to check with the look-outs. Within a quarter of an hour, he called back. *Vera* had been sighted off Plymouth at dawn the day before yesterday. She'd also been logged by an amateur watcher off Falmouth. She hadn't been sighted at Penzance. She was probably sheltering from the gale in one of the anchorages beyond Falmouth.

'Try Cowrie Cove.'

It was still half-light when Mr. Cork backed his silver Bentley out of the hotel lock-up. He'd left a message with the police telling Inspector Trelawny to follow him to Cowrie Cove as soon as possible. He'd assured Phoebe that he'd be back in time for Christmas presents after lunch. He was accompanied by one very bewildered burglar and one very jaded newspaper man.

They were climbing into Dartmoor, circling Plymouth to avoid the ferry which, at the crack of daylight on Christmas Day, was hardly likely to be working. A rime of frost silvered the winding, unwelcoming road. Dank mists swirled in the hollows and blotted out the hills. Nothing moved except the buzzards swinging lazily from the fence posts to make way for the passing car. Chris Sparrow was fast asleep in the back seat. Harry sat stiffly at the side of Mr. Cork.

'You know where we are, don't you, Harry?'

'No, guv.'

'Then, in your professional capacity, I hope you never become better acquainted with it. This is Dartmoor.'

'The Moor?'

'Yes.'

'Where are you taking me to?'

'Don't sound so anxious. You're on the side of the law this morning. I'm giving you the chance to make things straight with the police. It may not be pleasant.'

'I'll take m'chance.'

'We'll make an honest man of you yet. Now listen. You've heard from my conversation with Mr. Sparrow that we're going to a cove in Cornwall where we hope to find the motor yacht *Vera*. Aboard it, you may recognize the seaman who gave you the information which tempted you to burgle the Paradise. If you do, give no indication of it until I give you the signal. Is that clear?'

'O.K.'

'Now I'll take a chance. If you'll put your hand in my overcoat pocket you'll find your pistol. Put it in your own pocket. You won't produce it unless a pistol is drawn on us. You won't fire except in self-protection.'

'Are you sure this is a straight job?'

'It's one of the dirtiest jobs I've ever had to deal with. But, for once, you're on the clean end of it.'

On empty roads, the Bentley silently swallowed the miles through Two Bridges, Tavistock and Callington to Falmouth. Mr. Cork, who ordinarily never drove faster than thirty miles an hour, cruised at sixty and hardly noticed it. In his moments of serenity, his caution was exasperating. But, when he had a case, he could be as rash as a hunter on the brush of his fox.

Beyond the narrow, deserted streets of Falmouth, the car stretched herself on the coast road to Penzance.

'Look out on the left for a signpost to Cowrie Cove. According to the map, we're almost on it.'

They nearly overran it. The signpost was half-effaced by the pummelling of wind and weather. It hung over a narrow lane choked with dead brambles and bracken. It was a cart-track, not a road at all. But Mr. Cork bulldozed into it and, bumping Chris Sparrow into wakefulness, pushed the car over the frozen, rutted ground through windswept pasture into a steep descent towards the sea.

'Is this where we're meant to be?' asked Sparrow.

'This is where the Coastguards told us to look.'

'If de Raun's here, he's certainly picked a quiet hide-out. You're not taking the car much farther, are you?'

Chris Sparrow, completely imperturbable in the artificial air-conditioned surroundings of the Paradise, was as nervous as a lost child now that he faced the unknown perils of the open countryside.

'We'll park here,' said Mr. Cork.

An area of grass, close-nibbled by the rabbits, indicated where the tourists left their cars in the summer. Through a ragged, narrow gap in the cliffs, they glimpsed a slice of the white-crested sea. Mr. Cork ran the Bentley over the humpy turf until he found a spot where the car was hidden from the road. Then he stopped. He buttoned up his overcoat and, followed by Harry, he stretched his legs.

The salty wind came up to meet them with an enquiring, penetrating lick. Harry, peak-faced, sunk his head in his coat-collar. Chris Sparrow remained obstinately in the car.

'Are you coming?' said Mr. Cork gruffly.

Sparrow groaned.

'How I hate fresh air,' he said.

But, reluctantly, he got out of the car.

'Have we got far to walk?'

'You can see the sea.'

Together, the ill-assorted trio stumbled down the rocky lane, a trench walled in dry stone, to the shore. They passed a padlocked, iron-roofed hut advertising minerals and ice-cream. At the beginning of a stone groin running down to the beach, they saw a heap of rotting lobster-pots. Then they twisted through a dripping gutter in the grey stone cliffs on to the sandy beach.

In summer, Cowrie Cove is a Cornish beauty spot. In December, it is as lonely and hostile as a desert island. The gulls screaming with the anguish of lost souls, and the painted oyster-catchers, piping in shrill alarm, underline the desolation. Chris Sparrow hung back with the air of one in the presence of his Maker.

They stood there, like three castaways on the shore, gazing wide-eyed at the vision in the cove. A slim white motor yacht, with tapering bows and a tracery of fittings on her superstructure as delicate as a cobweb, was nodding like a graceful white ghost under the wall of the cliffs. *Vera* was painted in gold on her stern.

Beyond the shelter of the cove, the wind whipped the waves into a white fury. Inside it, behind the protecting arm of a curved headland, the sea lapped in oily quiet. The yacht was riding serenely in the embrace of a natural harbour. Her companion-way, lying fore and aft, was down. A sleek motor-boat with engine turning was moored at the foot of it.

Mr. Cork drew his two companions behind a seaweed-sticky boulder, where they were out of sight of the yacht.

'As we may not be welcome,' he said, 'we'll wait here until somebody comes ashore with the launch.'

It wasn't a long wait. A figure, wrapped in a duffle-coat, who was presumably one of the hands, came down the companion-way, and casting off, put the motor-boat in to the shore. As he tied up on a ring-bolt in the groin, Mr. Cork walked up to him.

'Good morning,' he said. 'I have urgent business with Mr. de Raun. No doubt you picked up the police message for him on the radio last night.'

'Radio's out of order,' said the hand.

'Indeed? Then that makes it all the more important that I should see Mr. de Raun immediately. Will you put us aboard?'

'Are you the police?'

'The police are on their way here. For my part, I have some urgent business to discuss with Mr. de Raun before they arrive.'

'You're not Press, are you?'

'No, it's a business matter.'

'Do these other gentlemen want to go aboard too?'

'They're with me.'

The seaman scratched his head.

'We're not supposed to do it without orders.'

'I assure you that Mr. de Raun will want to see us. I've already spoken to Mr. Dimitri. This is a serious business.'

The hand wavered.

'Is it Mr. Dimitri's orders?'

'Mr. Dimitri told us Mr. de Raun was aboard.'

'O.K., I'll run you out. After all, Mr. Dimitri's my proper boss and the sooner this damned Christmas cruise is over the better.'

They got into the boat and the hand started the engine.

'When did you start out?'

'Two days ago, just as we were on the point of going home for Christmas. Got orders to sail down to Exquay to pick up this party.'

'When did they join you?'

'Two nights ago. We had to lay off the harbour for 'em. They came aboard about midnight: or, rather, she did. He turned up later. We were supposed to set course for Monte Carlo, but the weather turned nasty, the lady got seasick, so here we are. Nice place to spend Christmas Day, I don't think.'

Chris Sparrow shuddered.

'If this is the way the film stars live, they can keep it.'

As the seaman held the launch steady at the companion-way, Mr. Cork pressed a pound into his palm.

'I'm obliged to you,' he said.

The seaman winked his thanks.

A tall, athletic man in a thick, roll-necked sweater and corduroy trousers appeared out of the cabin as Mr. Cork came aboard.

'What's all this?' he demanded.

He had blue eyes, sandy hair and a lean, sun-tanned face. He was probably over forty but he looked thirty-five, and he hadn't an ounce of spare flesh on him.

'Mr. de Raun?'

'That's me. I hope you're not Press?'

'No, sir, this is a business matter.'

'But I'm on my honeymoon. Can't it wait?'

'I'm afraid not.'

'All right,' said de Raun. 'Come into the saloon.'

As he held open the door for them under the covered sun-deck, he glanced suspiciously at Harry and Chris Sparrow, following in hangdog fashion in Mr. Cork's wake. But he made no comment.

'You're sure you're not Press men,' he said good-humouredly. 'That's what we came aboard this boat to avoid.'

'One of us is,' said Mr. Cork. 'Mr. Chris Sparrow, here.'

'I expect you've heard of me,' said Sparrow.

'Indeed, I have,' de Raun replied vaguely.

'But Mr. Sparrow isn't here to-day in his journalistic capacity.'

'Thank Heaven for that. Fanny and I have had too much publicity, you know. After the wedding we both felt that we simply had to escape. So, as we both like yachting, we chartered this one of Vic Dimitri's. We've had it before down in the South of France. Do you know Vic, Mr. Sparrow?'

'Sure; nice feller.'

'A very nice fellow. Do sit down, all of you. I'm sorry my wife isn't about. I'm afraid she's had a touch of seasickness.'

'I don't feel so good myself,' said Sparrow.

'Surely there's not enough movement to make you sick now. By the way, how did you find out where I was?'

'Dimitri told us.'

'Dear old Vic, eh? But he didn't know where we were sailing?'

'We checked with the Coastguards.'

'Indeed? Why so thorough?'

'There was a police message out for you on the radio last night.'

'For me?'

'If your radio hadn't broken down, you'd have heard it.'

'Yes, that was my fault. It's one reason why we're laying in here. The radio wasn't working properly so I started tinkering about with it and got the wires crossed. But never mind that. What's been happening in the great big world?'

The man oozed charm. His ease of manner was somehow sickening. As he talked, he admired his long-fingered hands and played casually with his signet ring. A smile, which was almost a sneer, played perpetually over his features.

'I'm sorry to have to tell you,' said Mr. Cork, 'that the jewels you were to have given to your wife as a wedding present have been stolen.'

'Stolen? Where? When?'

'Did you have an arrangement with your jeweller to deliver them to the Paradise Hotel?'

'Not necessarily at the Paradise. Guydamour simply arranged to contact me, either at Exquay or in London, when he arrived from Paris. We thought it just as well not to advertise his movements too widely.'

'Guydamour took the precaution of registering at the Paradise under an assumed name.'

'Good for him.'

'But it didn't save his life. He was murdered, battered to death with a tyre lever, two nights ago.'

'Guydamour murdered? But this is ghastly. Why didn't you tell me sooner? I can't believe it.'

'I'm afraid it's true.'

'Where did it happen?'

'In his bedroom at the Paradise.'

'Have the police any clue as to who did it?'

'They suspect one of the gangs operating in the South of France.'

De Raun gave a thoughtful nod.

'That's quite possible. Those jewels had altogether too much publicity for my liking. I told Guydamour so.'

'Yet you yourself made the announcement that you were giving Alouette's Worms to your wife?'

'Yes, it slipped out over a drink with one of the Press boys. At that time, I confess I didn't realize what a song and dance would be made of it. It's amazing what you chaps can dig up, isn't it, Mr. Sparrow?'

For answer, Chris Sparrow gave an ominous hiccup. The movement of the yacht might be slight, but his own discomfort was real enough.

'Is there somewhere I can go?' he said, with a green smile.

'Certainly,' said de Raun. 'The second door astern of this one. Don't lean over the side, it'll make a mess of the paintwork.'

'Thanks.'

Precipitately, Chris Sparrow made his retreat.

◇◇◇

'We'll have some hot coffee for you when you come back,' said de Raun.

'Your friend doesn't seem to be a very good sailor,' he went on cheerfully.

'He didn't have any breakfast. I expect that's upset him.'

'We'll soon fix that. By the way, that reminds me, I haven't asked you your name.'

'My name is Cork, Montague Cork of the Anchor Insurance Co.'

'Howdyedo?' He lazily stretched out his hand to be shaken.

'And your friends?'

'They're temporarily advising me.'

'Well, sir, what can I do for you?'

'Mine is the company which has insured these jewels of yours, Mr. de Raun. As I presume you will shortly be making a claim on us for the loss, it's important that I should make full enquiries.'

'We needn't bother about that now, need we? I confess I was quite unaware that you were even insuring me. That's all handled by my brokers. For the present, I'm much too concerned about poor old Guydamour. That's a bad business. We became quite close friends, you know.'

'Had you known him long?'

'A few years on and off. I remember I met him first in the *salle privée* at Monte Carlo.'

'So he was a gambler?'

'He liked a flutter, like most of us.'

'Did he play high?'

'I can't say I ever noticed. Why do you ask?'

'I just wondered what sort of man he was. But it doesn't matter. The *Sûreté* are checking up on him.'

'Ah, here's the coffee. How do you like it? *Au lait?*'

'Yes,' said Mr. Cork. 'And my friend too.'

'We must keep some for poor old Sparrow. He'll need it.'

'Did you ever see Alouette's Worms?'

'But of course,' smiled de Raun. 'Many times. I bought them, you know.'

'Has your wife seen them?'

'Certainly not. They were to be a surprise. You know, Mr. Cork, it's my own view that they'll be recovered. No thief could get away with a collection like that for long.'

'That's the opinion of the police, too. I hope you're both right.'

'I think you said the police have put out a message for me. I shall, of course, be delighted to see them, but I don't know that I can be of much help. I didn't actually know that Guydamour had arrived at the Paradise. In fact, I was wondering what had happened to him. He was supposed to contact me on the morning before the wedding.'

'He 'phoned your London hotel all right,' said Mr. Cork quietly.

'Did he? Well, he never got through to me.'

'I can quite understand that, at the last minute, you decided against going to the Paradise Hotel. But I'm surprised you never told them.'

'Really, that's my own affair,' laughed de Raun. 'But, if you must know, our idea, my wife and I, was that if we kept the hotel guessing we'd keep the Press guessing, too. Still, you'll be glad to hear that I'm putting them out of their misery to-day. I've sent one of the hands ashore to telephone. As soon as the weather improves, we're setting course for a warmer climate.'

'I hate to spoil your honeymoon, Mr. de Raun, but I fancy the police will want you to remain here, certainly until after the inquest.'

'You talk as if Guydamour's death were my personal concern. I'm terribly sad about it but, apart from the loss of the jewels, it's none of my business. By the way, I suppose there's no doubt that robbery was the motive; I mean you've got evidence that he had the jewels in his possession?'

'An empty jewel-box was found in the room with the body.'

'A heart-shaped case with a double-compartment and Fanny's initials on the lid?'

'I don't know about the initials but the rest of the description fits.'

'Then it's a bad business, all right. That's the jewel-case. We had it designed specially.'

'I suppose you realize that there'll be a lot more publicity over this.'

Anton de Raun threw up his hands in mock dismay.

'Poor Fanny,' he said. 'She's worn out with it.'

He poured himself some more coffee.

'Well, I think that's all,' he said, getting to his feet. 'In view of your sad news, I won't weigh anchor until I've given the police all the information I can. But I don't think there's much more that you and I can say to each other.'

'Would you think me impertinent,' said Mr. Cork, 'if I asked to meet the crew of this vessel before I leave?'

'What an extraordinary request. What on earth for?'

'If they're the regular crew, it's possible that my friend here may be able to identify one of them. If he can, it's of great importance to our case. That's so, isn't it, Harry?'

''Tisn't necessary, guv,' said Harry warily.

'Why not?'

''Cause 'e's 'ere. The chap what tipped me off on the job was him.'

He pointed accusingly at de Raun.

◇◇◇

De Raun gripped the edge of the table with long, strong fingers. He half rose from his swivel chair.

'You keep odd company,' he said to Mr. Cork.

'When I'm in odd company, I suit myself to circumstances. Please sit down.'

De Raun dropped stiffly into his chair.

'Are you sure you're right, Harry?'

''Course I'm right. He knows it, too. Him and his gentlemanly ways. He was dressed as a seaman when I met him.'

De Raun smiled again.

'I can't think what this fellow's talking about, but it's hardly likely that I should associate with a cheap little crook like him.'

'How did you know he was a crook?' asked Mr. Cork evenly. 'No, it's not your first mistake, de Raun. Your first mistake was when you said you didn't know that Guydamour had arrived at the Paradise; but you did know. Guydamour put through a call to you at your hotel in London, on the morning of your wedding. It wasn't an ordinary call; it was a personal one. It's recorded on the hotel bill that the call was completed. What did he tell you? All right, I'll tell you myself. He informed you that the insurance company was getting suspicious. He told you that he'd just had a call from Paris warning him that I'd been asking pertinent questions. He'd got cold feet. But you wouldn't call it off. You arranged to keep a secret rendezvous with him that night in his bedroom at the Paradise. I can't prove that yet, but the murderer was careless about finger-prints, because he never doubted that a celebrated honeymooner like himself would ever be suspected. Indeed, he was even stupid enough to use a tyre lever as a weapon which probably came from his own car.

I've no doubt Guydamour made you a prearranged signal to show you his room as you waited in the gardens.'

'You forget. I was with my newly-married wife.'

'Not at that moment. You sent your wife away to the yacht in the motor-boat while you held back on the excuse of parking the car or something of that sort. It didn't take long to accomplish your plan. Guydamour, your accomplice, was waiting to welcome you. When you shinned up the ivy, he opened the window and held out his hand…'

'All of which shows to what limits insurance companies will go to evade paying a claim. I don't want your money. Everybody knows that I'm a well-to-do man.'

'You mean everybody knows that you've got a well-to-do wife.'

'I can afford to ignore your cheap insults. What you don't explain, in this cooked-up story of yours, is what possible advantage it can be to me to lose the jewels and accept rather less than their proper value as compensation from the insurance company.'

'I don't believe you paid a farthing for the jewels, de Raun. Guydamour was in the conspiracy with you. You made a plot together to defraud my company. A very clever plot, too. By virtue of your social position and your engagement to Fanny Fairfield, you agreed with Guydamour to pretend to buy Alouette's Worms. You undertook to insure them and you took it on yourself to see to it that they'd be burgled the moment you got them. But you meant to do it properly. You wanted a real burglar and a real burglary. So you picked on poor little Harry here, a clever cracksman but a stupid man, as your tool. Because you were anxious not to introduce a third person into your plot, you took the foolish risk of dressing up as a seaman and tipping-off Harry yourself. You gave him the know-how on a plate, even to the position of a secret safe in the wall. You knew that, after the event, you could deal with Harry.

'In the end, Guydamour lost his nerve. But you couldn't afford to. So you made an even better job of it. You murdered your own accomplice. And you might have got away with it if you hadn't previously done such a good job with Harry. Because there were no newspapers, Harry knew nothing of the murder. Because I couldn't sleep, I caught him red-handed. Harry led me to you.'

'Have some more coffee,' said de Raun coolly. 'That lot's cold. I'll ring the bell for some.'

He put his hand under the table. When he lifted it again, he held a small automatic.

'I'm sorry to do this,' he said, 'but you're talking rather dangerously.'

'Don't move, Harry,' said Mr. Cork over his shoulder.

'Wise advice,' said de Raun.

'I must remind you that the police are on their way here, de Raun. That pistol is scarcely a recommendation of your innocence.'

'Get into that locker.'

With the muzzle of his pistol, de Raun indicated a large press in the corner of the saloon.

'Hurry up. Stand with your backs to the wall.'

He gave Mr. Cork a push, and launched a kick at Harry.

'You can shout your hearts out in there. Nobody will hear you. We're going for a long sea voyage together.'

He slammed the door and locked it.

'You told me not to shoot, guv,' whispered Harry in the dark.

'I'm glad you didn't try. De Raun, I'm sure, is a much quicker gunman than you are. But you can use your pistol now.'

'What for?'

'People who carry pistols always have one-track minds. I don't want you to shoot anybody. I just want you to blow the lock off this door.'

Harry felt about for the lock.

'If I had time,' he said, 'I could pick it.'

'If you took your time, we'd be half-way across the Channel.'

Harry let go with two shots from his gun. In the confined space of the cupboard, the noise was ear-splitting. The two of them burst out, in a cloud of powder smoke, like magicians in a pantomime.

They ran along the covered sundeck towards the bow of the ship. But they halted in time. The crew, eight of them, were standing on the fo'c'sle with their hands up watching the superstructure. Chris Sparrow was one of them. Mr. Cork took Harry by the arm, and drew him back.

'De Raun is obviously threatening them from the wheelhouse. Sparrow, I think, wasn't as green as he looked. He went out to make sure that the hands were on our side.'

'Can he start the boat, guv, without 'em?'

'I don't know enough about it, but I shouldn't be surprised.'

'What do we do?'

'We distract his attention, Harry.'

'How?'

'I'll see to that. You wait here.'

Mr. Cork quietly opened the door at the foot of the companion-way leading up to the wheelhouse.

'Do you want the gun?' said Harry in a hoarse whisper.

Mr. Cork shook his head. With hunched shoulders, he jutted out his chin and slowly climbed the creaking stairs. De Raun must surely hear him coming.

The door at the top of the dark companion-way was half-open, swinging gently with the movement of the anchored yacht. He could see the glittering brass of instruments in the wheelhouse and the gritty white enamel of the paintwork. But de Raun made no move.

Mr. Cork had only the vaguest notion of how to tackle him. It would be adequate if he could distract the man's attention long enough to give the crew on the fo'c'sle a chance to make a getaway. The risk that de Raun would shoot on sight couldn't be discounted; but the fact that he himself was unarmed was a certain protection. Normally, the best way of dealing with a man waving a pistol about was to reassure his immediate sense of security. Apart from that, there were very few people who could use one with any accuracy. He remembered with grim inconsequence that, in his own soldiering days in the First World War, he had failed completely to hit a tin hat with one of the old Webley revolvers at five yards range.

Outside the wheelhouse, he flattened his back against the wall of the companion-way. He slowly put out his hand and, with the tips of his fingers, he pushed the door wide open. Nothing happened.

'Are you there, de Raun?'

There was no answer.

'I'm coming in there with you. It's unnecessary to shoot at me because I'm unarmed. To reassure you, I'm going to show myself with my arms raised over my head.'

He took a deep breath. Raising his hands, he stepped into the glass-fronted cabin. As he crossed the threshold, he was grabbed round the waist. De Raun had been waiting for him behind the door. Half-thrown off his feet, he struggled in the hugging grip of de Raun's left arm; in his right, he still held the pistol levelled at the men grouped below on the foredeck.

'Keep still or I'll brain you.'

Wriggling in de Raun's grasp, Mr. Cork kicked him sharply on the shin. He was rewarded with a yelp of pain. De Raun fell down. Below on the deck, he heard a shout. The crew started running towards them. De Raun got to his feet, and he, too, ran.

He threw his leg over the rail and dropped overboard into the motorboat as the hands crowded in on him. But they fell back as, bending over the engine, he flourished his pistol menacingly.

The motor picked up with a gurgling hum. He cast off and, reeling back as the boat surged forward, he drove towards the shore. He was almost at the groin when a posse of police, led by Trelawny, came through the gap in the cliffs.

De Raun swung the boat away again. The launch was a fast one. With the throttle full open, it settled down on its stern with its bow slapping on the swell. With a spuming wake, it circled round the yacht in a wide arc and raced out of the shelter of the cove into the open sea.

Then, from a thing of fleeting beauty, it was reduced to the pathetic impotence of a cork. It rolled and plunged in the broken water, one moment with its bow pointing to the sky and the next with upraised stern showing the screw spinning aimlessly in the air. Against the crested cruelty of the ocean, it was lost. With every roll, de Raun was shipping water like a bucket dripping in a well. The seagulls crowded round, wailing like mourners at a wake. From the yacht and the shore, they watched him wrestling with the unconquerable. He went overboard a few seconds before the launch heeled over and, raising her cream bows in the air, slid to the bottom to make a bed for the congers and the other carrion-eaters of the sea. They didn't see de Raun again. They didn't expect to.

It was a quarter of an hour before they could swing out another boat to bring the police aboard. Fanny Fairfield woke up feeling so much better that she peered out of the porthole. Seeing so many men coming aboard, she took her time dressing and getting her make-up in proper order. When she came on deck, Inspector Trelawny had renewed the laborious business of taking statements and his officers had started the search of the yacht for the missing jewels.

◇◇◇

Chris Sparrow scooped the biggest story of his life as a newspaperman. Harry, until economic circumstances led him astray again, enjoyed for a while the strange experience of being an honest citizen. M. Aloysia, contrary to all his expectations, did a record New Year's business. Phoebe had an emerald ring from her husband to make up for the way he'd spoilt her Christmas. Fanny Fairfield married again, quite soon. Only Mr. Cork seemed discontented.

He called conference after conference with his chief executives. He harried his staff with a paper chase of memoranda dictated from the formidable sanctum of his private office. He was determined that there'd never be a de Raun case again.

But he couldn't avoid the publicity. Under great pressure, when the police proceedings were over, he consented to grant an interview to the Press. He'd never done it before and, after the event, he swore that he'd never put up with it again. At the conference, he explained, with his usual grave clarity, the main details of the fraud. He emphasized that people who try to cheat the insurance companies are pitting themselves against the experience of a business which survives by its capacity to distinguish the honest man from the dishonest one.

He answered all the questions which the Press reporters put to him on the de Raun Case, except one. When they pressed him, he smiled.

'That's my secret,' he said.

When they asked him why, he lit a Passing Cloud. Staring at them over his half-glasses, with his lined face wreathed in the blue smoke, he considered his answer.

'Gentlemen,' he said, 'there are certain cases of fraud, and this is one of them, when it would not be in the interest of the great insurance companies—and may I remind you that, for all the world, that means the insurance companies of the City of London—to reveal the whole truth. There are always dishonest people who might make improper use of the knowledge. Thank you, gentlemen, that's all. If you'll excuse me, I have a Board Meeting to attend.'

Over many a drink in the 'Cheshire Cheese,' in Fleet Street, Chris Sparrow has told the story of Alouette's Worms. But neither he nor his friends have been able to guess Mr. Cork's secret. Can you?

The solutions to 'Mr. Cork's Secret,'
as published by *Lilliput* magazine,
appear on page 307.

# The Santa Claus Club

## *Julian Symons*

Today, Julian Symons (1912–94) is best remembered as a crime fiction critic who was responsible for an outstanding history of the genre, *Bloody Murder*. Symons argued that the detective story had evolved into the crime novel, and in later life, he became rather dismissive of some of the traditional puzzle-mysteries which he had enjoyed in his younger days— although his admiration for the most talented exponents of the classic whodunit, such as Agatha Christie and Anthony Berkeley, never faltered.

*Bloody Murder* has proved so influential that it is easy to forget that, in addition to his achievements as a critic and historian, Symons was also a poet and a gifted writer of mystery stories. His finest novels, such as *The Man Who Killed Himself, The Plot against Roger Rider*, and *Death's Darkest Face*, show his skill at depicting character, but are also conspicuously well plotted, and his flair for the tricks and techniques of the conventional detective puzzle was evident early in his career, in books such as *Bland Beginning*, and in his twisty tales about private investigator Francis Quarles.

The Quarles stories have been neglected for many years, but this tale is a reminder that Symons was more adept at the traditional mystery than he might, in later life, have cared to admit.

◇◇◇

# 1

It is not often, in real life, that letters are written recording implacable hatred nursed over the years, or that private detectives are invited by peers to select dining clubs, or that murders occur at such dining clubs, or that they are solved on the spot by a process of deduction. The case of the Santa Claus Club provided an example of all these rarities.

The case began one day a week before Christmas, when Francis Quarles went to see Lord Acrise. He was a rich man, Lord Acrise, and an important one, the chairman of this big building concern and director of that and the other insurance company, and consultant to the Government on half a dozen matters. He had been a harsh, intolerant man in his prime, and was still hard enough in his early seventies, Quarles guessed, as he looked at the beaky nose, jutting chin and stony blue eyes under thick brows. They sat in the study of Acrise's house just off the Brompton Road.

'Just tell me what you think of these.'

*These* were three letters, badly typed on a machine with a worn ribbon. They were all signed with the name James Gliddon. The first two contained vague references to some wrong done to Gliddon by Acrise in the past. They were written in language that was wild, but unmistakably threatening. 'You have been a whited sepulchre for too long, but now your time has come… You don't know what I'm going to do, now I've come back, but you won't be able to help wondering and worrying… The mills of God grind slowly, but they're going to grind you into little bits for what you've done to me.'

The third letter was more specific. 'So the thief is going to play Santa Claus. That will be your last evening alive. *I shall be there*, Joe Acrise, and I shall watch with pleasure as you squirm in agony.'

Quarles looked at the envelopes. They were plain and cheap. The address was typed, and the word 'Personal' was on top of the envelope. 'Who is James Gliddon?'

The stony eyes glared at him. 'I'm told you're to be trusted. Gliddon was a school friend of mine. We grew up together in the slums of Nottingham. We started a building company together. It did well for a time, then went bust. There was a lot of money missing. Gliddon kept the books. He got five years for fraud.'

'Have you heard from him since then? I see all these letters are recent.'

'He's written half a dozen letters, I suppose, over the years. The last one came—oh, seven years ago, I should think. From the Argentine.' Acrise stopped, then said abruptly, 'Snewin tried to find him for me, but he'd disappeared.'

'Snewin?'

'My secretary. Been with me twelve years.'

He pressed a bell. An obsequious, fattish man, whose appearance somehow put Quarles in mind of an enormous mouse, scurried in.

'Snewin? Did we keep any of those old letters from Gliddon?'

'No, sir. You told me to destroy them.'

'The last ones came from the Argentine, right?'

'From Buenos Aires to be exact, sir.'

Acrise nodded, and Snewin scurried out. Quarles said, 'Who else knows this story about Gliddon?'

'Just my wife.' Acrise bared yellow teeth in a grin. 'Unless somebody's been digging into my past.'

'And what does this mean, about you playing Santa Claus?'

'I'm this year's chairman of the Santa Claus Club. We hold our raffle and dinner next Monday.'

Then Quarles remembered. The Santa Claus Club had been formed by ten rich men. Each year they met, every one of them dressed up as Santa Claus, and held a raffle. The members took it in turn to provide the prize that was raffled—it might be a case of Napoleon brandy, a modest cottage with some exclusive salmon fishing rights attached to it, a Constable painting. Each Santa Claus bought one ticket for the raffle, at a cost of one thousand guineas. The total of ten thousand guineas was given to a Christmas charity. After the raffle the assembled Santa Clauses, each accompanied by one guest, ate a traditional Christmas dinner. The whole thing was a combination of various English characteristics: enjoyment of dressing up, a wish to help charities, and the desire also that the help given should not go unrecorded. The dinners of the Santa Claus Club got a good deal of publicity, and there were those who said that it would have been perfectly easy for the members to give their money to charities in a less conspicuous manner.

'I want you to find Gliddon,' Lord Acrise said. 'Don't mistake me, Mr. Quarles. I don't want to take action against him, I want to help him. I wasn't to blame—don't think I admit that—but it was hard that Jimmy Gliddon should go to jail. I'm a hard man, have been all my life, but I don't think my worst enemies would call me mean. Those who've helped me know that when I die they'll find they're not forgotten.

Jimmy Gliddon must be an old man now. I'd like to set him up for the rest of his life.'

'To find him by next Monday is a tall order,' Quarles said. 'But I'll try.'

He was at the door when Acrise said casually, 'By the way, I'd like you to be my guest at the Club dinner on Monday night.'

Did that mean, Quarles wondered, that he was to act as official poison-taster if he did not find James Gliddon?

## 2

There were two ways of trying to find Gliddon—by investigation of his career after leaving prison, and through the typewritten letters. Quarles took the job of tracing the past, leaving the letters to his secretary, Molly Player.

From Scotland Yard Quarles found out that Gliddon had spent nearly four years in prison, from 1913 to late 1916. He had joined a Nottinghamshire Regiment when he came out, and the records of this Regiment showed that he had been demobilized in August, 1919, with the rank of Sergeant. In 1923 he had been given a sentence of three years for an attempt to smuggle diamonds. Thereafter, all trace of him in Britain vanished.

Quarles made some expensive telephone calls to Buenos Aires, where letters had come from seven years earlier. He learned that Gliddon had lived in the city from a time just after the war until 1955. He ran an import-export business, and was thought to have been living in other South American Republics during the war. His business was said to have been a cloak for smuggling, both of drugs and of suspected Nazis, whom he got out of Europe into the Argentine. In 1955 a newspaper had accused Gliddon of arranging the entry into the Argentine of a Nazi war criminal named Hermann Breit. Gliddon threatened to sue the paper, and then disappeared. A couple of weeks later a battered body was washed up just outside the city.

'It was identified as Gliddon,' the liquid voice said over the telephone. 'But you know, Senor Quarles, in such matters the police are sometimes happy to close their files.'

'There was still some doubt?'

'Yes. Not very much, perhaps, but—in these cases there is often a doubt.'

Molly Player found out nothing useful about the paper and envelopes. They were of the sort that could be bought in a thousand stores and shops in London and elsewhere. She had more luck with the typewriter. Its key characteristics identified the machine as a Malward portable of a type which the company had ceased producing ten years ago. The type face had proved unsatisfactory, and only some three hundred machines of this sort had been made. The Malward Company was able to provide her with a list of the purchasers of these machines, and Molly started to check and trace them, but had to give it up as a bad job.

'If we had three weeks I might get somewhere. In three days it's impossible,' she said to Quarles.

Lord Acrise made no comment on Quarles's recital of failure. 'See you on Monday evening, seven thirty, black tie,' he said, and barked with laughter. 'Your host will be Santa Claus.'

'I'd like to be there earlier.'

'Good idea. Any time you like. You know where it is— Robert the Devil Restaurant.'

## 3

The Robert the Devil Restaurant is situated inconspicuously in Mayfair. It is not a restaurant in the ordinary sense of the word, for there is no public dining-room, but simply several private rooms, which can accommodate any number of guests from two to thirty. Perhaps the food is not quite the best in London, but it is certainly the most expensive.

It was here that Quarles arrived at half past six, a big suave man, rather too conspicuously elegant perhaps in a midnight blue dinner jacket. He talked to Albert, the *maître d'hôtel*, whom he had known for some years, took unobtrusive looks at the waiters, went into and admired the kitchens. Albert observed his activities with tolerant amusement. 'You are here on some sort of business, Mr. Quarles?'

'I am a guest, Albert. I am also a kind of bodyguard. Tell me, how many of your waiters have joined you in the past twelve months?'

'Perhaps half a dozen. They come, they go.'

'Is there anybody at all on your staff—waiters, kitchen staff, anybody—who has joined you in the past year, and who is over sixty years old?'

Albert thought, then shook his head decisively. 'No. There is not such a one.'

The first of the guests came just after a quarter past seven. This was the brain surgeon Sir James Erdington, with a guest whom Quarles recognized as the Arctic explorer, Norman Endell. After that they came at intervals of a minute or two—a junior minister in the Government, one of the three most important men in the motor industry, a General promoted to the peerage to celebrate his retirement, a theatrical producer named Roddy Davis, who had successfully combined commerce and culture. As they arrived, the hosts went into a special robing room to put on their Santa Claus clothes, while the guests drank sherry. At seven-twenty-five Snewin scurried in, gasped, 'Excuse me, place names, got to put them out,' and went into the dining-room. Through the open door Quarles glimpsed a large oval table, gleaming with silver, bright with roses.

After Snewin came Lord Acrise, jutting-nosed and fearsome-eyed. 'Sorry to have kept you waiting,' he barked, and asked conspiratorially, 'Well?'

'No sign.'

'False alarm. Lot of nonsense. Got to dress up now.'

He went into the robing room with his box—each of the hosts had a similar box, labelled 'Santa Claus'—and came out again bewigged, bearded and robed. 'Better get the business over, and then we can enjoy ourselves. You can tell 'em to come in,' he said to Albert.

This referred to the photographers, who had been clustering outside, and now came into the room specially provided for holding the raffle. In the centre of the room was a table and on this table stood this year's prize, two exquisite T'ang horses. On the other side of the table were ten chairs arranged in a semi-circle, and on these sat the Santa Clauses. The guests stood inconspicuously at the side.

The raffle was conducted with the utmost seriousness. Each Santa Claus had a numbered slip. These slips were put into a tombola, and Acrise put in his hand and drew out one of them. Flash bulbs exploded.

'The number drawn is eight,' Acrise announced, and Roddy Davis waved the counterfoil in his hand. 'Isn't that *wonderful*? It's my ticket.' He went over to the horses, picked up one. More flashes. 'I'm bound to say that they couldn't have gone to *anybody* who'd have appreciated them more.'

Quarles, standing near to the General, whose face was as red as his robe, heard him mutter something uncomplimentary. Charity, he reflected, was not universal, even in a gathering of Santas. More flashes, the photographers disappeared, and Quarles's views about the nature of charity were reinforced when, as they were about to go into the dining-room, Erdington said: 'Forgotten something, haven't you, Acrise?'

With what seemed dangerous quietness Acrise answered, 'Have I? I don't think so.'

'It's customary for the Club and guests to sing "Noel" before we go in to dinner.'

'You didn't come to last year's dinner. It was agreed then that we should give it up. Carols after dinner, much better.'

'I must say I thought that was *just* for last year, because we were late,' Roddy Davis fluted. 'I'm sure that's what was agreed. I think myself it's rather pleasant to sing "Noel" before we go in and start eating too much.'

'Suggest we put it to the vote,' Erdington said sharply. Half a dozen of the Santas now stood looking at each other with subdued hostility. It was a situation that would have been totally ludicrous, if it had not been also embarrassing for the guests. Then suddenly the Arctic explorer, Endell, began to sing 'Noel, Noel' in a rich bass. There was the faintest flicker of hesitation, and then guests and Santas joined in. The situation was saved.

At dinner Quarles found himself with Acrise on one side of him and Roddy Davis on the other. Endell sat at Acrise's other side, and beyond him was Erdington. Turtle soup was followed by grilled sole, and then three great turkeys were brought in. The helpings of turkey were enormous. With the soup they drank a light, dry sherry, with the sole Chassagne Montrachet, with the turkey an Alexe Corton, heavy and powerful.

'And who are *you*?' Roddy Davis peered at Quarles's card and said, with what seemed manifest untruth, 'Of course I know your name.'

'I am a criminologist.' This sounded better, he thought, than private detective.

'I remember your monograph on criminal calligraphy. Quite fascinating.'

So Davis did know who he was—it would be easy, Quarles thought, to underrate the intelligence of the round-faced man who beamed innocently to him.

'These beards really do get in the way rather,' Davis said. 'But there, one must suffer for tradition. Have you known Acrise long?'

'Not very. I'm greatly privileged to be here.' Quarles had been watching, as closely as he could, the pouring of the wine, the serving of the food. He had seen nothing suspicious. Now, to get away from Davis's questions, he turned to his host.

'Damned awkward business before dinner,' Acrise said. 'Might have been, at least. Can't let well alone, Erdington.' He picked up his turkey leg, attacked it with Elizabethan gusto, wiped mouth and fingers with his napkin. 'Like this wine?'

'It's excellent.'

'Chose it myself. They've got some good Burgundies here.' Acrise's speech was slightly slurred, and it seemed to Quarles that he was rapidly getting drunk.

'Do you have any speeches?'

'What's that?'

'Are any speeches made after dinner?'

'No speeches. Just sing carols. But I've got a little surprise for 'em.'

'What sort of surprise?'

'Very much in the spirit of Christmas, and a good joke too. But if I told you it wouldn't be a surprise now, would it?'

Acrise had almost said 'shurprise.' Quarles looked at him and then returned to the turkey.

There was a general cry of pleasure as Albert himself brought in the great plum pudding, topped with holly and blazing with brandy.

'That's the most wonderful pudding I've ever seen in my life,' Endell said. 'Are we really going to eat it?'

'Of course we're going to eat it,' Acrise said irritably. He stood up, swaying a little, and picked up the knife beside the pudding.

'I don't like to be critical, but our Chairman is really *not* cutting the pudding very well,' Roddy Davis whispered to Quarles. And indeed, it was more of a stab than a cut that Acrise made at the pudding. Albert took over, and cut it quickly and efficiently. Bowls of brandy butter were circulated.

Quarles leaned towards Acrise. 'Are you all right?'

'Of course I'm all right.' The slurring was very noticeable now. Acrise ate no pudding, but he drank some more wine, and dabbed at his lips. When the pudding was finished he got slowly to his feet again, and toasted the Queen. Cigars were lighted. Acrise was not smoking. He whispered something to the waiter, who nodded and left the room. Acrise got up again, leaning heavily on the table.

'A little surprise,' he said. 'In the spirit of Christmas.'

Quarles had thought that he was beyond being surprised by the activities of the Santa Claus Club, but still he was astonished by sight of the three figures who entered the room. They were led by Snewin, somehow more mouselike than ever, wearing a long white smock and a red nightcap with a tassel. He was followed by an older man dressed in a kind of grey sackcloth, with a face so white that it might have been covered in plaster of Paris. This man carried chains which he shook. At the rear came a young middle-aged lady, who sparkled so brightly that she seemed to be completely hung with tinsel.

'I am Scrooge,' said Snewin.

'I am Marley,' wailed grey sackcloth, clanking his chains.

'And I,' said the young middle-aged lady, with abominable sprightliness, 'Am the ghost of Christmas past.'

There was a murmur round the table, and slowly the murmur grew to a ripple of laughter.

'We have come,' said Snewin in a thin mouse voice, 'to perform for you our own interpretation of *A Christmas Carol*—oh, sir, what's the matter?'

Lord Acrise stood up in his robes, tore off his wig, pulled at his beard, tried to say something. Then he clutched at the side of his chair and fell sideways, so that he leaned heavily against Endell and slipped slowly to the floor.

# 4

There ensued a minute of confused, important activity. Endell made some sort of exclamation and rose from his chair, slightly obstructing Quarles. Erdington was first beside the body, holding the wrist in his hand, listening for the heart. Then they were all crowding round, the red-robed Santas, the guests, the actors in their ludicrous clothes. Snewin, at Quarles's left shoulder, was babbling something, and at his right were Roddy Davis and Endell.

'Stand back,' Erdington snapped. He stayed on his knees for another few moments, looking curiously at Acrise's puffed, distorted face, bluish around the mouth. Then he stood up. 'He's dead.'

There was a murmur of surprise and horror, and now they all drew back, as men do instinctively from the presence of death.

'Heart attack?' somebody said. Erdington made a noncommittal noise. Quarles moved to his side.

'I'm a private detective, Sir James. Lord Acrise feared an attempt on his life, and asked me to come along here.'

'You seem to have done well so far,' Erdington said dryly. 'May I look at the body?'

'If you wish.'

As soon as Quarles bent down he caught the smell of bitter almonds. When he straightened up Erdington raised his eyebrows.

'He's been poisoned.'

'Bravo.'

'There's a smell like prussic acid, but the way he died precludes cyanide I think. He seemed to become very drunk during dinner, and his speech was blurred. Does that suggest anything to you?'

'I'm a brain surgeon, not a physician.' Erdington stared at the floor, then said, 'Nitro-benzene?'

'That's what I thought. We shall have to notify the police.' Quarles went to the door, spoke to a disturbed Albert. Then he returned to the room and clapped his hands.

'Gentlemen. My name is Francis Quarles, and I am a private detective. Lord Acrise asked me to come here tonight because he had received a threat that this would be his last evening alive. The threat said: "I shall be there, and I shall watch with pleasure as you squirm in agony." Lord Acrise has been poisoned. It seems certain that the man who made the threat is in this room.'

'Gliddon,' a voice said. Snewin had divested himself of the white smock and red nightcap, and now appeared as his customary respectable self.

'Yes. This letter, and others he had received, were signed with the name of James Gliddon, a man who bore a grudge against Lord Acrise which went back nearly half a century. Gliddon became a professional smuggler and crook. He would now be in his late sixties.'

'But dammit man, this Gliddon's not here.' That was the General, who took off his wig and beard. 'Lot of tomfoolery.'

In a shamefaced way the other members of the Santa Claus Club removed their facial trappings. Marley took off his chains and the young middle-aged lady discarded her cloak of tinsel.

'Isn't he here? But Lord Acrise is dead.'

Snewin coughed. 'Excuse me, sir, but would it be possible for my colleagues from our local dramatic society to retire? Of course, I can stay myself if you wish. It was Lord Acrise's idea that we should perform our skit on *A Christmas Carol* as a seasonable novelty, but—'

'Everybody must stay in this room until the police arrive. The problem, as you will all realize, is how the poison was administered. All of us ate the same food, drank the same wine. I sat next to Lord Acrise, and I watched as closely as possible to make sure of this. I watched the wine being poured, the turkey being carved and brought to the table, the pudding being cut and passed round. After dinner some of you smoked cigars or cigarettes, but not Acrise.'

'Just a moment.' It was Roddy Davis who spoke. 'This sounds fantastic, but wasn't it Sherlock Holmes who said that when you'd eliminated all other possibilities, even a fantastic one must be right? Supposing that some poison in powder form had been put on to Acrise's food—through the pepper pots, say—'

Erdington was shaking his head, but Quarles unscrewed both salt and pepper pots and tasted their contents. 'Salt and pepper. And in any case other people might have used these pots. Hallo, what's this.'

Acrise's napkin lay crumpled on his chair, and Quarles had picked it up and was staring at it.

'It's Acrise's napkin,' Endell said. 'What's remarkable about that?'

'It's a napkin, but not the one Acrise used. He wiped his mouth half a dozen times on his napkin, and wiped his greasy fingers on it too, when he'd gnawed a turkey bone. He must certainly have left grease marks on it. But look at this napkin.' He held it up, and they saw that it was spotless. Quarles said softly, 'The murderer's mistake.'

'I'm quite baffled,' Roddy Davis said. 'What does it mean?'

Quarles turned to Erdington. 'Sir James and I agreed that the poison used was probably nitro-benzene. This is deadly as a liquid, but it is also poisonous as a vapour, isn't that so?'

Erdington nodded. 'You'll remember the case of the unfortunate young man who used shoe polish containing nitro-benzene on damp shoes, put them on and wore them, and was killed by the fumes.'

'Yes. Somebody made sure that Lord Acrise had a napkin that had been soaked in nitro-benzene but was dry enough to use. The same person substituted the proper napkin, the one belonging to the restaurant, after Acrise was dead.'

'Nobody's left the room,' said Roddy Davis.

'No.'

'That means the napkin must still be here.'

'It does.'

'Then what are we waiting for? I vote that we submit to a search.'

There was a small hubbub of protest and approval. 'That won't be necessary,' Quarles said. 'Only one person here fulfils all the qualifications of the murderer.'

'James Gliddon?'

'No. Gliddon is almost certainly dead, as I found out when I made inquiries about him. But the murderer is somebody who knew about Acrise's relationship with Gliddon, and tried to be clever by writing the letters to lead us along a wrong track. Then the murderer is somebody who had the opportunity of coming in here before dinner, and who knew exactly where Acrise would be sitting. There is only one person who fulfils all of these qualifications.

'He removed any possible suspicion from himself, as he thought, by being absent from the dinner table, but he arranged to come in afterwards to exchange the napkins. He probably put the poisoned napkin into the clothes he discarded. As for motive, long-standing hatred might be enough, but he is also somebody who knew that he would benefit handsomely when Acrise died—stop him, will you.'

But the General, with a tackle reminiscent of the days when he had been the best wing three quarter in the country, had already brought to the floor Lord Acrise's mouselike secretary, Snewin.

# Deep and Crisp and Even

## *Michael Gilbert*

For many years, Michael Gilbert (1912–2006) combined a career as a busy Lincoln's Inn solicitor with that of a leading crime writer. His versatility was astonishing, as he moved from producing highly readable novels and short stories to working on television screenplays and stage plays, and proved himself equally adept in the fields of espionage, adventure story, courtroom drama, and classic whodunit. For good measure, he contributed incisive introductions to a series of classics of mystery and adventure, and edited a book of essays about the genre called *Crime in Good Company*.

Gilbert created a wide range of recurring lead characters, although his desire to avoid formula meant that none of them appeared in a long series of novels. The policeman Patrick Petrella, son of a Spanish cop and a British woman, combined, in his creator's words 'a Spanish temper and a British sense of equity. Such dangerous opposites were capable... of blowing Patrick Petrella clean out of the carefully regulated ranks of the Metropolitan police.' Fortunately, his career proved long-lasting, and he featured in many short stories, although only two novels. Amazingly, *Blood and Judgement* and *Roller Coaster* were published more than thirty years apart, in 1959 and 1993 respectively.

Eventually, therefore, Detective Sergeant Petrella spent most of Christmas Day in bed with influenza and a rocketing temperature, and it was well on in the New Year before he reported back for duty. And during the uncomfortable nights, while the disease sweated itself out and the patient slept and woke and slept again, one face seemed to dominate his imagination; a face at once strong and ruthless, touched by a dangerous humour, but unrelieved by any other weakness.

It started a week before Christmas, when Superintendent Haxtell went on seven days' special leave. Things were quiet enough. Quieter than usual, perhaps, because Chief Superintendent Barstow had at last been moved and his successor not yet appointed. A policeman's troubles do not all come from below.

The snow lay deep on North London that December. People were busy buying Christmas presents, laying in unusual quantities of food and drink, hanging holly over pictures and mistletoe in the front hall, devising excuses to prevent their in-laws coming to stay, and generally behaving exactly like everybody else all over the civilized world—except Scotland where, as is well known, is celebrated a curious deviationist festival known as Hogmanay.

Crime followed the seasonal pattern. A little shop-lifting in the crowded shops by day. A marked increase in brawling as the public houses stayed open for an extra half-hour to celebrate the season of goodwill; and the ever-present problem of people who went away and left their houses unguarded and at the mercy of housebreakers, who recognize no close season.

In Petrella's experience, the average Highside house-holder, on leaving for a few days in the country, omitted to inform the milkman—so that a lengthening line of milk bottles might clearly mark his house for preferential treat-ment—deposited his valuables handily arranged in unlocked cupboards, and was careful to leave a scullery window ajar.

On Haxtell's departure, Petrella came nominally under Detective Inspector Finch, at the adjacent Sub-station in Bridge Road, but that excellent officer was busy with his own affairs and happy to leave Petrella alone until he asked for help.

After a day or two of nervous attention to his enlarged command, Petrella felt easier. By Christmas Eve, indeed, he felt relaxed enough to accept an invitation from his old friend, the Reverend Philip Freebone, to join a carol-singing party.

The Reverend Philip Freebone, the curate of the Church of St. Peter and St. Paul, Highside, was an earnest and energetic young man, and, within the limitations of their different temperaments, the closest thing to a real friend that Petrella possessed. They met at the Boys' Club, well wrapped in coats, scarves, and gloves, and there they were issued with a carol book apiece, a storm lantern among six, and last-minute instructions.

'Take your time from me,' said the Reverend Freebone. 'All sing the same carol, and stop when I tell you. If they don't open the door at the end of the first verse we'll be wasting our time. Maurice'   this to a particularly angelic-looking member of the Harrington family—'you can hold the collecting-box. Remember to smile when you hold it out, and say Merry Christmas. The bottom's screwed on, by the way. All ready?'

Two hours later, their collecting-box full and their feet cold, they headed up the driveway of The Firs.

'There's a new man here, a Mr. Hazel. I believe he's a solicitor. His predecessor always used to give us a hot drink and a pound note. I hope this one'll co-operate. Oh dear! It looks as if he's out.'

'It's just that the curtains are very well drawn. There's a light on in the dining-room,' said Petrella. 'I can see a chink.'

'We'll give him *Silent Night*. That ought to wake him up. Plenty of support from the tenor and bass, please.'

The choir let itself go.

'One more verse.'

A light went up in the hall, the door opened, and a middle-aged man peered out. 'Very nice,' he said. 'Very nice indeed. I wonder if you'd all care to come inside and have a drink?'

'Why, how very kind of you,' said the Reverend Freebone. 'If you're sure we're not trespassing on your hospitality?'

'Not at all. I'm afraid I've only got the one room in use at the moment. But I'm sure we can find something for all of you. Come along, come along.'

He led the way into the dining-room. A big electric fire was burning at one end of it, but it could not have been long switched on, for the room, even on coming into it from the night air, struck cold. However, their host was soon bustling about, opening cupboards and unearthing bottles.

'I *think* there's some ginger beer in the larder,' he said. 'Whisky for you, sir, or would you rather have rum? There are some biscuits in that box. No, my mistake. They're figs. Here are the biscuits.'

Soon the room was warming up, and by the time the second drink had gone round, toes were thawing. Petrella, who was professionally interested in all who came to live in Highside, took unobtrusive stock of Mr. Hazel.

He noted a man of about fifty, large but not flabby, with a shrewd eye and a masterful mouth. He had the look of a lawyer; a lawyer who had seen perhaps, some active service during the war.

'We really must be getting along now,' said the Reverend Freebone. 'It's been very kind of you.'

'Not at all,' said their host. 'A seasonable duty. Oh—that's the collecting-box you're waving at me, is it?'

'Really, Maurice!'

'See if you can squeeze this in.' A pound note was folded and inserted into the box, and then the party were trooping out into the snow.

Back at the church hall the box was opened and the proceeds were counted.

'Nineteen pounds twelve and sixpence, a ten-franc piece, and an Irish shilling. That's nearly four pounds better than last year. Well sung, everybody. And well done, Maurice— only I don't think you should have stuck Mr. Hazel up quite so blatantly. We must have drunk more than a pound's worth of his whisky as it was.'

'That wasn't Mr. Hazel,' said Maurice.

'What do you mean?'

'I know Mr. Hazel. He's on my paper round. He's older an' he wears glasses.'

Petrella and the Reverend Freebone looked at each other.

'Well, whoever he was,' said the Reverend Freebone, 'he behaved very handsomely. Put your carol books in that cupboard, and the lanterns go on the shelf. Who do you think—'

But Petrella was already on his way. An uneasy suspicion had crept into his mind. However recently a man had taken over a house, would he really not know where the drinks were, and whether a box contained figs or biscuits?

He found Station Sergeant Rampole on duty in front of a roaring stove.

'Let's just have a look at the Notified Away List,' he said.

Almost the first item that jumped out at him was: *A. E. Hazel, The Firs, Crown Road*. And in the remarks column. *Touring*.

Petrella hesitated for a moment, and then, realizing that seconds might count, he banged his hat back on his head and took to his heels. Sergeant Rampole stared after him. He took a fatherly interest in Petrella's welfare, and suspected that he had been overworking.

◇◇◇

Petrella covered the distance to the front door of The Firs in two minutes and a half. The trampled footprints of the choir were visible in the snow. But superimposed on them was a new track: the track of car wheels. No light showed now from the chink between the curtains.

Petrella knocked, first softly, then loudly. He also rang the bell. The house remained silent and unresponsive. He walked round towards the back. The garage stood set back to one side of the house, and the fresh car tracks that he had noticed came from it. The doors were a-swing and the garage was empty.

It was all of a piece. A burglar with the nerve to entertain the choir to drinks could certainly use the garage to shelter his car.

Behind the garage the surface of the snow was unbroken, save for one double line of footprints leading towards the back quarters. Treading carefully to one side of them, Petrella followed. They led him to the kitchen door, which was shut.

He pressed, and with a click the door swung open. His torch showed him that the metal cup retaining the flange of the lock was hanging by a single screw. The slightest pressure unseated it and allowed the door to open.

He tried the light switch. The light came on all right. The kitchen was empty and had the tidy look of a room that was not in use. The stove was out, and the house was as cold as a mausoleum. He turned the light off and relied on his torch.

The dining-room was a little warmer, with the lingering heat of the electric fire that had been turned on for their benefit earlier in the evening. He looked around him. There were two obvious places for the household silver. A sideboard with drawers and a big oak corner cupboard. Covering his hand carefully with a handkerchief, Petrella opened the cupboard. It was empty. As also was the sideboard.

Petrella left the house, pulling the backdoor shut behind him, and made his way to the police station.

'Have you got any way of tracing Mr. Hazel?' he asked.

Sergeant Rampole studied the list. 'Touring,' he said. 'That's a fat lot of use. And he's new round here. So he hasn't had time to make a lot of friends.' He scratched his head. 'He's a solicitor, isn't he? We could look him up in the list and find his office. They might know where he's gone.'

'Of course,' said Petrella. 'I'll do that in the morning.' He was angry with himself for not thinking of such an obvious solution. There must be something wrong with him. He came to the conclusion that he was tired.

'There's another thing,' he said. 'What's the name of the little man we use to take off locks—Protheroe—could you get hold of him and ask him to put a new lock on the backdoor of The Firs?'

The Sergeant looked surprised. 'Some trouble down there?'

'That's just it,' said Petrella. 'I don't know.'

That night, for the first time for as long as he could remember, he slept badly. A face kept coming between him and his rest. A strong, sardonic face. The eyes seemed to be laughing at him, but the mouth was hard.

Next morning he located, without difficulty, the New Square firm of Marsham, Pratt, & Bailliwick of which Mr. Hazel was the senior partner; but such information as he got was vague and unhelpful.

'He never leaves any address when he goes on holiday,' said the junior partner, a cheerful young man with an H.A.C. tie and a rather less conventional style of dress than would have been tolerated in Lincoln's Inn before the war. 'If he does, he says we shall all be ringing him up with damned silly questions about his clients. And we should, too.'

Petrella thanked him politely, and withdrew.

That was Christmas Eve. As he came out into Chancery Lane the snow was coming down again, thick, slow-falling, enduring flakes, dropping from a steel-grey sky on to a blanched and shrinking world.

When he got back to the Station, Sergeant Rampole reported that Protheroe had duly fixed a new lock on the backdoor of The Firs. Protheroe didn't think that the old lock had been forced; it had just got like that.

'Some people,' said Sergeant Rampole, 'bloody well deserve to have their houses burgled.' When Petrella didn't answer, he looked up. The younger man was standing in front of the charge-room stove, his eyes shut. 'You all right?' said the Sergeant.

'Funny,' said Petrella. 'I blacked out for a moment. I expect it was coming in here out of the cold.'

'If I was you, I'd take a hot whisky and go to bed.'

'Can't do that,' said Petrella. 'Too much to do. I'll be all right.'

There was, in fact, work. He had a couple of visits to make immediately after lunch, in the residential area south of Helenwood Common. He didn't seem to have any appetite, so he lunched off a cup of strong tea, and then he set out. The snow had stopped falling and the clouds had cleared away. With their passing, some of his depression had gone too, and he felt a sort of delusive light-headedness.

As he came out from his second visit, he saw the man. Petrella was half hidden by the doorway of the house he was in, and was certain he had not been seen. The man was on the opposite pavement, walking slowly. Hungrily Petrella studied his face. There was no doubt about it. It was his host of the previous evening; walking easily, despite his bulk, and with something of the swing of one who had once been an athlete.

As innocent-looking as a family cat, thought Petrella, and perhaps as dangerous.

He followed cautiously. The big man was in no hurry; and since this was Petrella's home ground, and he knew every inch of it, he was able to anticipate his route, sidestep, circle round, and cut back in such a way that he kept on the heels of his quarry without ever seeming to follow him at all.

After about a quarter of an hour of this blindfold chess Petrella realized, with a prickle of excitement, where they were heading. It was the Clarendon Estate, the houses of the top Highsiders, the rich and the influential; big houses, each in its own half acre of garden and with its private back gate on to the heath.

The big man walked slowly up the approach. He made no attempt to disguise his interest. He might have been a benevolent tiger viewing a line of tethered goats. When he reached the end he stopped, tried a front gate, found it open, and walked in. As soon as he was out of sight Petrella pelted after him, his footsteps muffled in the piled snow. Apart from the two of them there was no one else in sight.

He reached the gate in time to see the big man disappearing round the corner of the house.

'He can't—!' thought Petrella. 'He can't—not in broad daylight!'

A board caught his eye, almost hidden in the snow-capped hedge: TO LET FURNISHED. Petrella stood undecided. The thing was to get under cover. But where? All the other houses looked horribly occupied. And the road was bare of cover. The solution suddenly occurred to him.

He opened the front gate, darted down the path, and dodged behind the line of laurel shrubbery that masked the point where the path turned round to the back of the house. It was not as thick as he could have wished, but it was better than nothing.

Three minutes. Five minutes. The silence of the late afternoon brooded over the snow.

Then, quite suddenly, the big man was there again. He had gone right round the house and was now moving, unhurried as ever, towards the spot where Petrella crouched. Unconsciously Petrella bent lower, and at that moment he knew he was slipping. There was nothing he could do about it. Not without grabbing one of the branches, and that would certainly give him away. He did the only thing possible. He let himself fall back, as softly and as slowly as he could, into the piled snow that filled the shallow dip behind him.

As he lay there, he heard the click of the front gate. And by the time he had rolled over, stumbled to his feet, and reached the end of the path, the roadway was empty.

Petrella himself retained little recollection of how he spent the rest of that day. Sergeant Rampole says that he came back to the Station, told him a long and involved story about having a fight in the snow with Father Christmas, and walked straight out of the room in the middle of the sentence without shutting the door. Mrs. Catt says that he came in looking like death, and she sent him to bed with a hot-water bottle. Later she took up his supper, found him fast asleep, and took it down again.

It was late the next morning when Petrella woke up. He had to think hard for a moment to remember that it was Christmas Day. He was bathed in sweat, but his head was a bit clearer. It was a beautiful day. The sun had come out, and was shining in glory on the fresh snow that had fallen during the night.

He felt curiously weak as he put on his clothes; and, although he had eaten nothing for nearly twenty-four hours, he was not hungry. He was not due at the Station until after lunch, so he decided to go to church.

There was always a good congregation at the Church of St. Peter and St. Paul, and on this fine Christmas morning the church was likely to be full. Ahead of Petrella two family parties, prayer books in hand, filled the pavement. As they turned into Rochester Road, a man fell in behind them.

Impossible to say where he had come from. One moment the pavement was empty, the next moment he was there.

Petrella felt himself going red. A moment later they had both turned in at the porch of the Church of St. Peter and St. Paul. His friend, Mr. Peggs, was there, solemn in suit of Sunday black. He handed Petrella a prayer book and a hymn book and said, 'Not much room downstairs. Why don't you grab yourself a seat in the gallery?'

Like many London churches, St. Peter and St. Paul had broad galleries across the back and two-thirds of the way down the sides; they were thrown open on festal occasions.

'Get a good view from there,' said Mr. Peggs.

Petrella hesitated. Through the glass doors he could see his quarry. He was being shown to a single empty seat, at the inner end of the sixth row. He said abruptly, 'Could you get a note to the Reverend Freebone? Before the service starts?'

Mr. Peggs looked at him for a moment, his eyes snapping with curiosity. 'I'm meant to be on duty,' he said. 'I take it it's important.'

'Yes,' said Petrella. 'Most important.' It seemed to him, at that moment, the most important thing in the whole world.

'All right. I don't suppose they'll court-martial me.'

Petrella was already scribbling: *He's sitting in the sixth row, on the south side, at the inner end of the row. If you or any of the choir recognize him...* What were they going to do? He had to know by the end of the service. Some action had to be taken. *Find some way of letting me know. I shall be in the north gallery, near the front.*

Petrella climbed the steep stone stair. The organ voluntary was reaching its climax as he slid into his seat. He peered over the parapet, felt unaccountably dizzy, and sat back hastily on his seat. The organ gave a final flourish, the big west doors swung open, and as the choir appeared, led by the People's Warden with staff in hand, the strains of *Adeste Fideles* broke from the massed voices below.

As the boys walked in solemn procession towards the altar they passed within inches of the big man. No head—not even an eye—turned. But Petrella knew. It was as clear to him as if it had been shouted. As clear as when, during the course of the service, head after head turned up from the choir to where he sat, clinging with hot hands to the gallery parapet.

'I'd better let him get outside,' thought Petrella. 'But he mustn't get away again. I'll walk to the end of the path, and tackle him as he comes out into the street. Always supposing I can get down those stairs. Something seems to have gone wrong with my legs.' The whole scene below him had broken adrift, and was floating on the surges of the solemn organ music, now rising, now falling, now circling in stately dance around that central figure to which his eyes were fastened.

Petrella rose to his feet as the service finished, and tottered down the stairs. A man looked up at him curiously as he cannoned into him, but said nothing. Then he was outside and heading for the lich-gate.

'I'll do it here,' he said. The stout oak gate-post was something to lean against in a reeling world, which suddenly steadied as he saw three figures walking together towards him, down the path. In the middle was the man he was waiting for. On his right, a tall grey-haired stranger, wearing glasses. On his left—Petrella blinked twice—Superintendent Haxtell.

'There is Petrella,' said Haxtell. 'I thought I saw him lurking in the gallery. Let me introduce you. Mr. Hazel you know, I think. And this is Chief Superintendent Causton. He's taking over Barstow's job.'

The big man smiled. 'I haven't had time to make myself known,' he said. 'I've been here unofficially for some days, house-hunting. Mr. Hazel let me base myself on him.'

Petrella found himself shaking hands.

'Sergeant Rampole gave me a bad report of you,' said Haxtell. 'He says you've been overworking. You don't look awfully fit.'

'I've got a car here,' said Mr. Hazel. 'Look here—I think we'd better give him a hand.'

The whole white world was rotating slowly round Petrella's head. He felt a strong hand under each arm, and then he was in a car. 'It's very good of you,' he said feebly.

'Hazel owes you that, at least,' said Chief Superintendent Causton, turning round from his seat by the driver 'It's a small exchange for that handsome lock you put on his backdoor. Invitation to burglars, leaving his house in that condition.'

Mr. Hazel laughed. The Chief Superintendent smiled, too. It was a smile that implied, perhaps, more than it stated. Or so Petrella thought. But he was in no real condition at that moment for logical thinking.

# The Carol Singers

## *Josephine Bell*

Josephine Bell was the pen-name of Doris Bell Collier Ball (1897–1987). Born in Manchester, she studied at Newnham College, Cambridge, and became a doctor, marrying a fellow physician in 1923. Following her husband's death, she started to publish detective stories. *Murder in Hospital*, her first book, made use of her medical knowledge, as did many of its successors. *Death on the Borough Council* introduced David Wintringham, who appeared in a dozen novels between 1937 and 1958.

Her non-series books included the atmospheric *The Port of London Murders* (1938). Freeman Wills Crofts, a prominent detective novelist of the Golden Age, and fellow resident of Guildford, gave her encouragement, and in 1954 she was elected to membership of the Detection Club, of which Crofts was a founder member. In the previous year, she had supported John Creasey in founding the Crime Writers' Association, which she chaired in 1959–60. Together with Julian Symons and Michael Gilbert, she edited the CWA's first anthology, *Butcher's Dozen*. Her interest in contemporary social issues is evident in much of her work, not least in this story.

Old Mrs. Fairlands stepped carefully off the low chair she had pulled close to the fireplace. She was very conscious of her eighty-one years every time she performed these mild acrobatics. Conscious of them and determined to have no humiliating, potentially dangerous mishap. But obstinate, in her persistent routine of dusting her own mantelpiece, where a great many, too many photographs and small ornaments daily gathered a film of greasy London dust.

Mrs. Fairlands lived in the ground floor flat of a converted house in a once fashionable row of early Victorian family homes. The house had been in her family for three generations before her, and she herself had been born and brought up there. In those faroff days of her childhood, the whole house was filled with a busy throng of people, from the top floor where the nurseries housed the noisiest and liveliest group, through the dignified, low-voiced activities of her parents and resident aunt on the first and ground floors, to the basement haunts of the domestic staff, the kitchens and the cellars.

Too many young men of the family had died in two world wars and too many young women had married and left the house to make its original use in the late 1940's any longer possible. Mrs. Fairlands, long a widow, had inherited the property when the last of her brothers died. She had let it for a while, but even that failed. A conversion was the obvious answer. She was a vigorous seventy at the time, fully determined, since her only child, a married daughter, lived in the to her barbarous wastes of the Devon moors, to continue to live alone with her much-loved familiar possessions about her.

The conversion was a great success and was made without very much structural alteration to the house. The basement, which had an entrance by the former back door, was shut off and was let to a businessman who spent only three days a week in London and preferred not to use an hotel. The original hall remained as a common entrance to the other three flats. The ground floor provided Mrs. Fairlands with three large rooms, one of which was divided into a kitchen and bathroom. Her own front door was the original dining room door from the hall. It led now into a narrow passage, also chopped off from the room that made the bathroom and kitchen. At the end of the passage two new doors led into the former morning room, her drawing room as she liked to call it, and her bedroom, which had been the study.

This drawing room of hers was at the front of the house, overlooking the road. It had a square bay window that gave her a good view of the main front door and the steps leading up to it, the narrow front garden, now a paved forecourt, and from the opposite window of the bay, the front door and steps of the house next door, divided from her by a low wall.

Mrs. Fairlands, with characteristic obstinacy, strength of character, integrity, or whatever other description her forceful personality drew from those about her, had lived in her flat for eleven years, telling everyone that it suited her perfectly and feeling, as the years went by, progressively more lonely, more deeply bored, and more consciously apprehensive. Her daily came for four hours three times a week. It was enough to keep the place in good order. On those days the admirable woman cooked Mrs. Fairlands a good solid English dinner, which she shared, and also constructed several more main meals that could be eaten cold or warmed up. But three half days of cleaning and cooking left four whole days in each week when Mrs. Fairlands must provide for herself or go out to the High Street to a restaurant. After her eightieth birthday she became more and more reluctant to make the effort. But every week she wrote to her daughter Dorothy to say how well she felt and how much she would detest leaving London, where she had lived all her life except when she was evacuated to Wiltshire in the second war.

She was sincere in writing thus. The letters were true as far as they went, but they did not go the whole distance. They did not say that it took Mrs. Fairlands nearly an hour to wash and dress in the morning. They did not say she was sometimes too tired to bother with supper and then had to get up in the night, feeling faint and thirsty, to heat herself some milk. They did not say that although she stuck to her routine of dusting the whole flat every morning, she never mounted her low chair without a secret terror that she might fall and break her hip and perhaps be unable to reach the heavy stick she kept beside her armchair to use as a signal to the flat above.

On this particular occasion, soon after her eighty-first birthday, she had deferred the dusting until late in the day, because it was Christmas Eve and in addition to cleaning the mantelpiece she had arranged on it a pile of Christmas cards from her few remaining friends and her many younger relations.

This year, she thought sadly, there was not really much point in making the display. Dorothy and Hugh and the children could not come to her as usual, nor could she go to them. The tiresome creatures had chicken pox, in their late teens, too, except for Bobbie, the afterthought, who was only ten. They should all have had it years ago, when they first went to school. So the visit was cancelled, and though she offered to go to Devon instead, they told her she might get shingles from the same infection and refused to expose her to the risk. Apart altogether from the danger to her of travelling at that particular time of the year, the weather and the holiday crowds combined, Dorothy had written.

Mrs. Fairlands turned sadly from the fireplace and walked slowly to the window. A black Christmas this year, the wireless report had promised. As black as the prospect of two whole days of isolation at a time when the whole western world was celebrating its midwinter festival and Christians were remembering the birth of their faith.

She turned from the bleak prospect outside her window, a little chilled by the downdraught seeping through its closed edges. Near the fire she had felt almost too hot, but then she needed to keep it well stocked up for such a large room. In the old days there had been logs, but she could no longer lift or carry logs. Everyone told her she ought to have a cosy stove or even do away with solid fuel altogether, install central heating and perhaps an electric fire to make a pleasant glow. But Mrs. Fairlands considered these suggestions defeatist, an almost insulting reference to her age. Secretly she now thought of her life as a gamble with time. She was prepared to take risks for the sake of defeating them. There were few pleasures left to her. Defiance was one of them.

When she left the window, she moved to the far corner of the room, near the fireplace. Here a small table, usually covered, like the mantelpiece, with a multitude of objects, had been cleared to make room for a Christmas tree. It was mounted in a large bowl reserved for this annual purpose. The daily had set it up for her and wrapped the bowl round with crinkly red paper, fastened with safety pins. But the tree was not yet decorated.

Mrs. Fairlands got to work upon it. She knew that it would be more difficult by artificial light to tie the knots in the black cotton she used for the dangling glass balls. Dorothy had provided her with some newfangled strips of pliable metal that needed only to be threaded through the rings on the glass balls and wrapped round the branches of the tree. But she had tried these strips only once. The

metal had slipped from her hands and the ball had fallen
and shattered. She went back to her long practised method
with black cotton, leaving the strips in the box for her
grandchildren to use, which they always did with ferocious
speed and efficiency.

She sighed as she worked. It was not much fun decorating
the tree by herself. No one would see it until the day after
Boxing Day when the daily would be back. If only her tenants had not gone away she could have invited them in for
some small celebration. But the basement man was in his
own home in Essex, and the first floor couple always went
to an hotel for Christmas, allowing her to use their flat for
Dorothy and Hugh and the children. And this year the top
floor, three girl students, had joined a college group to go
skiing. So the house was quite empty. There was no one left
to invite, except perhaps her next-door neighbours. But that
would be impossible. They had detestable children, rude,
destructive, uncontrolled brats. She had already complained
about broken glass and dirty sweet papers thrown into her
forecourt. She could not possibly ask them to enjoy her
Christmas tree with her. They might damage it. Perhaps she
ought to have agreed to go to May, or let her come to her.
She was one of the last of her friends, but never an intimate
one. And such a chatterer. Nonstop, as Hugh would say.

By the time Mrs. Fairlands had fastened the last golden
ball and draped the last glittering piece of tinsel and tied the
crowning piece, the six-pronged shining silver star, to the
topmost twig and fixed the candles upright in their socket
clips, dusk had fallen. She had been obliged to turn on all
her lights some time before she had done. Now she moved
again to her windows, drew the curtains, turned off all the
wall lights, and with one reading lamp beside her chair sat
down near the glowing fire.

It was nearly an hour after her usual teatime, she noticed. But she was tired. Pleasantly tired, satisfied with her work, shining quietly in its dark corner, bringing back so many memories of her childhood in this house, of her brief marriage, cut off by the battle of the Marne, of Dorothy, her only child, brought up here, too, since there was nowhere for them to live except with the parents she had so recently left. Mrs. Fairlands decided to skip tea and have an early supper with a boiled egg and cake.

She dozed, snoring gently, her ancient, wrinkled hand twitching from time to time as her head lolled on and off the cushion behind it.

She woke with a start, confused, trembling. There was a ringing in her head that resolved, as full consciousness returned to her, into a ringing of bells, not only her own, just inside her front door, but those of the other two flats, shrilling and buzzing in the background.

Still trembling, her mouth dry with fright and open-mouthed sleep, she sat up, trying to think. What time was it? The clock on the mantelpiece told her it was nearly seven. Could she really have slept for two whole hours? There was silence now. Could it really have been the bell, all the bells, that had woken her? If so, it was a very good thing. She had no business to be asleep in the afternoon, in a chair of all places.

Mrs. Fairlands got to her feet, shakily. Whoever it was at the door must have given up and gone away. Standing still, she began to tremble again. For she remembered things Dorothy and Hugh and her very few remaining friends said to her from time to time. 'Aren't you afraid of burglars?' 'I wouldn't have the nerve to live alone!' 'They ring you up, and if there is no answer, they know you're out, so they come and break in.'

Well, there had been no answer to this bell ringing, so whoever it was, if ill-intentioned, might even now be forcing the door or prowling round the house, looking for an open window.

While she stood there in the middle of her drawing room, trying to build up enough courage to go round her flat pulling the rest of the curtains, fastening the other windows, Mrs. Fairlands heard sounds that instantly explained the situation. She heard, raggedly begun, out of tune, but reassuringly familiar, the strains of 'Once in Royal David's City.'

Carol singers! Of course. Why had she not thought of them instead of frightening herself to death with gruesome suspicions?

Mrs. Fairlands, always remembering her age, her gamble, went to the side window of the bay and, pulling back the edge of the curtain, looked out. A dark-clad group stood there, six young people, four girls with scarves on their heads, two boys with woolly caps. They had a single electric torch directed onto a sheet of paper held by the central figure of the group.

Mrs. Fairlands watched them for a few seconds. Of course they had seen the light in her room, so they knew someone was in. How stupid of her to think of burglars. The light would have driven a burglar away if he was out looking for an empty house to break into. All her fears about the unanswered bell were nonsense.

In her immense relief, and seeing the group straighten up as they finished the hymn, she tapped at the glass. They turned quickly, shining the torch in her face. Though she was a little startled by this, she smiled and nodded, trying to convey the fact that she enjoyed their performance.

'Want another, missis?' one boy shouted.

She nodded again, let the curtain slip into place, and made her way to her bureau, where she kept her handbag. Her purse in the handbag held very little silver, but she found the half crown she was looking for and took it in her hand. 'The Holly and the Ivy' was in full swing outside. Mrs.

Fairlands decided that these children must have been well taught in school. It was not usual for small parties to sing real carols. Two lines of 'Come, All Ye Faithful,' followed by loud knocking, was much more likely.

As she moved to the door with the half crown in one hand, Mrs. Fairlands put the other to her throat to pull together the folds of her cardigan before leaving her warm room for the cold passage and the outer hall door. She felt her brooch, and instantly misgiving struck her. It was a diamond brooch, a very valuable article, left to her by her mother. It would perhaps be a mistake to appear at the door offering half a crown and flaunting several hundred pounds. They might have seen it already, in the light of the torch they had shone on her.

Mrs. Fairlands slipped the half crown into her cardigan pocket, unfastened the brooch, and, moving quickly to the little Christmas tree on its table, reached up to the top and pinned the brooch to the very centre of the silver tinsel star. Then, chuckling at her own cleverness, her quick wit, she went out to the front door just as the bell rang again in her flat. She opened it on a group of fresh young faces and sturdy young bodies standing on her steps.

'I'm sorry I was so slow,' she said. 'You must forgive me, but I am not very young.'

'I'll say,' remarked the younger boy, staring. He thought he had never seen anything as old as this old geyser.

'You shut up,' said the girl next to him, and the tallest one said, 'Don't be rude.'

'You sing very nicely,' said Mrs. Fairlands. 'Very well indeed. Did you learn at school?'

'Mostly at the club,' said the older boy, whose voice went up and down, on the verge of breaking, Mrs. Fairlands thought, remembering her brothers.

She held out the half crown. The tallest of the four girls, the one who had the piece of paper with the words of the carols on it, took the coin and smiled.

'I hope I haven't kept you too long,' Mrs. Fairlands said. 'You can't stay long at each house, can you, or you would never get any money worth having.'

'They mostly don't give anything,' one of the other girls said.

'Tell us to get the 'ell out,' said the irrepressible younger boy.

'We don't do it mostly for the money,' said the tallest girl. 'Not for ourselves, I mean.'

'Give it to the club. Oxfam collection and that,' said the tall boy.

'Don't you want it for yourselves?' Mrs. Fairlands was astonished. 'Do you have enough pocket money without?'

They nodded gravely.

'I got a paper round,' said the older boy.

'I do babysitting now and then,' the tallest girl added.

'Well, thank you for coming,' Mrs. Fairlands said. She was beginning to feel cold, standing there at the open door. 'I must go back into my warm room. And you must keep moving, too, or you might catch colds.'

'Thank you,' they said in chorus. 'Thanks a lot. Bye!'

She shut and locked the door as they turned, clattered down the steps, slammed the gate of the forecourt behind them. She went back to her drawing room. She watched from the window as they piled up the steps of the next house. And again she heard, more faintly because they were farther away, 'Once in Royal David's City.' There were tears in her old eyes as she left the window and stood for a few minutes staring down at the dull coals of her diminishing fire.

But very soon she rallied, took up the poker, mended her fire, went to her kitchen, and put on the kettle. Coming back to wait for it to boil, she looked again at her Christmas tree. The diamond brooch certainly gave an added distinction to the star, she thought. Amused once more by her originality, she went into her bedroom and from her jewel box on the dressing table took her two other valuable pieces, a pearl necklace and a diamond bracelet. The latter she had not worn for years. She wound each with a tinsel string and hung them among the branches of the tree.

She had just finished preparing her combined tea and supper when the front doorbell rang again. Leaving the tray in the kitchen, she went to her own front door and opened it. Once again a carol floated to her, 'Hark, the Herald Angels Sing' this time. There seemed to be only one voice singing. A lone child, she wondered, making the rounds by himself.

She hurried to the window of her drawing room, drew back the curtain, peeped out. No, not alone, but singing a solo. The pure, high boy's voice was louder here. The child, muffled up to the ears, had his head turned away from her towards three companions, whose small figures and pale faces were intent upon the door. They did not seem to notice her at the window as the other group had done, for they did not turn in her direction. They were smaller, evidently younger, very serious. Mrs. Fairlands, touched, willing again to defeat her loneliness in a few minutes' talk, took another half crown from her purse and went out to the main hall and the big door.

'Thank you, children,' she said as she opened it. 'That was very—'

Her intended praise died in her throat. She gasped, tried to back away. The children now wore black stockings over their faces. Their eyes glittered through slits; there were holes for their noses and mouths.

'That's a very silly joke,' said Mrs. Fairlands in a high voice. 'I shall not give you the money I brought for you. Go home. Go away.'

She backed inside the door, catching at the knob to close it. But the small figures advanced upon her. One of them held the door while two others pushed her away from it. She saw the fourth, the singer, hesitate, then turn and run out into the street.

'Stop this!' Mrs. Fairlands said in a voice that had once been commanding but now broke as she repeated the order. Silently, remorselessly, the three figures forced her back; they shut and locked the main door, they pushed her, stumbling now, terrified, bewildered, through her own front door and into her drawing room.

It was an outrage, an appalling, unheard-of challenge. Mrs. Fairlands had always met a challenge with vigour. She did so now. She tore herself from the grasp of one pair of small hands to box the ears of another short figure. She swept round at the third, pulling the stocking halfway up his face, pushing him violently against the wall so his face met it with a satisfactory smack.

'Stop it!' she panted. 'Stop it or I'll call the police!'

At that they all leaped at her, pushing, punching, dragging her to an upright chair. She struggled for a few seconds, but her breath was going. When they had her sitting down, she was incapable of movement. They tied her hands and ankles to the chair and stood back. They began to talk, all at once to start with, but at a gesture from one, the other two became silent.

When Mrs. Fairlands heard the voices, she became rigid with shock and horror. Such words, such phrases, such tones, such evil loose in the world, in her house, in her quiet room. Her face grew cold, she thought she would faint. And still the persistent demand went on.

'We want the money. Where d'you keep it? Come on. Give. Where d'you keep it?'

'At my bank,' she gasped.

'That's no answer. Where?'

She directed them to the bureau, where they found and rifled her handbag, taking the three pound notes and five shillings' worth of small change that was all the currency she had in the flat.

Clearly they were astonished at the small amount. They threatened, standing round her, muttering threats and curses.

'I'm *not* rich,' she kept repeating. 'I live chiefly on the rents of the flats and a very small private income. It's all paid into my bank. I cash a cheque each week, a small cheque to cover my food and the wages of my daily help.'

'Jewellery,' one of them said. 'You got jewellery. Rich old cows dolled up—we seen 'em. That's why we come. You got it. Give.'

She rallied a little, told them where to find her poor trinkets. Across the room her diamond brooch winked discreetly in the firelight. They were too stupid, too savage, too—horrible to think of searching the room carefully. Let them take the beads, the dress jewellery, the amber pendant. She leaned her aching head against the hard back of the chair and closed her eyes.

After what seemed a long time they came back. Their tempers were not improved. They grumbled among themselves—almost quarrelling—in loud harsh tones.

'Radio's worth nil. Prehistoric. No transistor. No record player. Might lift that old clock.'

'Money stashed away. Mean old bitch.'

'Best get going.'

Mrs. Fairlands, eyes still closed, heard a faint sound outside the window. Her doorbell rang once. More carol singers? If they knew, they could save her. If they knew—

She began to scream. She meant to scream loudly, but the noise that came from her was a feeble croak. In her own head it was a scream. To her tormentors it was derisory, but still a challenge. They refused to be challenged.

They gagged her with a strip of sticking plaster, they pulled out the flex of her telephone. They bundled the few valuables they had collected into the large pockets of their overcoats and left the flat, pulling shut the two front doors as they went. Mrs. Fairlands was alone again, but gagged and bound and quite unable to free herself.

At first she felt a profound relief in the silence, the emptiness of the room. The horror had gone, and though she was uncomfortable, she was not yet in pain. They had left the light on—all the lights, she decided. She could see through the open door of the room the lighted passage and, beyond, a streak of light from her bedroom. Had they been in the kitchen? Taken her Christmas dinner, perhaps, the chicken her daily had cooked for her? She remembered her supper and realized fully, for the first time, that she could not open her mouth and that she could not free her hands.

Even now she refused to give way to panic. She decided to rest until her strength came back and she could, by exercising it, loosen her bonds. But her strength did not come back. It ebbed as the night advanced and the fire died and the room grew cold and colder. For the first time she regretted not accepting May's suggestion that she should spend Christmas with her, occupying the flat above in place of Dorothy. Between them they could have defeated those little monsters. Or she could herself have gone to Leatherhead. She was insured for burglary.

She regretted those things that might have saved her, but she did not regret the gamble of refusing them. She recognized now that the gamble was lost. It had to be lost in the end, but she would have chosen a more dignified finish than this would be.

She cried a little in her weakness and the pain she now suffered in her wrists and ankles and back. But the tears ran down her nose and blocked it, which stopped her breathing and made her choke. She stopped crying, resigned herself, prayed a little, considered one or two sins she had never forgotten but on whose account she had never felt remorse until now. Later on she lapsed into semiconsciousness, a half-dream world of past scenes and present cares, of her mother, resplendent in low-cut green chiffon and diamonds, the diamond brooch and bracelet now decorating the tree across the room. Of Bobbie, in a fever, plagued by itching spots, of Dorothy as a little girl, blotched with measles.

Towards morning, unable any longer to breathe properly, exhausted by pain, hunger, and cold, Mrs. Fairlands died.

The milkman came along the road early on Christmas morning, anxious to finish his round and get back to his family. At Mrs. Fairlands's door he stopped. There were no milk bottles standing outside and no notice. He had seen her in person the day before when she had explained that her daughter and family were not coming this year so she would only need her usual pint that day.

'But I'll put out the bottles and the ticket for tomorrow as usual,' she had said.

'You wouldn't like to order now, madam?' he had asked, thinking it would save her trouble.

'No, thank you,' she had answered. 'I prefer to decide in the evening, when I see what milk I have left.'

But there were no bottles and no ticket and she was a very, very old lady and had had this disappointment over her family not coming.

The milkman looked at the door and then at the windows. It was still dark, and the light shone clearly behind the closed curtains. He had seen it when he went in through the gate but had thought nothing of it, being intent on his job. Besides, there were lights on in a good many houses and the squeals of delighted children finding Christmas stockings bulging on the posts of their beds. But here, he reminded himself, there were no children.

He tapped on the window and listened. There was no movement in the house. Perhaps she'd forgotten, being practically senile. He left a pint bottle on the doorstep. But passing a constable on a scooter at the end of the road, he stopped to signal to him and told him about Mrs. Fairlands. 'Know 'oo I mean?' he asked.

The constable nodded and thanked the milkman. No harm in making sure. He was pretty well browned off—nothing doing—empty streets—not a hooligan in sight—layabouts mostly drunk in the cells after last night's parties—villains all at the holiday resorts, casing jobs.

He left the scooter at the kerb and tried to rouse Mrs. Fairlands. He did not succeed, so his anxiety grew. All the lights were on in the flat, front and back as far as he could make out. All her lights. The other flats were in total darkness. People away. She must have had a stroke or actually croaked, he thought. He rode on to the nearest telephone box.

The local police station sent a sergeant and another constable to join the man on the beat. Together they managed to open the kitchen window at the back, and when they saw the tray with a meal prepared but untouched, one of them climbed in. He found Mrs. Fairlands as the thieves had left her. There was no doubt at all what had happened.

'Ambulance,' said the sergeant briefly. 'Get the super first, though. We'll be wanting the whole works.'

'The phone's gone,' the constable said. 'Pulled out.'

'Bastard! Leave her like this when she couldn't phone anyway and wouldn't be up to leaving the house till he'd had plenty time to make six getaways. Bloody bastard!'

'Wonder how much he got?'

'Damn all, I should think. They don't keep their savings in the mattress up this way.'

The constable on the scooter rode off to report, and before long, routine investigations were well under way. The doctor discovered no outward injuries and decided that death was probably due to shock, cold, and exhaustion, taking into account the victim's obviously advanced age. Detective-Inspector Brooks of the divisional CID found plenty of papers in the bureau to give him all the information he needed about Mrs. Fairlands's financial position, her recent activities, and her nearest relations. Leaving the sergeant in charge at the flat while the experts in the various branches were at work, he went back to the local station to get in touch with Mrs. Fairlands's daughter, Dorothy Evans.

In Devonshire the news was received with horror, indignation, and remorse. In trying to do the best for her mother by not exposing her to possible infection, Mrs. Evans felt she had brought about her death.

'You can't think of it like that,' her husband Hugh protested, trying to stem the bitter tears. 'If she'd come down, she might have had an accident on the way or got pneumonia or something. Quite apart from shingles.'

'But she was all alone! That's what's so frightful!'

'And it wasn't your fault. She could have had what's-her-name—Miss Bolton, the old girl who lives at Leatherhead.'

'I thought May Bolton was going to have *her*. But you couldn't make Mother do a thing she hadn't thought of herself.'

'Again, that wasn't your fault, was it?'

It occurred to him that his wife had inherited to some extent this characteristic of his mother-in-law, but this was no time to remind her of it.

'You'll go up at once, I suppose?' he said when she was a little calmer.

'How can I?' The tears began to fall again. 'Christmas Day and Bobbie's temperature still up and his spots itching like mad. Could *you* cope with all that?'

'I'd try,' he said. 'You know I'd do anything.'

'Of course you would, darling.' She was genuinely grateful for the happiness of her married life and at this moment of self-reproach prepared to give him most of the credit for it. 'Honestly, I don't think I could face it. There'd be identification, wouldn't there? And hearing detail—' She shuddered, covering her face.

'Okay. I'll go up,' Hugh told her. He really preferred this arrangement. 'I'll take the car in to Exeter and get the first through train there is. It's very early. Apparently her milkman made the discovery.'

So Hugh Evans reached the flat in the early afternoon to find a constable on duty at the door and the house locked up. He was directed to the police station, where Inspector Brooks was waiting for him.

'My wife was too upset to come alone,' he explained, 'and we couldn't leave the family on their own. They've all got chicken pox; the youngest's quite bad with it today.'

He went on to explain all the reasons why Mrs. Fairlands had been alone in the flat.

'Quite,' said Brooks, who had a difficult mother-in-law himself and was inclined to be sympathetic. 'Quite. Nothing to stop her going to an hotel here in London over the holiday, was there?'

'Nothing at all. She could easily afford it. She isn't— wasn't—what you call rich, but she'd reached the age when she really *couldn't* spend much.'

This led to a full description of Mrs. Fairlands's circumstances, which finished with Hugh pulling out a list, hastily written by Dorothy before he left home, of all the valuables she could remember that were still in Mrs. Fairlands's possession.

'Jewellery,' said the inspector thoughtfully. 'Now where would she keep that?'

'Doesn't it say? In her bedroom, I believe.'

'Oh, yes. A jewel box, containing—yes. Well, Mr. Evans, there was no jewel box in the flat when we searched it.'

'Obviously the thief took it, then. About the only thing worth taking. She wouldn't have much cash there. She took it from the bank in weekly amounts. I know that.'

There was very little more help he could give, so Inspector Brooks took him to the mortuary where Mrs. Fairlands now lay. And after the identification, which Hugh found pitiable but not otherwise distressing, they went together to the flat.

'In case you can help us to note any more objects of value you find are missing,' Brooks explained.

The rooms were in the same state in which they had been found. Hugh found this more shocking, more disturbing, than the colourless, peaceful face of the very old woman who had never been close to him, who had never shown a warm affection for any of them, though with her unusual vitality she must in her youth have been capable of passion.

He went from room to room and back again. He stopped beside the bureau. 'I was thinking, on the way up,' he said diffidently. 'Her solicitor—that sort of thing. Insurances. I ought—can I have a look through this lot?'

'Of course, sir,' Inspector Brooks answered politely. 'I've had a look myself. You see, we aren't quite clear about motive.'

'Not—But wasn't it a burglar? A brutal, thieving thug?'

'There is no sign whatever of breaking and entering. It appears that Mrs. Fairlands let the murderer in herself.'

'But that's impossible.'

'Is it? An old lady, feeling lonely perhaps. The doorbell rings. She thinks a friend has called to visit her. She goes and opens it. It's always happening.'

'Yes. Yes, of course. It could have happened that way. Or a tramp asking for money—Christmas—'

'Tramps don't usually leave it as late as Christmas Eve. Generally smash a window and get put inside a day or two earlier.'

'What worries you, then?'

'Just in case she had someone after her. Poor relation. Anyone who had it in for her, if she knew something damaging about him. Faked the burglary.'

'But he seems to have taken her jewel box, and according to my wife, it was worth taking.'

'Quite. We shall want a full description of the pieces, sir.'

'She'll make it out for you. Or it may have been insured separately.'

'I'm afraid not. Go ahead, though, Mr. Evans. I'll send my sergeant in, and he'll bring you back to the station with any essential papers you need for Mrs. Fairlands's solicitor.'

Hugh worked at the papers for half an hour and then decided he had all the information he wanted. No steps of any kind need, or indeed could, be taken until the day after tomorrow, he knew. The solicitor could not begin to wind up Mrs. Fairlands's affairs for some time. Even the date of the inquest had not been fixed and would probably have to be adjourned.

Before leaving the flat, Hugh looked round the rooms once more, taking the sergeant with him. They paused before the mantelpiece, untouched by the thieves, a poignant reminder of the life so abruptly ended. Hugh looked at the cards and then glanced at the Christmas tree.

'Poor old thing!' he said. 'We never thought she'd go like this. We ought all to have been here today. She always decorated a tree for us—' He broke off, genuinely moved for the first time.

'So I understand,' the sergeant said gruffly, sharing the wave of sentiment.

'My wife—I wonder—D'you think it'd be in order to get rid of it?'

'The tree, sir?'

'Yes. Put it out at the back somewhere. Less upsetting—Mrs. Evans will be coming up the day after tomorrow. By that time the dustmen may have called.'

'I understand. I don't see any harm—'

'Right.'

Hurrying, in case the sergeant should change his mind, Hugh took up the bowl, and turning his face away to spare it from being pricked by the pine needles, he carried it out to the back of the house where he stood it beside the row of three dustbins. At any rate, he thought, going back to join the sergeant, Dorothy would be spared the feelings that overcame him so unexpectedly.

He was not altogether right in this. Mrs. Evans travelled to London on the day after Boxing Day. The inquest opened on this day, with a jury. Evidence was given of the finding of the body. Medical evidence gave the cause of death as cold and exhaustion and bronchial edema from partial suffocation by a plaster gag. The verdict was murder by a person or persons unknown.

After the inquest, Mrs. Fairlands's solicitor, who had supported Mrs. Evans during the ordeal in court, went with her to the flat. They arrived just as the municipal dust cart was beginning to move away. One of the older dustmen came up to them.

'You for the old lady they did Christmas Eve?' he asked, with some hesitation.

'I'm her daughter,' Dorothy said, her eyes filling again, as they still did all too readily.

'What d'you want?' asked the solicitor, who was anxious to get back to his office.

'No offence,' said the man, ignoring him and keeping his eyes on Dorothy's face. 'It's like this 'ere, see. They put a Christmas tree outside, by the bins, see. Decorated. We didn't like to take it, seeing it's not exactly rubbish and her gone and that. Nobody about we could ask—'

Dorothy understood. The Christmas tree. Hugh's doing, obviously. Sweet of him.

'Of course you must have it, if it's any use to you now, so late. Have you got children?'

'Three, ma'am. Two young 'uns. I arsked the other chaps. They don't want it. They said to leave it.'

'No, you take it,' Dorothy told him. 'I don't want to see it. I don't want to be reminded—'

'Thanks a lot, dear,' the dustman said, gravely sympathetic, walking back round the house.

The solicitor took the door key from Dorothy and let her in, so she did not see the tree as the dustman emerged with it held carefully before him.

◇◇◇

In his home that evening the tree was greeted with a mixture of joy and derision.

'As if I 'adn't enough to clear up yesterday and the day before,' his wife complained, half angry, half laughing. 'Where'd you get it, anyway?'

When he had finished telling her, the two children, who had listened, crept away to play with the new glittering toy.

And before long Mavis, the youngest, found the brooch pinned to the star. She unfastened it carefully and held it in her hand, turning it this way and that to catch the light.

But not for long. Her brother Ernie, two years older, soon snatched it. Mavis went for him, and he ran, making for the front door to escape into the street where Mavis was forbidden to play. Though she seldom obeyed the rule, on this occasion she used it to make loud protest, setting up a howl that brought her mother to the door of the kitchen.

But Ernie had not escaped with his prize. His elder brother Ron was on the point of entering, and when Ernie flung wide the door, Ron pushed in, shoving his little brother back.

"'E's nicked my star,' Mavis wailed. 'Make 'im give me back, Ron. It's mine. Off the tree.'

Ron took Ernie by the back of his collar and swung him round.

'Give!' he said firmly. Ernie clenched his right fist, betraying himself. Ron took his arm, bent his hand over forwards, and, as the brooch fell to the floor, stooped to pick it up. Ernie was now in tears.

'Where'd 'e get it?' Ron asked over the child's doubled-up, weeping form.

'The tree,' Mavis repeated, 'I found it. On the star—on the tree.'

'Wot the 'ell d'she mean?' Ron asked, exasperated.

'Shut up, the lot of you!' their mother cried fiercely from the kitchen where she had retreated. 'Ron, come on in to your tea. Late as usual. Why you never—'

'Okay, Mum,' the boy said, unrepentant. 'I never—'

He sat down, looking at the sparkling object in his hand. 'What'd Mavis mean about a tree?'

'Christmas tree. Dad brought it in. I've a good mind to put it on the fire. Nothing but argument since 'e fetched it.'

'It's pretty,' Ron said, meaning the brooch in his hand. 'Dress jewellery, they calls it.' He slipped it into his pocket.

'That's mine,' Mavis insisted. 'I found it pinned on that star on the tree. You give it back, Ron.'

'Leave 'im alone,' their mother said, smacking away the reaching hands. 'Go and play with your blasted tree. Dad didn't ought t'ave brought it. Ought t'ave 'ad more sense—'

Ron sat quietly, eating his kipper and drinking his tea. When he had finished, he stacked his crockery in the sink, went upstairs, changed his shirt, put a pair of shiny dancing shoes in the pockets of his mackintosh, and went off to the club where his current girlfriend, Sally, fifteen like himself, attending the same comprehensive school, was waiting for him.

'You're late,' she said over her shoulder, not leaving the group of her girlfriends.

'I've 'eard that before tonight. Mum was creating. Not my fault if Mr. Pope wants to see me about exam papers.'

'You're never taking G.C.E.?'

'Why not?'

'Coo! 'Oo started that lark?'

'Mr. Pope. I just told you. D'you want to dance or don't you?'

She did and she knew Ron was not one to wait indefinitely. So she joined him, and together they went to the main hall where dancing was in progress, with a band formed by club members.

''Alf a mo!' Ron said as they reached the door. 'I got something you'll like.'

He produced the brooch.

Sally was delighted. This was no cheap store piece. It was slap-up dress jewellery, like the things you saw in the West End, in Bond Street, in the Burlington Arcade, even. She told him she'd wear it just below her left shoulder near the neck edge of her dress. When they moved on to the dance floor she was holding her head higher and swinging her hips more than ever before. She and Ron danced well together. That night many couples stood still to watch them.

About an hour later the dancing came to a sudden end with a sound of breaking glass and shouting that grew in volume and ferocity.

'Raid!' yelled the boys on the dance floor, deserting their partners and crowding to the door. 'Those bloody Wingers again.'

The sounds of battle led them, running swiftly, to the table tennis and billiards room, where a shambles confronted them. Overturned tables, ripped cloth, broken glass were everywhere. Tall youths and younger lads were fighting indiscriminately. Above the din the club warden and the three voluntary workers, two of them women, raised their voices in appeal and admonishment, equally ignored. The young barrister who attended once a week to give legal advice free, as a form of social service, to those who asked for it plunged into the battle, only to be flung out again nursing a twisted arm. It was the club caretaker, old and experienced in gang warfare, who summoned the police. They arrived silently, snatched ringleaders with expert knowledge or recognition, hemmed in their captives while the battle melted, and waited while their colleagues, posted at the doors of the club, turned back all would-be escapers.

Before long, complete order was restored. In the dance hall the line of prisoners stood below the platform where the band had played. They included club members as well as strangers. The rest, cowed, bunched together near the door, also included a few strangers. Murmurings against these soon added them to the row of captives.

'Now,' said the sergeant, who had arrived in answer to the call, 'Mr. Smith will tell me who belongs here and who doesn't.'

The goats were quickly separated from the rather black sheep.

'Next, who was playing table tennis when the raid commenced?'

Six hands shot up from the line. Some dishevelled girls near the door also held up their hands.

'The rest were in here dancing,' the warden said. 'The boys left the girls when they heard the row, I think.'

'That's right,' Ron said boldly. 'We 'eard glass going, and we guessed it was them buggers. They been 'ere before.'

'They don't learn,' said the sergeant with a baleful glance at the goats, who shuffled their feet and looked sulky.

'You'll be charged at the station,' the sergeant went on, 'and I'll want statements from some of your lads,' he told the warden. 'Also from you and your assistants. These other kids can all go home. Quietly, mind,' he said, raising his voice. 'Show us there's some of you can behave like reasonable adults and not childish savages.'

Sally ran forward to Ron as he left the row under the platform. He took her hand as they walked towards the door. But the sergeant had seen something that surprised him. He made a signal over their heads. At the door they were stopped.

'I think you're wanted. Stand aside for a minute,' the constable told them.

The sergeant was the one who had been at the flat in the first part of the Fairlands case. He had been there when a second detailed examination of the flat was made in case the missing jewellery had been hidden away and had therefore escaped the thief. He had formed a very clear picture in his mind of what he was looking for from Mrs. Evans's description. As Sally passed him on her way to the door with Ron, part of the picture presented itself to his astonished eyes.

He turned to the warden.

'That pair. Can I have a word with them somewhere private?'

'Who? Ron Sharp and Sally Biggs? Two of our very nicest—'

The two were within earshot. They exchanged a look of amusement instantly damped by the sergeant, who ordered them briefly to follow him. In the warden's office, with the door shut, he said to Sally, 'Where did you get that brooch you're wearing?'

The girl flushed. Ron said angrily, 'I give it 'er. So what?'

'So where did you come by it?'

Ron hesitated. He didn't want to let himself down in Sally's eyes. He wanted her to think he'd bought it specially for her. He said, aggressively, 'That's my business.'

'I don't think so,' Turning to Sally, the sergeant said, 'Would you mind letting me have a look at it, miss?'

The girl was becoming frightened. Surely Ron hadn't done anything silly? He was looking upset. Perhaps—

'All right,' she said, undoing the brooch and handing it over. 'Poor eyesight, I suppose.'

It was feeble defiance, and the sergeant ignored it. He said, 'I'll have to ask you two to come down to the station. I'm not an expert, but we shall have to know a great deal more about this article, and Inspector Brooks will be particularly interested to know where it came from.'

Ron remaining obstinately silent in spite of Sally's entreaty, the two found themselves presently sitting opposite Inspector Brooks, with the brooch lying on a piece of white paper before them.

'This brooch,' said the inspector sternly, 'is one piece of jewellery listed as missing from the flat of a Mrs. Fairlands, who was robbed and murdered on Christmas Eve or early Christmas Day.'

'*Never!*' whispered Sally, aghast.

Ron said nothing. He was not a stupid boy, and he realized at once that he must now speak, whatever Sally thought of him. Also that he had a good case if he didn't say too much. So, after careful thought, he told Brooks exactly how and when he had come by the brooch and advised him to check this with his father and mother. The old lady's son had stuck the tree out by the dustbins, his mother had said, and her daughter had told his father he could have it to take home.

Inspector Brooks found the tale too fantastic to be untrue. Taking the brooch and the two subdued youngsters with him, he went to Ron's home, where more surprises awaited him. After listening to Mr. Sharp's account of the Christmas tree, which exactly tallied with Ron's, he went into the next room where the younger children were playing and Mrs. Sharp was placidly watching television.

'Which of you two found the brooch?' Brooks asked. The little girl was persuaded to agree that she had done so.

'But I got these,' the boy said. He dived into his pocket and dragged out the pearl necklace and the diamond bracelet.

''Struth!' said the inspector, overcome. 'She must've been balmy.'

'No, she wasn't,' Sally broke in. 'She was nice. She give us two and a tanner.'

'She *what?*'

Sally explained the carol singing expedition. They had been up four roads in that part, she said, and only two nicker the lot.

'Mostly it was nil,' she said. 'Then there was some give a bob and this old gentleman and the woman with 'im ten bob each. We packed it in after that.'

'This means you actually went to Mrs. Fairlands's house?' Brooks said sternly to Ron.

'With the others—yes.'

'Did you go inside?'

'No.'

'No.' Sally supported him. 'She come out.'

'Was she wearing the brooch?'

'No,' said Ron.

'Not when she come out, she wasn't,' Sally corrected him. Ron kicked her ankle gently. The inspector noticed this.

'When did you see it?' he asked Sally.

'When she looked through the window at us. We shone the torch on 'er. It didn't 'alf shine.'

'But you didn't recognize it when Ron gave it to you?'

'Why should I? I never saw it close. It was pinned on 'er dress at the neck. I didn't think of it till you said.'

Brooks nodded. This seemed fair enough. He turned to face Ron.

'So you went back alone later to get it? Right?'

'I never! It's a damned lie!' the boy cried fiercely.

Mr. Sharp took a step forward. His wife bundled the younger children out of the room. Sally began to cry.

''Oo are you accusing?' Mr. Sharp said heavily. 'You 'eard 'ow I come by the tree. My mates was there. The things was on it. I got witnesses. If Ron did that job, would 'e leave the only things worth 'aving? It says in the paper nothing of value, don't it?'

Brooks realized the force of this argument, however badly put. He'd been carried away a little. Unusual for him; he was surprised at himself. But the murder had been a particularly revolting one, and until these jewels turned up, he'd had no idea where to look. Carol singers. It might be a line and then again it mightn't.

He took careful statements from Ron, Sally, Ron's father, and the two younger children. He took the other pieces of jewellery and the Christmas tree. Carol singers. Mrs. Fairlands had opened the door to Ron's lot, having taken off her brooch if the story was true. Having hidden it very cleverly.

He and his men had missed it completely. A Christmas tree decorated with flashy bits and pieces as usual. Standing back against a wall. They'd ignored it. Seen nothing but tinsel and glitter for weeks past. Of course they hadn't noticed it. The real thief or thieves hadn't noticed it, either.

Back at the station he locked away the jewels, labelled, in the safe and rang up Hugh Evans. He did not tell him where the pieces had been found.

Afterwards he had to deal with some of the hooligans who had now been charged with breaking, entering, wilful damage, and making an affray. He wished he could pin Mrs. Fairlands's murder on their ringleader, a most degenerate and evil youth. Unfortunately, the whole gang had been in trouble in the West End that night; most of them had spent what remained of it in Bow Street police station. So they were out. But routine investigations now had a definite aim. To collect a list of all those who had sung carols at the houses on Mrs. Fairlands's road on Christmas Eve, to question the singers about the times they had appeared there and about the houses they had visited.

It was not easy. Carol singers came from many social groups and often travelled far from their own homes. The youth clubs in the district were helpful; so were the various student bodies and hostels in the neighbourhood. Brooks's manor was wide and very variously populated. In four days he had made no headway at all.

A radio message went out, appealing to carol singers to report at the police station if they were near Mrs. Fairlands's house at any time on Christmas Eve. The press took up the quest, dwelling on the pathetic aspects of the old woman's tragic death at a time of traditional peace on earth and goodwill towards men. All right-minded citizens must want to help the law over this revolting crime.

But the citizens maintained their attitude of apathy or caution.

Except for one, a freelance journalist, Tom Meadows, who had an easy manner with young people because he liked them. He became interested because the case seemed to involve young people. It was just up his street. So he went first to the Sharp family, gained their complete confidence, and had a long talk with Ron.

The boy was willing to help. After he had got over his indignation with the law for daring to suspect him, he had had sense enough to see how this had been inevitable. His anger was directed more truly at the unknown thugs responsible. He remembered Mrs. Fairlands with respect and pity. He was ready to do anything Tom Meadows suggested.

The journalist was convinced that the criminal or criminals must be local, with local knowledge. It was unlikely they would wander from house to house, taking a chance on finding one that might be profitable. It was far more likely that they knew already that Mrs. Fairlands lived alone, would be quite alone over Christmas and therefore defenceless. But their information had been incomplete. They had not known how little money she kept at the flat. No one had known this except her family. Or had they?

Meadows, patient and amiable, worked his way from the Sharps to the postman, the milkman, and through the latter to the daily.

'Well, of course I mentioned 'er being alone for the 'oliday. I told that detective so. In the way of conversation, I told 'im. Why shouldn't I?'

'Why indeed? But who did you tell, exactly?'

'I disremember. Anyone, I suppose. If we was comparing. I'm on me own now meself, but I go up to me brother's at the 'olidays.'

'Where would that be?'

'Notting 'Ill way. 'E's on the railway. Paddington.'

Bit by bit Meadows extracted a list of her friends and relations, those with whom she had talked most often during the week before Christmas. Among her various nephews and nieces was a girl who went to the same comprehensive school as Ron and his girlfriend Sally.

Ron listened to the assignment Meadows gave him.

'Sally won't like it,' he said candidly.

'Bring her into it, then. Pretend it's all your own idea.'

Ron grinned.

'Shirl won't like that,' he said.

Tom Meadows laughed.

'Fix it any way you like,' he said. 'But I think this girl Shirley was with a group and did go to sing carols for Mrs. Fairlands. I know she isn't on the official list, so she hasn't reported it. I want to know why.'

'I'm not shopping anymore,' Ron said warily.

'I'm not asking you to. I don't imagine Shirley or her friends did Mrs. Fairlands. But it's just possible she knows or saw something and is afraid to speak up for fear of reprisals.'

'Cor!' said Ron. It was like a page of his favourite magazine working out in real life. He confided in Sally, and they went to work.

The upshot was interesting. Shirley did have something to say, and she said it to Tom Meadows in her own home with her disapproving mother sitting beside her.

'I never did like the idea of Shirl going out after dark, begging at house doors. That's all it really is, isn't it? My children have very good pocket money. They've nothing to complain of.'

'I'm sure they haven't,' Meadows said mildly. 'But there's a lot more to carol singing than asking for money. Isn't there, Shirley?'

'I'll say,' the girl answered. 'Mum don't understand.'

'You can't stop her,' the mother complained. 'Self-willed. Stubborn. I don't know, I'm sure. Out after dark. My dad'd've taken his belt to me for less.'

'There were four of us,' Shirley protested. 'It wasn't late. Not above seven or eight.'

The time was right, Meadows noted, if she was speaking of her visit to Mrs. Fairlands's road. She was. Encouraged to describe everything, she agreed that her group was working towards the house especially to entertain the old lady who was going to be alone for Christmas. She'd got that from her aunt, who worked for Mrs. Fairlands. They began at the far end of the road on the same side as the old lady. When they were about six houses away, they saw another group go up to it or to one near it. Then they were singing themselves. The next time she looked round, she saw one child running away up the road. She did not know where he had come from. She did not see the others.

'You did not see them go on?'

'No. They weren't in the road then, but they might have gone right on while we were singing. There's a turning off, isn't there?'

'Yes. Go on.'

'Well, we went up to Mrs. Fairlands's and rang the bell. I thought I'd tell her she knew my aunt and we'd come special.'

'Yes. What happened?'

'Nothing. At least—'

'Go on. Don't be frightened.'

Shirley's face had gone very pale.

'There were men's voices inside. Arguing like. Nasty. We scarpered.'

Tom Meadows nodded gravely.

'That would be upsetting. *Men's* voices? Or big boys?'

'Could be either, couldn't it? Well, perhaps more like sixth form boys, at that.'

'You thought it was boys, didn't you? Boys from your school.'

Shirley was silent.

'You thought they'd know and have it in for you if you told. Didn't you? I won't let you down, Shirley. Didn't you?'

She whispered, 'Yes,' and added, 'Some of our boys got knives. I seen them.'

Meadows went to Inspector Brooks. He explained how Ron had helped him to get in touch with Shirley and the result of that interview. The inspector, who had worked as a routine matter on all Mrs. Fairlands's contacts with the outer world, was too interested to feel annoyed at the other's success.

'Men's voices?' Brooks said incredulously.

'Most probably older lads,' Meadows answered. 'She agreed that was what frightened her group. They might have looked out and recognized them as they ran away.'

'There'd been no attempt at intimidations?'

'They're not all *that* stupid.'

'No.'

Brooks considered.

'This mustn't break in the papers yet, you understand?'

'Perfectly. But I shall stay around.'

Inspector Brooks nodded, and Tom went away. Brooks took his sergeant and drove to Mrs. Fairlands's house. They still had the key of the flat, and they still had the house under observation.

The new information was disturbing, Brooks felt. Men's voices, raised in anger. Against poor Mrs. Fairlands, of course. But there were no adult fingerprints in the flat except those of the old lady herself and of her daily. Gloves had been worn, then. A professional job. But no signs whatever of breaking and entering. Therefore, Mrs. Fairlands had let them in. Why? She had peeped out at Ron's lot, to check who they were, obviously. She had not done so for Shirley's.

Because she was in the power of the 'men' whose voices had driven this other group away in terror.

But there had been two distinct small footprints in the dust of the outer hall and a palmprint on the outer door had been small, childsize.

Perhaps the child that Shirley had seen running down the road had been a decoy. The whole group she had noticed at Mrs. Fairlands's door might have been employed for that purpose and the men or older boys were lurking at the corner of the house, to pounce when the door opened. Possible, but not very likely. Far too risky, even on a dark evening. Shirley could not have seen distinctly. The streetlamps were at longish intervals in that road. But there were always a few passersby. Even on Christmas Eve no professional group of villains would take such a risk.

Standing in the cold drawing room, now covered with a grey film of dust, Inspector Brooks decided to make another careful search for clues. He had missed the jewels. Though he felt justified in making it, his mistake was a distinct blot on his copybook. It was up to him now to retrieve his reputation. He sent the sergeant to take another look at the bedroom, with particular attention to the dressing table. He himself began to go over the drawing room with the greatest possible care.

Shirley's evidence suggested there had been more than one thief. The girl had said 'voices.' That meant at least two, which probably accounted for the fact, apart from her age, that neither Mrs. Fairlands nor her clothes gave any indication of a struggle. She had been overpowered immediately, it seemed. She had not been strong enough or agile enough to tear, scratch, pull off any fragment from her attackers' clothes or persons. There had been no trace of any useful material under her fingernails or elsewhere.

Brooks began methodically with the chair to which Mrs. Fairlands had been bound and worked his way outwards from that centre. After the furniture, the carpet and curtains. After that the walls.

Near the door, opposite the fireplace, he found on the wall—two feet, three inches up from the floor—a small, round, brownish, greasy smear. He had not seen it before. In artificial light, he checked, it was nearly invisible. On this morning, with the first sunshine of the New Year coming into the room, the little patch was entirely obvious, slightly shiny where the light from the window caught it.

Inspector Brooks took a wooden spatula from his case of aids and carefully scraped off the substance into a small plastic box, sniffing at it as he did so.

'May I, too?' asked Tom Meadows behind him.

The inspector wheeled round with an angry exclamation.

'How did you get in?' he asked.

'Told the copper in your car I wanted to speak to you.'

'What about?'

'Well, about how you were getting on, really,' Tom said disarmingly. 'I see you are. Please let me have one sniff.'

Inspector Brooks was annoyed, both by the intrusion and the fact that he had not heard it, being so concentrated on his work. So he closed his box, shut it into his black bag, and called to the sergeant in the next room.

Meadows got down on his knees, leaned towards the wall, and sniffed. It was faint, since most of it had been scraped off, but he knew the smell. His freelancing had not been confined to journalism.

He was getting to his feet as the sergeant joined Inspector Brooks. The sergeant raised his eyebrows at the interloper.

'You can't keep the press's noses out of anything,' said Brooks morosely.

The other two grinned. It was very apt.

'I'm just off,' Tom said. 'Good luck with your specimen, Inspector. I know where to go now. So will you.'

'Come back!' called Brooks. The young man was a menace. He would have to be controlled.

But Meadows was away, striding down the road until he was out of sight of the police car, then running to the nearest tube station, where he knew he would find the latest newspaper editions. He bought one, opened it at the entertainments column, and read down the list.

He was a certain six hours ahead of Brooks, he felt sure, possibly more. Probably he had until tomorrow morning. He skipped his lunch and set to work.

Inspector Brooks got the report from the lab that evening, and the answer to his problem came to him as completely as it had done to Tom Meadows in Mrs. Fairlands's drawing room. His first action was to ring up Olympia. This proving fruitless, he sighed. Too late now to contact the big stores; they would all be closed and the employees of every kind gone home.

But in the morning some very extensive telephone calls to managers told him where he must go. He organized his forces to cover all the exits of a big store not very far from Mrs. Fairlands's house. With his sergeant he entered modestly by way of the men's department.

They took a lift from there to the third floor, emerging among the toys. It was the tenth day of Christmas, with the school holidays in full swing and eager children, flush with Christmas money, choosing long-coveted treasures. A Father Christmas, white-bearded, in the usual red, hooded gown, rather too short for him, was moving about trying to promote a visit to the first of that day's performances of 'Snowdrop and the Seven Dwarfs.' As his insistence seeped into the minds of the abstracted young, they turned their heads to look at the attractive cardboard entrance of the little 'theatre' at the far end of the department. A gentle flow towards it began and gathered momentum. Inspector Brooks and the sergeant joined the stream.

Inside the theatre there were small chairs in rows for the children. The grownups stood at the back. A gramophone played the Disney film music.

The early scenes were brief, mere tableaux with a line thrown in here and there for Snowdrop. The queen spoke the famous doggerel to her mirror.

The curtain fell and rose again on Snowdrop, surrounded by the Seven Dwarfs. Two of them had beards, real beards. Dopey rose to his feet and began to sing.

'Okay,' whispered Brooks to the sergeant. 'The child who sang and ran away.'

The sergeant nodded. Brooks whispered again. 'I'm going round the back. Get the audience here out quietly if the balloon goes up before they finish.'

He tiptoed quietly away. He intended to catch the dwarfs in their dressing room immediately after the show, arrest the lot, and sort them out at the police station.

But the guilty ones had seen him move. Or rather Dopey, more guilt-laden and fearful than the rest, had noticed the two men who seemed to have no children with them, had seen their heads close together, had seen one move silently away. As Brooks disappeared, the midget's nerve broke. His song ended in a scream; he fled from the stage.

In the uproar that followed, the dwarf's scream was echoed by the frightened children. The lights went up in the theatre, the shop assistants and the sergeant went into action to subdue their panic and get them out.

Inspector Brooks found himself in a maze of lathe and plaster backstage arrangements. He found three bewildered small figures, with anxious, wizened faces, trying to restrain Dopey, who was still in the grip of his hysteria. A few sharp questions proved that the three had no idea what was happening.

The queen and Snowdrop appeared, highly indignant. Brooks, now holding Dopey firmly by the collar, demanded the other three dwarfs. The two girls, subdued and totally bewildered, pointed to their dressing room. It was empty, but a tumbled heap of costumes on the floor showed what they had done. The sergeant appeared, breathless.

'Take this chap,' Brooks said, thrusting the now fainting Dopey at him. 'Take him down. I'm shopping him. Get on to the management to warn all departments for the others.'

He was gone, darting into the crowded toy department, where children and parents stood amazed or hurried towards the lifts, where a dense crowd stood huddled, anxious to leave the frightening trouble spot.

Brooks bawled an order.

The crowd at the lift melted away from it, leaving three small figures in overcoats and felt hats, trying in vain to push once more under cover.

They bolted, bunched together, but they did not get far. Round the corner of a piled table of soft toys Father Christmas was waiting. He leaped forward, tripped up one, snatched another, hit the third as he passed and grabbed him, too, as he fell.

The tripped one struggled up and on as Brooks appeared.

'I'll hold these two,' panted Tom Meadows through his white beard, which had fallen sideways.

The chase was brief. Brooks gained on the dwarf. The latter knew it was hopeless. He snatched up a mallet lying beside a display of camping equipment and, rushing to the side of the store, leaped on a counter, from there clambered up a tier of shelves, beat a hole in the window behind them, and dived through. Horrified people and police on the pavement below saw the small body turning over and over like a leaf as it fell.

'All yours,' said Tom Meadows, handing his captives, too limp now to struggle, to Inspector Brooks and tearing off his Father Christmas costume. 'See you later.'

He was gone, to shut himself in a telephone booth on the ground floor of the store and hand his favourite editor the scoop. It had paid off, taking over from the old boy, an ex-actor like himself, who was quite willing for a fiver to write a note pleading illness and sending a substitute. 'Your reporter, Tom Meadows, dressed as Father Christmas, today captured and handed over to the police two of the three murderers of Mrs. Fairlands—'

Inspector Brooks, with three frantic midgets demanding legal aid, scrabbling at the doors of their cells, took a lengthy statement from the fourth, the one with the treble voice whose nerve had broken on the fatal night, as it had again that day. Greasepaint had betrayed the little fiends, Brooks told him, privately regretting that Meadows had been a jump ahead of him there. Greasepaint left on in the rush to get at their prey. One of the brutes must have fallen against the wall, pushed by the old woman herself perhaps. He hoped so. He hoped it was her own action that had brought these squalid killers to justice.

# Solution to Mr. Cork's Secret

The following was printed in *Lilliput* magazine, as the solution to the conundrum posed in 'Mr. Cork's Secret'. The author's solution was printed first, followed by the two winning entries (from the 'home' prizewinner and the 'overseas' prizewinner).

Alouette's Worms Never Existed. Mr. Cork was rightly suspicious as soon as he was consulted about the risk. The valuation, £75,000, was unusually high. Further, the Anchor were invited to give temporary cover on a mere description provided by a Paris jeweller and the doubtful evidence of the portrait of a singer named Alouette painted wearing the jewels over fifty years ago. His suspicions were confirmed when he discovered that Anton de Raun, the man who was supposed to have purchased Alouette's Worms, had put up a burglar to raid the private safe in the bridal suite at the Paradise. De Raun would never have risked losing jewellery as precious as Alouette's Worms to get the insurance money unless he knew that there was nothing to steal. But he had to have proof of burglary. Harry was to be the victim. The whole plot was only possible because, through his marriage to Fanny Fairfield, Anton de Raun's doings made news. The consequence was that the press played up the story until everybody, except Mr. Cork, believed in Alouette's Worms.

Guydamour, the jeweller, was the instigator of the plan. He somehow discovered, probably from Alouette herself in her old age, that her famous 'Worms' were made of paste. He put up the scheme to de Raun of insuring jewels which, because they never existed, could never be recovered if they were 'stolen.' Mr. Cork's pertinent inquiries when he telephoned Paris before the de Raun wedding put Guydamour on his guard. Guydamour warned off de Raun. But de Raun himself seized the chance of staging an even better fake robbery by murdering his own accomplice. If Harry hadn't arrived to burgle the safe as arranged, and Mr. Cork hadn't caught him by accident, de Raun might well have got away with it and the police would still be searching for the jewels. Mr. Cork kept the secret because he was alarmed lest it become widely known that the big London insurance companies constantly accept the risk on valuables for the existence of which they have no first-hand knowledge.

# *Home*

J. Carroll, *'Whiteholme,'*
*Grantham Road, Bracebridge Heath, Lincoln.*

Sparrow. Care Cheshire Cheese. Fleet Street, London. Regret unable to join you and Harry Christmas Eve as detained New York stop Due however general tightening insurance regulations am now able reveal missing link De Raun case stop My anxiety this cover first aroused by absence expert examination Alouettes Worms coupled knowledge De Raun's unsavoury financial record stop My cardinal rule these investigations is examine whether conditions favourable any of following three principal methods defrauding insurance companies stop Firstly phoney theft with view later underground sale insured articles stop Discarded this theory because convinced De Raun lacked wherewithal purchase jewels first place stop Secondly theft of imitations substituted for real jewels which usually sold beforehand stop Intriguing possibility here was manufacture by Guydamour of imitation Alouettes Worms for pre-arranged theft stop Nevertheless concluded this unlikely because Harry's subsequent attempts dispose of sham jewels would provide underworld concrete evidence fraud carrying distinct possibilities blackmail stop Came finally to third alternative of complete non-existence jewels real or false which proved to be solution in De Raun case stop Legend of missing Alouettes Worms provided De Raun Guydamour with ideal starting point their conspiracy stop They spread story that jewels reappeared lending authenticity by report of forthcoming public sale stop Alleged private sale to De Raun followed thus setting stage for fraudulent insurance of non-existent jewels and finally genuine burglary of precisely nothing stop This was the fact necessarily concealed from press.

Montague Cork

# Overseas

A. G. Yates, 2 *Seaview Parade,*
*Collaroy, Sydney, N.S.W. Australia.*

The Anchor Insurance Company
*Confidential memo to all Departmental Heads*
*from General Manager.*

This Memo is written as a solemn warning to all senior staff.

You have all read accounts in the Press of the de Raun case and, therefore, are familiar with the details. Perhaps some of the more observant among you have wondered why the obvious question was not answered, namely, 'Where were the jewels found?'

The answer is that the jewels were never found—because they never existed.

Ask yourselves—what proof was there that Alouette's Worms actually existed? Nothing more than newspaper reports, based on statements from de Raun and Guydamour themselves.

Guydamour described them as an exquisite collection of Siamese gems, he concocted a story of Alouette having been given them by a South African millionaire in her heyday. Alouette being dead, could not of course, deny this. De Raun, with a flourish of trumpets, announced to the Press that he had bought the jewels by private treaty as a wedding present.

De Raun, the brains of the partnership, contacted a professional burglar in the South of France and gave him exact details of a safe in a room of the Paradise Hotel and a date to commit the burglary, so that he would have a perfect setpiece.

De Raun planned the cold-blooded murder of his partner, Guydamour, for two reasons. Firstly, to substantiate the robbery as being genuine and secondly to save sharing the insurance money.

Let me not labour the point. I am sure, gentlemen, that you are satisfied with the generous salaries paid by this Company and wish to continue to enjoy them.

To receive a free catalog of Poisoned Pen Press titles, please provide your name, address, and e-mail address in one of the following ways:

Phone: 1-800-421-3976
Facsimile: 1-480-949-1707
Email: info@poisonedpenpress.com
Website: www.poisonedpenpress.com

Poisoned Pen Press
6962 E. First Ave. Ste 103
Scottsdale, AZ 85251